Sor Juana, My Beloved

Dedication

To Patty,

who always encouraged me,
no matter what.

Sor Juana, My Beloved

The poetry, the passion
that is Sor Juana Inés de la Cruz

Biographical Novel by
MaryAnn Shank

Publisher's Cataloging-in-Publication Data

Names: Shank, MaryAnn, 1943-, author.
Title: Sor Juana , my beloved : the poetry, the passion that is Sor Juana Inés de la Cruz / MaryAnn Shank.
Description: Includes bibliographical references. | Ashland, OR: Dippity Press, 2024.
Identifiers: ISBN: 978-1-7335819-3-6 (paperback) | 978-1-7335819-4-3 (ebook)
Subjects: LCSH Juana Inés de la Cruz, Sister, 1651-1695--Fiction. | Authors, Mexican--17th century--Fiction. | Nuns--Mexico--Fiction. | Mexico--History--Spanish colony, 1540-1810--Fiction. | Lesbians--Fiction. | Romance fiction. | BISAC FICTION / Historical / General | FICTION / Hispanic & Latino / Women | FICTION / LGBTQ+ / Lesbian | FICTION / Romance / LGBTQ+ / Lesbian
Classification: LCC PS3616 .H36 S67 2024 | DDC 813.6--dc23

Dippity Press, 321 Clay Street, Suite 24, Ashland, OR 97520

Table of Contents

Appendix:
After Word
Real? Or Not??
For Further Reading
I Bow My Head
If You Enjoyed This Story …
For thoughtful discussion

Viceroys and Archbishops in Sor Juana's Life

(Note: These are all historical people.)

	Archbishops	Viceroys	Juana's Journe
1664		Viceroy Antonio Sebastian de Toledo, Marquis de Mancera	
1665			Lady-in-Waiting
1666			
1667		**Vicereine Leonor** Carreto, Marquise de Mancera	Carmelite Conve
1668	**Archbishop Payo** Enrique de Rivera		Return to Palace
1669			
1670			
1671			Sor Juana at San Jeronimo's Convent
1672			
1673			
1674		**Viceroy/Archbishop Payo** Enrique de Rivera (Also Fray Payo and Bishop Payo)	
1675			
1676			
1677			
1678			
1679			
1680			
1681		Viceroy Tomas Antonio de la Cerda, Count de Parades, Marquis de la Laguna	
1682	**Archbishop Francisco de Aguiar** y Seijas y Ulloa		
1683			
1684			
1685			
1686		**Vicereine Maria Luisa** Manrique de Lara y Gonzaga, Countess de Parades, Marquise de la Laguna	
1687			
1688		Viceroy Gaspar de Sandoval Cerda Silva y Mendoza, Count de Galve	
1689			
1690			
1691			
1692			
1693		Vicereine Elvira Maria de Toledo, Countess de Galve	
1694			
1695			Died

Key Players in Sor Juana's Story

* Those marked with an asterisk are documented historical people. Others are representative of people who were part of Juana's life.

With her vibrant locutory gatherings, far-reaching family connections, as well as her status as a gifted poet and dramatist, Juana knew literally hundreds of people in la Ciudad de Mexico, and many travelers. This is but a small representation of those she influenced, and those whose lives touched hers.

Family and Friends

*ABUELO. Her grandfather, Pedro Ramirez de Asbaje

.

*MADRE ISOBEL. Isobel Ramirez, her mother had two lovers:
*PEDRO MANUEL DE ASBAJE. His two daughters, *MARIA and * JOSEPHA, were Juana's sisters.
    and
*DIEGO RUIZ LOZANO was Isobel's next lover. They had three children: *INES, *ANTONIA and *DIEGO

.

*TIA MARIA, Madre Isobel's sister, married *TIO JUAN DE MATA, and lived in Mexico City

.

DONA ANGELICA, the teacher at Las Amigas, the Girls' School

.

ROSITA. Cook and nurse at Panoayan.

.

At the Viceroy Palace:

(See chart of Viceroys and Archbishops for names and dates of Viceroys and Vicereines during Juana's time.)

.

LUCINDA, ALICIA, and **GLORIETTA.** Ladies-in-Waiting to la Vicereine Leonor

.

DON RODRIGO de Talaveras y Galve. Guest at Palace soirees

.

CONSUELA LOPEZ. Trusted servant of Maria Luisa

.

Others in La Ciudad de Mexico:

.

DONA SERAPHINA. Abuelo's lover

.

SARA. Juana's servant at St. Jeronimo's

.

DON MANUEL. Construction supervisor at St. Jeronimo's

.

***DON IGNACIO RUBIO.** Abuelo's friend. Paid for Juana's dowry

.

***DON PEDRO VELAZQUEZ DE LA CADENA.** Abelo's friend. Aided Juana many times, as did his son and heir, **DON IGNACIO VELAZQUEZ**

.

XIPIL and **TOCHLI,** and Tochli's son **XIPILLA** ("Jeweled Warrior"). Juana's Aztec friends

.

DONA CATERINA ROSA. The most beautiful actress in all of Nueva Espana.

.

DONA BONITA. Seamstress

.

The Religious Community

(See chart of Viceroys and Archbishops for names and dates of Archbishops during Juana's time.)

.

*__FRAY MIGUEL__ de Asbaje. Jesuit Padre at Juana's childhood parish

.

*__FRAY MIRANDA__. Antonio Nunez de Miranda. Jesuit. Confessor of Vicereine Leonor and of Sor Juana for many years. Chief Inquisitor of the Nueva Espana Inquisition.

.

__SOR BEATRIX__.. Nun at Carmelite Convent

.

SOR SOPHIA, SOR LUCIA, SOR GABRIELA. Nuns at St. Jeronimo

.

* __BISHOP OF PUEBLA__. Fray Manuel de Santa Cruz. Jesuit. Friend of Archbishop Payo and Juana

.

* __FRAY ARELLANO__. Juana's confessor for several years

The Story of
Sor Juana Inés de la Cruz

El regalo del abuelo (Abuelo's Gift)

Qaaaaak qakqak
　Thunder
　Chased lightening down the volcano
Sparks flew, like the snapping heels of a caballero,
　Down Popocatepetl, her mountain.
Rains … fed wild roses and plumeria.
　　Cougars … ripped the carcasses of deer
　　　　And eagles snared scared rabbits

Leaving but a trail of dripping blood over the land.

THIS WAS HER LAND, Juana's land, 17th century Mexico, Nueva España, where relentless passions merged with raw brutality to create a chaotic beauty. The peoples of Nueva España reflected this dichotomy in every sensual swing of their hips, in every syllable of prayer to la Virgen Maria.

Craaaack crak crakcrak. Juana heard the call of the blue heron before she saw it take off, its blue-grey wings melting into the summer clouds over Nueva España. She marveled at the mystery of flight, as though creatures of the sky were the rulers of the world, and we were but their invited guests.

She sometimes climbed Popocatepetl, reaching to the north, to la Ciudad de México, believing that if she reached far enough, she could touch the rooftops of this mystical city.

Across the grassland, alongside the marshes, the blistering Mexican sun embraced her slim aristocratic form. Juana knew this landscape well, having spent many youthful years exploring rocks and trees, devouring the books her grandfather, her Abuelo, lent her. Today she carried a treasure from Abuelo's biblioteca, a book that was now hers, a book by Plato only recently translated into Spanish, a handsome volume with pages hand sewn and bound in a stunning burgundy leather cover with silver imprinting.

She was intrigued by Plato's vision of the perfect state, but bristled at the notion of men owning women, for she wished to be "owned" by no one. He also wrote that "women and men have the same nature in respect to the guardianship of the state, save insofar as the one is weaker and the other is stronger." She smiled wryly, thinking how sad it was for men to be weaker.

She detoured to a hidden lagoon, a small swimming pool that captured cool water from a narrow waterfall that tumbled down the volcano, tossing to the winds the fragrance of the frangipani blooming by the pool's edge. Around a pile of volcanic rock and through a field of orange honeysuckle bushes, and there it was … her private swimming pond.

She wrapped her book in her summer frock, covering it yet again with her cotton slip, set the package under an agave plant, and slipped naked into the refreshing pool.

"Oh!" Startled, she froze as a circle of blood formed around her, a drippy moat in mortal battle, with her body as the castle standing tall. She stood on tip toe to get a view of the whole episode. Her first. Fear suddenly struck, not from the blood, but fear from the jack rabbits racing to their holes and the erratic shadows plunging down the mountainside to the water's edge. Men … no, boys … three young caballeros plummeted down the mountainside toward her, dizzy in their rush to prove their manhood.

"*¡Mira alli!*" sneered the tallest boy, his call setting blackbirds to flight. "*¡Una señorita bonita! ¡Esta sola!*" Two more boys appeared from behind the sycamore grove on the crest of the hill.

"*¡Vamos!*" challenged the tallest boy, a strapping teenager with ragged dark hair and a finely embroidered shirt. Their bumbling down the hill sliced through the afternoon's serenity with a flurry of birds and bugs and snakes escaping to hidden places.

The tallest boy began unbuckling his pants as he slid down the hill, reaching the edge of the pond as Juana spun and started toward the far side of the pool, hoping to escape. The last boy stumbled on the package protecting her book.

¡No! ¡No el libro! thought Juana. *Please not the book!*

"Look!" she challenged them. "Just try and get me!" She jumped straight up, her rounded breasts breaking through the water. She could handle losing her virginity, a quality she but little valued, but she would never forgive herself for losing a book so treasured by her Abuelo.

It worked. The boys focused their attention on her, forgetting that strange package. The tallest boy leapt into the water, heading for Juana, splashing with a commotion that sent fish and turtles hiding behind rocks.

"One kiss, little señorita," he oozed. "*Solo un beso.*"

Juana knew he wanted more than just one kiss. A scream froze in her throat, but it did not matter for there was no one to hear her.

She might have escaped; she was a decent swimmer, and a fast runner, but when she reached the middle of the pond she stopped. She could not leave. No… the burgundy bound book. The book was too important. She could not leave it to these childish ruffians to find.

A scratchy hand reached around her and grabbed her breast, so there, in the middle of the pool, she instinctively swirled, sweeping her arms in a big circle, catching up the surface blood and algae. Raising her arms to the sky, with blood oozing from her hair and from her fingertips to her armpits, dripping blood on the hand that had reached her breast, Juana screamed, a piercing wail.

"AAAAIIIIIIIIIIAAAAAAAOOOOO!"

"*¡Dios mio! ¡Es un demonio*, a devil witch!" The boys froze, then spun in unison, and naked as desert stones they escaped over the hill toward a field far away. Only one boy dared to stop long enough to retrieve their clothes. None of them cared a whit about the strange package under the agave plant.

Her scowl turned into a smirk. *So that is all it takes, a little dripping blood and men take flight.* Such was Juana's introduction to womanhood, a lesson now written in her heart.

She knew very well what the blood was. She had gotten her monthly; a dam had burst, her womanhood was released. Now she was a woman in the eyes of society; now she could marry and have children. Now she *should* marry and have children.

She had very mixed feelings about being a woman. She knew she would be regarded as an adult, which was good, but she did not want to marry or bear children. The notion of taking valuable time to wipe butts and runny noses turned her stomach. No, that was not for Juana. Juana's passion was to read, to study, to learn, to learn everything there was to know about poetry, philosophy, history, and languages, about plants and reading the stars.

There was just too much to learn, there was no time for children or running a household.

EVERYONE SAID she was a gifted scholar. When she was barely old enough to climb onto her pony, she began following her oldest sister Maria to school. She waited until Maria's buggy was out of sight, then she jumped bareback on her pony and flew over the hill to the only girls' school in the entire region.

She crouched down outside, below a window, unseen, alert, learning everything she could.

Her madre Isobel had three children, all daughters. Maria, the eldest, was allowed to attend school; Juana, the youngest, was not. This was *Las Amigas*, the girls' school, which was led by a woman, Doña Angélica, who was once a nun. Doña Angélica had left the convent a few years prior, to attend to her ailing madre she said. While boys could attend schools administered by the Church where they learned to read and write, and even do numbers, girls could not. The few schools that the Church offered for girls in La Ciudad de México were taught by nuns. Here is where girls learned embroidery and singing, and perhaps even cooking, with minimal instruction in reading, and none at all in writing or numbers. Church leaders could not imagine why a girl destined to run a household would need to know any more than that.

Doña Angélica, this former nun, this dedicated teacher, believed that girls deserved to learn to read and write and do numbers too, and so she formed Las Amigas. The school was not free; it was costly enough that only one Ramírez child could attend, so Juana took it upon herself to establish her own seat below the window sill.

Soon Doña Angélica looked out the window and saw Juana, sitting on a rock against the wall of the school. "What are you doing, little one?" asked the teacher, decidedly irked at this imp.

"Learning, Señora," responded Juana. "I want to learn everything."

Doña Angélica's frown vanished. "Everything? You will learn better, little one, if you come inside."

Inside, Juana's hand shot up to answer every question the teacher posed, even those questions intended for the older girls.

"Who can read this passage?" "Who knows who Socrates was?" Who can figure what fifteen times three is? Luna, do you know?" Luna, an older girl from a rich family, did not know. But Juana knew.

She not only joined in the daily classes, but also captured special tutoring. Doña Angélica immediately recognized the unique gifts that Juana possessed and helped her learn to read and to write, and even to do numbers, without charging Juana's madre anything at all. This was a gift that Doña Angélica gave herself: teaching a child blessed with extreme intelligence and kindness.

Learning to write was the gift that would create Juana's future, and learning numbers would solidify her prestige. "It will be our secret," said the pretty Doña Angélica.

JUANA ALREADY KNEW how to read before she met the kind teacher, for a year or so before she stole away to school, she had crept into la biblioteca that her grandfather, her Abuelo, had collected. The mysterious volumes sat on oak shelving in a spacious room, a room that reached all along one side of the hacienda. Even with more books than shelves, Abuelo stacked them gracefully, carefully guarding their spines.

Abuelo valued his books like nothing else he possessed. She knew without asking that they were treasured, for men came from haciendas many miles around, just to borrow these books and to talk with Abuelo as they drank cool beer on the veranda. Some books were in Spanish, and some in Portuguese, some even in Latin.

On special afternoons, Abuelo would take down a book and call to her to join him on the veranda. She curled up in his lap, enchanted with the stories he read to her. She heard stories about turtles and foxes, and even a magical adventure about a knight named Don Quixote.

Abuelo often left the hacienda for days at a time. When Abuelo was gone, she crept into this special room, climbed up a chair next to one of the shelves, and reaching up on tip toe, took down one of the glorious books to hold. She just held it, and very gently turned the pages. The red, green, and black leather bindings with the gold and silver embossed decorations on the covers enchanted her, but the magic inside enchanted her even more. She knew the tales of Aesop by heart, and she could almost make out the words on the page.

One day when she was kneeling in a dark corner of the room, totally enamored with the cryptic markings in one of the books, Abuelo burst into the room unexpectedly. The notion of a child defacing his book, even a child as dear to him as Juana, was an abomination to Abuelo, and his anger flared.

"Don't touch those books!' he shouted at Juana. He raised his hand as if to strike her, something he had never done.

"But, Abuelo," she said, "I have to touch them if I am to learn how to read."

Abuelo stopped short and put his arm down. He just stared at this child for a long moment. "You … you want to learn how to read?" he asked, incredulous at the thought of one so young wanting to learn so much.

"Oh, yes, Abuelo. I must. I *must*," she replied. She did not know how else to tell him how important it was that she learn how to read, but she knew from the tips of her toes to the crown of her head that it was very important, more important than anything else in the world.

Abuelo had already witnessed glimpses of the child's brilliance, how she recalled the name of each plant, each creature, each person after hearing it only once. He watched as she queried Rosita, the cook, on how eggs could have two colors, or how food could be both hot and cold while her dress always felt the same. The depth of her curiosity reached beyond what he had seen with any of his four children, or any of his dozen grandchildren.

Juana was different. And now she wanted to read.

Abuelo sat her on the desk. With both reservations and expectations, they shared the first steps of a new journey. He opened a book printed in Spanish, the tales of Aesop, and began to tell her what the markings on the page meant.

She was a brilliant student, knowing instinctively that each set of markings represented a word. Soon she saw a sentence that Abuelo had not read yet. "*El. Zorro. Lo. Escucho.*" She read her first words, her eyes dancing in pride and delight, as Abuelo sat, astounded.

He turned a few pages in the book, then pointed to a sentence in the middle of the story. Juana read, "*Vio … al … hombre …su amigo,*" and then she read the next line. She stumbled on the word "*sociedad.*" "I don't know that word, Abuelo," she said, looking up at him. He sat back in his chair, scratching his chin as in deep thought.

"My child, my little Juana, I will help you learn how to read. And I will allow you to borrow books from my biblioteca. But I have one condition." Here he raised his voice as if giving orders to a regiment. "You must treat these books like precious jewels, for indeed that is what they are. Each one is a pearl, a turquoise, a diamond. Let no harm come to these treasures, and you may learn as much as you like."

And so the lessons began. The world of books was slammed shut to her madre Isobel, and even to her sisters, but that world of books burst open a world of dreams for Juana.

Not only did she learn from books, but she learned from the dozens of compadres who came to talk with Abuelo. They sat on the veranda, drank beer or lemonade, and challenged each other on politics and policies, on religion and the real world. She soaked up these discussions as if they were written in gold, even the parts she did not fully understand. At first, she sat in a corner by herself, but with Abuelo's invitation, she came to sit beside him on his favorite bench.

She remembered the first time Abuelo turned to her and asked, "Is that what Ovid really said?" The three men on the veranda were in a rather heated argument on what Ovid wrote, from a work that Juana had read. One man said that Ovid wrote that we could never learn from our enemies; another said that Ovid's thought was that we learn only from our enemies.

Don Pedro Velázquez de la Cardena, a frequent guest at these gatherings, tugged at his pointed goatee, making his long moustache wiggle up and down. He turned to Juana, asking, "What do you think Ovid said?" Truly, he did not expect Juana to reply, but she did.

With a toss of her head, she replied. "Ovid said that one should learn, even from one's enemies."

She did not understand why no one else knew this, it was such a simple statement. "I'll show you." She jumped off Abuelo's lap, raced into the biblioteca to retrieve the book of Ovid's writings. She gently turned a few pages, grinning when she found the proper page. She handed the book to Abuelo

Abuelo broke into a broad smile and bowed to Juana.

"The prize is yours, my little scholar," said Abuelo. "That is exactly what Ovid said." The men roared approval, and Abuelo beamed. This was his granddaughter who knew the real answer to their riddle. He was immensely proud of her.

JUANA DID NOT KNOW her own padre; he had returned to España when she was very young. She thought perhaps her madre Isobel harbored a hatred of her because it was Juana who pushed him away, but in truth she was just a babe and did not remember what she might have done to distress him. In fact, she rarely even saw this "Don Pedro Manuel de Asbaje y Vargas Machuca," this padre. She remembered that he was a tall, robust man who came to eat and sleep and drink beer on the veranda, and often wrote in the record books of Panoayan and told the farm workers what to do, and then he was off again. One day he left and never returned.

It was not as if her madre Isobel mistreated her. No, she had pretty dresses, just like her sisters, with shawls in the vibrant colors of the fields surrounding her. But she was different from her sisters who flaunted their plump breasts peeking through lace mantillas. They were about her age, but they looked like grownups in her eyes. Her slight form and youth suited her romping through the countryside, not coyly baring her shoulders for men. Her madre Isobel told her that she was smaller because she was born early, and that she even had to take her to a wet nurse for several months to build up her health.

She had no father to command that she act "like a lady," and no brothers to tell her how skinny she was. She had only Abuelo. Abuelo treated her differently, with something she would learn to call "respect." When Abuelo told her that he would help her learn to read, she literally cried with joy. There was no other gift in the world that could have pleased her more.

And she did learn. The lessons came easily to her. She learned how to read in Spanish, and in Portuguese. With only a few lessons in each language, her own brilliance illuminated a world of lessons. She read all the stories of turtles and foxes that Aesop wrote and scampered through the tales of the errant knight Don Quixote. She even read the stories about the pilgrims who met on the road. She devoured all of these, and more. Then, with the grace of Doña Angélica at *Las Amigas*, she held both reading and writing, as well as arithmetic, in her hands, a unique accomplishment for one so young, and particularly unique for a girl. By the time she was six or seven, she could quote poets and philosophers, and in time learned the messages in their writings.

AS SHE STEPPED OUT of the cool pool that hot August day, she rinsed off her body in the freshness of the waterfall, letting her hands gently massage her breasts where the caballero's rough hands had scratched her, then pulled the cotton slip over her head, her damp breasts and hips molding the slip to her soft form. She kept the burgundy book wrapped in her summer frock lest some errant drops of blood that streamed down her thighs found their way to the treasured pages.

She walked toward Panoayan, her home, her hacienda, stretching her head high, feeling the power of her new found womanhood.

Panoayan sat by itself, clinging to the base of Popocatepetl, the volcano that commanded the countryside, and, like Juana herself, a cauldron of fire and ice poised to erupt at any moment. The volcano had been quiet for as long as anyone remembered, giving time for the grasses to fill in the mesa, orchids and frangipani blooming profusely. She plucked a wild rose, counted the petals, and marveled at the symmetry so common in all trees and flowers.

Why, she wondered, is all life so symmetrical – flowers, wolves, snakes, even people – but things that are not alive, like rocks and waterfalls, are not symmetrical?

She heard a green parakeet call and believed that, if she listened closely, she could decipher its language. Her spirit echoed the subdued complexity, the seething majesty of Popocatepetl. Her restless, commanding nature called on the power of this spot.

Panoayan was one of the two haciendas that Abuelo leased from the Dominican order, the recorded owners of the Spanish land grants for all the land around. Each hacienda was to remain in the Ramírez family for three generations, for Abuelo's lifetime, for his daughter Isobel's lifetime, and for her children's lifetimes. Then ownership would revert to the Dominicans, a common arrangement in Nueva España. The Catholic Church itself, along with assorted orders, brotherhoods, associations, monasteries, and convents – there were hundreds of them -- owned over seventy percent of the land in Nueva España, the rest being owned by Spanish nobility. The original owners, the native Aztecs, owned nothing, and worked as servants and farm workers and mine workers, all for little pay.

The Church could only manage that much land by leasing it to Criolles, part of the ruling class of Nueva España. Juana was herself Criolle, one born in Nueva España with direct Spanish heritage, as was her madre Isobel. They both inherited the Spanish bloodline from Abuelo, who was pure Spanish, having been born in Andalusia, as were Abuelo's madre and padre. She never knew her abuela, Abuelo's wife, but she too was of pure Spanish blood. Juana's father was also full-blooded Spanish.

"Wear your Criolle heritage with pride," Abuelo had told her, and she did. As Criolles, the Ramírez family enjoyed privileges, like land leasing, that only those of pure Spanish blood could touch. They also shared a judicial and economic status with those born in Spain, something that no lower caste could boast. The Criolles were the privileged class of Nueva España.

Panoayan was a self-sufficient farm and ranch with cows, goats, chickens, and fields of maize and hot peppers and tomatoes enough for everyone, while a huge harvest of sugar cane tended by slaves found its way to the market in la Ciudad de México each year. Managing such a hacienda was no small task, requiring physical strength and leadership authority. Abuelo was not only the manager responsible for the hacienda itself, but was also head of the local community comprised of his slaves and servants. He wore this mantle well, boasting lush fields and rich harvests.

Juana sometimes accompanied Abuelo as he managed the fields, and sometimes skipped off on her own adventures, sometimes to visit her pet lizard, Tepin, for that is what she named him. "Tepin" means "small" in Nahuatl, the Aztec language, and her lizard was a small creature indeed. She found Tepin on a solitary rock on the far side of the duck pond, near the corral.

"*Buenos días*, Tepin," she always greeted him, and Tepin always flicked his tail in acknowledgment.

Tepin and Juana became great friends, and she went nearly every day to greet him, sharing her adventures with this delightful creature. She knew that he was magical, for Rosita, the cook, had told her that lizards are magical in the Aztec world.

"Did you know that all animals have tails?" she asked Tepin. "It's true. Cows, birds, ducks, deer, even butterflies – they all have tails. Me? No, I don't have a tail." She stretched her neck to look behind her, just to be sure. "Maybe that's how God made people different from animals."

One day Abuelo pointed out that Tepin's tummy looked bigger than usual. "Perhaps," said Abuelo, "perhaps Tepin is a *she*, not a *he*, and perhaps she is going to lay her eggs soon."

The next day Juana rushed out at dawn to see if Tepin had laid her eggs. No, not yet. She looked the same. That afternoon she went out again to Tepin's rock, just in case. Tepin flicked her tail as Juana came around the corner of the corral. But Juana saw something else too – Huerto, one of the burly ranch hands, was flinging his saddle right onto that rock … right on top of Tepin.

"Noooooo!" screamed Juana. But it was too late. The saddle crashed down on Tepin, with parts of her tiny body squirting out from under the saddle. Juana ran over to Huerto, kicking him fiercely on his legs, pounding his thighs with her ratatat fists.

"You devil! You evil devil!" she screamed. "You have killed my Tepin, my lizard." Hot tears filled her eyes, blurring the world.

Huerto picked her up by her waist, her arms and legs pounding empty air. "A lizard?" said Huerto. "All this fuss for a slimy lizard?" Huerto laughed, a mean, dominating laugh, with the half dozen other ranch hands nearby joining his chorus. It was fierce, dark laughter, laughter that ridiculed Juana.

With all the strength she could muster, she kicked back her right leg, then flung it forward like a javelin, her boot hitting Huerta's nose and making it bleed. More surprised than hurt, Huerto dropped her, and she flew off to the comfort of Rosita's kitchen, her refuge in all things upsetting. From fights with her sisters to runaway ponies, Rosita always knew what to do.

"*Por que*, Rosita? Why did he kill my little lizard? Why did he laugh at me?"

Rosita settled Juana on her generous lap, rocking her until the tears stopped. "Sometimes, Juana, sometimes people are just cruel. Often, we cannot change them. All we can do is pray that we will never be cruel like them."

She accepted this explanation as best she could, and vowed that she would never let another evil person see her tears.

A few minutes later Rosita grabbed her huge butcher knife and marched out to the corral. She aimed the knife about three inches below Huerto's belt.

"If you ever again make my Juana cry, I will remove every inch of manhood from your ugly carcass." Rosita meant it. More to the point, Huerto knew that she meant it.

RARELY DID THE RAMÍREZ family leave the hacienda. Sometimes on holy days they went to the local church, a small church suited to the small population of the area, and sometimes they went to the town of Amecameca for shopping, perhaps to see a dressmaker or hire a blacksmith.

Their greatest adventures were the fiestas at surrounding haciendas, a never-ending source of music and merriment. Here is where mariachi guitars tossed caution to the clouds as señoritas in low-draping ruffles teased all with glistening breasts and swirling hips, while men's clicking heels and gazes made it obvious what they sought that night. Juana twirled her skirts with the best of them, flirting with propriety, even in the open sensuality of Nueva España. Juana's slim form flaunted a sexuality of its own.

Everyone's favorite fiestas were those at the hacienda of Don Pedro Velázquez de la Cadena, a sharp witted, gracious landowner who often joined Abuelo on the veranda for spirited debates. The Velázquez estate stretched for hundreds of acres in all directions, with quarters for slaves and ranch hands and house workers. The music and feasts at these fiestas prompted tales of legendary extravaganzas, with whole families camping out for a weekend of celebration, finding resting spots all over the ranchero.

"*¡Hola, Maria!*" called out Juana to her sister. Maria was rushing off with a local boy, in the direction of the barn. He pulled at her blouse while she giggled like a chicken. "*¿A donde vas, Maria?*"

"Go back to dancing, Juana. You are too little," called out Maria.

She did turn back, but only briefly. Following her sister in the shadows, she soon heard laughter and cow-like groans, or perhaps the braying of asses coming from one of the stalls. She was not sure which it was, but peeking around the enclosure, she clearly saw what was happening. That is what pigs and horses did, but pigs and horses never made so much noise. She had not realized that people do it too.

Startled, she crept away soundlessly. When Maria and the boy returned to the fiesta, grinning, Juana decided that the laughter and the groans, and that other stuff, were all okay. Juana kept after Maria until she explained that this was "sex," a new word in Juana's expanding vocabulary.

WHILE THE FAMILY did not travel, Abuelo was riveted on showing Juana all the glorious sights of Nueva España. Once she stood beside him as clouds of monarch butterflies tickled her cheeks, their wings singing a siren's song.

"Abuelo, I can fly with the wings of a butterfly!" She spun around, wishing that she could indeed fly with the butterflies.

"You can do whatever you choose to do, Juana."

In Veracruz they watched the dancers in gossamer lace, mimicking the flight of butterfly wings, their red, orange, and black girdles and crowns honoring the flamboyant beauty of these winged creatures.

In Guadalajara she stood in wonderment at the huge Catedral, its twin spires springing from a façade of sculpted cherubs, angels, saints, and sinners. They visited altars dedicated to Nuestra Señora de la Asunción, La Virgen de Guadalupe, and others, each created with more care than the others, each bestowing its own aura on the Catedral. The stained-glass windows imported from France cast a mystical light on all the altars.

But what caught Juana's attention was a small painting set off by itself, almost in shadow, showing a blessed woman alongside a many-spoked wheel.

"That," said Abuelo, "is our beloved Santa Caterina. She lived over a thousand years ago, a princess who became a Christian herself and who brought hundreds of others to worship Christ as well. The Emperor hated her for her wisdom and her devotion and so demanded that she be executed on the spiked wheel, a most slow, excruciating death. This was an immense iron wheel that reached from the tips of her toes to her outstretched fingers." Abuelo showed Juana how far Santa Caterina had to stretch, then continued.

"Yet, when her blessed hand touched that huge wheel, it miraculously fell apart, its spokes tumbling down, the rim laying worthless on the ground. Clearly, she could not be painfully executed on that wheel. The Emperor had no choice but to give her a kinder death, a beheading. Christ made sure that, if she were to die, she should die quickly and painlessly. And so it was."

Juana was not sure that being beheaded was such a great way to die, but having the magic in her hand to make a huge wheel fall apart impressed her immensely.

Another time they stood against bitter winds on the Pacific. "Look there," called out the captain of their small vessel. "Those are whales."

A huge spout of water shot to the sky, then another, and another.

"They are celebrating that they have met you, Juana," beamed Abuelo.

"And I celebrate you, my glorious creatures," she said as she twirled around and around.

Walking on the beach after their ocean adventure, she discovered a beautiful pink shell. It was nestled among the heart-shaped pink, grey and lavender shells sprinkled everywhere, but this shell was unique.

"It is a conch shell," he explained. "Here. Listen to its song." He placed the conch shell against her ear, and she burst into smiles.

"Where does that song come from?" she asked.

"*Muy, muy lejos.* From far across the sea." He placed the shell in her hands, and she held it close to her heart the rest of the day, bringing it to rest by her ear every few minutes, listening for its songs.

That evening they opened the book by Machiavelli that he brought. Sometimes Abuelo brought books of Virgil, Ovid, Horace, Persius or Seneca. Tonight they read Machiavelli. "Here. Read this paragraph, Juana."

She read. "All courses of action are risky, so prudence is not in avoiding danger (it is impossible), but calculating risk and acting decisively. Make mistakes of ambition and not mistakes of sloth. Develop the strength to do bold things, not the strength to suffer."

"Does that mean that you punch someone in the nose, just because they are being mean to you?"

"No, Abuelo. That's not it. It means that if the person who punched you is a giant, you probably cannot punch back, unless he really deserves it. But if he is a midget, you should punch back."

Abuelo laughed, his huge guttural laugh, and gave her a hug, recalling when she did punch a giant in the nose because he killed her lizard.

ABUELO OFTEN TRAVELED to La Ciudad de México, but always went by himself, a two-day journey each way. One day, miraculously, he took Juana with him.

It was a normal day, no more special than any other, when he announced at breakfast, "I am going to La Ciudad de México today. Isobel, you are in charge while I am gone. No books are to leave the house until I return." Juana's face fell, she knew she would be left behind. Then he added, "Juana, pack your most beautiful dresses and you will come with me."

Isobel was accustomed to running Panoayan whenever Abuelo was away, but she was not accustomed to his taking Juana with him to La Ciudad de México. Abuelo did as Abuelo wished, and although Isobel was startled, she dared not challenge him.

Juana was too stunned to move at first, then she fled up the stairs to her room, threw her prettiest dresses into a basket, along with several beautiful shawls, ribbons, and petticoats, and raced down the stairs to meet him at the carriage that was already at the front gate, the driver poised to head off.

She tossed her two sisters a smug smile as she flew out the door. They never invited her to join their games and childish conspiracies, but Abuelo never took them anywhere special, so she reveled in their envy that morning.

"*¡Voy a la Ciudad de México!*" she said to Rosita, as Rosita lifted her up in her generous arms and plunked her into the seat next to Abuelo.

"Don't forget your lunch!" Rosita smiled as she set a big basket of baked ribs, tortillas, fruits, and sweet cakes in the carriage next to the jug of wine.

"*¡Vamos!*" Abuelo called out to the driver, and they were on their way.

Abuelo seemed to know everyone in Nueva España, and he greeted many on the road to Amecameca.

"Don José, *mi amigo*," he called out. "What's a good price for cows this season?"

"Don Pedro," replied Don José, "A bit more than last year, but alas! as you know, it is never enough," They shared a smile, and a wave for good fortune.

"Pedro, mi amigo" called out a neighbor tending his sugar cane. "Where are you headed this bright day, my friend?"

"*Buenos días*, Don Pedro Ramírez de Santillana," called out another as he doffed his hat.

These were all neighbors and friends of the Ramírez family. The lowest classes, the Indians and mulattos, remained silent, and respectfully kept their eyes lowered. Once there were but a few defined lower classes in Nueva España – the Aztecs, the African slaves, the Chinese – but through generations of intermarriage they now comprised a broad pallet of hybrid bloodlines, while the Spanish and Criolle jealously guarded their own pure blood.

Juana enjoyed the swaths of color that swept over the road. All but the poorest sported vibrant reds, blues, yellows and oranges, each shirt more colorful than the next, each skirt with more flounces. The lower the class, the more basic the clothing, with the lowest class of Indians wearing only a dust-colored loin cloth or loose, ragged pants with a *tilma*, a rectangular loosely-woven cloth, tied around their necks.

All along the journey fields of maize, sugar cane and beans reached to the horizon. Wagons pulled by slaves and donkeys, and herders chasing cackling geese, shared the road with their carriage, all stepping aside for Don Pedro.

In Amecameca they stopped by the shipping office to see if any packages had arrived for Abuelo.

"*Sí*, Don Pedro," said the shipping clerk. "Two heavy boxes are waiting for you."

"*¡Maravilloso!*" Abuelo declared as he glanced at the boxes. "*Nuevos libros*. We shall have some exciting new books to read when we return." He sent the boxes home with his carriage driver while they went to board the stagecoach bound for Chalco. Seven passengers crowded into a coach made for only six, but Juana did not mind being crowded at all, for the rest of the journey was new and terribly exciting.

"Why are there so many soldiers?" she asked.

"Because there have been so many bandits on the road to La Ciudad de México lately that the government assigns soldiers to protect us. But, here, let's enjoy this journey with a bite of lunch. *Amigos*, would you like some?"

Abuelo shared the generous lunch that Rosita had packed, with enough ribs, chicken, tortillas, and wine for all, all the while talking about the regional governor and even singing a few popular songs.

A burly middle-aged man with calloused hands sat across from them, sitting tall as he realized who his fellow passenger was. "Am I in the company of Don Pedro Ramírez de Santillana, he of the famed *Biblioteca y Grupo de Filosofos*?"

"Yes!" volunteered Juana. "He is my Abuelo. And he has the most incredible biblioteca in all of Nueva España!"

Abuelo and the man with the calloused hands smiled at her enthusiasm, but she was right, her Abuelo did have the most incredible biblioteca in all of Nueva España, with the possible exception of *La Biblioteca de la Real y Pontificia Universidad de la Ciudad de México.*

"Please," said Abuelo, "won't you join us on the veranda some Sunday afternoon?"

"Alas!" spoke the gentleman. "I am the captain of a trading vessel, and I rarely reach the interior of Nueva España ..."

"You travel?" interjected Juana. "Please tell us about where you have been."

And he did. The rugged sailing captain teased her imagination with tales of far-away islands peopled with beautiful women, of exotic fruits picked by monkeys, of waves battering the sea that were taller than the tallest building. She now understood why Abuelo enjoyed these trips so much.

The stagecoach stopped at Talmanalco that evening. Even with the military escort, it was not safe traveling at night. Juana and Abuelo spent the night just outside town, at the hacienda of Don Pedro Velázquez de la Cardena, Abuelo's good friend.

The following afternoon they reached Chalco, a bustling town for merchants and travelers. They joined other travelers as they loaded everything into *canoas*, large dug out boats constructed from México's giant *abuehuete* trees.

As rowers drove the canoas toward the docks at the edge of la Ciudad de México, haciendas sprouted into view, then clusters of homes, then la Ciudad de México itself shone like a rainbow of opals, bursting up against a blue blue sky. Thousands of birds perched on red tile rooftops, swooping to snatch a morsel from a passing basket or picking up a crumb dropped on the street. Abuelo arranged for donkeys and native Indian carriers to haul their luggage. Juana sat tall on a donkey so she could see all La Ciudad de México.

As their entourage lumbered along cobbled streets, Abuelo broke into non-stop praises of La Ciudad de México delights. "Down that street is the *Iglesia de la Inmaculada Concepción*, one of the most beautiful churches in the whole city…. There is the *Capilla de San Salvador* with artwork that will amaze you …. Here is the best bootmaker in all of Nueva España, the one who made the boots I am wearing…There is the silversmith who created the jewelry that I gave you and your sisters last Christmas…. Over there is *Plaza Mayor* with *la Universidad, la Catedral de la Ciudad de México*, and government buildings. All around the Square are the printers, and bookshops, lots of bookshops…"

"Stop! Stop!" laughed Juana. "Abuelo, this is too wonderful! I can't remember them all." She did desperately want to remember them all. She wanted to soak up all that was La Ciudad de México, embrace it as her own.

"Don't worry, little one. We will come back and visit them all again."

He expertly maneuvered the small caravan around hundreds of merchants congregating along streets and in shops in the fresh evening air, and pulled into a lovely boulevard bordered by two- and three- story homes, each dripping in its own shade of bougainvillea intertwined with brightly painted Talavera planters and frescoes. A couple of kilometers down this street they stopped in front of one of the opulent three-story houses. Servants poured out of the magnificent house, some to take care of the luggage, some to bring glasses of lemonade for them both.

"Padre! Padre!" It was Tia Maria. "And Juana! You bless our home by coming here. I am so glad to see you both." She led them up the stairs, through the ornate doorway and into the parlor where plush leather chairs and more lemonade waited for them. "Juan will be home soon and we will all have a bite of dinner. Can I get you something until then?"

As Abuelo's second daughter, Tia Maria was delighted to leave the family hacienda, for she had fallen in love with the handsome Don Juan de Mata, as he had fallen in love with her. She enjoyed nothing more than turning their home into a luxurious, welcoming place, with artwork bursting from all corners.

"Come along, Juana, let's find you your room." They went up to the second floor where Tia Maria showed Juana a room overlooking the large patio where fountains and floral fantasies snuggled into every inch, nestled against adobe benches and carved tables. The central fountain was a statue of la Virgen Maria pouring water from an urn, the Christ Child playing at her feet.

"Here is another that you might like," said Tia Maria, leading her across the hallway to a room with a large window reaching out toward la Ciudad de México and la Gran Catedral de la Ciudad de México.

"Which one do you think you would like, Juana?"

She glanced out the window. "Your patio is so pretty, but I will choose this room, the one facing La Ciudad de México." She picked up an embroidered pillow on the bed. "This is beautiful, such bright colors. It is like some that we have at Panoayan."

"That was created by one of our favorite nuns. I sent some to Isobel, hoping she might like them too."

"Nuns do embroidery work?" Juana had never met a nun, except for her teacher Doña Angélica who had left the Order.

"Yes, indeed. And paintings, and small statues, and lacework. Sometimes we hear hymns that nuns have composed."

EACH MORNING, just before dawn, the boisterous birds set off an alarm in her window. She rushed to dress and ran downstairs where the servants had already set out her breakfast. The dining room was elegant, with one side opening to the lush courtyard, and an elaborate mural on the opposite side.

She paused to look at the vibrant mural with a dynamic scene of a city plaza in early Nueva España with Aztecs in full regalia, showing off their tall ostrich feathered headdresses and bright tunics. Some of the Aztecs were dancing, some were strolling through the plaza, their costumes decorated with the angular depiction of Aztec deities, especially Quetzacoatl, the supreme God of the Aztecs. Spaniards and Criolles were there too, but off to the sides of the mural. Something was wrong.

Tio Juan and Abuelo arrived for breakfast too, and saw her studying the mural.

"These are Aztecs, aren't they?" she asked.

Tio Juan nodded.

"But I've never seen any that look like this," she said. "Any Aztecs that I have seen wear grey tilmas, and none that I know would walk so arrogantly in the city plaza."

"You are right, Juana. This mural is not historically correct. Few Indians walk with such pride now, at least not in our Plaza Mayor."

"Then why is this mural painted like this?" She was clearly puzzled.

"This mural was painted by Aztecs," Tio Juan explained. "The artists were selected by Fray Bernardo himself. Not only did he know what they were painting, but he encouraged it. You see, most in the religious community do not know how to paint, so they bring in Indian slaves to monasteries and teach them how to paint, and the Jesuits believe that such representations as these should be encouraged, to better blend Indian ways and Catholic ways, and aid Indians in their conversion to Catholicism."

"But Indians are so …" she struggled to find the word. "So poor. They can't read or write, and don't even have the same laws as we do."

"That's true," said Abuelo as he took a cup of coffee. "But teaching Indians how to paint gives them a kind of status, even dignity, that they could not have any other way. The priests even tried to teach the Aztecs how to become priests so they could minister to the Indian population, but it didn't work."

"Why not?" she asked. "Weren't they smart enough?"

"Oh, yes, they were smart enough," explained Tio Juan. "They were smart enough to know they didn't want to be celibate the rest of their lives."

"But then, neither are most priests," laughed Abuelo. "But hurry along, Juana," he prodded, "for today I have a very special treat for you."

She grabbed a sweet roll, gulped a quick cup of frothy cocoa, and scampered along as they headed toward the city. Each morning they walked to the city, each morning taking a different route.

"*BUENOS DÍAS*, Doña Romina," Abuelo said as he introduced her to the mask maker. "This is my granddaughter Doña Juana Ramírez, the brilliant scholar. Do you have a beautiful mask that she can wear to the fiesta?"

They had stepped into a world of fantasy and reality. Deer masks covered in deer skin or blue paints sat next to jaguars and imps and devils, all a riot of merriment, with streamers and robes in every color. Everyone could hide behind masks on fiesta days, poking fun at the aristocracy, the government, the clergy, and the simple silliness of life, and everyone did, even some of the aristocracy and clergy themselves.

"Of course, Don Pedro Ramírez," Doña Romina replied. "Here is one of la Virgen de Guadalupe with red roses in her hair that would be beautiful on your granddaughter." She reached onto the wall covered with masks of la Virgen de Guadalupe, each more beautiful than the next. Juana had to agree, the one that Doña Romina selected was beautiful. The adobe mask was painted in bright colors with red roses dripping down the bamboo stick handle that she would hold. A blue robe covered in golden stars completed the disguise.

"But wait," said Juana as another mask caught her eye. "May I have the purple fox, the grinning one?" There was a fox family on her mountainside that she was fond of, and she liked the notion of playing with foxes in the fiesta. She chose the purple fox with red roses behind his ear, the one showing his teeth in a mischievous grin.

"AH, DON FELIPE, mi amigo," said Abuelo to the bookseller. "I've brought my brilliant granddaughter Doña Juana Inés Ramírez to see your glorious books."

"Do you read?" inquired Don Felipe, fully expecting her to say No.

"She reads nearly as well as I do," said Abuelo, "and she is even more curious."

"Then welcome to my humble shop, Doña Juana Inés Ramírez."

"Here, Abuelo, here's the book of poetry by Lope da Vega, just like the one you have."

"Yes, Juana, I bought that book here. Look over here," said Abuelo as he stood by a table of smaller books. "These are treatises and homilies that philosophers and clergy of Nueva España have written. Some are from *España* itself, and even Portugal." He picked up one in Portuguese, glancing through it.

"Are they good?" she asked.

He laughed. "Well, they are not *Don Quixote*, but some of them are quite good. You will enjoy them more as you grow older. Here, Don Felipe, I'll take this one today," handing his friend payment for the book.

SHE FELT SO PROUD walking beside Abuelo as they met more merchants -- tailors, tortilla vendors, leather craftsmen, mask makers, and of course book merchants. Abuelo seemed to know everyone well, people in the Spanish and Criolle castes as well as those in artisan guilds and independent shopkeepers. Everywhere he introduced her as "his brilliant granddaughter," or as "my granddaughter, the scholar."

One evening as they were walking home through an alleyway that she did not know, a brawl broke out at an inn, spilling out into the street, with half dressed women and men with pants pulled down to their knees amid the madness. Bottles ricocheted off walls, even an errant knife got flung with no apparent target. She had seen many such brawls break out at the fiestas, usually among drunk caballeros fighting over a señorita. But this fight seemed to be advancing toward them.

For a moment she was confused in all the mayhem, but Abuelo grabbed her, hiding her behind some huge crates, protecting her with his own body.

Her eyes grew bigger as she watched through a crack, as one nearly naked woman got tossed against Abuelo. This woman draped one of her sweaty hands behind his neck, her other hand pushed her sagging breast into his mouth. Abuelo did not push this woman away very quickly. In fact, he used his own hands to grind her fleshy hips into his groin, laughing like a drunken bandit. The sounds of rutting pigs and braying asses echoed off the walls of the alleyway, adding to the sounds of Abuelo's deep laughter, the laughter that began in his gut and echoed to the skies, a laughter that had always made her smile.

As the ruckus died down, she crawled out from behind the crates and asked who these people were, the ones causing so much trouble.

"*Esas son putas,*" explained Abuelo, with a smirk, and in response to her question about "whores," said only, "They take money for sex."

"Both the men and the women?" she asked, her eyes popping open.

"Yes, both the men and the women, whores and homosexuals. The Church may preach that there is sin in prostitution, especially between the men, but these people don't think so. In a kind of truce between the Church and the people, the police are banned from entering these places, even to stop drunken brawls. People do as they wish behind closed doors." He shrugged his shoulders, grinning. "And once in a while it breaks off into the streets."

Later she asked her sisters if they had ever seen a whore, and neither had. "But what about our madre Isobel?" she asked. "Madre's new lover, Captain Diego, gets sex from Madre, then he pays her by working around the hacienda. Isn't that the same as paying her pesos for sex?"

Juana's sisters hid their raucous laughter behind their hands, but never gave her a straight answer. She could not see any difference. She was sure that Captain Diego would not be there to do things around the hacienda if Madre stopped providing sex, so in her mind, it was providing sex for money, just like a whore.

That night she included a simple request in her prayers.

> *"Dear Virgen Maria, thank you for showing me the whores and prostitutes of La Ciudad de México. I will try to understand them better."*

EACH DAY THEY EXPLORED a different section of la Ciudad de México, and today they were headed directly to the center of la Ciudad de México, to the Plaza Mayor.

She stood in awe at the edge of the Plaza. It was huge, easily comprising twenty or thirty city blocks in size, and it was all open. This was indeed where all of Nueva España mingled. Colorful costumes from every province of the empire sprinkled through the crowd, bright colors dashing around street vendors like a multi-colored serpent, while children chased each other everywhere, belonging to no one and to everyone.

"*¡Aquacates!* Fresh, ripe avocadoes!"

"Hot *enchiladas* today!"

"*¡Tortillas!* Hot from the oven by my own madre's hand!"

Street vendors called out delicacies, while other vendors' carts showed off serapes in striped oranges, reds, blues, and greens beside cotton lengths for women's flounced skirts, woven baskets and hats. Indians, Negros, and mulattos of all shades found a spot on the Plaza Mayor, to talk, perhaps to sing or to stomp to the music.

"*¡Jalapeños! ¡Ardiente jalapeños!*" called out a street vendor.

"Come, Juana, these are truly the best jalapeños in the whole city." Abuelo got them several and they sat on a bench to enjoy them.

They watched the boats that floated along the Central Canal, the broad waterway that the Spanish built to carry produce and products in and out of La Ciudad de México, the huge mercantile exchange sitting on the far side of the canal. Everywhere was laughter; even serious statesmen paused and smiled. This was the La Ciudad de México that she had only glimpsed in her dreams, and here she was, beside Abuelo. Then he began to tell her the story of the creation of the Plaza.

> "Many years ago," he began, "the Aztecs built their capital city, Tenochtitlan, on this very site. It was immense, and glorious. Temples covered in gold reached to the clouds. Had Europeans known of Tenochtitlan, they would have envied it, but Europe was very far away and all they heard were vague rumors of this City of Gold.
>
> "The Aztec nation was ruled with a barbed fist by their king, Montezuma, a miserably cruel king who demanded human sacrifice."

"Why would he kill his own men?" she asked, startled.

> "I don't know what makes someone that cruel, that bitter. He sacrificed women and children too. Thousands and thousands of them were sacrificed to the gods. The people feared Montezuma tremendously, and hated him even more. When our grandfathers, the Spanish conquerors, invaded a couple of hundred years ago in search of *la Ciudad de Oro*, the native Indians, the Aztecs, were glad to help them defeat Montezuma. The 'conquerors' became 'liberators,' liberating the Indians

from the brutal rule of Montezuma. These Spanish liberators had guns, and so that victory came quickly for us as we employed our superior weapons and knowledge." Abuelo paused.

She nudged him on. "What has that got to do with the la Gran Catedral de la Ciudad de México, Abuelo?"

"Well, child, Montezuma's palacio was constructed right here, right on this spot. It was a fantastical palacio, covered in gold, with towers that reached beyond the clouds."

He reached up, as if to touch the clouds.

"Right here. There were hundreds of fine houses too, for the dignitaries of Montezuma's court. The houses and the palacio grounds reached for leagues around."

Here he swept his arms wide to include the whole plaza.

"Our Spanish grandfathers tore down that palacio, they tore down the houses and buildings around el palacio, leaving nothing but piles of stones – and gold -- all over this area."

She imagined tall palacio walls tumbling down, crashing treasures all along the floor of the city.

"Then our stone masons set to work. They took the most beautiful stones and one by one, building layer upon layer, they created the foundation of this majestic Catedral de la Ciudad de México. Goldsmiths worked beside them to drape la Catedral in golden garments."

The Catedral was not yet finished, and when she looked up, she saw stone masons as they worked, and watched the spires climbing higher and higher, foot by foot. She traced the façade of golden lace mantillas, twisting and turning around the spires, saints and ghouls alike peeking out. She would return many times to this spot, always enchanted by the mysteries of the golden spires on the Catedral. She desperately wanted to understand how such a structure could be built and how the gold craftsmen created this mystique.

"Remember, Juana, that la Ciudad de México is a very special place. It is more beautiful than even Madrid. It welcomed the first print shop in the new world, the first university, and the first biblioteca. Now it is here to open its arms to one lively little señorita that I know!"

Juana's eye caught the flamboyant twirl of a young señorita's purple skirt, her eyes challenging Juana to join her, her hand beckoning in a flirty twirl. "*Ven, ven a bailar conmigo,*" called the señorita. "Let's dance!"

Juana felt a warm surge of energy as she joined the sassy little senorita, as a guitarist nearby urged them to spin faster and faster. Two nuns dashed over, their black and white habits blowing in the breeze. "May we join you?" asked one.

"*¡Sí! ¡Sí!*" said the dancing girl.

Each nun took the hands of one of the girls, skipping around and around with them, cheerfully singing the little song that went with the music, a song about a traveler who finds his love under an apple tree. Abuelo clapped while the girls spun in circles of red and purple and orange, with black and white in between, Juana finally collapsing back on the bench beside Abuelo. Abuelo gave the girl and the guitarist several loose coins, thanking them for the joy of the dance, and handed the nuns a few coins too

"My sister Tochtli, and I, Xipil, thank you kindly, señor. May many blessings fall upon you," said the young guitarist, with a proper bow. The two youngsters smiled broadly as they skipped away. Juana liked them immediately, for they were proud of who they were.

"Yes, blessings upon you, father and little ones!" called out one of the nuns as they headed on their way, waving.

These were the first nuns that Juana had met, and she liked these singing, dancing nuns. She had heard of nuns, but her parish church was too small to have any living there.

"Over there is *el Palacio del Virrey*," said Abuelo as he pointed to the left. "Such elegance, such luxury. I don't think anyone has ever counted how many rooms there are in el Palacio de Virrey. The Viceroy and his wife, la Vicereine, live there, and there are dozens and dozens of rooms, perhaps even hundreds of rooms, for all the top-level government officials.

"And there," he said, straightening his back and pointing to the right, "is *la Real y Pontificia Universidad de la Ciudad de México*, the only university in the new world. It was established by the Catholic Order of St. Augustine. That is where I will place most of my books when I die. It has a glorious biblioteca that holds hundreds of volumes, some even more magnificent than mine. Some of my books will also go to you, Juana. I know how you treasure them."

She refused to entertain the notion that her dear Abuelo would ever die, and so would not speak of it. Goats die. Sometimes even fields of crops die. But not Abuelo; he would never die.

"Abuelo, please, Abuelo, may we go visit *la Biblioteca de la Universidad?*" she begged.

"Juana, you know la Universidad is for men only. La Biblioteca is part of la Universidad and it too is forbidden to women."

Her heart fell, her smile vanished. She reached out as if to capture its wonder on the wind. How could this mystical spot be so close, and so far away? "But come, Juana," he said. "I have a surprise for you."

THEY WALKED a few blocks to a tailor's shop. "*Buenos días*, Doña Bonita," he said as he touched the brim of his hat. "Meet my granddaughter, Doña Juana Inés." Juana gently curtsied.

"It is always such a joy to see my favorite customer," said this handsome woman, her wrinkles deepening even more from decades of smiles. Don Pedro was indeed one of her favorite customers, always choosing the finest shawls, fans, and gowns as gifts for his ladies. Juana looked in wonder at the rich-blue gown that Doña Bonita was working on.

"Do you have the clothes we talked about, Doña Bonita?"

She nodded and reached under the counter and brought out a parcel tied up in string, handing it to Don Pedro. "Here, Juana," said Abuelo as he handed her the package. "Take this to the back and change into it."

She expected a pretty new dress, and that would have been wonderful, but that was not it at all. She emerged a few minutes later, smiling broader than she ever had in her whole life.

"Doña Bonita," said Abuelo with a flourish, "meet my grandson, Don Diego!"

Doña Bonita clasped her hands in front of her round tummy, rolling forward in laughter. Juana's slim figure fit perfectly into the loose-fitting burgundy cotton trousers and embroidered white shirt, and the leather vest with inlaid decoration finished it off.

"One more thing," noted Doña Bonita as she crowned Juana/Diego with a cap, a feathered blue one fit for a Criolle, tucking Juana's hair under it.

"Perfect!" declared Abuelo. "Remember, this is just our secret," he said as he closed his lips. Doña Bonita and Juana beamed, nodding in agreement.

JUANA COULD NOT have been happier, constraining her joyful giggles as they marched across the Plaza Mayor to la Universidad. She strutted beside Abuelo as they walked up the marble stairs and entered la Biblioteca de la Real y Pontificia Universidad de México, then froze in wonderment. Such immense beauty! La Biblioteca was even bigger than Abuelo's biblioteca at Panoayan. Bookshelves covered the walls, stuffed to the ceiling with books of all sizes and colors neatly aligned.

She turned to see that the door they just passed through was part of a large mural of San Jerónimo, the patron saint of libraries, at his biblioteca. The real door was cleverly designed to fit into the mural itself. In the middle of the room was a group of desks and chairs where scholars sat and studied. Three men stood in the corner, arguing in hushed whispers, whispers that turned to laughter as they shook hands and parted, like a kettle of hawks flying off.

"*Reverencia*, Fray Payo Enríque de Rivera, I am so glad you are here today," said Abuelo to a stately padre as he approached. "I have brought my grandson, Don Diego Ramírez, to visit la Biblioteca. He will be doing some research for me."

Fray Payo stood nearly six feet tall, slender with a scruffy beard and moustache. He would have looked imposing were it not for his ready wink and his quick wit. An illegitimate child, he had learned to soften his approach to many who erred, and he smiled at all. Neither a Jesuit nor Dominican, but of the Order of St. Augustine, the Order that built la Universidad, he offended no one in Nueva España's hierarchical clergy and lived among them as an honored friar. Fray Payo had once been an instructor in the School of Theology at la Universidad. Plodding the halls and Biblioteca in his black cassock, he personified the values of his Order, the Order that valued education so dearly that it had its own printing presses. King Philip IV of España held him in high regard, trusting his evaluation of the Nueva España territory, one of which he was completing right then.

Fray Payo stopped instantly, with a broad smile to greet them. "Don Pedro Ramírez de Santillana, it has been too long since we have talked. Don Diego Ramírez, it is an honor to meet the next generation of the Ramírez family."

Juana started to curtsy, but stopped herself. "Reverencia," she said, with as much authority as she could muster, touching the brim of her hat.

"Will you be here long, Fray Payo?" asked Abuelo.

"Sadly, no. I am returning to España. Our expedition leaves for Veracruz tomorrow morning, and we will set sail in about ten days. I do wish we had time for one of our vibrant conversations, Don Pedro." His voice had turned sad at missing this opportunity.

"As do I, Reverencia." Abuelo was truly sad in not being able to converse with his friend. "But you will be returning soon?"

"I do hope so. I love la Ciudad de México. And you, Don Diego, do you plan on staying in la Ciudad de México?" asked the good friar.

Juana was caught off guard, gazing longingly at rows of books. "For a little while, sir," replied Juana/Diego, standing as tall as she could.

"Then I hope you enjoy our glorious Biblioteca while you are here."

"I will, Reverencia, I will!"

"Excuse me, Fray Payo," interrupted Abuelo. "Since you are returning to España soon, might I impose on you to take some funds that I owe to a bookseller in Madrid? I am sure my deposit is used up by now, and I do want to thank him for all the magnificent tomes he sends me. This is too much money to trust to most travelers."

"Of course, I am humbled to represent you, Don Pedro. I will send a messenger to pick it up this evening. Are you staying with your daughter, Doña Maria?"

With nods and handshakes, they parted. Fray Payo even shook the hand of Juana/Diego, leaving her frozen in excitement.

Juana could not have imagined how important this serendipitous meeting would be in her life. But for now, she simply soaked up the joy of being in the La Biblioteca de la Universidad.

She had so much to thank la Virgen Maria for that night that her head did not touch her pillow until the small hours of the morning.

ABUELO DIED a few months later. His last words wove themselves into her very soul.

"Come, Juana," he said, as he lightly touched the side of the bed. He looked small, but still strong, against the embroidered pillow. His greying hair had been combed lovingly, an heirloom blanket draped gently over his chest, leaving his arms resting on top.

"You must rest, dear Abuelo."

"Soon."

Juana tiptoed to his side and sat gently on the bed beside him. He tapped softly on his heart as she reached to hold his hand one more time.

"Heart," he said softly. "Follow your heart. Fly. Fly, Juana."

Don Pedro Ramírez de Santillana closed his eyes. He had done all he could do for his family, ensuring they had a strong hacienda to live in, rich fields for nourishment, and a biblioteca, a world of knowledge for the little treasure who now held his hand.

Juana's beloved Abuelo never opened his eyes again, and in a few hours, he took his last breath.

She was inconsolable. She wandered the fields of Panoayan, somehow looking for Abuelo, and sometimes finding him, sitting on a tree stump, his pipe in his hand. He always smiled and tipped his hat. She always made a gentle curtsy. It felt natural to find him there.

They walked, and talked. "Go, my child. Follow your heart. One day your dreams will light the world."… "Be kind to your madre and sisters, Juana. They were not blessed with your talents." … "Know that you are different from others, and wear that difference with pride."… "Fly, Juana, fly!"

Then one day he stopped coming.

Abuelo had given her all the guidance he could give. Now it was up to her to find her path.

When she discovered the art of reading, she knew she had stepped into a world that few knew. When her Abuelo got her the boy's clothing, she felt the world at her fingertips. Now she could do as Abuelo asked of her: She could follow her heart, follow her own path.

Except for her madre Isobel.

Madre Isobel truly did not know what to do with her. She was pretty enough to attract a lover who would give her children, as Isobel herself had done when she met Don Manuel Ramírez de Asbaje, and then Don Diego Ruiz Lozano, but Juana did not want a lover. Even without a dowry she was socially acceptable as a wife to a town merchant, but she did not want that either.

"What a waste for a beautiful young señorita!" she had once heard madre Isobel arguing with Abuelo. "You did this to her,

Papa. All that she wants to do is stick her nose in a book and read. I don't want her," said Isobel as she slammed her fist on the table. "She can't stay here. The saddle maker wants her, so let's give her to the saddle maker. At least we would have good saddles for our ranch hands."

"No!" said Abuelo, equally adamant.

"Why?" demanded Isobel. "Why can't someone else control her arrogant temper?"

Abuelo's voice softened. "Because she is special, my daughter. She has gifts for learning that God himself has given her. You have known that for a long time, Isobel."

"You know she is a burden, and always has been. I don't want her in this house the rest of her life." Isobel was adamant.

Abuelo was equally adamant. "She is to stay here for as long as I live. Then let her go to La Ciudad de México. I will arrange for her to live with Maria and Juan. Let her attend la Universidad if she wishes."

Abuelo won the argument, at least for the time being. She was so glad that Abuelo defended her, for she could not imagine a life with the saddle maker. *I can attend la Universidad!* Her heart leapt with pure joy. *"I have Abuelo's permission to attend la Universidad!"*

SOON AFTER Abuelo's funeral, she approached her madre.

"I must go to la Ciudad de México," she stated.

"No," insisted Isobel. She was in no mood to bargain. "You will stay here and help with the running of the hacienda, and you will stop riding off on your pony every day."

"But I must ride off if I am to learn how to read and write and do numbers."

"You already know enough. You are to stay home." Isobel's incisive stare said she meant it.

"No, Madre. I won't stay home." Juana's equally taut spine signaled her intentions too.

"Be kind to your madre," Abuelo had asked of her.

Although she did not stay at home all day, she was home long enough each day to help her madre with the paperwork of Panoayan.

Since her madre Isobel could not read or write, or do numbers; she needed this help, especially when her new lover, Captain Diego Ruiz Lozano, was not there. She was a strong woman, proud of her figure even after having children, but with a temperament better suited to dancing at fiestas than to doing bookwork. She knew the workings of Panoayan, for she managed it whenever Abuelo was not there, but now, day after day dealing with all the financial issues and managing all the workers was exhausting.

But then, when the work was finished, Juana sped across the fields in time to catch some of the day's lessons from Doña Angélica.

Afternoons found her wandering the fields and forests, discovering synchronicity in the leaves and in the feathers of the pretty little yellow warbler, hearing sound patterns in bird calls and river rocks, watching the shifting shapes of the clouds and mists from the waterfall. Everywhere she felt the cohesion, the interaction of the natural world and wondered how she fit into this world.

And Abuelo's biblioteca. Always she went to Abuelo's biblioteca, devouring book after book, searching for answers when she had not yet formulated the questions.

She made herself useful with the paperwork needed for the hacienda for a time, until Captain Diego Ruiz Lozano began to spend more time at Panoayan. Captain Diego smiled a lot more than she remembered her padre smiling, and he even asked her to read to him sometimes, a simple delight for him on hot afternoons. He stepped in and took over the management of the hacienda, leaving her with no reason to remain at Panoayan. It was agreed that it was time for Juana to leave.

Before leaving for La Ciudad de México, she approached her madre one more time. *"Por favor, mi madre,"* she begged, "let me attend la Universidad. I can dress as a young man, and no one will know who I really am." She had made this request before, and had always gotten the same response.

"Why should a girl go to la Universidad? And dress like a man?" demanded Isobel. "Why pretend to be a man?" Isobel turned her back, closing the conversation.

"Because I need to learn."

"No!" Isobel spun around. "No daughter with a Ramírez name will ever dress as a man. No daughter with a Ramírez name will ever pretend to be someone else. I have given you a good home, a good name, social status, and a respectable future. You snub your nose at all of this?"

"No, mi madre, I do not snub my nose at all your gifts. But this is not the life for me. I don't want some strange man to come and go as he wishes, while I do all the work." Isobel grabbed Juana by her shoulder and slapped her on her cheek. Hard. Juana spun around with the force of the blow.

"Do not criticize my way of life." Isobel's voice was bitterly cold, her back straight, her face set in stone.

"But, madre, Abuelo said ..."

"I know very well what your Abuelo said. I never questioned his wisdom. But this time – this time -- I say NO. Now go and pack for your trip before I toss you out in the gutter."

The topic was closed. Isobel simply would not consider this option, ever.

JUANA DID LOVE La Ciudad de México. Everything about it fascinated her, especially la Biblioteca de la Universidad. Her uncle and aunt gave her a great deal of freedom and most mornings found her detouring to Doña Bonita's shop to change clothes, then slipping into the La Biblioteca de la Universidad, her nose in Greek philosophers or Spanish poets or any of the dozens of other philosophers, scientists and poets represented there. She soon discovered treasures in Theology, Laws, Fees, Medicine, and Arts, the five schools of study at la Universidad. She wanted to know them all, to soak up knowledge from every line of study, from every book. She read Plutarch, Archimedes, St. Augustine,

Valerius, Gongora, and so many more. She found old favorites from Abuelos's biblioteca here, books that he had donated, and she found some new ones too. The books that Abuelo had given to her personally remained at Panoayan until she had a home where she could house them.

One day Fray Payo paused by Juana/Diego in La Biblioteca de la Universidad, smiling acknowledgment, acceptance. She treasured this acceptance since it was her dear Abuelo who had introduced her to this very learned man. She respectfully stood and nodded her appreciation.

"I have heard of the passing of your Abuelo," said the good friar. "I am so sorry. He was a very special friend."

"Thank you, Fray Payo. Yes, he was indeed very special." Then Juana/Diego ventured, "Reverencia, what finds you in la Ciudad de México at this time? When last we met, you were on your way back to España." She felt very grown up asking such a personal question.

"Ah, yes, Don Diego, I did return to España. Our Most Honorable Pope Alexander VII told me that our King has granted me the honor of appointment to the post of Bishop of Guatemala, and I am now meeting with the Archbishop of Nueva España to review our priorities for developing Guatemala."

"Fray Payo…" she began, then stopped herself. "I mean 'Bishop' Payo, the people of Guatemala are blessed indeed to have such an honored Bishop as yourself."

She thought the meeting was finished, but the next day Bishop Payo came again, this time holding a package. "Do you write, Don Diego?" asked the good padre.

"Only a little," she replied, uncharacteristically modest.

"Here is something for you," he said, setting on the desk a sheaf of fine parchment likely imported from Europe, along with ink made from iron salts and tannic acid, and goose quill pens, already sharpened. The gift overwhelmed her.

"What shall I write?" she asked.

"Write anything you want. Anything at all. Write about whatever is important to you. Write an essay, or a poem perhaps, or even a play. You don't even have to show it to anyone, unless you want to. Just write."

With that introduction, she began her writing career. Words that once imprinted themselves in her memory now burst onto pages as if writing themselves. She wrote about the people she met in la Ciudad de México, about ideas that she read about in the library books. She kept notes on who she met, and let her fancy fly with the birds in the Plaza Mayor.

She began her excursion into writing poetry first by reading as many of the poets as she could find – Homer, Montoro, Menander, Virgil, and everything that had been translated into Spanish. When poems referenced Greek or Roman Gods or Goddesses that she did not know, she learned about them too. First, she mastered writing short quatrains, then modeled longer poems from the masters, reaching for their ideas in different words.

Soon she mastered the complex structure of Spanish poetry and wrote about notions of Gods and Goddesses and sins. All forms of poetry flew from her pen as if she were born of poetic speech.

When there were only a few sheets of parchment remaining, she wrote a special poem, one just for Bishop Payo, a poem about the blessedness of God and the beauty of la Biblioteca with ideas erupting from its shelves, captured in rivers and clouds racing through Neuvo España. It began:

> Thunderbolts – Zeus' quill –
>   Shot over His cathedral
>   To fill the world
>   To turn asunder
> All who challenged His domain.

… and continued for twenty more verses, entwining Greek deities, la Biblioteca de la Universidad and the Church. Incorporating Zeus and the Catholic Church into the same thought came naturally, for many of the songs they sang in Church, and many of the fiesta plays did much the same.

"I will get this wonderful poem published!" proclaimed the Bishop.

"No. Please no," she begged. "That poem is just for your eyes. Truly."

"As you wish, young Don Diego, but one day I would like to see your work in print."

TIO JUAN AND TIA MARIA could not have been more gracious to Juana, filling her closet with lacy dresses and inviting men to dine, always introducing her as their "talented, beautiful niece."

None of the men came more than once or twice. She did not know if her lack of dowry or quick wit frightened them off more, and she did not care. Her life was reading, learning, and now writing – that was all she wanted to do.

Tio Juan and Tia Maria simply did not know what to do with her, and her madre Isobel was no help at all. The men they introduced her to did not become suitors, either in marriage or as lovers. Men did not bed women who read books and counted numbers.

There was no place for Juana.

"She did it again." Tia Maria stomped her foot in exasperation. "She flew off on an analysis of some obscure philosopher, clearly irritated that Don José couldn't say a word."

"I know, my dear," said Tio Juan, trying to soothe his wife's temper.

"How many has it been now? Ten? Fifteen? Twenty? No matter how many suitors you bring here, she intimidates them all. She knows well how to entice a suitor – I have shown her myself," insisted Tia Maria. "She just won't do it. All she does is talk philosophy and politics. We must do something, Juan. A withered virgin is a curse on a house." Tia Maria spat on the floor to ward off the evil spirits that might linger there.

"Perhaps we should have encouraged Don Ignacio," Tia Maria commented. "He didn't care that she doesn't have a dowry, or that she talks too much."

"No," interjected Tio Juan. "You were right to reject him in the first place. He does whip his slave girls, and his first wife died under suspicious circumstances. No, that is not a husband for our Juana."

"Perhaps it is time we introduced her to the la Vicereine Leonor as a possible lady-in-waiting." Tia Maria's voice held a tone of sadness, but finality.

"Do you know la Vicereine?" teased Tio Juan. "I didn't know you spent time at el Palacio."

"No," said Tia Maria. "I do not know her. I have only met her briefly. But I do know people who do know her well, so I should be able to manage such an introduction. Doña Estella has placed her daughter there, so I believe I can arrange the introduction."

It was settled. She would be introduced to la Vicereine, the Viceroy's wife, the beautiful Doña Leonor Caretta, as a possible lady-in-waiting. While all of this sounded exciting, Juana certainly did not expect that she would soon be plunked into the center of La Ciudad de México's elite society, but she was.

Tio Juan and Tia Maria knew well what waited for her. Juana did not.

Noches (Nights)

JUANA REMEMBERED WELL the first time she saw Doña Leonor Caretto, Marquise de Mancera, the first time she saw cheeks that were too rosy, lips that were too red, hair that was too blond, breasts that were so bountiful they nearly popped out of her too expensive gilded gown. It was at the end of the procession honoring the new Viceroy as he arrived in Nueva España, the Honorable Don Antonio Sebastian de Toledo y Salazar, Marquis de Mancera.

After a stormy three-month voyage from España, the new Viceroy and Vicereine were greeted on the coast of Nueva España, in Veracruz, by civil and military leaders, the governor and clergy – hundreds of them. After many dozens of handshakes, salutes and blessings, Viceroy Mancera mounted a fiery black stallion festooned with orange and green ribbons, while his wife, Vicereine Leonor Caretta was settled in a plush open coach pulled by a team of milk white horses, riding midway back among the militia. Ceremonial trumpets blew, banners were hoisted, and a regiment in full regalia materialized on the beach.

Thousands of Indians, slaves and Criolles converged along the coastline, waving flags, sombreros, and handkerchiefs. The grand fiesta overflowing with political symbolism for the new Viceroy had begun. For the next several weeks the whole country celebrated.

In Veracruz the keys to the city were presented to the new Viceroy, as they were at every town along the way. The new Viceroy stood tall on a dais, while la Vicereine stood off to the side. All along this journey, he was the one honored, but she was the one who captured the most attention.

"They say she is the most beautiful woman in the world ..."

"I heard he married her only because of her political connections, since what he really wants is to be Chancellor of España..."

...and the people cheered.

Several days later, led by bugles and standards, the whole entourage traveled along a road sprinkled with flowers to Jalapa, then to Tlaxcala and Puebla. In a country that needed little excuse for a fiesta, this procession burst with music, feasts, bull fights and hundreds of formal introductions.

"She is Austrian, not Spanish, so why do we treat her as royalty?"

"Her family is actually Germanic, but she served in the Austrian court of Queen Mariana ..."

...and the crowds shouted "Ole!" and tossed their hats into the air.

In Otumba, a city closely associated with the conquest of the Aztecs, the outgoing and incoming viceroys exchanged the scepter of command.

"They say he paid thousands of pesos for the post of Viceroy..."

"He is from one of the richest families in all of España, I've heard, as is she..."

...and the bugles blew, and cannons were fired and celebrations echoed through the hills.

Several more stops and they arrived at la Capilla de la Virgen de Guadalupe, bowing their heads and knees in homage to the patron saint of Ciudad de México, as they had at a dozen other churches along the way.

...and the people prayed and drank wine and sang and stomped their heels.

A few more days of a religious pause and they were ready to enter la Ciudad de México itself.

Every step was choreographed to demonstrate the power of España and the Catholic church. A purple canopy with gold fringe emerged, riding high on tall poles held over the Viceroy himself as he approached the Plaza Mayor, an honor bestowed upon only kings and conquerors.

One of the stops was at the celebratory arch at the entrance to Plaza Mayor, an elaborate arch created by an honored poet and a respected artist of Nueva España. It was here that the keys to la Ciudad de México were ceremoniously handed to the Viceroy.

A second elaborate ceremonial arch met them at the portico to la Gran Catedral de la Ciudad de México where he swore allegiance to the Catholic Church.

Finally on the steps of el Palacio del Virrey he swore allegiance to the Crown and to the laws that governed Nueva España. By the time the journey was finished, ceremonies had included nearly everyone – the Audiencia, the Church, la Universidad, the military, religious orders, guilds, and brotherhoods.

Now it was time for the huge celebration.

The Plaza Mayor, a riot of color and festivities on any given day, now burst with the hues of a thousand birds and ten thousand flowers, all in celebration. The people from all of Nueva España relished the music and the wine that flowed so freely that day, with every fine costume from every corner of the empire screaming for attention, raging rivers of rainbows merging, flowing, re-merging. People shouted and cheered and sang and rejoiced, rivaled only by the fiesta of the Virgen de Guadalupe each December.

"Look at the emeralds in her necklace…"

"…and the pearls on her breast…"

"…and the rubies in her hair…"

"…and that glistening gown!"

The people of Nueva España could not get enough of this woman who rode in the pale white carriage embellished with alabaster.

Juana was in that crowd in La Ciudad de México, a young señorita enraptured with the decorum, the fiestas, the music, the joy of the entire city. There she saw this blond beauty who was just too ... too.

IT WAS A YEAR later when Tia Maria escorted her to el Palacio de Virrey, a cold, imposing building with its facade of granite and gold. It sat on one side of the Plaza Mayor, near la Gran Catedral de la Ciudad de México, on the far side from la Universidad. This was her formal introduction to la Vicereine Leonor.

Tia Maria and Juana were escorted up a broad staircase bounded by gilded sconces and resplendent portraits of the kings of España, the gold and silver frames capturing reflections of the intricately carved ceiling.

La Vicereine's chamber was large, nearly as large as Tio Juan's entire house. The Persian carpet led from the entrance of the room up to la Vicereine's red velvet settee. All around her were beautiful Criollas in gowns of blues – golds – purples – and reds, with laces and ribbons billowing down. Peacock fans caught the morning breeze, as did the lace mantillas draped over crowns of flowers and gilt.

She was being presented as a possible lady-in-waiting to la Vicereine, a position held by some of the loveliest Criolla señoritas in all Nueva España. The constant wars in the northern provinces pulled young men out of Nueva España, creating a generous pool of beautiful señoritas vying for husbands and for lovers. These ladies-in-waiting were the most desirable of them all.

La Vicereine was unmistakable, a portrait of opulence in a blue cotton gown with embroideries and laces hugging her breasts and scampering down to her waist, chasing down her very full skirt and around the hem. The off-shoulder cut of the gown emphasized la Vicereine's full round breasts. The ladies near her fanned her gently, wispy strands of golden hair flirting with her face.

The walls of the room were covered in rich tapestries, stories of Gods and Goddesses of ancient worlds, as was the fashion. Juana's eye settled on a tapestry of the Goddess Diana with her bow and arrow drawn, leaping through the woods on a hunt with her dogs, and was caught off guard when La Vicereine addressed her directly.

"You've read Plutarch and Machiavelli?" asked Doña Leonor, impressed with this girl standing before her.

"Juana, answer la Vicereine," prompted Tia Maria.

"Yes, Excelencia, Plutarch and Machiavelli and many more distinguished philosophers," she replied, not too modestly.

"How has one so young learned so much?" asked Doña Leonor.

"My Abuelo taught me," Her eyes shone as she spoke of her Abuelo and his biblioteca. "He had a magnificent biblioteca of several hundred volumes, and it was he who introduced me to the wonders of reading and learning."

"Not only that," interjected Tia Maria, "but Juana writes elegant poetry as well."

"Do you write dramas too?" inquired la Vicereine.

"I have not done so as yet, but in your honor, I would be pleased to try."

La Vicereine smiled broadly. "Such talent! Such beauty. I am pleased to welcome you to el Palacio, Doña Juana Inés Ramírez." As a well-read woman herself, la Vicereine appreciated the talents of this young woman.

JUANA'S ROOM faced the east. Brilliant sun rises and a cacophony of birdsong wakened her each morning as she rushed to meet the new day.

Stunning French tapestries and lush brocades covered the walls of her room, with a bed that was bigger, and softer, than any she had ever seen. Every pillow, every piece of décor was chosen by Doña Leonor herself, and much of it was imported. What Doña Leonor lacked in artistic skill, she atoned for in opulence. Everything, from pillows to carpets, was all that it needed to be, and more.

Doña Leonor had even thoughtfully provided her with an intricately carved walnut writing desk, a box of parchment, and writing tools waiting for her touch.

"What are you studying so intently, *carina*?" Doña Leonor stopped by her room as she began unpacking, as she had paused to linger on the songs of the green parakeets on her window sill.

"Just the parakeets, Excelencia. I love the lilt of their melody."

"Please, Juana, my ladies call me Doña Leonor, or simply Señora."

"Of course, Señora. And thank you so much for so graciously providing a desk and paper and pens, and even ink. I hope that I may compose a play or two worthy of your viewing."

"I don't doubt that you will." She picked up one of the dresses that Juana was unpacking. "But first let us call in my tailor and see what he can do. This will be fine for afternoon teas, but I think we need something special for the evenings."

That dress, one of the lovely new ones that Tia Maria had made for her, just did not fit into el Palacio. Even in their first meeting she had felt like a poor country cousin amid the Palace ladies' finery.

"Augusto, there you are. This is my lovely new lady-in-waiting, Doña Juana. I would like you to create some glorious new gowns for her, three, I think. Let us have one out of that stunning crimson China silk that arrived last week, and one in deep purple brocade, and a third one with rich cream and gold velvets. What do you think, my dear?"

"It sounds like more than I ever could deserve, Doña Leonor."

The tailor did just that. Each gown was accented with gold or silver threads in laces and bows, with rich embroideries on the bodice or flowing skirt. Her breasts were too modest to create alluring fields for admiration, so the tailor had her demure mounds peeking out of laces or out from behind bows. Each gown shouted, "Here is a jewel. Honor her!"

She was intrigued with el Palacio de Virrey, this palace of a thousand rooms, this treasury of art and artifact. Her new young friend, the smiling Glorietta, showed her all the galleries, all the back stairways, all the secret hiding places.

Hundreds of paintings, statuary, ceramics, and murals covered every wall, a feast for eyes and souls. Some were of religious themes, especially la Virgen de Guadalupe, but many were politically toned, with portraits of all the Viceroys of Nueva España pieced together along a corridor like a huge mosaic, a whole regiment of leadership. The current Viceroy was the twenty-fifth Spaniard holding that title, and many of his predecessors subsequently flew to even greater heights. No Criolle could hold the position of Viceroy; that position was reserved for one of pure Spanish blood, one born in España.

Along one wall in the Grand Salon was a map showing the expanse of the Spanish empire in the New World, reaching from *La Florida*, the region that Ponce de Leon discovered, to Peru, the Incan empire conquered easily by Francisco Pizarro, both put under the Spanish flag over a century earlier.

In between was the coastline of the gulf that now commanded the enlistment of so many soldiers from Nueva España. And along the west, Juana smiled seeing *"Las Californias"* and the lower peninsula that Cortes once believed to be the mythical isle governed by Queen Calafia.

Armies were marching north now, a huge magnet pulling them further and further, claiming region after region for the Spanish crown, and claiming young men to serve in this massive army. With communications so slow, no one ever really knew the total expanse of the empire of Nueva España; they only knew it kept expanding.

THE FESTIVITIES of the Court seemed endless – afternoon teas, evening receptions, dinners that stretched out over several long walnut carved tables. Servants bustled about continually refreshing the wine and fruit and abundant delicacies within an arm's reach of all guests.

"Duke Hightower, may I introduce Doña Juana Inés Ramírez, one of the jewels of our realm?" Her reputation spread rapidly, and the Viceroy took immense pleasure in introducing her to his titled guests, guests it is said, who traveled hundreds of miles just for this introduction. Her wit and whimsy served her well at these gatherings where she enchanted men and women alike.

Duke Hightower bowed gracefully and asked, "Is Nueva España educating its women now?"

"Only slightly, Your Grace," replied Juana.

"I trust you are in favor of such education, Señorita."

"Indeed, Your Grace. England, as you know, led the way when your own Sir Thomas More advocated such education a century ago, insisting that his own daughter Margaret be schooled in languages and the classics, then wrote about it in his *Utopia*."

The Duke smiled at the fount of knowledge in front of him. "Since you are so familiar with King Henry VIII, you must have considered the issue of the King's annulment from Queen Catherine. Tell me, was Leviticus or Deuteronomy the proper text to follow?"

"I am not a religious scholar, sir, but I do see validity in both arguments. I see even greater validity in Sir Thomas More's argument that the King took a vow, a sacred oath to follow the edicts of Rome, and that he failed to do so in divorcing Queen Catherine."

"Aha. A broken vow. So, the Church of England is a renegade religion?"

Juana shook her head, aware of the political glass she was treading on. "Not a renegade, Your Grace, just a unique approach. I am certain we have much in common."

Viceroy Mancera took delight in asking learned men to interrogate Juana, and watched her exceed their expectations time after time. Never once did he see her falter.

She also enchanted the women of el Palacio society, once learning of women in the Japans. "A secret language just for women?" Juana's curiosity was indeed piqued. "In the Japans?"

She had joined a duchess from Andalusia, one of the honored guests at dinner that evening, and la Vicereine Leonor as they sipped a sweet wine after the dinner.

"Indeed." The Duchess smiled, a conspiratorial smile. "It is a narrow, fluid script, quite lovely. The women use it to write messages to each other in the folds of their fans. Men consider this frivolous writing," she continued, whispering, "but you and I know it is a great deal more than that." The women shared a conspiratorial smile behind their fans.

The Duke and Duchess from Andalusia had traveled further than anyone Juana had ever met, and their stories intrigued her. "Women in ancient Athens, and now in the Japans, seem to have a great deal more power than we honor," she noted.

"In ancient Greece too?" asked la Vicereine Leonor.

"Indeed," explained Juana. "Aristophanes, an ancient Greek playwright, wrote about Lysistrada, a woman who organized the whole city of women to stop the constant wars. Athens became peaceful only through the efforts of the women."

"Isn't that a comedy?" asked the Duchess.

"Yes, it is," said Juana. "But there must be truth in it, or it wouldn't be so funny."

"Perhaps," noted the Duchess, "if we could organize our women as the ancients did, and forbid conjugal rights until fighting stopped, we too could live in a peaceful world."

"But my dear Duchess," interjected la Vicereine Leonor, "how could we ever handle the population explosion of babes that would ensue when the fighting stopped?"

"Isn't it odd," Juana commented to la Vicereine Leonor after the guests had left, "that men often pretend to know so much, and know so little, while women often pretend to know so little, and know so much."

"That's just fine, my dear," she replied. "Let's let them do all of the work, while we have all of the fun."

Juana thoroughly enjoyed these diplomatic gatherings, tossing wits with the worldly travelers, and as those travelers returned to España and Portugal, word of Juana's brilliance and wit began to grow.

Had Juana but had a dowry, she could have had her choice of any number of ambassadors or business leaders or even learned men that she met at these dinners. She did not have the regal bloodline to become a duchess, but she could have done well.

Alas, she had no dowry.

AND LA VICEREINE'S balls! The dazzling gowns of the ladies-in-waiting at the evening balls captured more hues than all the rainbows that ever were from magenta deep as a cavern to a whisper soft pearl pink, from deep iris blues to pale dawn lavender. Silks and brocades, and laces with gold and silver accents stuffed the ballroom with hardly room for the equally regaled men of the court.

Fashion was dictated by the Spanish court in Madrid, which in turn was dictated by the French court. Unlike the ladies of the Court at Versailles, the señoritas of Nueva España were far more likely to enjoy generous hourglass figures, so the ladies of Nueva España flaunted their figures with décolleté necklines. Tight bodices flattened a lady's breasts creating mounds of flesh usually hidden. A huge skirt in very expensive imported silks and brocades emphasized a señorita's small waist, with matching curved high heeled shoes peeking out below. Voluminous sleeves with ruffles and bows, with a lace mantilla and a jeweled fan, completed the silhouette.

The first time Juana joined the evening ball, she wore the red silk gown, the China red sleeves set low on her shoulders, with a red and black mantilla and gold jeweled fan. The boisterous room fell to a murmur as she entered down the red carpeted stairs.

The richly framed mirrors all around the room captured light from dazzling crystal chandeliers, creating a fantasy world swirling in reflections, truly a fairyland of courtship. She was stunning, yes, but it was the saucy walk and flirty shoulders that captured such attention. This was how la Vicereine Leonor taught her to walk, and what an entrance it made. She followed the instructions la Vicereine gave her, for she relished the palace glamor and the attention she was capturing. She did not want to be told to leave.

"Doña Juana Inés Ramírez, your beauty illuminates the entire palacio." An elegant man stood on the step below her and offered her his arm, leading her to the ivory tiled floor.

"I am afraid you have the advantage, señor. You know my name, but I know nothing of you." She tipped her fan to her lips, letting him know that she indeed found him very interesting, another trick la Vicereine taught her.

"Don Roderigo de Talaveras y Galve, at your service." He bowed from the waist, swinging his right arm in the French manner, showing off the gilt-edged laces on his jacket sleeve. She curtsied low, teasing Don Roderigo with a fine perspective for her not-so-hidden breasts.

The guests had just completed a minuet and were taking their places for a lively gavotte. The shush of silks mingled with snapping heels as the couples took their places. Don Roderigo led Juana to the double circle of about forty couples, with women forming the inside circle, and men forming the outside circle, capturing the women in their collective strength. In proper French society men and women did not touch while dancing, but teased each other with tightly choreographed advances and retreats. They seemed to advance close enough for a kiss, but such a kiss was not allowed in proper French society. Even the sensual arm movements were designed solely to tease one's imagination. Eyes and smiles spoke volumes on this floor.

This, however, was not a proper French ballroom. This was Nueva España, and while the steps were similar, the men did indeed partake of a kiss, or let their hands wander curiously over a señorita's curves. On this, Juana's first ball, the men were more respectful.

She danced several times with Don Roderigo that night, and many other nights. She also flirted with dozens of other men of the court, each more attentive and complimentary than the others.

She quickly determined that all the men were Criolle, and nearly all of them were married, but their wives were never in attendance at these balls. Most of the señoritas who were guests at the banquet that evening were not at the ball, not even la Vicereine

Leonor. The ladies-in-waiting who attended the balls were all young and beautiful Criollas, and none of them had dowries, just like Juana. The men were a conglomeration of dinner guests and new guests as well. Most of the men at both events were older, for the younger men of Nueva España were engaged in military activities of one form or another.

By the end of that first ball, she knew why she was there.

The ladies-in-waiting were there to serve la Vicereine Leonor, of course, but the elite ladies-in-waiting, the ones from illustrious families, the ones with large dowries and titles, did not attend these balls. She surmised that the ladies who did attend these balls were there as the elegant bordello for the privileged men of Nueva España, and she was indeed correct.

Some men were looking for only a brief and passionate affair. Others, she discovered, sometimes offered a lady-in-waiting the opportunity of becoming his personal lover, with a hacienda and servants at her command. The women's families had deposited the women here because they were un-marriageable, and becoming such a kept lover would at least shift the responsibility for upkeep away from the woman's family to a lover far away.

For most of the señoritas, this was an elegant, even desirable path for their lives, especially since they were being introduced to the elite men of México. With the scarcity of men due to the persistent wars, this was an excellent option, a way for them to bear children and create a family while living in luxury.

Not Juana.

She felt like she was put on a slaver's block, going to the highest bidder, and all she had to do was provide sexual adventures the rest of her life. She saw no escape. Her madre Isobel did not want her sitting around their house, no matter how smart she was. Tio Juan and Tia Maria certainly made it clear that they did not want her. With no dowry, she had no respectable marriage prospects. So here she was.

She needed time, time to sort things out, time to find another path.

For the moment, she opted to become the brightest star of the ball, the one who could join in their games, and best them. There were lots of games. The soiree often played word games, and she excelled at these. Someone might propose a rhyme scheme, or a first line, while everyone jotted down humorous poems. One of the poems that she wrote openly scolded men, those men who corrupted women's virtue and then blamed women. That poem was a huge success, but there were many others.

When one of men dared to question her Criolle heritage, Juana spat out a sweetly scathing poem questioning his background as well, praising his madre for providing so many choices, ending

Look about, you'll find, señor,

Your father, I guess, and many more!

There were many other parlor games and pastimes. Often each gentleman tossed one of his gloves into a hat, and a lady-in-waiting blindly pulled a glove out of the hat, thus choosing her partner for the evening.

The lovely Lucinda was a much-desired partner for these games. Lucinda hid her eyes behind her fan as she reached in the hat, pulling out a soft doe-skin glove embellished with rubies, waving it softly over her head.

"Who might this belong to?" she cooed.

"'Tis mine! 'Tis mine!" called out a portly older man from the midst of the crowd. This man was known to gift his lovers with jeweled trinkets, so they both won. Lucinda added a jewel to her collection, and the gentleman was guaranteed a beautiful companion that night.

The revelry of the soiree continued well into the night, with men coming and going throughout the ladies' wing of el Palacio, barroom songs echoing off the walls. Juana blocked her door with a heavy chair to keep drunken men from stumbling in. She shared her wit and whimsy with her evening partners, but not her bed. She gave them clever conversation and seductive dances, and that was enough for her.

The men of the soiree took it as a challenge to see who might bed her first.

ON HOT AFTERNOONS la Vicereine Leonor called for palace carriages to take el Palacio ladies to a lovely secluded lake just outside of La Ciudad de México. There, in light undergarments, or in no garments at all, they swam and lounged in sunshine, giving each other full body massages, and kisses.

"Come and join us," whispered Lucinda. "This is how we show men how we like to be pleasured."

Sometimes she did join them, and she did enjoy the pleasures. A woman's touch was gentle, following the natural curves of her body.

When she looked closely, she could see the bulging eyes of men in the bushes, but she did not care. She flaunted her form and desirability in long tall stretches and in playful games with the other ladies. She let her slip fall gently off her shoulders and down to her ankles before jumping into the water, and savored the delicious massages after the swim.

The men might desire her, but they would never approach her at the lake. She felt only the safety of the entourage, and the glorious warmth of the sun.

MEN'S GAMES were far more brutal. In addition to hunting and jousting, they created bull fights that tore a bull apart, piece by piece. The huge central patio of the Palais Virrey was a favorite spot for bull fights. The hot southern sun blazed down on the open courtyard. Beer and liquor flowed freely as two or three hundred men squeezed around the perimeter of the courtyard, large bales of hay protecting them from the bull.

Up above on the balconies, the women looked down as a huge black bull was let into the arena, followed by a matador with his snapping red cape.

The matador flung his cape, teasing the bull, again and again, luring him closer. Men around the perimeter popped out to jab the bull with long pointed iron sticks, egging it on to fierce anger.

The bull knew his purpose: he was to kill the matador before he was killed himself. He lowered his head, rushing the matador, quickly learning that the matador neatly side-stepped his passes. The constant barbs from the perimeter ... the skillful footwork of the matador ... 30 ... 40 ... 50 minutes of battle ... the bull grew weary ... he let his guard down for but a moment. The matador rushed at the bull, thrusting his javelin into the animal's neck.

Bellow as he might, the fight was over. Men rushed from all sides, glad to finish the job, geysers of murky blood shooting up, soaking all their fine garments.

They thought this was great fun.

El PALAIS VIRREY boasted dozens of patios, some cozy nooks, some elegant gardens with lush fountains. One afternoon Juana sat by the Magi fountain in one of the resplendent patios of el Palacio, a quiet chill settling over everything. That afternoon the ladies were especially subdued at la Vicereine's tea time. Juana asked Glorietta if she had felt it too.

"Haven't you heard?" asked Glorietta.

"Heard what?"

"That Lucinda got pregnant. She left yesterday to have an abortion and she never came back."

Everyone knew that abortions were available, but only in stinking rooms with untrained women who knew little about human anatomy. When all went smoothly, all were happy. But when there was trouble, even death might ensue before help would arrive. Legitimate doctors would not do abortions from fear of reprisal from the Church, so the midwife was on her own.

"Lucinda took a servant with her," explained Glorietta, "but the servant hasn't come back either. La Vicereine Leonor has sent out people to find them, but so far no one knows what happened."

"Didn't she tell anyone where she was going?" asked Juana.

"No," said Glorietta softly. "No."

Of course not, thought Juana. No one would want to intrude on Lucinda's privacy, so no one would ask. No one wanted to ask, knowing full well that she could be the next one looking for an abortion. Now no one could find them.

Anything could have happened. They could have been accosted before, or after, the abortion; they were, after all, two well dressed women in a questionable area of La Ciudad de México. Lucinda could have died from the abortion, while her servant might have disappeared in the labyrinth of the city, too frightened to even tell anyone. Lucinda could still be at the clinic, perhaps bleeding to death, too weak to move, with her servant beside her. No one knew.

That night she prayed fervently to her dear Virgen Maria.

Dear beloved Virgen Maria, please protect Lucinda. Dear Señora, why have you brought me here? I have done no good for Lucinda, or for anyone else. Do you truly want me to end up like Lucinda, on a cold forgotten cement table somewhere?

There were no palace parties for the next week. The hallways in the ladies' wing fell silent as the search continued. Gradually men came back to the ballroom and the ladies came down the stairs. Within a couple of weeks, the candle-lit hall again mingled with laughter and the rustle of silk gowns.

No one mentioned Lucinda.

Juana felt overwhelming sorrow for her. The jewels that Lucinda was gifted would have paid for the abortion, but they would never have comprised a dowry, for el Palacio señoritas were not considered marriageable. Juana came to hate the soirees, the devil's dances, the witty repartee, the pseudo courtship. She hated the notion that she was there to please men, whether in the ballroom or in the bedroom.

"Juana, why so glum?" asked Don Roderigo as he ran his finger from her lips down her throat and along her breast, slipping his fingers under the sparkling lace of her bodice to squeeze her nipple.

She slapped his face and when he removed his hand she said, "I worry about Lucinda."

"Don't worry about her," he shrugged. "She is probably on her family's veranda, soaking up sunshine."

"Why do you think so? Have you seen her? You know that baby she aborted might have been yours."

He raised his eyebrows in feigned alarm. "Mine? No, not mine, little señorita. I am always careful."

Roderigo was referring to the practice of pulling out before he climaxed. She had doubts that the trick worked. It certainly had not worked with Lucinda.

In time Lucinda was mentioned no more, Doña Leonor even giving her room to a new lady-in-waiting.

JUANA BEGAN wandering away from el Palacio de Virrey, sometimes creeping silently into the pews of the incomplete Catedral de la Ciudad de México, letting the sun's rays encircle her as they burst through the newly installed stained-glass windows. She looked in awe upon the six-piece altar carving at the front of the Catedral, the one depicting the life of la Virgen Maria, accented in inlaid gold with painted Talavera touches, especially the brilliant blue robe that la Virgen Maria wore.

Sometimes she walked out to the countryside, to the lovely small Capilla de la Virgen de Guadalupe, lighting a candle and softly asking for la Virgen's guidance.

She kept coming back to the same questions: Why were the women of her family – her madre Isobel, her sisters, even her aunts – content to live as whores, and she was not? Why were the ladies of the Court so anxious to find a man who would support them, and she was not? Her Abuelo had told her she was different, but Why? Why was she just different? The only answers that she had were those she could not admit to, not even to herself.

"Doña Juana! Doña Juana!" The sweet call came from across the plaza where she was sitting, enjoying the parade of people as she had with Abuelo. It was the voice of Xipil, the native Aztec boy she had first met when Abuelo brought her to La Ciudad de México. He had played the guitar while she spun in circles with his sister. She had seen him sometimes in the plaza, always joyously smiling. She always had a few pesos to thank him for his songs.

Today Xipil was waving his arms and running toward her. Her eyes softened. Xipil was a good boy, and she was glad to see him.

"What is it, Xipil? Why are you so excited?"

Xipil was grinning and spinning in circles. "Doña Juana, do you remember when you gave that beautiful mantilla to my sister Tochtli?"

"Sí, I do remember." His sister was to be married. Her family was so poor they could give her little. She gave Tochtli a rose-colored mantilla for her wedding day, and a few pesos to help with the festivities.

"Doña Juana, they have had a baby! A baby boy! They have christened him 'Pedro,' in honor of your Abuelo. Is that okay?"

"It is splendid. Abuelo would be pleased that you remembered him."

In a burst of pure joy she took his hands, laughing with him. "Xipil, I am so happy," she beamed. "Tochtli and little Pedro, they are fine?"

"They are wonderful!" he assured her.

"What is little Pedro's Aztec name?" she asked. She loved the lyrical names given to Aztec children. "*Xipil*" meant "warrior" because his madre said he came out fighting, and his sister was named "*Tochtli*," meaning "rabbit," because her tiny legs were ready to jump around right away, or so the children were told. All children were christened with Biblical names, but native children were also given beautiful Aztec names.

"Pedro's other name is 'Xipilli'," he said.

Jeweled prince. She knew some of the Aztec language, Nahuatl, from stories her nurse Rosita had told her when she was young. She reached into her sleeve, letting loose a trinket that she had tied there. Don Roderigo had given her the trinket a few days earlier as a bribe to get to her bed. She gave Don Roderigo a poem instead, and he was furious. Now she knew why she had tied it in her sleeve this day.

"Here," she said. "Here is a little something for our little Xipilli, for his food, his clothes, his schooling, for whatever you think he needs."

The trinket probably cost Don Roderigo a hundred pesos, but Xipil could easily get fifty or sixty pesos for it in the merchants' market behind them. Fifty or sixty pesos would do a lot for a family like Xipil's.

He dropped to his knees and began kissing the hem of her skirt. "Come, come, Xipil. That is enough. Now go kiss Tochtli and Xipilli for me. Tell them that I will keep both in my prayers."

A cooling breeze wrapped itself around her, and she smiled as she watched him run off, waving.

WITH HER SPIRITS brighter than they had been in a while, she decided to go to the ball that evening, even fluffing her red silk gown. Her lovely friend Glorietta caressed her hair into sensuous curls, so altogether she looked, and felt, spectacular.

She avoided dancing with Don Roderigo that evening, feeling a chill down her spine every time he looked at her, as though he were calculating just what it would take to rip off her gown.

When the time came for the game with men tossing their gloves into a hat she quietly stepped aside, drifting to the dark back stairwell leading to the ladies' chambers. She just did not want the inevitable confrontation about sexual favors the men felt they deserved, so she stepped away. She climbed the stairs faster than usual with ominous shadows chasing her every step. Reaching the third floor she stepped onto the elegantly tiled corridor of the ladies' wing, down the deserted hallway.

Then she stopped.

There was Don Roderigo, leaning against a pillar, slapping one of his gloves into the palm of his hand. Once. Twice. Three times he slapped the glove into his hand. "Come, my little señorita," he whispered. "It is time. Remember? You picked my glove tonight."

She knew it was a blatant lie. She had not picked anyone's glove that evening. She walked faster and tried to rush past Roderigo.

"Get out of my way!" she demanded.

The hallway was too narrow. He grabbed her around the waist and flung her against the wall, knocking the breath out of her. He pinned her there, his mouth covering hers so she could not scream. One arm held her in place while the other hand expertly ripped open her skirt. He let his arm loose for a moment to pull down his trousers. She took that moment to pull away, and when she could not escape, she pounded him with her fists and rammed her knee into his groin.

His face registered pain for an instant then transfigured into revenge as he flung her to the tile floor, banging her head. Then he jammed himself into her …

then again …

and again, each time banging her head harder on the tiles

… again … harder … harder …

She tried to raise herself up, but every time she tried, he only slammed her head down on the tiles again … yet again. What had become a blurry nightmare morphed into a black chasm, ending in a desolation of pain.

She woke as a servant was gently cleaning the sticky goo and the blood from around her stomach and legs, the world a blur. Her head ached beyond reason, her face blue and battered. She was in la Vicereine Leonor's chambers, on a soft sofa. Her beautiful red velvet ball gown lay in tatters on the floor nearby. A doctor stood nearby, pulling a vial out of his case, but it was la Vicereine who was clearly in charge.

"No," said la Vicereine Leonor. "Not yet. I do not want her to sleep just yet. She needs a warm, soothing bath and a cup of warm wine. Then she can sleep."

La Vicereine saw Juana's eyes blink open, with fear still racing through her pain. "Don't worry, little Juana," she assured her. "Roderigo has been banned from el Palacio. I have warned him that if he ever touches you, or any of my ladies, ever again, I will have him pulled apart piece by piece on the rack." La

Vicereine Leonor meant it. "He will never hurt you again, Juana. Tonight, you will stay here with me."

Roderigo knew, as did la Vicereine, that the rack had not been used in Nueva España in decades. But Roderigo also knew that la Vicereine Leonor had the power to have a rack constructed that would rip him apart, limb by screaming limb. He did not want to contemplate which appendage would be pulled out first.

She drifted in and out of consciousness all night, barely aware that all night long there was at least one lady-in-waiting holding her hand, and that la Vicereine sat on a chair nearby. For the next few days one of the ladies-in-waiting slept in Juana's room, helping her chase away the nightmares that sometimes erupted. Each one slept next to her, holding her close when the screams came, and then the screams came less often.

ON THE THIRD day she looked at herself in the mirror, an ashen reflection of herself, and set to the business of setting herself right. No quivering coward like Roderigo was going to control her life. She bathed; she set her hair in soft curls; she dabbed a bit of rouge on her cheeks; she chose a soft, revealing gown for afternoon tea. She set her shoulders square and rejoined the life of el Palacio.

But for years her heart abruptly paused whenever dark shadows wavered.

As her life at el Palacio returned to normal once again, she found herself spending more time with la Vicereine Leonor, and writing poems in her honor. La Vicereine was truly one of the loveliest and most caring people she had ever known. The only way that she knew to thank her was to present her with elegant heart-felt poetry.

She wrote of la Vicereine Leonor's legendary beauty, her fair golden crown, the divine harmony of her form. She wrote of her eternal devotion to one so blessed by the gods … and she meant every line. Leonor had been gracious and kind beyond belief, bestowing upon her a comfort and protection unlike any other.

A diadem crowns your brow,
A stem of stars surrounds,
A bough of blessings
from Bethlehem

La Vicereine Leonor loved these poems. They spent many hours together with Juana reading stories and poetry of ancient and contemporary luminaries, and sometimes telling her own stories and poems. They had lively conversations about Machiavelli and Gongora, while Juana helped la Vicereine with translations of Portuguese, and la Vicereine helped her with some glorious writings in French.

Now, except for la Vicereine's siesta in the afternoon, they were together from dawn to dusk. This arrangement suited them both well. La Vicereine had never had a lady-in-waiting so versed in languages, in philosophy, in poetry. As a well-educated woman herself, she treasured every moment. Juana, for her part, let go all the pretense of flirtation and simply enjoyed la Vicereine's company.

THE LADIES OF THE COURT gathered one afternoon to present a play for La Vicereine Leonor's pleasure, one of Juana's plays, a play where the Goddess Aphrodite tricked Eros into hypnotizing the entire country into loving only themselves, but Eros misunderstood and ended up giving the wrong command under hypnosis, proclaiming the command that everyone should love everyone else. Women chased men … and women; while men chased women … and men.

La Vicereine loved the mayhem that ensued, laughing and clapping, and declared without hesitation, "My dear, this is such a splendid play! Here is what we shall do. We shall hire Doña Caterina Rosa to come play the lead role, and we will present the play to the whole Court!"

So it was that Doña Caterina Rosa came to el Palacio de Virrey in one of her resplendent gowns. No one knew if the "Doña" was a proper title for Caterina, and no one cared, for she commanded a room when she walked in, flaunting her jewels and laughter. Doña Caterina could not read, so Juana read her lines for her, and within two readings, she knew her role. The date was set, the stage was created, and over three hundred guests squeezed into the ballroom to see the famed actress.

The ladies of the Court took their places on the stage, then Doña Caterina entered, her sizzling azure gown accenting every nuance of her voluptuous figure. She took her place on the stage as everyone applauded and roared. Then all fell silent, waiting for the play to begin.

Doña Caterina raised her hand, as if to speak, then stopped. For a long few seconds, she stood there, unable to utter a word. Doña Caterina had forgotten her lines.

Juana rose from her seat in the front row and, as if it were planned, said simply, "Welcome to our play about love and romance. It begins with the Goddess Aphrodite gathering around her all the Gods and Goddesses on Mount Olympus."

Doña Caterina nodded. That was all she needed.

"Gather around, all ye Gods and Goddesses of Mount Olympus," proclaimed Doña Caterina in the persona of Aphrodite.

"Come, Circe and Selene. Come, Ares and Pan.

Let us shed joy throughout the whole land!"

The play was a huge success, and as she exited after her bows, Doña Caterina flung her arms around Juana, lifting her off the ground in a huge hug. "You are indeed a brilliant woman!" declared Doña Caterina.

Doña Caterina came several more times to the Palace to play roles in Juana's plays. Once she played the role of the Greek Goddess Venus to absolute perfection, and another time was Chantico, the Aztec Goddess of home and hearth. One of the plays told how men of the court drew lots from a pot, not for the ladies' love, but for their scorn.

Doña Caterina loved Juana's plays, and loved sharing laughter and accolades with her. Doña Caterina also loved the jewels that men slipped into her bodice and into the pockets of her stockings.

One of the most popular plays was "Love Is A Labyrinth," with the story based on the tale of Theseus and the Minotaur. No serious sermon, this was a raucous, and raunchy, play with mix-ups and merriment as Minas' daughter plots to help Theseus, while Phaedra and Ariadne, and Lidorus and Racino cause nothing but mayhem. In the end Virtue triumphs, and all is well.

With the plays and the poetry, and her friendship with La Vicereine Leonor, Juana's life settled into an unexpected flow, but she knew that this arrangement could not last forever. One day the Viceroy would be recalled to España, and she would once again be on her own. She had to find her future.

ON A SPRING day when wild roses tickled the countryside, la Vicereine Leonor invited Juana to join the Viceroy's party on a journey to the southern provinces, past the region where she grew up.

This was the opportunity she was waiting for. The Viceroy might review his broad domain, but she could investigate a part of her past that had puzzled her for a long time. Her madre Isobel had told her that she had no dowry. She understood that her father left nothing for her, or her sisters, when he left Panoayan abruptly soon after she was born. And she understood that her dear Abuelo put most of his money into properties for his children and books for his biblioteca, and by custom he had no responsibility to provide dowries for his many granddaughters.

But she did not understand why her madre told her she had no godparents, no godmother, no godfather. Her two sisters had godparents, and, if she could identify her own godparents, perhaps they could help her acquire the dowry she needed to have a noble marriage. If indeed she had to be married, she wanted to be rich enough to hire nannies and cooks, and slaves to do the housework, leaving her time to study and to write, and only a dowry could promise that. She thought she could find the answer at the church where she was baptized.

There were answers there; she just had to find them.

THE EIGHT CARRIAGES of the Viceroy's party left at dawn and headed out over the road toward Amecameca, accompanied by a whole regiment to protect them. They pulled onto the wide, cobbled semi-circle that was the entrance to the Velázquez hacienda, the largest and most elegant hacienda in the region, the home of Don Pedro Velázquez de la Cadena, one of Abuelo's closest friends.

Juana had visited this hacienda when she traveled with her Abuelo, and had enjoyed many of the Velázquez fiestas.

The sun was just slipping away, and the fiesta had begun. Three mariachi bands roamed the estate while guests swirled their hips and clapped their hands. Everyone wanted to welcome the Viceroy and his beautiful wife. A pig was in the pit in the ground, slowly baking, and half a cow was being churned on the rotary pit. The huge flat open fire was stuffed with thick steaks, spiced chicken, lamb, and goat. Beer was flowing, and every imaginable delicacy was offered to the hundreds of guests.

The Aztec servant spoke with respectful authority as he led the ladies up the broad staircase at the Velázquez hacienda so they could freshen up for the fiesta. "Excelencia, you and your ladies have rooms in the hacienda, as does the Viceroy. The men will sleep in guest cottages that we have set up for them."

An older gentleman appeared at the foot of the staircase. "Excelencia, Señora Vicereine, you do us more honor than our poor home can bear. Please let me know if I can make your stay more enjoyable." His long moustache jumped up and down as he spoke, just as Juana remembered when he sat with her Abuelo on the veranda.

La Vicereine Leonor nodded. "I will indeed, Don Pedro. Thank you for your hospitality."

Don Pedro Velázquez turned to leave, but caught a glimpse of Juana. "Doña Juana Inés Ramírez, what an honor to have you grace our home once again."

"Don Pedro Velázquez de la Cadena!" She smiled broadly, standing proudly. They had not met since her Abuelo's passing nearly ten years previously. His long hair was now grey, but his smile was as she remembered it, broad and contagious. "How gracious of you to welcome us." Don Pedro's sharply trimmed white goatee unquestionably identified the one who had visited with her Abuelo so often, and who had so often challenged her to join the lively conversations.

"I very much miss the splendid debates with your Abuelo. Tell me, are his books still at Panoayan?"

"Some of them are. He bequeathed many to la Biblioteca de la Real Universidad Pontificia de México, but for now at least the ones he has left in my care are at Panoayan. You are, of course, welcome to borrow them any time."

In but a few minutes the courtyard rustled with the hundred-hued petticoats of the ladies' fiesta gowns. She knew most of the Criolles in the region, for had the entourage taken the other fork a few miles back, they would have gone right past Panoayan.

Juana's eyes teased the caballeros at the fiesta. These were the celebrations of her childhood, danced with abandon under bright stars. The ruffles on her tiered skirt hardly settled all evening. She was delighted to see señoritas she knew, even some of the girls from Las Amigas. Many were married now, most of their husbands away with the military.

DOÑA LEONOR had given her permission to go on an errand "to see her family" the next day, so she rose before dawn, grabbed her satchel, and headed to the stables. The groom had a pretty little mare waiting for her.

"No," she insisted. "I'll take that one," pointing to a regal black stallion.

The black stallion in the adjacent stall pawed his foot, demanding attention. He was a young horse, about four or five years old, and a good height, about sixteen hands tall. He looked straight into her eyes, challenging her for an adventure.

"But the stallion is hard to handle, señorita," said the groom. "It is a horse for a caballero, not for a pretty señorita."

"It is okay," said Don Pedro Velázquez de la Cadena stepping out of the shadows. "I have seen Doña Juana ride. She is a good equestrian, especially for a pretty señorita. I think Thunder would enjoy such an adventure. Tell me, Juana, why were you riding so fast when I saw you as a child?"

"I was rushing to get to school. My sister rode in the pony cart, but I loved riding bareback across the mesa. Well, Thunder," she said, "what do you think? Do you want to go on an adventure today?"

Thunder pawed at the ground, tossing his mane, ready to go.

"Okay, then, *vamos!*"

She was an excellent equestrian and, with the black stallion racing, she soon found herself miles away from everyone, slipping through back roads and byways.

She stopped Thunder to rest by a secluded creek while she changed into the men's clothing that she had brought in her satchel. The priest at her church knew her, but on this day, she did not want to be recognized. She rubbed some dirt on her face to look a bit more rugged.

She sat tall in the saddle as she approached the church. "Excuse me, sire, are you the friar of this church?" she asked, knowing full well that this short man with the large brimmed hat was indeed the friar.

"Sí, señor," he said. "I am Fray Miguel de Asbaje. What can I help you with?"

She had always known him as "Fray Miguel." The "de Asbaje" part was new to her. Was he a relative of her father, Don Manuel de Asbaje? A cousin perhaps? Or just someone from the same region in España? This was not the time to ask.

"Would it be possible, Fray Miguel, to look at your church records? An old ledger perhaps? I want to look up some old baptism records, perhaps from sixteen or seventeen years ago."

"Of course, señor, Don ….?"

"Don Diego Esteban Ramírez. I am a cousin of the Ramírez family." She did not know how she came up with "Esteban," but it sounded good.

"Ahhh, so that is why you look familiar. Welcome to our humble church." Fray Miguel flourished his hat in a regal bow and led Juana/Diego to a back office.

He pulled a large black leather-bound book from the shelf and set it on the sole table, a rickety table barely big enough to hold the large ledger. A sliver of light from the one window fell on the ledger. "Here. Take your time, Don Diego. May I get you some coffee?"

"Yes, please." She opened the ledger, gently turning the pages until the births, deaths and marriages of 1651 were listed. She ran her finger down the page, looking for November 12, her birthday. Her name was not there. She read down the list, slower. No, her name was not there. There was no entry that could even be a variation of her name. Perhaps there was an error.

She followed the listings to 1652. Nothing.

Then 1653. Nothing. Nothing. It was as though she did not exist. She started to panic. What was wrong?

She turned back to 1651, and went backwards. 1651 again. Nothing.

1650. She ran her finger down the list very slowly. Nothing.

1649. Again, nothing. She was ready to give up, but she turned back one more year.

1648. Nothing. But wait... here was an entry. "Juana Inés, baptized December 2, 1648." There was no listing for "Madre" and none for "Padre," but there were two people listed as godparents: her madre Isobel's brother and sister, Miguel Ramírez and Beatrix Ramírez, the aunt and uncle she hardly knew. This child was listed as a "daughter of the Church," a phrase often used as a child of a religious person, a bastard.

She quickly turned back the pages to find the entries for her sisters. Those entries listed "Doña Isobel Ramírez" and "Don Pedro Manuel de Asbaje" as the parents of her sisters, and listed the same uncle and aunt as godparents. Her sisters had a madre and a padre, and although she was listed with godparents, she was only "a child of God." None of this made sense. Her head began to spin.

Fray Miguel returned with the coffee. Her questions blurted out before she could even think.

"Who is this child?"

"One of the Ramírez children. You must know her."

"Why isn't her madre listed? Her padre? Who chose these godparents?"

"I do not know, señor."

"Was she baptized?"

"All children are baptized, señor."

"Why is she listed as a child of God? Do the godparents know they are designated the godparents of this child?" She hit the table with her fist, nearly toppling the ledger to the ground.

Startled, Fray Miguel shot to attention. "I do not know, señor."

She leaned over the table, staring into the padre's eyes. "Are you the father of this child?"

Fray Miguel literally shook in fear. "No! No, señor! *Por favor*, please, Don Diego, I had left this parsonage for the hospital in La Ciudad de México at that time. I was very ill." Fray Miguel pointed to the year 1648 on the ledger. "I do not know the circumstances of this child's birth."

She saw the deceit in the padre's eyes as he stared at the ground and turned away from her. He was clearly an outright liar. No matter whether this padre was or was not at the parish, he did know something about that entry in the ledger. He just was not telling Don Diego.

She could not push too hard for she was not sure she really wanted to know the truth. What if that entry really was her? Why was it listed three years earlier than she was born? Or was she born three years earlier than she thought? Or was neither date correct? Could she have been born prior to 1648, or after 1651? Was she 18 years old? Or 15? Or some other age entirely? It was not unusual for an illegitimate child to be listed as "a child of God," but why wasn't her madre listed when her uncle and aunt were named, and why did the Padre deny any knowledge of it?

She got back on Thunder, commanding him to get out of there, knowing she would discover no more from Fray Miguel.

Fray Miguel peered out from his small window, watching Don Diego send his horse galloping off, angry and rushed, much as he had watched Fray Antonio Miranda spur his huge black stallion and gallop off many years ago.

***

WAS IT FIFTEEN years ago? Or eighteen years? Fray Miguel could not remember exactly. Fray Antonio Núñez de Miranda, who even then was a powerful force in the Church hierarchy in La Ciudad de México, had arrived in the early hours of pre-dawn, riding all night with a basket, a basket carrying a small, sickly newborn.

Fray Miranda had slipped into the San Jerónimo Convent under cover of a dark moon, and was handed this baby wrapped in sheep's wool, a tiny package in a small reed basket. He rode all night, pushing his horse to reach the parish priest before daybreak. He did not want to be spied in this region, at this hour.

The babe wailed for food, and Fray Miguel immediately sent for a local wet nurse, while his servant nudged some milk from the she-goat in the enclosure at the back of the church. The servant moistened a bit of cloth, squeezing one drop after another into the small babe's mouth.

Fray Miguel and Fray Miranda had met a couple of years earlier when they shared sleeping quarters on a boat from España to the new world. Fray Miranda was assigned to the corridors of intrigue in La Ciudad de México; Fray Miguel came to this small country parish.

"They have to be Criolle," insisted Fray Miranda.

"I know just the place. Doña Isobel ..."

"Stop!" Fray Miranda held up his hand. "I do not want to know where the child goes. Just make sure it is raised properly. Is this woman trustworthy?"

"Oh, certainly," replied Fray Miguel. "Very trustworthy. She doesn't come to church often, but the fear of God is in her heart." Doña Isobel Ramírez was the perfect choice. She already had two illegitimate daughters; one more would not raise an eyebrow. Her lover Don Pedro Manuel de Asbaje, the Fray's countryman, had decided to return to España soon, even carrying some letters on behalf of the Padre, so he could never say anything. Yes, they were the perfect choice.

"But we must enter the babe into the ledger," noted Fray Miguel, taking out his inkwell and a sharpened quill, and opening the ledger to the current date. He poised his pen to write.

"What is its name?" asked Fray Miguel.

"It has no name. Just give it one. And not there! Not on the current page. I do not want its arrival to be on this date." Fray Miranda turned a couple of pages in the ledger. "Here. Put the entry here. Any name you want."

With no more instruction than that, Fray Miranda mounted his horse and rode off, angry and determined, just as Don Diego had done now.

***

A FIERCELY ANGRY Juana spurred Thunder on. Was Isobel really her madre? And Don Pedro Manuel de Asbaje, was he truly her father? Did she have sisters? Aunts and uncles?

And Abuelo. Was he truly her grandfather? That doubt plunged like a rusty butcher knife in her gut. What if he was not her grandfather? What if ....

She reined in Thunder at Abuelo's grave at the edge of Panoayan, racing to ask him. She fell to her knees at his grave, fiercely begging,

"Please, Abuelo, tell me the story. Tell me what happened. Dear Abuelo, I truly don't care how old I am ... that means nothing. But you. You. I so desperately need you as my Abuelo. Please, please, I beg of you. Tell me what happened."

The breeze was silent, whisking its secrets beyond her reach. She knelt for half an hour or so, then anxious that no one should see her, she kissed the cross on Abuelo's grave, and, pained that he would not share this bit of knowledge with her, she rode Thunder back to the creek where they had stopped that morning.

She talked to Thunder while she re-created herself as a proper señorita. "Well, Thunder, what do you think now? Who am I? Am I the bastard child of a nun, or a priest? Or both? Am I even Criolle? What if I am a gutter child that has been rescued? But if so, why? And who reached down to rescue me?"

A thousand questions smashed up against her brain. She needed to ask someone, but who? Fray Miguel clearly was not going to share anything he knew which, if the news was bad, was a blessing. Her dear Abuelo might have told her once, but now he was gone. Her madre? Would Isobel tell her? More importantly, would Isobel tell her the truth?

Suppose that Isobel told her she was an abandoned child, a gutter child that someone brought to her. Who would she be then? One's family determined everything in Nueva España, the social position, the financial options, the legal status of a person. It was acceptable to be an illegitimate child, if your parentage was Criolle or Spanish. She knew that even Bishop Payo was illegitimate, but born in España, so she knew this to be true.

Once her madre Isobel was aware that she knew the truth, there would be no more pretense. She would have no family, no connections, no position in society, no financial options, and would be tossed to the bottom of the social and legal systems. Just like slaves and beggars, she would have no honor whatsoever and would leave the service of la Vicereine Leonor in disgrace, to do … what? Become a whore? a beggar? But surely her madre Isobel would never have accepted a gutter child into her home. Would she?

Juana's life was a lie.

One thing seemed certain: her uncle and aunt certainly did not know they were listed as her godparents. It was likely that her madre Isobel did not know, for Isobel could not read and likely never saw the ledger.

A parakeet flew past, its emerald wings brushing her brow. *Of course!* She thought. *Of course! You will fly*, her Abuelo had told her. *Just follow your heart.* The choice about the future was hers, and hers alone. There were no more Roderigos to rape her, no padres with secrets. There was only her future. HER future. No matter what the future held, it was her decision.

She turned toward Thunder. "What should I do, Thunder?" she wondered out loud as she stroked her steed's neck. He simply pawed the ground, then flung back his head, looking off to the distance.

She smiled despite her distress. "You're right. All I can do is keep on going and not look back."

SHE RODE BACK to the Velázquez hacienda in silence, barely noticing the people along the roadway, sometimes pushing Thunder, and sometimes holding him back, not knowing if she wanted to go to la Vicereine Leonor or not.

It was evening by the time she got back. At the doorway she paused, erased the wrinkle in her brow and set her lips in a calm smile. This was her new persona, a señorita with a calm smile. It would be many years before her eyes sparkled as they had at the fiesta just yesterday.

She followed the laughter to the parlor where la Vicereine and her ladies were telling stories and singing. "Juana, come sit by me," implored la Vicereine Leonor "Tell me a story."

"Perhaps not this evening," she said. "Indeed, I am weary."

"*¡Sí, por favor! ¡Por favor!*" begged the ladies surrounding la Vicereine, for they enjoyed her stories so.

"Just one story, please, Juana," said la Vicereine.

She relinquished. "For you, Señora, yes. Just one, a short story this evening."

"*¡Maravilloso!* You grew up in this lovely countryside, didn't you?" asked la Vicereine.

Yes, she thought. A simple adventure from her youth.

"Indeed, I did," said Juana as she settled into the goose feather cushions next to la Vicereine. "Look out the window, over there, under those trees. That is where I met a group of wanderers from Spain, the ones with the color-splashed wagons – the Roma."

"Ooooo!" "Didn't they eat you?" "Didn't they steal you?" Everyone chattered at once. Juana raised her hand gently for quiet, and began.

"No, they didn't eat me, or abscond with me. There were about twenty of them. It was evening, about this time. They had just finished dinner and were beginning to strum their guitars and sing, their crimson and golden painted wagons on one side of the clearing and a robust fire climbing sky high on the other side of the clearing. I crept up to listen, through those bushes to the left.

"Alas! A man materialized out of nowhere, grabbed my arm and nearly dragged me down to the campfire. He plunked me down next to him, making it clear that I was not to move, and he picked up his guitar.

"You should have seen this guitar; it was glistening with mother of pearl and abalone shells that lured the light of the fire. It was carved from a rich red wood, with the decoration all around it. Even the strap was woven in bright crimson and ivory silk threads with designs of roses and peacocks.

"The man began to play, very slowly at first. I knew I should have run away, for my madre warned me about the Roma. But I couldn't. I was mesmerized by the rhythm of his guitar."

She stood and began to beat a syncopated rhythm on the chair. *Beat – Pause – BeatBeat – Pause – Beat – Pause – BeatBeat – Pause.*

"He was a dashing man, his raven hair almost reaching his shoulders. And his eyes … his eyes burned as ebony coals set aflame. His fingers flew over the strings, and beat a rhythm on the back of his instrument."

The ladies leaned in closer, their eyes growing ever larger, as she softened the guitar syncopation.

"Then from the far side of the circle, a señora rose. Such a woman you've never seen. She was tall, and old – about my madre's age – with robust breasts and dancer's thighs."

She stood tall and proud, becoming this intriguing creature.

"Her flounced skirt hugged her hips as she began to swirl them in rhythm to the music, first slowly, then gradually faster, until she was a whirlwind of purples and reds."

She raised her skirt, revealing her own shapely thighs.

"Her shawl spun around her breasts, the silver fringe pretending to hide her curves, while her skirt flirted with her long legs. She arched her back, flinging one hand over her head. The other hand lifted her skirt to show her bare legs as if shouting out to God, 'Look, see how beautiful I am!'"

"Ooooooo." A shared shock and fascination flew through the room, dreamers hungry for Juana's vision.

"Then she reached down, taking the hand of another stunning beauty."

Here she reached down, pulling up feisty Glorietta beside her.

"They dipped into deep plunges, like this."

Glorietta followed her lead.

> "All the while long gold earrings dripped to their shoulders and bracelets reached half way up their arms. They even had bracelets on their ankles!"

"Oooooh!" An appreciative surprise flew around the room. She led the ladies in a syncopated clapping as she and Glorietta aligned side by side, their hips and shoulders melting into each other

Then they turned to face each other, and with their arms over their heads, brought their breasts to tease the other, slowly … seductively. Then she grabbed Glorietta around her waist, and Glorietta grabbed her. Everyone clapped in time, going faster, then going even faster. She spun, as if to shake off all horrendous memories.

Then they stopped.

> "In a whirlwind of twirls, they both stopped dancing. They flung their arms around each other, and brought the dance to a close. Everyone around the campfire roared approval."

She settled Glorietta back on the pillows. As the ladies began to clap, she held up her hand, alerting them that the story was not finished. Their eyes were glued on her as she continued.

> "Then the most mysterious thing happened.
>
> "A woman as ancient as the moonbeams casting shadows on her face, and as young as the blossoms in her hair, sat on the far side of the circle. She motioned me to approach her. Her ebony hair was pulled back in a red ribbon. Even she wore the rich blue colors of royalty, with a midnight blue shawl woven in silk and embroidered with birds of a thousand colors.

"She sat me on a tree stump across from her and told me to open my hand, like this."

She opened her right hand, palm up.

"And she gazed into it, tracing the lines."

This was why the story of the wanderers came to mind this evening. She had not thought of this incident in years. But it was the old woman, the wanderer from Spain, wrapped in the midnight blue shawl who told her that she was alone in the world, that she had no brothers or sisters, no family.

She had laughed at the old woman then, thinking it simply the tale of a delusional woman, for she knew she had two sisters and two more half-sisters, and might have a brother one day, and she was indeed part of the Ramírez family. But the ledger book at the church told her something very different this very afternoon. It told her that she was alone … sans brothers … sans sisters … sans family.

There was something else this old woman told her. "You will have a long life, much longer than your years on earth. You will be honored."

Then the woman's face went cold and she quickly folded Juana's fingers over her palm, dismissing her. "What is it, Sabia?" someone asked. "Nothing," said the woman. "I see nothing more. Now go."

The woman sounded cold, almost frightened, as she abruptly turned away from her. Juana quickly thanked the strangers for their music and continued on her way home. She had not told this story to anyone at all, until tonight.

"Juana, Juana, what did the woman say?"

"She told me I would have a long life." She closed her hand as the old woman had closed it.

She knew she was omitting much of what the woman said, but that was okay. Fray Miguel at the church today had omitted a lot too.

"Juana, this story is so enchanting," said la Vicereine. "You must turn it into a play."

"Perhaps someday," she said. But she did not think she ever would, not this story. She did not want people looking at her life that closely, for just that day she had discovered much that she never wanted known. She suddenly felt like she was naked at a costume ball, a very discomforting feeling.

She looked around the room. The ladies circling her that evening were all younger, her earlier friends having dispersed to haciendas with lovers, to mask maker's shops as apprentices, even to bordellos. Her sweet friend Glorietta was packing to leave, to manage a coastal retreat of a wealthy merchant, to become his lover. A few of the ladies went to convents to serve as nuns, as arranged by Fray Antonio Munez Miranda, la Vicereine Leonor's confessor. Juana felt ... old. Her time at court had passed.

And now, she thought, it is time ... time to make decisions.

La Monja Descalza (The Barefoot Nun)

There was received as a Sister, Sor Juana Inés de la Cruz,
legitimate daughter of Don Pedro de Asbaje and of
Isobel Ramírez, his wife, a native of Nueva España,
this Sunday, August 14 of anno 1667.

From the Records of
el Convento de San José de las Carmelitas Descalzya

"SO WHAT NAME will you take, Juana?" Madre Superiora of el Convento de San José de las Carmelitas Descalzya, the Barefoot Nuns of the Carmelite Order, tapped her finger on the large oak desk, anxious to get past these formalities. The Dominican priests had appointed this Madre Superiora, but she chose this room where heavy dripping shadows hung like dirty underwear. No windows, so no sunlight came here. It suited her granite mask well.

There it was again. Who was she? Fray Miranda had presented her to the convent as the legitimate daughter of a Spaniard and a Criolla, as la Vicereine Leonor had presented Juana to him. That much was settled. But her name as a nun? She had not given that much thought.

"You can keep your own name, 'Sor Juana Inés Ramírez.' " Madre Superiora's suggestion was a logical one, but No, it would cast a bright light on her dubious background. Even she no longer believed she was a Ramírez or an Asbaje. Juana shook her head.

"Then we will use your place of birth: 'Sor Juana de Panoayan.' " Madre Superiora was getting impatient and started to write it down.

"No. That's not it either," Juana insisted.

"Very well. Then you will choose a different name entirely. You will be 'Sor Piadoso.' That is an honorable name."

"No," she said again, emphatically. That would not do at all. She had come to terms with her madre Isobel's deceit, believing that her madre acted as best she could under the circumstances, no matter what those circumstances might have been. Someone had named her "Juana" and so she wanted to hold onto that name.

"Good heavens, child. If you don't even want a name, perhaps you don't even want to be a nun at all." Madre Superiora's voice had turned colder, edgier. "Well, what is it to be?"

Juana's eyes darted about the room, settling on the crucifix on the wall behind Madre Superiora. "De Jesus"? No, that was far too presumptuous. But the cross … yes, the cross.

"My name is Juana Inés de la Cruz." She spoke it slowly, deliberately.

That is the name she would be known by for the rest of her life. Yes. That was it. It just felt right. It did honor her madre, for she believed that "Juana Inés" was the name her madre Isobel had given her. The name "de la Cruz" foreshadowed the many crossroads of her life, some of the roads leading to great joy, and some presenting her with a heavy cross to bear. She smiled, vaguely recalling another Sor Juana de la Cruz, a Spanish nun who escaped from a violent father by wearing men's clothing. *How ironical*, she thought, *that this name is now coming to me, for I am running away from nothing.*

"Your veiling will be in one hour," said Madre Superiora.

Fray Miranda had already paid the three thousand pesos that the convent demanded, and everything was signed. Don Juan Sentis de Chavarria, her Abuelo's colleague, had provided the three thousand pesos for Juana's dowry. He was a noted philanthropist and member of the Knights of the Order of Santiago, one of Fray Miranda's many elite groups. Juana had met him at Vicereine Leonor's dinner parties, and was impressed with his understated elegance, as he was impressed with her brilliance.

As a poor institution, the Carmelite Convent did not usually require a three-thousand-peso dowry, but with Fray Miranda involved, Madre Superiora knew they could demand more than usual, and did so.

La Vicereine Leonor did not want her to enter a convent.

"You could be so much more," la Vicereine Leonor had said.

"I must learn. I must write. Joining a convent is truly my best option," Juana had replied.

"Come with me to España, enjoy all the glories of palace life, perhaps even find a duke or lord as enchanted by you as I am. You can write, and we will present your plays so all of España knows your brilliance. You can live with us, and I will present you as my Criolla daughter."

"Thank you. Truly, thank you, but la Ciudad de México is my home. Every breath, every guitar, every word of poetry is here."

LA VICEREINE arranged for Juana to meet with her personal confessor, the powerful Fray Miranda.

She sat in the confessional at the Catedral de la Ciudad de México, la Vicereine Leonor's confessor on the other side, streams of sunlight dimmed by the curtains. This was Fray Antonio Nunez de Miranda, the priest who could not bother himself with "little sins," only the big ones would do. He basked in the tales of scandalous sins of Nueva España's elite, doling out penances like cups of vinegar. This was the priest who vowed to never look upon a woman, and so he always sat behind a wall, or lowered his eyes to the floor.

Fray Miranda's eccentricities, his simple title, and simple friar's attire belied his extraordinary standing as a blazing shadow over Nueva España. He was an imposing figure by any standard, except physical stature. He was short, of slight build, with sunken cheeks and thick eyeglasses that only partially helped his near-sightedness. With his hunched shoulders and simple brown robes, he could have been mistaken for a huge mole prowling the halls of la Gran Catedral de la Ciudad de México, but his commanding persona more than compensated for his small physical presence.

When just a child, Fray Miranda got dumped into the midst of a clerical den of learning and subservience. As a boy of only six years, he served the whims of the priests in España, discovering early that his brilliant analytical skills put him in the limelight of monastic life, garnering attention he never sought. He rapidly adopted the machinations of devious minds, finding his only guardian in an innate ability to charm priests to his own will. If this was the life he was destined for, he determined to lead it on his own terms.

"Sinner! Destined to hell!" was what his confessor screamed at him as he stood on the thresh hold of becoming a priest. His life had carved a pit so deep, so dark that it seemed unlikely he would ever escape. But he did escape. With an almost miraculous determination he became the second most powerful cleric in all of Nueva España.

It was not his illustrious background as a scholar, a professor, and homilist, that gave him such power, although those accomplishments were remarkable.

It was not that he carved a spot for himself as confessor to nuns, even writing a handbook to guide their actions.

It was not even the fact that he was appointed a Censor for the Tribunal of the Inquisition. No, this appointment was a reward for his other efforts.

Many claimed that Fray Miranda was a "Fisher of Souls," treasuring the hundreds, or even thousands, of orphans, ill people, and parishioners he saved in building orphanages, hospitals, cathedrals, and schools.

But Fray Miranda could only enjoy the luxury of the title "Fisher of Souls" because he was a master "Fisher of Fortunes."

He had formed dozens of committees comprised of Nueva España's most elite businessmen and politicos, and he served most importantly as Prefect of the *Congregacion de la Purisima Concepcion de la Virgen Maria,* The Brotherhood of la Virgen Maria. He led the nine priests of the Brotherhood, one for each month of Mary's pregnancy, calling all members together each Tuesday morning, all the priests and lay men alike, providing them with homilies on charity, prayer, and soul cleansing. Here is where money flowed into church coffers, a wild river of guilty gifts guaranteed to ensure salvation.

The voice that screamed "Sinner!" pursued his every step, forcing him to seek salvation for his own soul in his peasant's attire, his self-imposed menial dishwashing and floor cleaning chores, and his thrice weekly flagellations so severe that his cell was covered in dry blood.

This misery was not just for penance. He also soaked up doses of power like jugs of fine wine. Fray Miranda prepared himself as the most-qualified cleric to be the next Archbishop of Nueva España, and in fact expected such an appointment when the time came.

MADRE SUPERIORA tapped on her large desk to get Juana's attention. "Sor Beatrix will show you to your cell."

Sor Beatrix, a generously built woman with strong creases in her forehead and stubborn stains on her apron, had appeared at the doorway, and without a word, Juana followed her down a long hallway, up a flight of stairs, down another hallway and to a room at the end of the row.

There was a heavy wood door on the cell and, like the exterior of the building, the interior walls were all adobe, scrubbed clean of the lichen and worms that gathered there.

An image of the Crucifixion was painted on the wall over the cot in her cell, the small room that she was to call her own. A single straight-back chair sat in the corner. One small square window nudged the ceiling, letting in a dim light. She noted that she would need to ask for a small table, and perhaps a few more candles so she could read.

Her satchel held only one book, a treasured volume of the poetry of Ovid from her Abuelo's library, along with the boy's clothing that he had given her. She did not know why the clothes were important, she just knew she had to have them, perhaps only as a memory of other times. She also brought some writing paper, quills, and ink; she did not expect the Convent to pay for those items. Finally, she had brought some of her early writings, poems mostly, and some plays that had been presented at el Palacio, the ones she was especially proud of, the ones she wanted to work on further.

She put her satchel by the chair and changed into the formless habit that Sor Beatrix had left for her, leaving the hairshirt on the cot for nighttime.

The habit was two pieces of large rectangular cloth. The smaller cloth was much like a pauper's tilma, rough-hewn oatmeal-colored and tied at both shoulders. The other, much longer, one was a muddy grey, and she draped this one over her head, resting it on her left shoulder before letting it tumble to the ground, just as she had seen Sor Beatrix do.

Yes, she decided, this would do well. Her cell was quiet so she could read and write. Her friends would bring her more books. Yes, this small room would do fine. She sat in the sole chair, surveying her new surroundings.

She had already given away most of her worldly possessions, like the elegant gowns that la Vicereine had gifted her, and had put other treasures, like her Abuelo's books, into safe keeping with friends and family. She had money in reserve so friends could purchase books and writing materials for her when she was ready to call for them. Yes, this kind of life was what she wanted.

She was ready for a new life.

Sor Beatrix interrupted Juana's contemplation when she marched unannounced into the cell, picked up the hairshirt and threw it at her. "You will wear this all the time!" Her voice was not kind. Skin that was accustomed to silks and soft cottons nearly bled from the thorny bristles on the hairshirt, but if this was what was required, she could do it. She held onto her quiet smile, a long-established habit by now.

"Do you think this is a joke?" demanded Sor Beatrice.

"Oh, no," she replied, confused.

"Then wipe that insipid smile off your face." Sor Beatrice was not joking. Juana assumed a more serious demeanor, one, she thought, that was more in tune with the severity of the occasion.

The interminable ceremony meant lots of standing, lots of laying on the floor with her arms and legs spread out, lots of prayers. At one point she was led into a confessional where she confessed her sins to a priest she did not know, then returned to the church where the priest placed the ring of Christ on her finger, then communion. La Vicereine Leonor was the sole guest allowed, and even she was pushed into the shadows where Juana could not see her. They never had a chance to say good-by.

Finally, Madre Superiora led her out of the church, and Sor Beatrix led her to the dining room where all the nuns sat on benches for the evening meal. She smiled at the nuns around her, but no smile was returned. One nun had only bread and water, but when Sor Juana offered her some of her own meager meal, an elder nun appeared behind her shoulder and struck Sor Juana's hand with a wooden stick. Sor Juana pulled her plate back and watched the young nun, her eyes downturned, looking only at her piece of bread, a single tear resting on her cheek.

The silence continued unabated. No one spoke a word except for the prayers before and after the meal. No one smiled; no one nodded acknowledgment.

After dinner the nuns returned to the church for more prayers, and after a very long day, she followed Sor Beatrix back to her cell. She felt immediately that something was wrong. In just a glance she saw that the dress she wore that morning was gone, but she expected that. But the satchel! The satchel was gone.

"Sor Beatrix!" she called out. Sor Beatrix was already half way down the hall, but spun abruptly and shushed her. "Sor Beatrix," whispered Sor Juana as she rushed down the hall. "This must be the wrong room. My satchel isn't there."

Sor Beatrix motioned her back to her room. "There is no savage shouting in these sacred hallways," she sneered. "This is not the wrong room. It is your room for the rest of your days."

"But my satchel."

"Your satchel and everything in it has been burned." Sor Beatrix left, closing the door behind her.

Her mouth fell open and she collapsed onto the cot, stunned, lost. Burned? Why? Her writing materials gone? Why? Her treasured book of poetry, gone? Why? The boy's outfit that she brought with her, that was gone too? Why? Who else could ever have any use for it?

She was so confused she did not know what to say. She sat on the cot all night, four dark walls staring back at her, hardly a single star stepping across the window sill, weeping uncontrollably. Sor Beatrix had to be wrong.

SOR BEATRIX was not wrong. The next morning Madre Superiora called Sor Juana into her office. "Well, Sor Juana, I understand that you were upset that your satchel was missing," she said sharply.

"Yes, Muy Venerada Madre Superiora, indeed I was. I had a few treasures in that satchel, as well as writing paper and ink."

"A book of lurid poetry? Obscene writing? And men's clothing? Is that what you call treasures? Just what abomination did you have planned for the devil's poetry and men's clothing?" Madre Superiora spat out the words.

"No abomination at all, Muy Venerada Madre Superiora. I simply wanted to read …"

"Read?" Madre Superiora nearly shouted. "If you want to read, you can read the verses in your room." Juana recalled seeing a few pages of verses, from the Psalms perhaps, on smudged parchment.

"And men's clothing?" she continued. "What did you intend to do with that?"

"I don't know, Muy Venerada Madre Superiora. Truly, I don't know." Huge tears fell down her cheeks. "But the ink and paper, so that I can write a bit…" implored Sor Juana.

"Nuns do not need to write. Everything you need to know is already written in the Bible."

THE NEXT FEW WEEKS were a unique kind of hell. If she was not praying or eating or sleeping from exhaustion, she was scrubbing the floor, washing dishes, washing diapers from the orphanage next door, or nudging vegetables from a pallid garden. She came to welcome the click-click of metal plates being stacked, the shush of her scrub brush on the floor, the rattle of the wheel barrow bringing dirty laundry from the orphanage. She treasured the time outdoors in the garden for she could listen to the melody of the birds that gathered there.

The austere architecture of the convent, the grounds bereft of a single tree or bush, even the location of the convent in a dilapidated corner of the city – all of this should have alerted her to the kind of convent this was, but she did not know a place like this could exist. Her Ciudad de México world was stuffed with music, conversations, and lush gowns.

Now every nook and cranny of her day was scheduled to precision, day after day after day. Each day began at 5:30am when bells echoed through the halls, when the nuns rose and dressed for Mass at 6:00am, followed by a breakfast of bread and milk, and sometimes an egg. At 9:00am everyone returned to the chapel for Matins prayers, then met in the communal room for work assignments, perhaps to work in the garden or in the laundry or scrubbing the floors. At noon were more prayers, then lunch. An hour or so of work followed before prayers at 3:00pm. The evening found the nuns in the communal room, silently embroidering or doing other chores. At dusk they usually had a piece of fruit, then went for Vespers at 7:00pm. Dinner followed, with evening prayers and Lauds to complete the day. By 9:30 every nun was in her cell, exhausted, ready for bed. This schedule followed day after day – no diversions, no reading, no writing, no conversation.

The only respite from work and prayer came on Friday afternoons when all the nuns gathered in the dining hall for the "communal gathering." In this gathering every nun was held accountable for misdeeds during the previous week, with penance imposed by Madre Superiora. One nun slept through a mass, and got five lashes on the palms of her hands. Another spoke disapprovingly to Madre Superiora; her penance was to clean the dining hall floor with her tongue. A nun who had pulled up three young carrots from the garden and eaten them was subjected to three days without any meals at all. The sins and omissions seemed trivial to Juana, but huge punishments were doled out every week, week after week.

Even if she had a room full of books, there was no time to read, or write. And rules, so many rules. No talking. No touching. No thinking. The nuns marched from task to task, eyes lowered, hands clasped at their waist.

Everywhere, every moment, the silence screamed like the silent wail of wolves on a bitter cold midnight.

Only the Sunday routine was different, for on Sundays the nuns knelt on the stone floor of the church and prayed, all day. Her knees bled from the rough stones tearing through her habit and piercing her flesh, callouses quickly forming to protect her.

Yet even in this infernal pit, she could not stop herself from learning, from listening and observing. She saw the angled ceiling above walls that were straight, and wondered how the walls and ceiling could shift sizes as they marched toward a distant point. She heard the birds sing different melodies – morn and night – and wondered what they meant. She listened to the words of the prayers and wanted to study them, to truly understand them. She wanted her silence to find refuge in poetry.

But none of that was possible.

A morbid pall had crept into this space long ago, and it crawled upon itself day by day. The walls were covered in a putrid gray, as were the habits the nuns wore, the food they ate, and flesh itself. There was not one inch of vitality to be found… anywhere.

She could only wonder if it were her own eyes that had changed, or if the world had morphed into an eternal muck.

ONE MOONLESS, starless night she jolted from her restless sleep, startled by the measured screams of a nun. It came from somewhere down the hall. Three … four … five sharp piercing screams, then the world fell again into a bottomless silence. She could not ask anyone what had happened, for no conversation was allowed, nor did she even know the names of the nuns. She did discover that one nun, a pretty, young nun, was not at services or at meals for several days.

It was not as if she were singled out for punishment, for all nuns kept the same schedule, did the same tasks, ate the same meals. She did notice that sometimes particular nuns received an extra potato or slice of carrot at meal time. It was always the same few nuns, but she did not know why those nuns were singled out. They all punished themselves in this foul purgatory, even the ones who got an extra potato, and Sor Juana was the only one who seemed to care.

What were these nuns atoning for? What could they possibly have done that would warrant this? What had she done? These were not the singing, dancing nuns that she had seen so many times on the Plaza Mayor.

ON A GLOOMY AFTERNOON Sor Beatrix motioned her to follow, and they went into a room where la Vicereine Leonor was seated behind iron bars that defined the locutory of this convent. She rushed to the barrier, thrilled beyond belief that her dear friend was there.

"Señora Leonor, what a joy! What a joy to see you!" La Vicereine's gown of deep purple, with her golden cape, made Juana's heart literally leap for joy. Life itself burst forth in la Señora's eyes.

La Vicereine glared at Sor Beatrix, stating, "You will excuse us."

Had it not been la Vicereine Leonor, Sor Beatrix would not have left. Had it not been la Vicereine Leonor, Juana would not have been allowed a visitor at all, for novices were allowed no visitors at all for three long years. After three years of isolation, most of the world gladly forgot about the nuns cloistered here, while the locutory sat empty. La Vicereine Leonor looked like a painted puppet to Sor Beatrice, but even Sor Beatrice recognized her status and left.

They spoke in soft raptures, words piling on top of words, sentences and thoughts piling on top of each other.

"Oh, Juana, I am so glad to see you …"

"And I, you …"

"Your dirty habit …"

"Yes, I was scrubbing diapers …"

"Diapers?" They both broke into laughter, the first time Juana had laughed since coming to the convent.

"I thought nuns studied." la Vicereine raised an eyebrow quizzically.

"So did I." Juana's voice carried a deep sadness.

"I didn't have a chance to congratulate you at your initiation ceremony…"

"You were there?"

"Yes. They sat me in the back, in the shadows, where I could barely even see you. I wanted so desperately to pull you out of there and take you back to el Palacio." The pain of that missed escape left Juana speechless.

"Bishop Payo has inquired about you, Juana."

"He did? How very kind of him. Is he well?" She recalled so fondly the day he had gifted her parchment and inks that day in the La Biblioteca de la Universidad.

"He is quite well…"

"And the others? Have you heard from any of the ladies?"

"All are well, and we all miss you so much … so much. Even our dinner guests are distraught to discover that you are sequestered in a convent."

Her eyes fell. She too was distressed to discover just how sequestered she was.

"I almost forgot," said la Vicereine. "Here is something you might like." She handed Juana a small book through the bars of the barrier. Juana held it tenderly in her blistered hands for a moment then quickly tied it up in her hairshirt, far from scathing eyes. La Vicereine reached for Juana's hand through the bars, turning it over to see the callouses. "These hands were once so beautiful, enchanting el Palacio, holding a silk fan."

Just before leaving, la Vicereine looked quietly at her. "You look sad, my dear." Even through the bars of the locutory, Juana felt the tender embrace, the arms of a weeping willow wrapping her in compassion.

"I am sad," she whispered. "But this is the life I chose, and I will find a way to make it work." La Vicereine threw her a kiss through the bars of the locutory, and with this soft gesture they parted. Juana held that moment of springtime in her heart a very long time.

AFTER MORNING PRAYERS the next day, she was called to the convent office. There on the huge desk was the book la Vicereine Leonor gave her.

"You stupid child, did you think we wouldn't look in your bed after someone like la Vicereine saw you?" Madre Superiora's stare shot arrows to her gut.

She was caught. There was nowhere to hide even this small book, so she had to put it under the sole sheet on her cot.

"Do you, or do you not know the rules?" Madre Superiora stood tall, peering down at her. She had never felt so intimidated, and all she could do was quiver. "Well?" shouted Madre Superiora. "Speak, you stupid idiot."

"Yes, Muy Venerada Madre Superiora, I do know the rules." Her voice was soft and shaking.

"Then bend over this desk." Madre Superiora raised the leather strop that she held, ready to attack.

"What?" She was incredulous. What could be happening?

Sor Beatrix grabbed her by her wrists, forcing her face down on the huge desk. Madre Superiora threw Sor Juana's habit over her head and pulled up her hairshirt, leaving her naked from her shoulders down.

Then WHACK! Once.

WHACK! Again.

And again.

Five times Madre Superiora whipped her with the thin leather strop. Five times her whole body sank into the desk. Five times she could not even muster the strength to scream.

"The next time it will be ten lashes," said Madre Superiora as she marched out, pleased that she had done a good job with this recalcitrant girl. Sor Juana would give her no more trouble.

Sor Juana froze in total disbelief and pain. All of this because of one small book of poetry?

Sor Beatrix half led, half carried her back to her cell, stripped off her habit and hairshirt, shoving her face down on her cot. She took out a vial of ointment that she had carried in the pocket of her apron and began rubbing Sor Juana with the ointment of aloe and mint, all down her back, over her legs, then between her legs. This was not the sensuous massage of the ladies at the swimming pool, but an obnoxious invasion, a disgusting, demanding assault that sought out all the private places of Sor Juana's aching body.

"Stop. Stop!" she demanded. No matter how healing the ointment may have been, she felt like she was oozing through dark crevices, further and further into an endless pit. It was wrong; it was so wrong.

Sor Beatrix did not stop.

"You know, Juana," came Sor Beatrix's silky voice. "You could be favored and have a comfortable life if you let yourself."

No! No! thought Juana. *This is not worth getting an extra potato.* She raised herself up on her elbows and spat on Sor Beatrix's shoe.

"That's enough for now," said Sor Beatrix.

Juana vowed to never allow such abuse again. When Sor Beatrix came the next day, Juana took the bowl of tepid soup and threw it at Sor Beatrix, her fat belly an easy target. Sor Beatrix's face scrunched like an angry troll.

"So that's what you want, Juana. Fine. Don't eat. Starve to death if you like. I don't give a damn, and I doubt that Christ does either. You are a worthless turd in this convent."

Sor Beatrix did not return for two days, and when she did return, she simply plunked the meager meal on Juana's table and left. She did not tell Juana that Madre Superiora had instructed her to give food to Juana, at least until la Vicereine Leonor and Fray Miranda had forgotten about her.

Sor Beatrix left no ointment, and without this medication, Juana's wounds turned to ugly scars. But she stood smugly proud that she had won the battle against Sor Beatrix.

She vowed to never again do anything that would dump such misery on her. Throwing herself into the work of the convent, she worked relentlessly, always doing more than her share. She fervently believed that if she could show Madre Superiora what an outstanding nun she truly was, then Madre Superiora would allow her a few minutes each week to read or write. And with that writing, she could earn money for the convent and become a valuable nun as she had originally planned.

MORE DAYS CREPT by. Ten? Fifteen? She was not sure. All she could do was put one foot in front of the other and keep on going.

Then one day Sor Beatrix motioned her to follow again, this time to the confessional just outside the chapel. She was not surprised; she certainly had many sins to confess. Sor Beatrix left and Juana entered the confessional. "Forgive me, Padre, for I have sinned."

"I understand that you have suffered more than you have sinned." It was a familiar voice. She knew that voice!

"Fray Miranda, Reverencia, I am so honored that you are here!"

"La Vicereine Leonor would give me no peace until I promised to come see you. You have strong willed friends in high places, Sor Juana."

"La Vicereine! How is she?"

"She is well, but she tells me that you are not. What is wrong, Juana?" His voice carried a good dose of smugness, but she did not care. He was there. He might be able to help.

With dejected humiliation, she opened her heart. "Everything is wrong, Reverencia. Everything. I've made a wretched mistake becoming a nun. This is not the life I longed for. I am allowed no books, no writing materials, no visitors. I have no life." She omitted the part about the lashing and about Sor Beatrix, for her pride would not allow her to talk about that to anyone, certainly not to a priest. Nor did she tell him about all the menial work, for that was designed to improve her soul, or so she had been told.

"I feel trapped. Please, Reverencia, what should I do? What can I do?"

"As you recall, Juana, I warned you against coming to the Carmelite convent."

SHE DID REMEMBER. They had had a vicious fight, two towering egos, each determined to win, she an irreverent señorita who needed to find the best home possible for herself, and he, a highly respected member of the clergy, one not accustomed to being challenged, especially by a girl.

Fray Miranda's powerful presence wrought fear, even terror, into the hearts of his charges, and kept his coffers full. He had the power to pick and choose who he wanted to support, and who he did not. When la Vicereine Leonor called upon him to help one Doña Juana Inés Ramírez, he knew it was more than a simple request; it was a command. Within days he had a large dowry arranged, three thousand pesos, enough so that the finest convent in all of Nueva España would gladly accept her.

But Juana had ideas of her own.

"The Carmelite Convent is a den of demons!" Fray Miranda had shouted. "The silence is deafening; the work is inhuman. You will hate it there!" Fray Miranda was speaking from behind a wooden screen at el Palacio de Viceroy, situated so that he could not see her, as was his habit.

Juana recalled the dancing nuns she often saw in the Plaza Mayor during the festivals

"Is there a biblioteca?" she demanded.

"Probably. A small one."

"A garden?"

"Yes, if you can call their anemic vegetables a garden."

"Is there a locutory where nuns can welcome visitors?"

"Theoretically, yes, but no one goes to visit the rejected nuns of that convent. Do you want to languish in obscurity, child?" Fray Miranda demanded.

"My writings will lift me out of obscurity." She stood firm.

"You won't even have time to write at that convent,"

"I will have all the time I want when they see the recognition – and money – that I bring to them." She spat out the arguments to him like a hunk of bacon spewing grease over a hot fire.

Fray Miranda was astounded, shouting at a girl. Was this the same girl who the Viceroy and Vicereine swore to be a genius? Fray Miranda had wondered. Is this the young philosopher that the whole of la Ciudad de México was talking about, the one reputed to be an astonishingly gifted poet? Who was this child to challenge his years of wisdom? His influence? His intelligence? Who was she to turn her back on his generosity in helping her?

Viceroys and lords cowered when he spoke – why was this girl challenging him?

Juana was equally astounded. Who was he to challenge her choice for her life? It was her life, not his. She knew that convents, and the priestly order they were affiliated with, benefitted from nun's creations, and she assumed that Fray Miranda was insistent so that the honorariums for her poetry and writing would go only to the Jesuits, his Order, not to the Carmelites who were affiliated with the Dominican Order of priests. Rivalry between the Jesuits and Dominicans fueled constant battles in la Ciudad de México, and Fray Miranda would not, of course, relinquish Juana Inés, this prized income source, easily.

One ego countered the other like two bulls fighting to the death.

She could not even reveal to Fray Miranda why she fought so hard. She needed a convent that would not look at her background very closely. She simply could not risk being judged "non-Criolle," the repercussions would have driven her to madness. The Carmelite convent was known as a poor convent, one that would overlook a lot to get her 3,000 pesos and the income she would provide.

There was another reason too. Of all the people in her life, her dear Abuelo and Doña Angélica, the kind teacher at Las Amigas, were the two that she loved the most, the two she trusted the most. Most importantly, since Doña Angélica had chosen this convent, then so should she.

She would not allow Fray Miranda's obstinance to get in the way of her future. After all, it was the Dominicans who leased Panoayan to her family, and the Dominicans were affiliated with this convent. How could such affiliations foretell such torment?

Fray Miranda finally gave up. Juana's determination would not bend an inch, and so she became a Carmelite nun.

She was partially correct in her assumption that Fray Miranda wanted the financial benefit of her writings. She also knew now that he was also being bluntly honest in his assessment of the Carmelite Convent.

"I DO REMEMBER what you told me, Reverencia," replied Juana meekly. She looked sadly at the wall between Fray Miranda and herself. "You told me I would hate it here, and you were so right. My stubborn nature overpowered my better judgment, and now I am trapped."

"You are not truly trapped, Juana. You can walk out those iron gates any time you want. Even the Carmelites cannot keep you prisoner."

She sat up at attention.

Fray Miranda continued. "The issue is, What do you do once you step outside? Do you go back to your madre and padre? They do not want you. To your uncle and aunt? They pushed you out too. To el Palacio de Virrey? Hasn't la Vicereine Leonor done enough for you? Even if they took you in, do you think any of them will take care of you forever? Would you want to be a burden to any of them?

"If you did not depend on them, how would you support yourself? It is unlikely that any man will want you for a wife, except perhaps a village pig butcher – remember, you still have no dowry. Another convent is not likely either. Although I may be able to convince another convent to accept you, I cannot ask for a second dowry donation for you, and any decent convent will require a dowry. Your options are limited on the other side of the gate, Juana."

She knew that he was right, that no respectable hacienda would ever house an old, unmarried woman, a woman obviously diseased or loco. Women who could not marry were sent to convents. Being a widow was acceptable. Even being a woman whose husband deserted her was acceptable, and being a woman supported by another man was certainly acceptable. Being an old, unmarried, unattached woman was not.

"Will the Carmelites return my dowry? That three thousand pesos would go a long way to re-establishing me somewhere." She did not know what she would do with the three thousand pesos, but she did know she could make better use of the money than the Convent could.

"I doubt it, Juana. You signed a commitment to the Carmelite Convent, and the dowry was paid. If this were another convent, I could intercede on your behalf, but I have little influence with the Carmelites. Think about your options, child. Then act accordingly. You have so much to offer the Church. Find a way to make that offering."

He blessed her, and left. He did in all sincerity believe that she had a great deal to offer the Church. but she had to want a different future enough to walk out that gate and find a different way.

He could not help her if she would not help herself.

Never once had Fray Miranda looked at her; he remained behind the wall, keeping his eyes to the ground as he always did. She regretted that she likely would not see him again, and she sorely regretted that she had not followed his advice. She thought that perhaps the Carmelite convent had changed since Doña Angélica was there, and that even Doña Angélica herself would not recognize it now.

She left the confessional determined to make her life better. On her way back to her cell, she heard the distant strumming of mariachi guitars, no doubt for one of the many fiestas de la Ciudad de México, but she had lost all track of time and had no idea what fiesta it might have been. As weary as she was, she longed to sing, to throw herself into joy. It was not to be.

Instead, she threw herself even more fervently into the work of the convent, capturing whatever spare moments she could to ponder her choices. She fell completely exhausted into her cot each night, and each morning rose just a bit more drained.

Sor Beatrix had cut her meals to little more than oily broth, without so much as a potato. Her energy seeped out like a leaking bucket. Finally, one morning she slept through Matins and woke with a start to find the chapel empty, the nuns getting work assignments.

The next day she fell asleep in chapel, curling into a thorny ball on the floor when everyone else stood to leave.

HER TRANSGRESSIONS had become too obvious to ignore, and once again she was called to Madre Superiora 's office.

"I believed we had an understanding about the rules, Sor Juana."

"We do, Muy Venerable Madre Superiora. I am so sorry I fell asleep."

"Perhaps this will keep you awake. Lean over the desk." Madre Superiora reached for her leather strop, and Sor Beatrix reached for her wrists, a twisted sneer forming on her face.

She pulled away, with more strength than she thought she had. "NO! NO! I won't be punished. It was a simple mistake, that's all."

"No punishment? Perhaps I should reward you. Is that what you suggest?" Madre Superiora glared at her.

She knew what she had to do, no matter what. She straightened her back and boldly glared at Madre Superiora. "I suggest that you return my dowry, and that I leave this convent." She spoke with finality.

Madre Superiora was equally blunt. "You are welcome to leave; you are too troublesome and much too weak for this convent. But you may not have your dowry back. Was that not you who signed the commitment of service to this convent?" The sweetness of her voice mocked Juana's predicament.

"Yes, that was me, before I knew what you truly are." She stood straight, not giving an inch. Neither did Madre Superiora.

"That commitment was predicated on a dowry being paid. If you choose to break your commitment, that is your choice. But the dowry remains. Give me the ring."

Juana gladly removed the ring that was placed on her hand during her initiation ceremony, slamming it on the table. Her back arched, a lynx ready to rip the throat of its prey.

"Sor Beatrix, give this child a dress to wear and show her the door."

That is exactly what Sor Beatrix did. She tore the habit and hairshirt off Juana's aching body, pushed a filthy beggar's dress into her hands and shoved her out the side door without a peso to her name.

"But the dress I came in," she protested. "I want that dress."

"Selfish child," sneered Sor Beatrice. "Haven't you heard of charity? That dress was given to truly poor people long ago. Now get out!" Sor Beatrice slammed the door in Juana's face, leaving her clutching only a torn, dirty dress, without so much as shoes on her feet.

Said Sister did not profess and
on November 18, 1667, left the convent.

From the Records of the
Convent of San José de las Carmelitas Descalzya

SHE STEPPED into a vile corner of La Ciudad de México with garbage and excrement covering the path, filthy people lolling about crippled doorways. She pulled the stinking dress over her head, then, dressed as a beggar herself, her shoulders began to droop and her feet ached for she had no shoes. She tripped on a slimy stone and fell into a disgusting slush, getting her dress even filthier, if such were possible. She was so exhausted she could hardly stand, the encounter with Madre Superiora squeezing the last dram of energy out of her.

She was broken, but tears would never do for Doña Juana Inés Ramírez. She recalled the advice that Thunder, the tall black stallion, had given her: Look straight ahead, and keep on going. It took but a few minutes for her to straighten her shoulders, look straight ahead and begin her trek to somewhere, but she did just that. She kept an eye out for her young friends, Xipil and Tochtli, but did not see them.

No, she thought, Xipil and Tochtli would not live in such filth.

Even the poor section of the city, the section for native Aztecs, mixed breeds and servants, the section that was not filthy, went on for blocks and blocks in all directions.

She found her way back to the center of town, going to the only place she could think of. She stumbled into the tailor's shop, to Doña Bonita, the seamstress who had made the boy's clothing for her so many years ago.

"Out!" shouted Doña Bonita "We don't allow beggars in here."

"Please, Doña Bonita, please … I am Doña Juana Inés Ramírez, the granddaughter of Don Pedro Ramírez de Santilliana. I came here the first time with my Abuelo to wear the boy's clothes that you had made. That was when you called me 'Don Diego.' I have been preyed upon, dear Doña Bonita, and I need your help."

"Yes, I see," said Doña Bonita, smiling. "You are indeed a very dirty Doña Juana Ramírez. Come, Doña Juana, let's find something for you to wear, and some soap for your dirty face and those filthy feet."

Now, in a respectable modest dress in muted blues and greens, and proper shoes, she headed to the Viceregal Palace. La Vicereine Leonor would understand. More than anyone, her dear Leonor would understand.

La Virgen de Guadalupe

February 24, 1669

WAS IT ONLY two years ago that Juana stepped with such trepidation over the threshold of the Viceregal Palace, once again asking for shelter? Now here she stood, in a large chapel at the magnificent Gran Catedral de la Ciudad de México, hundreds of slim tapered candles hugging every niche, with a cascade of candles at the altar, all poised to be lit in her honor, creating waltzing shadows for her celebration.

"Fray Miranda placed the altar candles himself," said Sor Sophia, the kind nun who had met her when she first arrived at San Jerónimo Convent. "He came last night when no one was around so he would not risk seeing an errant nun. He also arranged for the celebration after the ceremony, and I understand that some very important people will be there."

Sor Sophia was among the small group of nuns who joined the convent for religious reasons, and Juana found herself wrapped in their meditations from time to time, basking in the joy of Christ. The love of Christ was so much a part of Juana that she never doubted it, so she treasured the meditative aura of these blessed nuns.

Juana stood in wonderment at la Gran Catedral de la Ciudad de México.

WAS IT ONLY two years ago, or a lifetime ago, that la Vicereine Leonor welcomed her back so graciously, so kindly? La Vicereine did not ask why she had returned. She did not need to ask, for she had seen the absolute despair in Juana's eyes when they visited at the Carmelite convent. La Vicereine Leonor simply embraced her as a prodigal daughter and settled her in a quiet room dipped in sunlight, had her meals brought to her room, and ordered a simple wardrobe for her. There was a ball gown too, but Doña Leonor assured her that she was not to attend a ball or a banquet until she wanted to.

Fray Miranda arranged for a Latin tutor for her, Martin de Olivas, hoping that mental challenges would help set her mind at ease, and it did help. With but twenty lessons from the tutor, she had Latin grammar and style well in hand and proceeded to master the classics of Latin literature, and began her adventures in reading the Bible itself. She was so grateful to this splendid tutor that she dedicated a complex acrostic sonnet to him, comparing him to Archimedes, the ancient Greek scientist whose studies of geometry were indeed revolutionary.

Hardly a month had passed when work was nearly completed on the largest and most astonishing cathedral in all the new world. After nearly a century of building, la Gran Catedral de la Ciudad de México was ready to accept visitors. While work would continue for decades, it was time for an elaborate opening celebration.

Gold and silver images of Our Lady, large and small, embedded with rubies, emeralds, and diamonds flew from every corner of the Christian world, from Charles V and Pope Pius V, from kings and emperors, from dukes and bishops, from lords and artists.

The floor plan was in the shape of a cross; the massive main door featured a relief of the Assumption of la Virgen Maria, to whom this Catedral was dedicated.

The huge main chapel was surrounded by fourteen smaller chapels, a choir, and crypts. The five altar pieces in the main sanctuary were the Altar of Forgiveness, the Altar of the Kings, the main altar, the Altar of Resurrected Jesus, and the Altar of the Virgen de Zapopan. Rich organ music rang throughout this sanctuary at every opportunity.

Magnificent poetry flowed through the streets of La Ciudad de México on rivers of opulent praise in honor of this celebration, in books bound in crimson leather. One poem was signed by "Doña Juana de Asbaje." It prefaced a book by the renown poet Diego de Ribera, a friend of la Vicereine.

She peeked into the gay celebrations for the new Catedral, but for the most part Juana's days gently flowed, one to another, as she began to reach out, to wander the courtyard and nod greetings to all along the way, like a deer in the forest gracefully seeking a new meadow. One afternoon she found herself in la Vicereine's parlor, telling stories to the ladies-in-waiting. She told them Don Quixote's tale of the wedding of Quiteria, one that they especially enjoyed, and soaked up the laughter that filled the room. It was good to be back.

SHE HAD BEEN BACK at el Palacio but a year when the new Archbishop of Nueva España was announced, and it was not her confessor, Fray Miranda. It was her dear friend, Bishop Payo, the bishop who had so generously encouraged her to write. Juana, thrilled with this choice, pondered what her life should be and how she could fit into this glorious new burst that was Nueva España.

"Please, Juana, come back to España with me," la Vicereine Leonor begged once more. "My husband's term as Viceroy will end soon. You need a home, and I need you. You are my Criolla daughter, and I would be so proud to introduce you to Spanish society. I will build for you a special hacienda with vistas that reach forever. You can write all day if you like. Juana, your gifts are wasted on parlor games at the balls. You can be one of the most celebrated women writers of all time. Come with me. You can do so much more."

Yes, the security of la Vicereine Leonor's protection was tempting. The glorious gowns, the witty conversation of society life, the extravagant dinners, the elegant balls – all of that appealed to her. It was a life she had become accustomed to. And broad vistas to entice her creative powers. It was a tempting invitation.

But there was something missing in palace life, a challenge, a spice, rather like leaving jalapeños out of enchiladas. In palace life she was still a sheltered woman, a curiosity, a woman who was there to please men. She enchanted the palace with her witty and erudite poetry, but the sophistication of its message was lost on unhearing ears, her ideas unheard, being those of only a woman. More than that, this place, this Ciudad de México, was her home. No, there had to be another way, one where she could plant her feet solidly on Mexican soil.

WAS IT ONLY a few months ago that she had sat under the glowing pink bougainvillea vines by the Magi fountain at the Viceregal Palace, remembering the times when she had been happiest? She recalled the times with her Abuelo, listening to his stories, and learning how to read. La biblioteca held such magical mysteries, many that she had yet to discover. And attending Las Amigas, the school for girls, and learning from the kind Doña Angélica – that was a happy time too. What a joy to see Doña Angélica's face light up as she solved another mathematical problem or read a complex section in a new book. It was these memories that brought back her smile, the smile that was beaten out of her at the Carmelite Convent.

As for her future, she loved visiting bookstores in la Ciudad de México with Abuelo and she thought that she too could open such a store. That would be a most honorable, and profitable, way of supporting herself. She presented the idea to Don Felipe, Abuelo's favorite bookseller, and he literally laughed in her face. "Who do you think would ever buy a book from a señorita? Reading is not for women, and operating a successful bookstore is certainly not for women! Bah! Go get married, señorita."

She first thought that Don Felipe just did not want the competition, but in the end she knew that he was right, that few men would ever buy a book from a female bookseller, especially an unmarried one, no matter how brilliant she was. They would compliment her pretty dresses, and laugh at a witticism, and perhaps even offer her a jeweled bracelet, but they would not buy books from her. She had to look elsewhere.

SHE LOVED Las Amigas with Doña Angélica. *Yes! perhaps that is the answer, to open a school of my own, just like Doña Angélica had done,* she thought. She could teach in the morning, but have all afternoon and evening to read and study, and even write. She had to talk to Doña Angélica. Doña Angélica was a good person, and it was Doña Angélica who had said that she was once a Carmelite nun, and that she left the convent only to care for her madre. It was because of Doña Angélica that she had insisted on joining the Carmelite convent.

She felt a jarring disconnect. How could someone so innately kind join such a brutal group, a group that seemed to have no respect for life or learning? It did not make sense. It was a puzzle that she could not answer. Before she embarked on establishing her own school, she had to talk with Doña Angélica.

Doña Angélica greeted her like the long-lost friend that she was. After a long lovely embrace and a warm kiss on her cheek, Doña Angélica settled her comfortably on her veranda, her servant bringing coffee and sweets, while the two women told stories of their adventures.

"No, Juana, no!" Doña Angélica's whole body sagged, her brow splintered into rows of distress. "Oh, no, Juana, I never wanted you to join the Carmelites."

"But you said that the only reason you left was to care for your madre."

"That wasn't true, Juana. You were so young. You didn't deserve to hear the truth. I see that you have left the Carmelites, just as I did, so I know that you too have discovered what they truly are – deranged devils intent on inflicting misery on all." She stopped abruptly, waving her hands as if to shoo away the memories. "I am sorry. I simply have nothing good to say about them."

"Then why did you join them?"

Doña Angélica spoke truthfully, and softly, of something she had never told anyone. "It was the only convent that my family could afford," she said. "The Carmelites accepted my family's five hundred pesos gladly. My mediocre dowry didn't give me many choices. I had no prospects for marriage, so I opted for a nun's life."

She reached to hold Doña Angélica's hand. They knew. They both knew.

They sat in silence for a few moments, then Juana said, "I thought I might open a school like Las Amigas, as you did. I so loved learning from you ..."

"No, Juana, the Carmelite convent was not the right path for you, and such a school isn't the right path either." She paused to consider her thoughts, then continued. "Juana, I am a smart woman. Very smart, and I have a very good school. Even with my success, I could not afford to live like this. This," as she waved her arm around her, "all of this belongs to Don Enríque. I live here and keep him company. He even brings me jewels and pretty clothes, and sometimes books. It was being a bordello whore or this, so I chose this life, and I am happy with that choice. You have a different choice to make, Juana. You are not just 'smart,' you are brilliant. Gifted. I have never known another like you. Just as importantly, you have strong allies, la Vicereine Leonor and Fray Miranda among them."

"But what can I possibly do?"

Doña Angélica slowly picked up her cup and took a sip of coffee. She looked intently into Juana's eyes. "I believe that Fray Miranda advised you well about joining a convent."

She jolted. "No! no more convents."

"There is a great deal about convent life that suits you well, especially since you have no desire to marry. It is just that the Carmelite convent was the wrong one."

"Which one is the right one?"

"There are over twenty convents in La Ciudad de México, each with its own personality, and several that would suit you better, convents that would encourage you to explore your talents and learn how to share your gifts with the world. Trust the advice of Fray Miranda. You have a very influential advocate with him on your side. Listen to him, Juana. My guess is that he will choose the Hieronymite convent at San Jerónimo. He has strong ties there, both religiously and financially. Trust me, Juana, the nuns at San Jerónimo are so very different. You will hear laughter in their hallways, have time to study and to write, and be able to meet with people in the locutory nearly every day."

"But will there be an issue with my dowry? I have none. The Carmelites have refused to return my money to me."

"Yes, that will be an issue. San Jerónimo's Convent prides itself on admitting women from the finest Criolle families, and a dowry will be required. You will need money to buy a cell, money to hire at least one servant, and money to support your household until you can earn enough money on your own."

"But how can I earn that much money of my own in a convent?" She knew she could earn some money, but Angélica was speaking of supporting a whole household.

"With your writings," explained Doña Angélica. "Patrons and churches will pay you well for your elegant poetry, and even for plays for the feast day celebrations. Juana, I would be so honored to hear a *villancico* that you wrote." Doña Angélica spoke of the complex religious play presented at many of the larger cathedrals. "Many nuns earn a bit that way, but I think you could earn a lot, and having the ability to earn a lot of money for the convent marks you as a very desirable nun. The Carmelites were too smug to look for ways to make income, but other very reputable convents seek out talented women."

"Before I can earn money for the convent, or for myself, I still must get admitted. That, alas, may not happen."

"I believe it will happen, Juana. You know, I teach the daughters of some of the finest – and wealthiest – families in all of Nueva España. Let me see what I can do to help you raise your dowry."

Doña Angélica beamed, feeling like this was a task she was meant to accomplish, and despite her reluctance, Juana smiled as well. She still was not convinced on the advisability of returning behind gated walls, but she was willing to consider the option, and in the end a dowry might not be possible at all, so she did not want to hope for too much.

As they embraced their good-by, a very fashionable middle-aged woman turned into the pathway to the hacienda. Her broad smile and strong stride told Juana that this woman was someone she wanted to know.

"Angélica! Doña Angélica! How are you this bright day?" asked the woman.

"Doña Juana Inés Ramírez, meet Doña Seraphina," said Doña Angélica, beaming with pride as two of her blessed friends met.

"Juana? Juana Ramírez?" asked Doña Seraphina. Her eyebrows shot up as she stepped back to take in this woman.

"Yes, that is my name."

"Are you the granddaughter of Don Pedro Ramírez de Santillana?"

"Yes ..."

"Oh, heavens," interrupted Doña Seraphina. "Pedro bragged about you day and night. He was so proud of all that you knew. He had such high hopes for you, Doña Juana. He felt death tapping him on his shoulder and he was frantic to teach you everything that he could. He knew he had little time, and you needed to know so much. In fact, I was even jealous of you because he spent so much time with you!"

"You knew him well."

"Sí. Indeed. I knew him, I loved him, for many years," said Doña Seraphina. "He was a kind and generous man who made sure that I always had a house to live in, and food to eat. I miss him dearly, as no doubt do you, Doña Juana." Doña Seraphina would never have spoken so boldly while Don Pedro lived, but now she could share a special memory with his cherished granddaughter.

It was an open secret that Abuelo had a lover, but Juana did not even know her name until that moment.

"Your Abuelo was a good man," said Doña Seraphina softly.

"Indeed, he was. I am so glad he had the company of someone as gracious and kind as yourself." They embraced briefly as they parted, as though they had known each other for years, which in a sense they had.

Juana pondered Angélica's recommendation as she traveled back to la Ciudad de México, and that night she prayed long and deeply to la Virgen Maria.

Dear blessed Virgen Maria, am I truly supposed to be a nun? What if they discover my true heritage? What would I become then? Would you intercede with sweet Glorietta, the lady-in-waiting who went to the coast, and ask her if I might be a maid at her hacienda? If I housed the books that my Abuelo left me at the hacienda of Don Pedro Velázquez de la Cadena, would he allow me to live in a small shack in a forgotten corner of his fields?

Ultimately, she opted to continue as Doña Angélica had suggested and be patient. When she met with Fray Miranda, she told him about the invitation from Doña Leonor to go with her to España.

"No," he said firmly. "You cannot go to España. This is your home. This is where you need to be."

She surely agreed with him, but said simply, "Reverencia, what do you recommend that I should do? My friend Doña Angélica, the teacher I had at Las Amigas, suggests that a different convent might be the best path."

"Yes, she is right. A different convent is the best path for you. It will give you a real opportunity to contribute your talents to the Church." He paused. Fray Miranda did not want another pathetic confrontation with Juana about which convent she should choose.

She said respectfully, "Reverencia, which convent would you suggest?"

If Fray Miranda was surprised at her humility, he did not show it. He simply said, "The Hieronymite convent, San Jerónimo's, would be the best choice for you." Never once had Fray Miranda looked at her, holding his position behind the confessional screen, but she knew he was sincere.

"Why, Reverencia, would you choose that one?"

Without hesitation Fray Miranda jumped into an explanation of the benefits of San Jerónimo Convent, speaking slowly at first, then a bit faster and faster. "Wait until you see la biblioteca, Juana, with books overflowing the shelves, and nuns who know how to read and study them. The locutory gatherings at San Jerónimo's are legendary, popular with La Ciudad de México's intelligencia. The Sisters manage one of the finest girls' schools in the entire country, and their hospital is an invaluable asset to everyone. There is so much there, Juana, that you will find your place without difficulty."

Personally, Fray Miranda needed something more austere, but for Juana, yes, for Juana San Jeronimo's Convent was the best option. "Sadly," he noted, "there is still the issue of your dowry. I have not been able to convince the Carmelites to return your dowry."

Fray Miranda paused. Her shoulders drooped, anticipating defeat. "Let me see what I can do," he assured her.

Hardly two weeks passed before she received a note from Doña Angélica.

> "Dearest Juana, When your brilliant smile graced the veranda of my home, my heart leapt in joy. You have brought an honor to my life that no teacher could anticipate. Your intelligence, your sensitivity, your compassion – with all this, and more, I am certain that our Ciudad de México will shine for you.
>
> I was honored indeed to seek the assistance of a local family in your quest of a literary future, and I am so pleased that the most honorable Don Ignacio Rubio has said that he would be proud to sponsor you to enter a convent of your choice. I but mentioned your name to his lovely wife Doña Josepha, and noted your desire to join San Jerónimo's, and she smiled her glorious smile, saying her family must be the one to provide whatever you need. Don Ignacio agreed instantly.
>
> Don Ignacio recalls so fondly the times you joined your Abuelo and him on the veranda at Panoayan for lively conversations, and how proud your Abuelo was of you. In honor of your Abuelo, he will contact Fray

Miranda when he is in La Ciudad de México and arrange it.

With deepest love, your Angélica."

She could not help it, she wept. So much kindness, and Abuelo was still with her. She indeed remembered Don Ignacio's deep belly laugh when she tugged at his bushy beard so long ago, and she felt honored that he remembered her.

A week later Fray Miranda contacted her. He had arranged the payment of the dowry, the message said, and she was to meet with Sor Gabriela, the Abbess, the following Monday at four o'clock. She smiled. It was so like Fray Miranda to take credit for arranging the dowry, but it did not matter. It was arranged. She felt like her life was beginning again.

SHE ARRIVED at the Convent of San Jerónimo the following Monday, a few minutes before four o'clock, with far more trepidation than she expected. Constructed with the austerity of a fortress, its bleak appearance startled her. The tall thick walls stretching the length of several blocks screamed at her to run away. A wide door was open and she pushed herself through, to be greeted with smiling eyes from a nun walking rapidly toward her.

This small nun with bird like hands held up her skirt as she ran. A huge smile lit up her dark eyes. As she drew nearer, Juana could see that she was older than she first appeared, perhaps around forty.

"You must be Doña Juana Inés Ramírez! I am sorry for being late."

"Oh, no, you are not late. I think I may be a bit early."

"No matter, Sor Gabriela, the Abbess, is anxious to meet you. I am Sor Sophia. Come, let's go this way."

The interior of this fortress told a story of lush trees and flowers bursting into bloom, all through the dozens of alcoves and passageways, the meeting rooms that Fray Miranda had told her about, through a maze of walkways and galleries to the main building where Sor Gabriela had her office. All along the way, she saw groups of nuns, padres, and businessmen, and heard bits of conversations and laughter, yes, even laughter in convent hallways.

She liked Sor Gabriela, the Madre Superiora, immediately, her crinkly laugh lines speaking of years of joy.

"You grew up in the countryside near here, didn't you, Juana?"

"Yes, Muy Venerada Madre Superiora …"

"No, Juana. Please, simply 'Sor Gabriela' will do fine, and when we are Sisters, please call me simply 'Gabriela.' I am the Abbess for a short time, so I don't want to get accustomed to fancy titles." Sor Gabriela saw the confusion on Juana's face. "We elect our convent leaders at San Jerónimo, for two-year terms. We work closely with the Jesuit order, but we treasure our independence."

Juana smiled, and relaxed. Independent nuns. She liked that. She liked it a lot.

"You were telling me about where you grew up."

"Yes, Sor Gabriela, I was raised in Panoayan, south of here at the base of Popocatepetl. It is a land truly bursting with fields of sugar cane and corn, and thousands of birds, with brilliant wild flowers in every hidden nook. I used to run through the countryside, chasing butterflies and bugs." She laughed at herself for remembering so vividly the joys of her childhood. "When my Abuelo died, I moved to La Ciudad de México and lived with my aunt and uncle for several years. They introduced me to la Vicereine Leonor, who invited me to become a lady-in-waiting at el Palacio." She paused.

"And the Carmelite convent?"

She blushed. She had hoped this would not come up. "Yes, Sor Gabriela, I was there for two months."

"Why did you leave?"

How much could Sor Gabriela already know? Did the various convents communicate with other? Was she labeled as a weak nun who could not handle the rigors of living in a convent?

She was not surprised at the question, and she answered it as honestly as she could. "I am afraid that I was not a good Carmelite. I wanted desperately to read, to learn, to write, to converse, and these things were not part of the Carmelite way. I tried to become what they needed, but found myself wanting. Even one small book of poetry that la Vicereine Leonor gave me as a gift was burned. Ultimately, it was in their best interests that I leave, for I was too much of a trouble." She did not mention the lashing, but there was no need, for Sor Gabriela knew the reputation of the Carmelites. In fact, Sor Gabriela respected the fact that Juana did not speak of those things.

They took a leisurely stroll through lovingly tended gardens and orchards, down hallways painted with murals so vibrant they nearly jumped off the walls, and even peeked into a few rooms. Sor Gabriela opened an ornately carved door and stepped aside so Juana could see. La biblioteca. Fray Miranda was right, it was small, but the shelves indeed overflowed with intriguing titles. She glimpsed a title or two that had even been banned by the Inquisition.

They also visited the dining hall splashed with stunning murals, one mural reaching out to tell the story of la Virgen de Guadalupe, and another mural celebrating San Jerónimo and Santa Paula, founders of this, the Hieronymite Order. Her Abuelo had a portrait of San Jerónimo in his biblioteca. She knew San Jerónimo and Santa Caterina as the patron saints of libraries, so instantly felt grounded here, at home.

"Most nuns prefer eating in their cells," said Sor Gabriela. "The dining hall is used mostly by some slaves or protected women, and we have our communal meetings here on Fridays." Juana cringed at the mention of "communal meetings." This convent doled out punishments too. That was not a good sign.

They strolled through the labyrinth of the locutories to an open area where a large well sat, surrounded by vibrant herbs and spices and exotic fruits.

"We are blessed to have our own fresh water well," explained Sor Gabriela, "so our slaves and servants don't have far to go for fresh water. It gives us generously for all our needs, and keeps our gardens fresh."

"How many nuns are here, at San Jerónimo's?"

"There are about fifty nuns, and about one hundred and fifty more women, some protected women, some servants, some slaves. The nuns don't do much physical work. We teach, we write plays and songs, we manage the hospital, we help the poor, we sew, and we pray. We do pray a lot." Sor Gabriela smiled, as did Juana.

Their walk had covered but a small part of the nearly four acres of the Convent grounds, and barely touched the many acres more of nearby orchards and fields, all of it bursting with life, reaching far into the countryside. As a wealthy convent, San Jerónimo's also owned hundreds of buildings in La Ciudad de México, sometimes whole blocks of houses and shops, as well as dozens more haciendas and lands that were leased to farmers. The Sisters managed an impressive empire.

Sor Gabriela knew that it was not yet a good fit for Juana, but she was impressed with her and wanted to make it right. "I want you to be happy here, Juana. A discontent still rests on your shoulders. I want you to take your vows, comfortable in knowing that you will be happy here for the rest of your life, so I have an invitation for you. I have never extended such an invitation before, but I think it is important now. Come and live with us for a month or two, for as long as you need to settle any hesitation you have about joining us. When you have decided that this is how you truly want to spend the rest of your life, then you will take your vows."

"That will give you time to evaluate me as well."

"I don't need time to evaluate you. Fray Miranda's strong recommendation included mention of your inspired poetry and literary gifts. We only accept one or two Sisters a year, and I would be honored to have you be the one."

"Your invitation is incredibly generous, Sor Gabriela. Yes, I would be pleased to accept." She spoke humbly, and sincerely.

WHEN SHE SAW the cell she was to live in during her visit, she stood in the doorway, unable to speak. It was a spacious area of several large rooms – a common area, a kitchen, a bedroom containing a bed dressed with a relatively soft mattress and bedding, a private bathroom, a bathing cubby with a bath tub, sleeping quarters for her slave, and most miraculous of all, a desk with paper and ink sat by the large window that invited sunlight. It was unlike anything that she envisioned. With easy access to the patios and locutories, this was a spot that she could indeed call "home." She soon learned that all the nuns had apartments like this one, some larger than others, but all spacious and well lit.

Calling upon her time at the Carmelite Convent, she fell quickly into the routine at San Jerónimo's. She woke with the bells at 5:30 am and Doña Monica, a woman of about thirty years, one of the protected women, helped her dress.

"Monica, you perform your duties so gracefully. Have you never wished to become a nun?"

"Indeed, I have," replied Doña Monica, "but I had no dowry, and so I could not formally join the Convent as a Sister. I feel honored that San Jerónimo's has so generously accepted my service in exchange for my care."

Juana felt it much too presumptuous to sit with the nuns during the services, so she found a spot toward the back, and quickly discovered that the chapel was nearly empty. Many of the nuns did not attend early services, and no one seemed to mind.

On her way back to the guest cell, she caught the enticing aroma of café de olla with cloves and cinnamon, and chilaquiles with salsa verde drifting from several rooms, and found a tasty breakfast waiting for her.

At 9:00am she returned to the chapel for Matins prayers, a service that called to many more Sisters, and she embraced the warmth of their camaraderie. Then she joined them in the communal room where they formed work assignment groups. No one told them what to do, they just seemed to know what needed to be done, and knew what they could contribute.

"Come visit our school," called out one nun. "Sor Sophia tells me you are a poet and a writer, so perhaps you can join us there." She did just that. She visited the school famous for teaching girls a bit of reading, but mostly embroidery arts, music, and drama, charmed by the youthful energy of the students. She even composed a little play, one based on the Greek myth of Eros, that the girls presented for locutory guests.

After prayers at noon, they parted for lunch. "Can you join me for lunch?" asked another nun. Sor Lucia, a delightful nun who had become her guide, made certain that a slave or protected woman like Doña Monica was in attendance to Juana while she was a guest, cooking her meals and cleaning her apartment, but she did not often need such assistance. The nuns were generous in their offers of companionship and shared meals, so she rarely found herself eating alone.

Afternoons drifted by in additional work assignments, or in needlework or personal pursuits until 3:00pm when there was another prayer service. She had immense discretion all during the day to do as she wished, to work, to study, to write, to converse, as did all the Sisters, a freedom that she did not take for granted.

Most nuns were simply women beyond marriageable age who had nowhere else to go. These nuns were not particularly religious, they simply needed a respectable place to live, so they chose the convent. They often worked in the hospital or the school, or directed the farming endeavors of San Jerónimo. The Sisters' embroideries and weavings were much desired by churches and cathedrals throughout Nueva España.

Sometimes a nun flaunted a ring or bracelet that an admirer gave her, but most often she gifted it to the Convent, which in turn invested it. San Jerónimo's was proud of the fact that it earned five percent annually on its investments, making this one of the wealthiest convents in all Nueva España. They were financially beholden only to themselves, and worked hard to maintain that independence.

The greatest joy was in the evenings. Guests from la Ciudad de México joined the Sisters for Vespers services at 7:00pm, then everyone broke into groups in the locutory gatherings. There were no bars separating the nuns from the guests, just open spaces with adobe walls creating a maze of gathering rooms, some small for a few guests, and some larger rooms for dramatic presentations and music. Everywhere were tables of sweets and savories, coffees and wine, and delicacies that even the finest bakeries did not possess. She used her freedom to wander through many of the locutory gatherings, marveling at the variety of presentations, from studied analytical discussions to bawdy barroom singing and banter. Some priests came and lolled around the locutories all afternoon, sunning themselves and munching on assorted delicacies as they appeared, chatting with various nuns and each other. The evening locutory gatherings were so popular that they burst the extensive walls of the ground floor patio and flew up to the rooftops of the main building. Juana began planning how her locutory gathering could attract the curious and learned, resident and traveler alike.

"Indeed," said Sor Lucia, her young friend, "many here do not seek a life as religious as mine, and few are as talented as you. Sometimes you will hear us floating through the hallways like a gaggle of geese, sometimes winging our way silently, and sometimes bickering like so many chicks in a nest. The thick walls, the incessant idle chatter in the locutories, the groups of women who isolate themselves – these things and more do cause me distress. It is not a perfect place, but all in all, I prefer it to anywhere else."

So did Juana. She sometimes slipped into the chapel late at night, seeking the image of la Virgen Maria, kneeling, and again and again thanking her for bringing her to this place, this Convent of San Jerónimo. She felt intensely grateful that because of her family she had been introduced to la Vicereine Leonor and subsequently to Fray Miranda. It was only because of her familiar connections that she was not required to scrub floors or do laundry as a Protected Woman, or worse. It was only because of those connections that she would have the freedom to study, to read and to write.

"COME ALONG, Juana!" called out Sor Lucia one morning. "It is fiesta time! We don't want to be late!"

Such a fiesta it was! It was the fiesta of la Virgen de Guadalupe, the patron saint de la Ciudad de México, the most beloved of all religious icons. After morning prayers and breakfast, Juana left with Sor Lucia and several other nuns, darting through the city from clapping with mariachis players to joining rivers of women and children, everyone holding a painted mask, perhaps of their beloved Virgen de Guadalupe or even a blue fox like the one that Juana had when her Abuelo first brought her to this great fiesta. Everyone from across Nueva España had come, dressed in vibrant local finery. Swirling skirts and leaping young men were everywhere. Clicking heels rumbled on cobblestone streets even beyond the Plaza Mayor.

With thousands of visitors on Plaza Mayor, there was hardly room to move, but the crowd made way for the entrance of the parade! Decorated carts pulled by donkeys and oxen inched their way around the Plaza, each cart festooned with flowers and gilt, each cart with a troupe of actors and singers. Poets and playwrights vied for the honor of producing plays for this fiesta. The plays were about palace life, or Greek myths, or Aztec stories, or all of it stirred together. No one could hear the dialog over the music and laughter of the crowd, but no one minded – the carts would remain there all day, with audiences coming and going to hear the stories told.

The nuns made a point of watching the play that Doña Caterina Rosa was in, for she was after all the most glamorous, and most popular actress, in la Ciudad de México. She flaunted jewels of all colors on her wrists, on her fingers, and around her neck, and was indeed the envy of every woman there, even the nuns. She paused in the play to accept a new jewel from an admirer, and caught sight of Juana. Doña Caterina Rosa jumped down from her stage, flinging her arms around Juana, swinging her in pure delight.

"Doña Juana Inés Ramírez, my little parakeet," said Doña Caterina Rosa, "I was so lonely when you left el Palacio. I had no more of your wonderful plays. Will you write another play for me soon? Please? A play with a sexy, beautiful woman, of course!" People all around were indeed curious about this young woman in the midst of nuns who had captured Doña Caterina Rosa's complete attention.

"Of course I will!" promised Juana. The nuns were clearly impressed with her rapport with Doña Caterina Rosa, the crowd nearly crushing them all.

"Here, my little chickadee," said Doña Caterina Rosa as she hid a jewel in Juana's hand. "This is a little payment for your promise, so you must write a new play for me!" Juana later gifted the jewel to San Jerónimo's in appreciation of the Sisters' hospitality and generosity, a gift that was most graciously accepted.

She had been to the Fiesta de la Virgen de Guadalupe many times, but never had she felt so much a part of it. They feasted on enchiladas, buying enough to share with peasants along the edges of the crowd. One wine maker crossed himself as they approached, saying his whole crop would be blessed if they would accept his hospitality, which they were pleased to do. The nuns laughed and twirled with children from all classes, the richest and the poorest. They barely made it back to San Jerónimo before the doors were locked for the night.

"Not to worry," Sor Lucia assured her. "They would have opened the gate for us."

THEN FRIDAY AFTERNOON arrived, the "judging time," and all nuns were required to attend. She did not want to attend this meeting, but she knew she had to discover what miseries it held.

The proceedings surprised her immensely, even shocked her. Two nuns had been elected to keep records of the sins of the Sisters. One such nun stepped forward in the assembly hall to announce their transgressions. Sor Bianca had missed five prayer services this past week; she was commanded to say ten Hail Marys. Sor Delores stayed out all night one time without approval; her punishment was to remain in the Convent for the next two weeks. Sor Soledad missed serving her shift at the hospital on Tuesday; she was commanded to serve two additional shifts the coming week. And so it went.

The judging nun, who was elected by all the nuns, dispensed punishment consisting of additional Hail Marys or Beatitudes or special prayers. That was all. Not a single lashing was ever dispensed, no matter how grave the misdeed. Juana did not believe it the first time she saw it, but week after week, there were no lashings. None, not even for a nun who had left the convent without permission and had stayed out for two days.

"Juana," said Fray Miranda, "Don Pedro Velázquez de la Cadena in his overwhelming generosity has offered to provide funds to support your first year at San Jerónimo's." This was a gift beyond the three thousand pesos that had already been provided to San Jerónimo's as her dowry, and Juana was simply overwhelmed by the generosity.

"My dear," said la Vicereine Leonor, "I haven't seen your eyes sparkle like that in a very long time. I would be so pleased to purchase your apartment for you, the corner one looking out toward Popocatepetl."

"My dear niece," said Tio Juan, "Maria and I would be honored to have shelves built in your cell so that your Abuelo's books may be with you for the rest of your days."

"Juana," said her madre Isobel, "you will need help. Please accept Sara, my most talented servant, to help you in your new surroundings."

Everyone, it seemed, knew that this was the right step for Juana to take.

It did not take long for her to approach the Abbess with her decision, and she had one request. "Please, Sor Gabriela, may I be excused for a time before taking my vows? I want to go home to see my family, and I want to say good-by to a few friends and let them know that I have finally found my way."

"Of course. Let's plan the ceremony for the end of February. That will give us time to finish up the paperwork and get you settled in. Fray Miranda said that he would like a bit of time to plan an appropriate celebration, so that should work fine. You are welcome to remain in the guest cell until you have your own cell, if you like. Your joining us is a very special Christmas joy for me"

"Thank you, Sor Gabriela, it is a gift for me as well."

WAS IT ONLY yesterday when she stepped into her own cell, the one la Vicereine Leonor had purchased for her? Her study and her sleeping room were to be upstairs, with the bath tub in a cubby all its own, while downstairs was the kitchen, the common area and a room for her servant Sara.

Sara, a strong, bright teenager, had been in Nueva España for nearly a year, quickly learning the new language. There were about fifty slave girls housed at San Jerónimo's. Some came from East Africa, captured by Arabs, and shipped via the Silk Road sea route, from Zanzibar on the eastern coast of Africa to India to China, then the Portuguese traders took them across the Pacific Ocean in slave ships to Puerta Vallarta in Nueva España.

Other slaves came from West Africa, across the Atlantic Ocean in the trade triangle of Africa to England to Veracruz on the eastern coast. Those who survived the interminable journey from either direction arrived at coastal slave markets in Nueva España, to be deloused and inspected and baptized.

Now, with Biblical names like Josepha and Sara, they were sold. Haciendas, farms, churches, monasteries, and convents all made use of these slaves. The greatest demand came from silver mines, which ate up slaves, feeding them to worms. Slaves could be granted freedom, but rarely were.

Sara did not know where she came from, except that there was lots of rain, and monkeys as pets. It was hot in Sara's homeland, but lush vegetation absorbed a lot of the heat. Without ocean breezes to break the heat in La Ciudad de México, she sometimes found this heat difficult to bear.

Juana's first chore was to unpack the boxes that she had packed on her trip to Panoayan. She set Sara to the task of setting up the kitchen with pans, dishware, and cookware that Rosita had selected, while she unpacked her books, ceremoniously arranging them on the beautiful oak bookshelves that Tio Juan and Tia Maria had built for her. She felt so at home with all these splendid volumes around her. Kircher, Ovid and Gongora all took their rightful places, along with nearly two hundred others, and still there was room for more.

There was one basket that she did not remember packing. It looked to be stuffed with fabric, but as she unwrapped the fabric, she discovered a statue of la Virgen de Guadalupe. This was not just any statue of la Virgen de Guadalupe; it was the statue that had guarded the kitchen at Panoayan as long as she remembered, blessing all who entered. There was a small note that said simply, *"From Rosita. To keep you safe."* Rosita, her beloved cook and nurse, must have searched far to find someone who could write even this small note.

She held the carving to her breast, blessing Rosita again and again. Of all the wondrous gifts she had received, this statue was the most precious. Rosita had been the cook at Panoayan since before she was born, making the kitchen her second most favorite room at the hacienda. La biblioteca, of course, was her favorite, but the kitchen exuded aromas and delights that teased her imagination. She rushed from her bed in the morning to hear the stories that Rosita told her, the stories of her Aztec ancestors, and the story of la Virgen de Guadalupe.

How many times ... dozens of times ... hundreds of times had Rosita told her the story of la Virgen de Guadalupe.

Once a poor peasant dressed only in a faded tilma, a young man on his way to get help for his ailing father, had been blessed with a visit by la Virgen Maria, la Virgen standing on the crest of a deserted hill with a burst of golden sunbeams surrounding Her. Her sky-blue robe was sprinkled with images of stars, and Her hand reached out to the peasant in mercy.

La Virgen told the peasant to go to la Ciudad de México and tell the Archbishop there to build a church in Her honor on that spot, and She would care for people who came to Her in prayer.

The poor peasant did just that. He went to la Ciudad de México, to the Archbishop and, falling on his knees, told the story of the appearance of la Virgen Maria and Her request.

The Archbishop turned him down immediately, considering him nothing more than a crazy peasant. The peasant returned to the hill where he saw la Virgen and told Her what had happened. She told him to go again, that he must plead even harder.

The peasant did as la Virgen asked. He pled so deeply at the Archbishop's feet that the stones in the wall wept. Still the Archbishop would not budge. Broken hearted, the peasant once again returned to the hill where he saw la Virgen.

The peasant stood on the empty hill, the weeds all turned to scraggly nubs in the summer blaze. He waited until the next morning, when la Virgen came again. Tears flew down his cheeks as he told Her again of his defeat.

La Virgen spoke softly. "Give me your tilma." She blessed the ragged piece of cloth and swept Her arms over the hillside, now bursting with flowers -- crimson flowers, golden flowers, lavender flowers … all so beautiful, all so alive.

"Pick some flowers," She said, "and take them to the Archbishop in your tilma." She handed him back his tilma, which he tied around his neck, and as he collected a bundle of beautiful flowers, he felt exuberant, as though the blessing of God had come upon him, for indeed it had.

This time as he approached the Archbishop, he stood and released the bounty of flowers he carried in his tilma. Flowers flew across the tiled floor, bursting into bloom before their eyes – delicate orchids, tiny pink cactus flowers, bold chocolate cosmos, orange honeysuckle, purple passion flowers, the fragile frangipani, and so many more. The flowers scattered on the floor in a fantastical array, but the entourage and the Archbishop were not looking at the flowers on the floor. No, they were looking at the tilma that had carried the flowers. There on the tilma was the image of la Virgen Maria herself, with stars on Her sky-blue robe and golden rays of the sun bursting around Her. She held out a hand, inviting all to come to Her.

Everyone fell to their knees, begging Her forgiveness for not believing Her messenger.

The Archbishop did have Her chapel built, just as She wished, and as She promised, She heard the sorrows of people, as many as there are stars in the sky, and helped everyone.

The Archbishop also placed the tilma with this image of la Virgen above the altar of the chapel. This was the tilma, the piece of shoddy cloth from a poor peasant, that now never aged, unlike all other tilmas that fell apart in a year or two. Despite the thousands of candles lit around this altar, this tilma never got smoky. Despite the many thousands of people who touched it, this tilma never showed a spec of dirt. La Virgen had made it pure. The blessed Virgen, la Virgen de Guadalupe as She came to be called, simply stretched out Her hand, inviting all to come to Her for mercy.

It would be over six hundred years before the mystery of the stars on her cape would be deciphered, or the hidden secrets in her eyes would begin to be revealed, but from the moment the tilma displayed her image to the Archbishop, the tilma was revered. She was La Virgen de Guadalupe.

Rosita's great grandfather had carved this lovely statue, and had touched the gold paint with glints of gold dust. It was certainly Rosita's most valuable possession, and now she wanted to protect her dear little Juana forever.

Holding la Virgen de Guadalupe brought back so many memories, the simple joys of her childhood … running in from the field to capture one of Rosita's sweet cookies, listening to tales of the great Gods and Goddesses of the Aztecs, while Rosita made tortillas, or listening to Rosita's little song about the blue bird as she chopped peppers with her big knife. And chilly mornings always found Rosita at the stove with a big cup of hot chocolate, wrapping her in a toasty warm shawl, and telling her stories. She told stories about Cihuacoatl, the Snake Woman, and Cacahuatl, the God of Chocolate. Rosita always loved picking up little Juana and tipping her upside down, and little Juana loved it too.

"COME, JUANA, it is time to get ready for the ceremony." Sor Lucia nudged her shoulder gently, luring her from her reverie.

Sor Lucia and two other nuns dressed her in her white tunic and tucked her hair under the white cap and tiara. Over that went a finely loomed white cotton ceremonial gown with large sleeves and free flowing skirt. A white cross was embroidered in silk thread on each shoulder of the ceremonial gown. The Sisters tied a slim black braided leather belt at her waist and laid the black cotton scapular over her shoulders.

She expected a tedious ceremony like that at the Carmelite convent, but it was not like that at all. This was a beautiful ceremony, one worthy of a bride of Christ. The Sisters flowed into a procession that placed them in an alcove to the side of the main chapel, each dressed in ceremonial habit. Sor Lucia and Sor Gabriela walked with her, leading her up the center aisle to the altar. Candlelight glowed on every wall, smiles and nods flowing from every direction.

During the ceremony of prayers and songs Sor Gabriela placed a large rosary around her neck and positioned a large brass medallion of the Annunciation on her breast, while two of the younger nuns positioned her stiff white headdress. These were the design touches that distinguished the Sisters of San Jerónimo, the Hieronymite nuns. The nuns wore them with pride.

The last piece of her uniform was the simple gold ring that she would wear as a bride of Christ. She watched, frozen, as Archbishop Payo himself stepped forward and placed the ring on her finger and blessed her as "Sor Juana Inés de la Cruz." She had not noticed the Archbishop standing on the side of the altar until that moment. She was so moved; she truly did not know what to do or what to say. She need not have worried, for immediately following that, each nun, each Sister of San Jerónimo's Convent, stepped forward and one by one they gently kissed her fingers, as she returned each honor in kind. Sor Gabriela was the last, and she whispered to her, "Now we are sisters forever."

Sor Gabriela led the processional out of the Church, followed by Sor Juana, and then by the other nuns. The guests were next. The Jesuit priests were last, acting as honorary hosts to all. She and Sor Gabriela stood by the door of the church, greeting their guests as they spilled into the large patio that was bursting with guests and with tables of sweet cakes, fruits, cheeses, sausages, tacos, enchiladas, vintage wines, and lots of delicacies that she had never even seen before, like some salty worms that were a true delicacy in Nueva España.

She knew many of the guests, and presented a proper curtsy to honored guests from the government, but enthusiastically embraced la Vicereine Leonor.

Doña Angélica, her beloved teacher, stepped up to greet her, but she would not accept a formal greeting from Angélica and instead embraced her joyously too. "May I present Don Enríque Hernandez de Castelan," Angélica said, as Don Enríque presented a courtly bow and kissed Juana's hand.

"Don Enríque, what a pleasure to meet you," she said sincerely. "Our Angélica has told me how kind and generous you are."

Many priests came to honor her, the whole Jesuit order of la Ciudad de México it seemed, and she bowed to each, thanking them for the honor of their presence. Some priests came from further away, like Fray Manuel Fernández de Santa Cruz, the Bishop of Puebla, a most respected member of the clergy; he kissed her hand, as did the other priests, then held her hand for a moment and told her how truly honored he was to meet her.

Successful local merchants, guild presidents and those who had distinguished themselves as leaders in their fields were well represented too -- book sellers, poets and artisans of all ilk stopped to greet her. She had met some of them previously, but many were new to her. She thanked each of them for coming and making this day so special for her.

Finally, Archbishop Payo stepped forward.

"Reverencia … Reverencia," she began. Rarely was she at a loss for words, but she was speechless now.

Archbishop Payo smiled. "It was my honor to be here," he said graciously as he kissed her fingertips. "I could not say No to Fray Miranda, and he insisted." They both smiled, knowing well Fray Miranda's persuasive powers. Then the Archbishop winked. "By the way, Sor Juana, is your brother Don Diego here?"

Juana blushed, remembering when she and Archbishop Payo first met in the La Biblioteca de la Universidad, years before he became the Archbishop. "Only in spirit, Reverencia."

The Archbishop laughed, a great belly laugh. "I hope he will be with us in spirit for many years to come," he said as he stepped away to greet other guests.

Her family stood to one side, along a wall of the patio. Even her madre Isobel's typical commanding presence was subdued by the gallantry of the gathering. Juana rushed over to greet them, one by one. Her sisters Maria and Josepha looked dazzling in new gowns. Both had married, and both were now left alone, deserted by their husbands, raising bastard children as had their madre Isobel. Her madre Isobel's new lover, Don Diego Ruiz Lozano, was there with her young half-sisters, Inés Ruiz Lozano and Antonia Lozano, both looking delightfully charming.

"It is so nice to see you," she said to Inés and Antonia. "How do you like la Ciudad de México?" They glanced up at Don Diego, their father, and he nodded, giving them permission to speak.

"I saw a juggler in the Plaza Mayor today," said Inés, the young woman who would one day wed a university professor. Two of her daughters would also enter San Jerónimo's as nuns, with Fray Miranda's assistance, and under Juana's watchful eye. One of Inés' daughters, Isabel Maria de San José, would fall completely under the protective arm of her aunt, Sor Juana Inés de la Cruz.

"I really liked the candy that Tia Maria had," said Antonia. She would wed a wealthy landowner and manage a large, beautiful hacienda. Both Inés and Antonia had doweries of 1,500 pesos, so they each had many suitors.

"Please do stop by before heading home, and I'll show you around my new home," she told the girls, "and we might even find some candy!"

Juana now had a half-brother, too, also named Diego -- Diego Ruiz Lozano -- who was presently at a military academy, and who would no doubt follow his father into military service.

Along with uncles and aunts and cousins from far away, her new Sisters, the clergy of the Jesuit order, and all the noblemen who surrounded her on this, her special day, Juana felt … happy. Secure.

Fray Miranda was not, of course, in attendance. He could not have navigated such a gathering with so many females, and he remained steadfast in his vow to never look at a woman. Yet Fray Miranda was quite present, in the guests he invited, in the splendor of the feast, in the joy of the occasion. She knew she had a great deal to thank him for. For his part, Fray Miranda knew that the souls – and treasuries – that she would bring to the Convent and to the Jesuits would far surpass any amount that could be spent on her celebration. For Fray Miranda, it was a solid investment.

As the bells rang for Lauds everyone paused and bowed their heads as the Archbishop led them in a service, followed by a hymn sung by the nuns. Around midnight the guests began to leave, each again stopping by to say *"Buenos noches."*

It had been a long day, a good day. A very good day. She could not sleep that night as she watched the silvery fog crown the moon, then crawl between the buildings surrounding San Jerónimo's, wrapping the world in swaddling clothes..

Serenade

"KNOWING MUSIC is as important as knowing Latin when studying the Bible," insisted Sor Juana. She stood in her locutory at San Jerónimo where she hosted gatherings several times a week.

The large open space, the largest at the Convent, boasted seating for twenty or more guests, with room for servants to set out coffee, beer, wine, barbequed meats, and peppers, with treats and delicacies too. Sara proved to be invaluable at these gatherings, serving exotic delicacies and managing extra help with finesse.

Here, the locutory, was the university education that Juana longed for. This was the Golden Age of Spanish Poetry, the age of Luis de Gongora, the age of Juana Inés de la Cruz. The brightest minds of Nueva España came to call at Sor Juana's gatherings, the poets, the writers, the philosophers, the statesmen, the financiers, the composers. Many of the men that she had met at la Vicereine Leonor's gatherings came to this locutory gathering, but now they came for political and economic connections, rather than social dalliance. Even distinguished visitors from España, Portugal, England and the northern provinces of California and Texas came to call.

Many of these guests were ones that she had personally invited, for whenever she read something she especially enjoyed, which was often, she dashed off a letter of praise to the author, luring the greatest minds of her time to her locutory gatherings.

Wives and women of el Palacio were welcome too, although few but la Vicereine Leonor came, and even she was nearly always accompanied by her husband.

This spot, Sor Juana's locutory, became a polarizing spot in la Ciudad de México for liberal literati, rising politicians and men of power.

Sor Juana's locutory was where discussions on Hellenistic classics, Ovid's "Metamorphosis," Avicenna, Aquinas, Maimonides, Cicero and so many others found a robust home, and tales from all over the world settled here too. A traveler once came who told about the redwood trees in California, trees that reached far into the clouds, nearly as tall as the towers of la Gran Catedral de la Ciudad de México. Everyone sat in wonderment, afraid to believe something so majestic could exist, yet knowing the traveler could not be wrong. Another well-traveled gentleman raved about the joyful commedia del'arte performances in the Italian court.

All were welcome at Sor Juana's locutory, and all listened in rapt attention when she spoke.

"You mean learning music for singing the Psalms," said Fray Jacinto from the nearby Catedral de México.

"No," she replied confidently. "We don't study music just for singing, but for understanding." She was in her element … a smile that welcomed all, eyes that laughed, a piercing intellect of pure wonderment.

Music and sound had intrigued Juana from the time she sat enraptured by the songs of birds in her Panoayan countryside. She cherished, too, the conch shell with its windy whisperings that her Abuelo had set in her hands at the edge of the Pacific Ocean one bright day. That conch shell still sat on her bookcase, and it still whispered memories from so long ago. She ached to delve into the complexities of sound and music as presented in some of the several hundred books that she now owned, especially the theories of Aristotle.

This day she spoke with her usual strength of conviction in explaining the essence of the story of Abraham to her guests. With sophisticated math, and a knowledge of music that few possessed, she explained how Abraham begged God to save Sodom and

Gomorrah, if he could but find fifty righteous people, and then took it step-by-step down the octave when he asked only for the lives of forty-five righteous people, then forty, then thirty, then twenty, then just ten righteous people. That was as far as he could go.

"You see," she explained, "Abraham could ask for no fewer than ten righteous people, for he had reached the end of the octave."

"Splendid!" decreed Fray Jacinto. "I shall never read that passage the same way again. I thank you, Sor Juana!" He ceremoniously rose and bowed to her eloquent analysis, as the other guests followed his example.

Sara took the opportunity of the pause in conversation to flow graciously among the guests, delighting them with sweets spiced with the rare, complex vanilla bean found only on the Tonka tree in the plains of Nueva España. She also brought in a pitcher of spiced wine, and other pitchers of hot chocolate, ale, and Brazilian coffee. Today's treats included fish in a savory sauce, and even some caramels.

Juana glanced around the setting, seeing many faces she knew well, and half expecting la Vicereine Leonor to walk through the gateway beside her husband, the former Viceroy, the Marquis de Mancera, as they had done nearly every day the past few years. The Viceroy's term had ended two months earlier and although they had just left la Ciudad de México, they had not yet left Nueva España, winding their way leisurely to Veracruz for a ship to España.

"I suppose you would claim that even philosophers should study common philosophies more." This from one of the professors at the University. He intended it as a joke, but Juana did not see it that way.

"Absolutely," she said. "While I marvel at the distinct properties of egg whites and egg yolks, even Aristotle would have done well to study the properties of heat in the kitchen!"

Amid a round of communal laughter, a small commotion erupted at the gate of the locutory. The Bishop of Puebla, Fray Manuel Fernández de Santa Cruz, made his way to the front of the gathering, directly toward Juana. Archbishop Payo had introduced Juana and the Bishop of Puebla at Sor Juana's initiation rites, but there were so many new faces at that ceremony that Sor Juana forgot about him until Archbishop Payo made one of his rare visits to the locutory, bringing the Bishop of Puebla with him.

She and the Bishop of Puebla joined a very elite group that Archbishop Payo called his circle of friends. The Bishop of Puebla arrived at this august group because Archbishop Payo had been his Principal Consecrator, and they had become strong allies and friends. Juana came to the circle some years after her happenstance meeting with the Archbishop in the La Biblioteca de la Universidad. As they each deeply respected Archbishop Payo, so they came to respect each other.

"Forgive me, most honored Sor Juana Inés de la Cruz. Please forgive me. I am but a humble servant carrying a message from the Marquis de Mancera." The Bishop turned to face the guests. "Forgive me, gentlemen, but may we continue this discussion another day?" There was no questioning the urgency of the Bishop's message, and so the guests filed out silently.

The Bishop had delivered many such messages, but few rested as heavy on his heart as this message. He reached into his vest, pulling out a sealed letter. "It is a letter from the Marquis de Mancera," he said quietly.

A letter from the Marquis de Mancera, the former Viceroy? Juana had exchanged many letters with la Vicereine Leonor, and with the Marquis, but none held the urgency of this missive. She reached for the letter. Then stopped. Her shoulders drooped. She knew that she did not want to read this letter. She also knew she had to read it. Slowly she broke the seal on the letter. It was dated two days earlier, April 22, 1674, and written in the town of Tepeaca.

"My dearest and most exalted Sor Juana Inés de la Cruz, I write to you with extreme sadness. My heart is broken, my soul so

weak that I can barely lift this quill. My wife, our dearest friend, our Leonor, has passed away. Our honored Bishop of Puebla, Fray Manuel Fernández de Santa Cruz, was with her last evening, as was I. She rested on a bed of golden velvet, her hand wearing the glorious ruby ring you bestowed upon her last Christmas. Her last words were to speed a message to you, to tell you that her heart was with you, to thank you for the million kindnesses you gifted her ..."

She could read no more. It was la Vicereine Leonor who had gifted her a million kindnesses. It was la Vicereine Leonor who brought her to el Palacio, who protected her, who encouraged her writing and her learning, even commissioning plays to be performed in el Palacio. It was la Vicereine Leonor who once taught her how to float down the stairs to the ballroom, how to use her silk fan to send seductive messages. It was Leonor who cared for her after the brutal attack that night. It was Leonor who introduced her to Fray Miranda. It was Leonor who went to the Carmelite Convent to see her, and it was she who persuaded Fray Miranda to visit her as well. And it was her dear Vicereine Leonor who took her in when the whole world shut its doors against her, took her in and let her find her own path, here to San Jerónimo's.

Now she was gone. Gone.

The Bishop of Puebla saw the tears flowing on Juana's cheeks. He gently stood beside her, then wrapped his arm around her shoulders in comfort. "Come," he said, "let us go to the chapel and pray for her."

Juana chose a spot in front of the gilded Virgin statue. They each lit a candle, and knelt side by side. An hour passed, perhaps two. Then Juana spoke, whispering. "Why does God take those who are so kind? I needed her so."

"Perhaps the angels needed some kindness too," said the Bishop of Puebla. "He brought her to you when you needed her most of all, and now He has taken her home. But, Juana, know that He has not taken all of her, that some of la Vicereine Leonor will remain in your heart, forever. I think she would be pleased to know that your memory of her has brought goodness to the world."

She relaxed a bit, and even smiled a bit. "Of course. You are right. I feel I must let this sadness soar into poetry in honor of that blessed soul." She rose slowly, as did the Bishop of Puebla.

"You were there to bring our dear Vicereine Leonor to rest, weren't you?" It was a simple affirmation. The Bishop nodded.

"Thank you for bringing this message, and for staying by my side. Your warmth and understanding mean more than you can imagine." It was true. With the passing of la Vicereine Leonor, there was no one else in the world who would have stayed by her side as had the Bishop of Puebla.

"It is always my honor to be here for you," said the Bishop. "I will advise Archbishop Payo of la Vicereine Leonor's passing and arrange for a service in her honor."

She looked up. "Perhaps …" she began.

"Yes," agreed the Bishop. "Perhaps several services would better honor a woman who was so remarkable. I will see to it. I will personally lead the services in Puebla."

SHE ACCOMPANIED the Bishop of Puebla on his return to his parish where he led a special mass in the unfinished *Capilla de Nuesta Señora del Rosario* in the Church of Santo Domingo. The Chapel was already glistening with the Mysteries of the Rosary, the Virtues associated with it and la Virgen de Rosario herself. It would not be complete for another fifteen years, but the love and devotion in its every stone were already evident. It was the perfect spot for a remembrance of la Vicereine Leonor.

Then for several days she joined the Marquis de Mancera on the arduous trek to the coast, and strolled with him along the waterfront, recalling the hundreds of times that the beautiful Leonor had touched their hearts.

When it came time for the Marquis de Mancera to leave, she accompanied him to the small boat that would ferry him to the ship. He started toward the boat, then stopped, reaching in his pocket.

"I am sure Leonor wanted you to have this," he said as he placed the ruby ring in her hand, wrapping her fingers to hold it tight. It was the ring that she had gifted Leonor the last Christmas that she was in la Ciudad de México.

She bowed deeply as he left the shore, a gesture he treasured.

On her way home, the modest resting place of her dear Vicereine Leonor, the Church of San Francisco, tugged at her heart still, and again she stopped to pray at la Capilla del Rosario in the church of Santo Domingo. Something treasured in her life was gone.

Juana wept, and through her tears she wrote not one, but three, glorious poems celebrating her Leonor, calling on the morning stars to crown her in her heavenly home. Archbishop Payo performed several masses in honor of la Vicereine Leonor, having Juana's elegant poetry read at each service, while her Sisters at San Jerónimo's offered their prayers as well. She recognized the emptiness in her heart. It first appeared on the death of her cherished Abuelo, and now forged deeper on the death of her dear Vicereine Leonor.

SO MANY MOMENTS reminded Juana of la Vicereine Leonor, moments that came and went like spikes of sunlight dancing on the wall. The appointment of the new Viceroy was one of these times. The last letter Juana received from la Vicereine Leonor spoke of the new Viceroy. She had met him at Otomba, the traditional spot where the former Viceroy hands the scepter of command to the new Viceroy, effectively handing off power and position. La Vicereine Leonor called the new Viceroy a "popinjay," and seemed amused by his appointment.

The new Viceroy held the post for but a very brief time, for four days only. After paying the Crown fifty thousand ducats for the honor of the position, he arrived in la Ciudad de México with all the pomposity of a new Viceroy – the parades, the parties, the Triumphal Arch that greeted him as he entered La Ciudad de México. Then four days later, he died. La Vicereine Leonor would not have missed the comic irony.

The Crown turned to the one man it trusted the most, the man it had called upon for decades for special projects and reports on Nueva España, a man thoroughly trusted, and loved, by the people of Nueva España as well. It called upon Archbishop Payo to add the post of Viceroy to his existing duties as Archbishop. It was not unusual for an Archbishop to be appointed on an interim basis, but it was unusual for an Archbishop to serve a full term simultaneously as Viceroy.

The treasury was still in a shambles after the exorbitant spending of the Viceroy Mancera and la Vicereine Leonor, for they had left the government of Nueva España in serious debt, over a hundred thousand pesos in debt. The Crown trusted Archbishop Payo to bring a fiscal responsibility to Nueva España, as well as a sense of political stability, and they were right. Accepting a salary that was but a fraction of that of his predecessors, and with a modest installation ceremony, Archbishop Payo added the responsibilities of Viceroy of Nueva España to his equally demanding duties as Archbishop of Nueva España.

One man now represented both the religious life of Nueva España, and its political/economic life, and for Juana it was truly a blessing. While the Archbishop generally oversaw the activities of all the convents, the nuns knew that if they did not like a ruling from the Archbishop they could always go to the Viceroy, whose authority was unquestioned. But now the Archbishop and the Viceroy were the same person, Juana's longtime supporter and friend, Fray Payo. La Vicereine Leonor would have so enjoyed the fact of the appointment of Juana's friend, for it certainly had its rewards.

"SOR JUANA! Sor Juana! Have you heard?" Sor Josepha raced toward the fountain where Juana spent many afternoons.

"Heard what?"

Sor Josepha, a vivacious nun with a wagging tongue, could hardly contain herself. "Do you remember how you called Madre Superiora a stuffy old woman?"

Juana smiled. "Indeed, I do remember. And she deserved it."

"Well, Madre Superiora was so angry she went to the Archbishop and demanded that he reprimand you for being so disrespectful." Sor Josepha bent over laughing. She simply could not hold the laughter in.

"So, what penance did the Archbishop declare?" asked Juana, a bit skeptical about hearing the rest of the story.

"None! He told Madre Superiora that if she could prove you wrong, he would then reprimand you!"

Juana broke into laughter too. And it was true, the current Madre Superiora was a stuffy old woman. La Vicereine Leonor would have agreed, for she considered many of the nuns too stuffy for their habits.

DAY PASSED into day, a peaceful time. With Archbishop Payo as Viceroy, there were no balls at el Palacio, no soirees, and few elegant dinners, but Juana's life assumed a comfortable step all its own. The arts of Nueva España inspired every moment of life, with dynamic music, plays, poetry, stained glass creations, and statuary of all forms creating a wonderment of joy.

While the good fathers of the Church were busy constructing new schools and hospitals, Juana was busy teaching the girls at San Jerónimo's school. She taught them how to write plays, how to stand straight and declare their lines, how to graciously accept the compliments from the locutory guests who saw their performances – no small skills for the señoritas de la Ciudad de México. She also told them the stories of the Gods and Goddesses in Greek, Roman and Aztec worlds.

Juana helped at the hospital too, as did most of the nuns, bestowing comfort to all who came. She learned a bit of the art of medicine, she let her heart wrap the poor and the sick in an aura of a Pacific breeze. More than once she helped someone ill step over the threshold to the other world, comforting those left behind.

ONE AFTERNOON her melancholy took her to a corner of the locutory, a small area with a charming fountain of the Christ Child playing with a lizard, a magical creature in Aztec myth. She called this lizard "Tepin" too, in honor of the small creature she called a friend when she lived at Panoayan.

She thought she heard the call of the blue heron, but when she turned the corner, she saw her friend, Sor Sophia, now stepping graciously into the role of an elder nun, playing a small flute, her tiny fingers flying over the piece of bamboo. Here was a nun whose wrinkles only made her more beautiful, her ageless eyes seeing only the good. Each set of notes that she played called to a special bird, and sometimes the birds even replied. The two women had been friends since Sor Sophia had first greeted her at the gate of San Jerónimo's on Juana's first visit.

"Sophia, you play so charmingly."

"Thank you, Juana, but I do not play charmingly at all. It is the birds themselves who toss such enchantment into the air. I only mimic their sounds."

"Please, Sophia, do mimic them some more." They sat together that afternoon, the elder nun and the younger one, sharing the beauty of nature's songs.

"Sophia, so many times I have heard the melody of birds in this patio. Was that you?"

"Perhaps. But more often I walked to the meadows on the outskirts de la Ciudad de México and sang with the birds there. Now my legs are becoming weaker, so I come here for companionship."

"I have heard those bird songs since childhood," said Juana.

"As have I."

A few days later Juana found a small flute on her doorstep. She tried playing it a few times, eking out only a few feeble notes on the first attempt, but soon sending sweet melodies to the birds on her window sill. Whenever Juana felt need of a quiet conversation, she stole into the hidden courtyard where she and Sophia whispered conversations to the birds, and to each other. Their flutes sang of love, of joy, of the wonderment of the world, while birds of blue feathers and gold told them of tales from far away.

JUANA HONED her skills as a writer, studying the works of contemporary poets and playwrights, learning the complexities of Spanish poetic forms from Lope de Vega, Quevedo and St. John of the Cross.

As her locutory became well known, guests brought gifts of books, inventions, arts, and curiosities that prodded her imagination every minute of her day. Her bookshelves overflowed with music boxes, magnets, Aztec artifacts, magnifying glasses of all sizes, helioscopes and mirrors, each piece finding its proper spot among the hundreds of books.

"You work too hard." Sara, Juana's devoted slave, cared for all Juana's daily needs, her meals, her cleaning, her cooking, and she watched over her mistress like the Greek Goddess Amphitrite watches over the dolphins in the sea. "You were up very late last night, Señora. I saw your light when the whole world was quiet."

"I was up late, Sara. I must finish this play that is being presented at the Fiesta next week. And it is not work. Every time I write a hymn, or a poem celebrating the birth of a child, I feel content."

It was true. While the commissions were all very nice, her joy came in the creation, in knowing she was celebrating the faith that spilled from inside her.

This play was centered around the tale of Hathor, the Egyptian Goddess of sky and sun, of music and dance. Egyptian mythology was very much alive in Nueva España. The silversmith guild of La Ciudad de México had commissioned her to write this play, so the wagon would be overflowing with silver decoration. The leaves of the forest trees were silver, the costumes of the players were decorated in silver, the platform itself was trimmed in silver relief work.

Not only that, but Doña Caterina Rosa, still the most popular actress throughout Nueva España, was playing the lead in this play. Of all the actresses throughout the country, Doña Caterina Rosa still flaunted more jewelry of more colors from curly coif to wiggly toe, and flirted outrageously with more rich patrons than any other actress in the whole city. Men adored her; women envied her.

Juana stopped by the preparation area the day before the Fiesta as Diego, the stage manager, helped the players learn their roles.

"Sor Juana! You beautiful woman! You should be up here on the stage presenting this play!" Caterina rushed over and threw her arms around Juana, spinning her around joyously. Juana treasured this unlikely friendship. Caterina Rosa did not like many women, but she did like Sor Juana's gutsy approach to life. "Just wait until you see the gown that I have designed for the fiesta." Caterina raised her eyebrows. "It is the color of rubies, and comes down to here." She held her hand level with her nipples.

"I know it will be beautiful," said Juana, laughing, "and you will be beautiful. You are always beautiful!"

"Sor Juana, I hear that you are friends with this new Viceroy, this Fray Payo. True?" asked Doña Caterina Rosa.

"Very true. We have been friends for years."

"But to be the Viceroy and the Archbishop – so much power in one man." Caterina Rosa wrinkled her brow.

"He wears that power well. You and I can both be grateful that he is there, in power."

It was true. Archbishop/Viceroy Payo ruled with fiscal responsibility and a generous spirit. Public projects sponsored by the government meshed with the good works of the Church, creating a vibrant city that cared for all its citizens. Nueva España indeed entered a period of intense peace and prosperity. The arts flourished in this inviting environment, launching Juana on a life of public writings as she began rising to the upper echelon of all writers of Nueva España. Her sassy wit flourished; she flew through la Ciudad de México with an independence she had only dreamed of, her locutory gatherings, and her plays, becoming legendary.

"If he is your friend, he is my friend." Doña Caterina Rosa smiled broadly as she threw her arms around Sor Juana again.

"Sor Juana," called out Diego, the stage manager. "I need Caterina for one last run through before we finish for today."

"Don't worry, little Sister," called out Caterina Rosa as she returned to rehearsal. "I won't forget my lines!" Juana smiled, remembering the time that Caterina Rosa totally forgot her lines during a play at el Palacio de Virrey. Juana did not worry about it any longer, for if Caterina forgot a line, she improvised, something that Juana would do herself.

The ruby red gown did come down to there, with garlands of rubies and emeralds and diamonds and pearls sprinkled over Caterina Rosa's breasts, around her wrists, and crowning her hair. She was spectacular, garnering more attention than any other player at the fiesta. The silversmith guild was more than pleased, doling out bonuses to everyone. La Vicereine Leonor would have enjoyed the spectacle dearly. The Hieronymite nuns of San Jerónimo's, and the Jesuits too, deeply appreciated the generous donation that Juana presented to them.

JUANA RACED across the broad campus of San Jerónimo, stopping only as she reached the hospital doors. Sor Sophia was desperately ill and had called for her. They had become special friends since sharing the songs of the birds, as Juana sought out Sophia's gentle notes amongst the locutory maze, letting her spirit soar to the open fields of Panoayan. She felt like she had known Sophia forever.

She was no stranger to the hospital. Hardly two years after taking her vows, she became so grievously ill with typhoid fever that she wrote a poem to Archbishop Payo, gently begging for absolution. Even on the edge of death, Juana could think only in poetic terms. Now it was Sophia who was grievously ill.

Sophia looked peaceful against the white sheets, only her brow showing signs of distress. She took Sophia's hand in hers, softly kissing her fingertips.

"I knew you would come," said Sophia softly, the wrinkles in her brow fading away.

Juana sat beside this dear nun way into the night, sending word that she could not attend the locutory gathering. Around midnight Juana turned aside to get a cup of coffee, and when she turned back, Sophia had crossed her arms over her chest and was moving her lips as if calling to the angels of the world, smiling gently. Only a few hours later Juana heard the whisper of Sophia's soul as crystalline doves came to claim it.

She sat there all night, pondering life … and death. When nuns came to wrap the body in a white linen shroud, she returned to her cell, feeling something so deep, so unexpected, that even as she sat at her desk ready to write a poem in memory of Sophia, she could not. She could not put these feelings into words. Finally, she picked up a piece of exquisite parchment and wrote carefully.

> *Dear beloved Virgen de Guadalupe, my soul and my salvation, the benefactor of so many millions of blessings, I know you understand. I know you will wrap your loving arms around our beloved Sor Sophia forever. Please fill this parchment with the words that I cannot find. Thank you.*

She took the parchment to la Capilla de la Virgen de Guadalupe, blessing each blade of grass as she walked along the way. She set the parchment in a silver bowl in front of the tilma showing the image of la Virgen de Guadalupe, and burned it as a small offering.

She began to stand, but felt la Virgen de Guadalupe gently tugging, softly urging her to stay a bit longer.

> *"Why didn't you ask her?"* la Virgen de Guadalupe whispered.

> *"What could I ask? What could she say? That she once had a child? That she did not know if it was a boy or a girl? And when she asked when I was born, what could I tell her?"*

Juana was certain that she would never really know who her parents were. *"May I pretend, may I believe, that she was indeed my madre?"*

> *"Yes, Juana, dream a dream that is right for you, and keep it close to your heart, always."*

Brujeria (Witchery)

WORD HAD ERUPTED. Sor Juana Inés de la Cruz had been selected as the creator of the Triumphal Arch to be placed at the Catedral for the new Viceroy, which came as no surprise to the Bishop of Puebla, nor to Juana herself, for she knew she had earned this honor. And, while she was busy before, now she was inundated with requests.

"I beg of you, Sor Juana, my wife will give birth to our first child in about a month, and I know a poem from your blessed hand would soothe her delivery immeasurably." The man on bended knee, a regular at Sor Juana's locutory gatherings, pled as enticingly as he knew how, and she knew he would reward her generously.

"My heart bleeds to say that I would treasure the opportunity to write such a poem for your wife, but alas! My desk overflows with requests right now. Perhaps we can plan on celebrating the first-year anniversary of this blessed child."

The literati and elite of La Ciudad de México stuffed her locutory gatherings and ached for new commissions for poems and songs, some for a special lady, some for cathedrals, some to bless a newborn, and some just wanted to claim that Sor Juana Inés de la Cruz had created a piece just for them. The aristocracy and bishops of Nueva España called upon her day by day for new plays, new poems, new hymns, and chorales. Juana welcomed these commissions like wild flowers welcome spring rain. The more she concentrated on writing, the less time she had to think about the kindness of la Vicereine Leonor, and the loneliness she sometimes felt now, yet still in the quiet of night or in the crack of a thunderbolt, Leonor was there, her sure steady gaze reaching deep into places Juana did not let herself ponder. She felt so blessed that it was la Vicereine Leonor who had been at el Palacio; no one else could have been so kind.

One brilliant night the stars themselves took the shape of la Vicereine Leonor and whispered, *You see, Juana, I told you that you could do so much more.*

She remembered that conversation well. She had recited one of her witty poems that she wrote at the evening ball. Leonor had smiled, and simply said, "Juana, you can do so much more."

That simple statement had prompted her to reach so much further. She had become lazy at el Palacio, being more witty than wise. Now she drew upon the mysteries of the ancient tales of Gods and Goddesses, finding truths and merriment where she never saw them before. With this encouragement, she had even written "The Trials of a Nobel House," her first play, the one presented at el Palacio.

It was at St Jerónimo's that her full talents burst open. The locutory guests brought books, curiosities, and inventions to thank her for her hospitality, with her shelves now boasting rare copies of Erasmus, St. Thomas Aquinas, and Euripides, as well as exotic new inventions like kaleidoscopes and sea-faring compasses. La Vicereine Leonor had given her many treasured gifts – a painting made from hummingbird feathers, a gold plate embossed with the image of the Virgin, an Aztec mask rescued from the ruins of their city. Nothing was too unusual or too complex for Juana; it all captured her imagination. In fact, the more complex an invention seemed, the more she enjoyed it.

The hundreds of gifts that she received burst the walls of her cell, imploring her to purchase the empty cell adjacent to her own, and converting it to a private library and museum. Her desk and her cherished statue of la Virgen de Guadalupe were there too, creating a comfortable and private place for her to work.

SEVERAL MONTHS earlier she and her dear friend, the Bishop of Puebla, had visited Archbishop/Viceroy Payo and learned of his resignations, both from his duties as Archbishop and from his duties as Viceroy.

"He looked weary, didn't he?" Juana asked, almost to herself that September morn. Archbishop Payo had served thirteen years as the Archbishop of Nueva España and seven years as its Viceroy. He was exhausted. The dual yoke of responsibility had finally worn him down and he would be retiring soon to a small parish in the south of España near his home town.

"You know, my friend, he does want you to become the next Archbishop of Nueva España," she said to the Bishop of Puebla.

"Stop, Juana!" said the Bishop. "Do not say that. Do not even think it." The Bishop was adamant, but she heard a hint of desire in his voice. She had known him too long to not know the dreams of his heart. The Bishop was a good man, and would be a great Archbishop, following in the footsteps of Archbishop Payo.

"Juana, you know well that we accept the challenges, and gifts, that God gives us, no matter what they are."

She knew. She also knew that Archbishop Payo had provided the Bishop of Puebla with every opportunity to demonstrate his superior administrative abilities and his deep faith. The Bishop of Puebla had built several cathedrals and churches, tended to the plight of solitary women with new convents, developed properties for Aztec natives and orphans, all with sharp financial skills and the innate magic that opened the pocketbooks of the wealthy. Rarely did the Bishop of Puebla have fewer than five or six major projects in process at any given time. He walked with respect and honor throughout Nueva España. Archbishop Payo made certain that the Spanish Crown, King Carlos II, knew of the Bishop's accomplishments, for it was King Carlos who appointed both viceroys and archbishops in Nueva España.

"The decision rests with the Crown," the Bishop reminded Juana. "But you, Juana, with the Archbishop recommending you as the creator of the Triumphal Arch for the new Viceroy, your star will soar like a glorious shooting comet!"

"Not so quick, my friend. It has not happened yet."

"But it will, Juana. If I were you, I would start work on it immediately. Tell me, what theme will you use?" He smiled as he asked, and she took the challenge.

"I would create a majestic Triumphal Arch of Gods and Goddesses and saints from ancient Greek, Egyptian and Aztec traditions, as well as from Christian." Her eyes sparkled as ideas flashed into her head.

"And you will start this afternoon?" The Bishop of Puebla winked.

"Yes, my incorrigibly optimistic Padre, I will start this afternoon."

THE BISHOP of Puebla was right, as he was about most things. She was indeed awarded the commission from the Church to create a Triumphal Arch for the new Viceroy. She was to design the Arch itself, identify the artists who would do the actual work, as well as create a book of poetry and songs about the images and writings on the Arch. She was also to create a new play to be presented to the Viceroy after he arrived. It was a huge commission.

Since it required nearly three months for Archbishop Payo's resignation to reach España as it traveled across the Atlantic Ocean, and several months more for the new Viceroy to be named, plus a few more months for the new Viceroy to arrange to bring his household to Nueva España, it was nearly a year before the new Viceroy, Don Tomas de la Cerda, Count of Parades, Marquis de la Laguna, arrived in La Ciudad de México.

A strapping forty-one-year-old aristocrat, the new Viceroy had already served as the Captain General of the Andalusian Coast and as Counselor of the Indies. What he lacked in administrative ability – and he lacked a great deal – he atoned for through his personal heritage, for he was of the House of the Dukes of Alcala, one of the richest families in España, and a heritage that he shared with Archbishop Payo. His wealth and familiar connections made him the perfect choice to be the new Viceroy. He invested 50,000 ducats to acquire this position, but with its annual salary of 20,000 ducats, and the treasury of Nueva España at his disposal, he would recapture that investment in but a year or two.

Also, the royal matchmakers had woven a good cloth. What the Count of Parades lacked in political influence, his wife's family provided. The new Vicereine, Maria Luisa Manrique de Lara y Gonzaga, Countess of Parades de Nava, was reputed to be one of the most beautiful, and most powerful, women in the world, and justifiably so. On her paternal heritage, Maria Luisa was a princess of the House of Mantua. Her father was the Viceroy of Valencia, so she had been trained well in the interminable dinners and receptions and courtly duties of a vicereine. She inherited the title "Countess of Parades" from her madre, an honored distinction that her husband assumed as well. Maria Luisa and the Count had married five years earlier in the royal Palacio in Madrid.

On its ritual journey to La Ciudad de México, the regal entourage celebrated Sunday mass at la Catedral de la Puebla where Juana's friend, the Bishop of Puebla, arranged for one of Juana's brilliant *villancicos* to be presented, the one that presented la Virgen Maria as the Master Tatterer of the entire universe, weaving wonders in all lives. This vision of la Virgen spoke Truth to the new Vicereine Maria Luisa as la Virgen Maria wove robes of amber, emerald, ruby and pearls, wrapping them on souls everywhere, even on the shoulders of Aztecs. The Bishop had decked la Catedral in garlands of plumeria and wild roses, with candlelight accenting each work of art.

Maria Luisa thanked the Bishop for arranging the performance. "Never have I so enjoyed such a magnificently beautiful and inspirational service," she said quite honestly. "Tell me who created this masterpiece?" She suspected that it might have been composed by one Sor Juana Inés de la Cruz, a poet whose reputation was already leaping over oceans, and she was right. She knew that this poetic nun would be as beautiful as her poetry.

"Is she here?" she asked.

The Bishop smiled. "She is waiting for you in la Ciudad de México, Excelencia."

The crowd parted as la Vicereine Maria Luisa left la Catedral, for she commanded the corridors of power and society with the grace and intelligence that was gifted her by birth. The ferocity of her beauty and her power became abundantly clear to Juana on their first meeting.

THE COMMISSION for the Triumphal Arch was incredibly important for Juana, for it would confirm her status in the political and artistic society of Nueva España for years to come. While she could write all that she wished, her works would not be presented, nor be published, nor even commissioned, without official patronage.

She had previously relied on the protection of the former Viceroy Mancera and la Vicereine Leonor, then for many years on the approval of Archbishop Payo. Her dear Vicereine Leonor had passed away. Her guardian Archbishop Payo would soon be leaving for España, stepping aside from political concerns. The former Viceroy Mancera still marched with considerable political power in Madrid, but those who most fervently held her prestige high were gone.

Juana's political and social support in Nueva España was crumbling. She needed to re-establish a strong connection with the powerful new Viceroy and Vicereine if she had any hope of retaining her exalted position in la Ciudad de México. This Triumphal Arch had to make a tremendous impression; it had to open doors. She was more than adept at cultivating political alliances, and knew she could do it again.

"LOOK! THEY are coming!"

"Such beauty!"

"Such majesty!"

The thousands of people jammed into the Plaza Mayor roared with approval. In a city that relished every moment of festivity, this was a grand day as the royal entourage came into view, high stepping black stallions leading the Viceroy's own steed, la Vicereine Maria Luisa's glistening white coach just behind. The new Viceroy and Vicereine sat calmly, each protected from the midday sun by gold fringed canopies held high by soldiers on white stallions, he in a resplendent gold uniform, she in a gown of deep purple, reflecting the deep violet of her eyes, and together presenting the colors of Nueva España's flag.

The custom of creating a Triumphal Arch in honor of a new Viceroy reached back over a hundred years. These arches were always created by the most outstanding poets and artists of Nueva España, with titles like "Mythological-Political Star," "Catholic Mars," and "The True Ulysses." Custom now dictated two such Arches, one at the Plaza Mayor, and one at the portico to la Gran Catedral de la Ciudad de México.

On that Saturday morning, November 30, 1680, the entourage had already passed through the Arch created by Don Carlos de

Siguenza y Gongora, a popular poet in La Ciudad de México. Siguenza y Gongora was an odd choice to create this arch, for although he was a rising star in the literary circles of Nueva España, he had been banished from the monastery for his inappropriate behavior, and was twice denied re-entrance. He was, however, a pious man who objected to creating a "Triumphal" Arch since that implied a military conquest, so his was simply an "Arch."

Siguenza y Gongora titled his Arch "Theater of Political Virtues That Constitute a Ruler, Observed in the Ancient Monarchs of the Mexican Empire, Whose Effigies Adorn the Arch Erected by the Very Noble Imperial City of México." It overflowed with praise for Nueva España, even as being superior to España itself, calling the Arch a monument to truth and the art of governing, using native Mexican rulers as his prime examples. He featured Irtzcoatl, Tizoc, Montezuma and Ilhuicama among the sovereigns depicted in his arch.

Juana's Triumphal Arch sat at the west door of the nearly completed Catedral de la Ciudad de México, reaching thirty feet high, creating a dramatic frame for the view of la Catedral.

The Arch created by Juana was no less ambitious. It was titled "Allegorical Neptune, Ocean of Colors, Political Simulacrum, Erected by the Noble, Holy and August Metropolitan Church de la Ciudad de México, in the Magnificent Allegorical Concepts of a Triumphal Arch Solicitously Consecrated and Lovingly Dedicated to the Joyful Entrance of the Most Excellent Don Tomas Antonio de la Cerda, Count de Parades, Marquis de la Laguna, Viceroy, Governor, and Captain General of Our Nueva España." Choosing the "Neptune" theme tied together the new Viceroy's title of "Marquis de la Laguna" ("Marquis of the Lake") with the historical fact that la Ciudad de México was constructed on a lake, a construct that now needed serious attention.

If there was any competition or jealousy between Siguenza y Gongora and Juana, they hid it very well. In fact, they considered themselves colleagues. As far as the new Viceroy was concerned, he was being doubly honored, as he was.

As the Viceroy's entourage slipped through the crowd on the Plaza Mayor, he and la Vicereine Maria Luisa were presented with the view of the stunning design of Juana's Triumphal Arch. She had worked with set designers and painters for her plays, so she knew just which ones to call upon to create this celebratory seven panel arch. The panels of her Arch represented various stories of Neptune, cleverly alluding to the need to finish construction of the la Catedral de la Ciudad de México, and the need to drain the ocean waters out of la Ciudad de México.

The center panel of the Arch featured images of Neptune and his wife Amphitrite entering their realm, riding on a sea shell, naked. The accompanying book explained that these images were intended as representations of the Viceroy and Vicereine, but once Juana glimpsed la Vicereine Maria Luisa, she was acutely aware of how even the most respected artist of La Ciudad de México could not anticipate la Vicereine's hypnotic beauty. This was a beauty whose waving fingers halted a regiment, whose raised eyebrow brought crowds to silence, whose deep violet eyes calmed the wildest ocean.

As the regal carriage approached, Juana stood in the first row of dignitaries, beside the Bishop of Puebla, clutching a copy of the book that she created, the one with loas and lyrics inspired by all the great Gods and Goddesses in the Triumphal Arch, with stories about how these idols personified the Viceroy and la Vicereine.

She could not take her eyes off the spectacle, but she was not looking for the Viceroy. She was looking at la Vicereine Maria Luisa. She believed that she had found the greatest artist in La Ciudad de México to paint the glorious image of Amphitrite in this Triumphal Arch, but it was not glorious enough. Maria Luisa's ebony coif cascaded over shoulders the color of sun-kissed sand. A square chin framed the face of an Italian beauty, her arms slim and graceful, her fingers artistically slender, her smile regally accepting the accolades of the crowd.

La Vicereine Maria Luisa scanned the crowd, not certain what she was looking for. Then her deep violet eyes stopped, looking at a solitary nun, a nun with the presence of knowing exactly who she was, and being proud of it.

With but a nod to the footman, Maria Luisa signaled for the carriage to stop. She glided down and walked toward Sor Juana, the crowd parting to let her pass. Maria Luisa and Sor Juana stood but a few feet apart, speaking softly, a crystalline aura encapsulating them.

"You are Sor Juana Inés de la Cruz." *You are the one I am looking for.*

"Yes, Excelencia." Yes, Maria Luisa. *I have looked long for you as well.*

"Archbishop Payo spoke about you, and told me I must make your acquaintance at the first opportunity." *But he did not tell me how beautiful you are.*

"The Archbishop is a kind and generous person." *How did he know that I was destined to meet you?*

"You designed this magnificent Triumphal Arch." The Lady smiled wryly, glancing at the naked Amphitrite. *Is that truly how you imagine me?*

"I designed it, Excelencia." *But I had no notion that you were so much more stunning than anything I could dream.*

"Will you come to el Palacio and tell me about all these images?" *Soon. Come.*

"Of course, Excelencia." *Dear Maria Luisa, I would follow you to the furthermost star, if you but asked.*

"Sor Juana, perhaps Su Excelencia would like the book of poetry that you have created for this occasion. The one you have in your hand." The voice of the Bishop of Puebla tossed a smoke screen in their revelry.

"Reverencia, it is good to see you again." La Vicereine forced herself to turn and nodded at the Bishop. Her gaze returned immediately to Sor Juana.

"Yes, Excelencia," said Juana. "I totally forgot about the book. Here is where you will find descriptions of the images in the Triumphal Arch. But this scribbling does not do you justice. It is the work of a school girl." *I have met you, and now I am someone new.*

Juana held out the book for la Vicereine.

"Then don't give it to me now, Sor Juana," said Maria Luisa. "Bring it with you when you come to visit." *And do come soon. Soon.*

Juana dropped to a full curtsy, her eyes awash in in a lavender aura. La Vicereine reached down to cradle Sor Juana's hand in hers, as Juana felt the breeze of a down feather caress her fingertips. Juana stood and watched la Vicereine take her place in the royal carriage. La Vicereine Maria Luisa willed herself to not look back, to not rush back to the slender form draped in white. Juana did not know if five seconds had passed, or five years. Time was suspended. Thought was suspended. The lightness in her head did not match the iron in her shoes that kept her riveted to that spot. The Bishop of Puebla grabbed her elbow.

"Juana, are you alright?" the Bishop asked.

This must be what a river feels, rushing to a precipice, terrified, yet anxious to crash over the edge as the resounding waterfall, to rush to its destiny in the swirling pond below.

"Yes, my friend," she replied. "I am fine."

THEN A WEEK passed. Two weeks. Three.

Juana had not yet ventured to el Palacio. She tried to re-write the verses in the book about the Triumphal Arch, but every time she picked up her quill, her hand quivered so severely that all she could do was drip ink on the parchment. Even her commissions languished, blank pages begging for a sonnet or a loa.

"Sor Juana! Sor Juana! Have you heard?" Juana's slave Sara rushed into the cell, carrying fresh produce from the market. Sara worked morn to night with never a complaint, and Juana had come to rely on her ingenuity in the kitchen, and her discretion in her speech. Sara was also the one who kept her in touch with the gossip in San Jerónimo's, bits of which she was glad to share with her mistress.

"Heard what?"

Sara set her basket down, then leaned in, speaking in a hushed whisper. "She's a witch!" Sara immediately threw salt over her left shoulder to ward off any lingering spirits and, just to be certain, she also crossed herself.

"A witch? Who?" demanded Juana. This was a serious charge, one that the Inquisition would investigate.

Blessedly, witch tortures had not reached the shores of Nueva España, for Aztecs, with all their faults, had no concept comparable to witches. Juana had heard of the excruciation of witches in Germany but these torments did not emanate from the Inquisition of Nueva

España. In fact, the Inquisition in Nueva España had been relatively quiet for decades. Yet, women lived with the knowledge that such a panic could erupt at any moment.

"Who?" repeated Juana. "Who is a witch?"

"Oh, Señora, do not say that word so loudly. You might call the evil spirits to this house."

"But who is it?" she demanded again.

"La Vicereine," whispered Sara, as if to say it softly would make it less real. "The new Vicereine, Maria Luisa. They say she can look into someone's soul and toss them into purgatory."

Juana shot to attention. "Stop that, Sara! Never, never say anything like that again. Ever. EVER. Do you understand, Sara?" She raised her hand as if to strike Sara.

Sara backed up against the cupboard. She had certainly seen Juana angry, but not like this, not directed at her personally, not with the intensity of hot coals in the fire.

"Do you understand, Sara?" she repeated.

"Yes," whispered Sara, "I understand."

She took a moment to compose herself, then stated a bit more calmly, "I have met la Vicereine Maria Luisa, and I can assure you that she is no such thing."

"But her eyes ..." protested Sara.

"Her eyes are the color of the passion flowers that we place on the altar to celebrate Christ. There is nothing evil in her eyes. La Vicereine brings only kindness and beauty into this world." She was not sure this was true, but la Vicereine needed a defender just then.

An insistent knock on the door interrupted the conversation. Sor Gabriela, currently the Treasurer at San Jerónimo's stood there, looking stern.

"I must speak with you, Juana. Now. Privately." She tossed but a glance at Sara, and Sara disappeared out the door and down the hallway. Sor Gabriela closed the door behind her, and just stood there a moment.

"May I get you some tea, or coffee perhaps?" Juana had stood her ground with several Madre Superioras since joining San Jerónimo's, but at that moment she felt her ground was shaky.

"No," said Gabriela "No tea. No coffee. Just some answers."

"Of course. What questions do you have?"

"First, why haven't you called on la Vicereine Maria Luisa at el Palacio? I understand that she invited you on the day she arrived in la Ciudad de México, most insistently I understand."

"Yes, Gabriela, she did invite me to call on her, but it was, I believe, just a bit of polite conversation, not a true invitation." She knew it was a lie, and so did Gabriela.

"Oh? Then why has she called on Archbishop Payo, specifically requesting that you call on her?"

"I didn't know she had done so." Juana looked away, confused.

"She met with him this morning, just before I saw him. The Archbishop was angry, saying that you are plotting to make la Vicereine feel unwelcome. The Archbishop knows your little schemes well, Juana, and he is not going to stand for your self-serving temperament on this issue. It doesn't matter if you personally like her or not. Good, bad, indifferent, we welcome all viceroys and vicereines to La Ciudad de México. ALL of them."

'I'm … I am so sorry. Truly I meant no disrespect." Sor Juana – this nun so completely in control -- was close to tears, for she indeed did not intend to insult la Vicereine. In truth, she did not even know why she had not called on la Vicereine Maria Luisa. Every time she took a step in that direction, her stomach tightened up, like she was getting ill.

"Good. The Archbishop told her that you will be there at four o'clock this afternoon."

Juana's mouth opened, but no objection was said. It did not matter that her stomach was in knots again. She had to go; it was commanded by Archbishop Payo.

As Gabriela turned to leave, she paused for one more question. "You do know astronomy, among your other skills, don't you?"

"Yes, I do. I have been intrigued by the skies since childhood."

"Good. La Vicereine has been frightened by the comet passing overhead. Perhaps you can persuade her that la Ciudad de México has not been cursed."

SOR JUANA HAD faced down Madre Superiora at the Carmelite convent; she had met the challenges of Fray Miranda, one of the most powerful men in Nueva España; she had even been assaulted, and emerged triumphant. But as she stood on the threshold of el Palacio de Virrey, she had to wipe her sweaty hands on her crisp white linen ceremonial habit. Her mouth was dry, and she had no ready repartee for the new Vicereine. She had a small gift in her pocket, a miniature image of la Virgen de Guadalupe created from hummingbird feathers, with traces of gold dust. She thought that this gift, created by one of la Ciudad de México's most celebrated artists, and a gift she had treasured herself, would convey her overflowing thoughts, but even this gift now felt like a cheap ceramic.

The door opened before Juana realized she had knocked. As she followed the servant through the Grand Gallery, a spot she had passed hundreds of times, she hardly recognized it. The once gaudy hall was now clothed in deep blue, the portraits of all the Viceroys of Nueva España arranged chronologically around the room, while elegant terra cotta, copper and silver vases held bouquets of plumeria, orchids and ferns. The opulence of la Vicereine Leonor was set aside for the elegance of a Vicereine who cherished every piece of art.

The servant escorted Juana to the second floor, then along the long hallway decorated with contemporary Aztec and Mexican art, past the rooms that the former Vicereine had called her own. They turned down a nearly hidden hallway to a large door opening onto a suite of rooms that Juana had never seen before.

Juana's crinkled brow softened. This was a room of light, a room of discovery with shelves of books and treasures and artifacts, not unlike her own biblioteca. This was a room exploding with love for beautiful things, blessed by one whose curiosity slipped easily from Egyptian art to Aztec wonders, a room exploding with honor for the natural world of mystical stones, and a tapestry with riotous bougainvillea. One whole wall held bookcases, floor to ceiling, filled with all manner of leather-bound books and artifacts and statuary. The opposite wall had a large fireplace bounded by marble statues of Egyptian deities, and an arch that opened into another room, a bedroom perhaps. Near the fireplace sat an intricately carved cherry wood desk, with pens and parchment on it. Here was a room where she could feel at home.

The far wall held a glorious glass door with blue and green panes, and some panes painted with images of peacocks, hummingbirds and plumeria. La Vicereine stood by that door, looking out over La Ciudad de México. She turned.

"Welcome to el Palacio, Juana. Come in, please." She noticed Juana looking around. "This is my garden room, my writing room, my personal retreat from Palacio society. You once lived in this Palacio, didn't you?"

"Yes, Excelencia. I served as a lady-in-waiting to la Vicereine Leonor. But I do not recall this room at all."

"Please, Juana, call me Maria Luisa. Everyone else can address me as 'Excelencia,' but I would like you to call me by my Christian name, and I would like to call you by yours." Maria Luisa welcomed this brilliant woman, this woman who was more than her equal. All the others – the wealthy landowners, the politicians, the businessmen – they were all her subordinates. This poet, this philosopher, this proud nun, this was no subordinate. Juana was in all respects her equal and, she hoped, a great deal more.

Juana smiled. "Yes, Maria Luisa, I am pleased to address you as such. That is such a lyrical name, like it was caught on a butterfly wing and carried away."

"Thank you, Juana. I have always blessed my madre for gifting me with such a name." Had Juana seen Maria Luisa's face at that moment, she would have seen her blush. But Juana was captivated by the multi-colored leather-bound books on the shelves. Maria Luisa continued. "This room was part of some kind of storage area, but I love the breeze that drifts in here, and the huge fireplace. The view stretches off to the east, toward España, and I can linger over coffee in the morning with the sun rising toward my homeland."

"Yes, I understand," said Juana. "My cell faces south, toward Panoayan, my home. Sometimes I feel like I can hear the rumble of Popocatepetl, the volcano near my home." There were a million things that Juana wanted to say to Maria Luisa, but she could not think of even one thing to say. She could not even look at her, for the lady's eyes were far too deep to be real. Then Juana felt something in her pocket.

"Oh, I almost forgot," she said, holding out the small gift wrapped in lavender lace.

Maria Luisa smiled in anticipation, opening the gift with immense expectation and care. "Oh, She is so beautiful! So delicate." She held the gift to her breast, then placed it ceremoniously on her desk, next to another miniature, a painting of the Goddess Diana. "I am not sure I believed the story of la Virgen de Guadalupe until we paused there on our way to la Ciudad de México. It was there, in Her Capilla, that I truly felt Her presence, Her miracles. Do you go there often, Juana?"

"As often as I am able." Juana was still looking at Maria Luisa's desk. "The other miniature, the exquisite Goddess Diana. Who painted that?"

"That is one of my modest creations."

"You painted this? She is so strong, so stunning. Would you teach me how to paint?" She blurted out the question without stopping to think, for she had no right to ask such time and attention from la Vicereine.

"I would be honored to do so," she replied. "I wish I could ask you to teach me how to write poetry, but I fear that such gifts are bestowed upon one, not learned. Archbishop Payo gifted me a selection of your poems, and I knew instantly that you indeed have a special talent. But come, Juana, look over here." Maria Luisa spoke as she stepped back to the large glass door. "Look up there. Archbishop Payo also told me that you have studied the stars." The two women stood, their shoulders lightly touching.

"Yes, since childhood when my Abuelo showed me how to read the stories in the night sky, but I still don't know as much as I would like to know."

"There," said Maria Luisa. "That star, the one with the long tail. What can you tell me of it? I have heard from some scholars that its presence is a harbinger of misfortune on the world. Since it followed us over the Atlantic Ocean to la Ciudad de México itself, I fear it foretells a time of great misery for Nueva España."

"I am certain your scholars have good reason to speak as they do, but perhaps the stars of Nueva España differ from the stars of España."

"As we were preparing to leave España, we spoke with Fray Kino, the Jesuit priest who is charting the course of that star."

"Did he come with you?" asked Juana. "I would love to meet him."

"No. He stayed behind to take more measurements of this phenomenon. He expects to arrive next year, and promises to provide more definitive information then. But since the star followed us, seemingly as a harbinger of great evil, I went to see Archbishop Payo. He told me that you are the true expert in matters of the stars."

'I am indeed flattered that Archbishop Payo considers me such. I am but a fascinated student. I am sure Fray Kino can tell us a great deal when he arrives, but I can tell you this now. That star with a long tail is called a comet, and it is not to be feared. Comets come to our skies from time to time, often as a messenger of good will, not evil."

Maria Luisa looked skeptical, so Juana continued. "Do you recall the story of the star that stood over the manger in Bethlehem? That was likely a comet with a long tail, much like this one, pointing the Magi to the spot where they would find the Christ Child. There was no evil in that comet, only great goodness. I do not know why this comet has come to our world just now, but I do not feel evil. I only feel joy and happiness. Were Archbishop Payo here, I believe he would agree."

Maria Luisa visibly relaxed. "Do you believe our fate is written in the stars?" she asked.

Juana replied honestly. "I believe there are millions of mysteries in the stars, many of which we may never be able to decipher. It is very possible that our fate is written there, but I know of no one who can read it. Not yet."

When Maria Luisa smiled, she continued. "There is a wonderful book that my Abuelo gave me called 'The Theater of the Pagan Gods.' It tells us of the origin of the Milky Way.

"It happened that Jupiter and Alcmeme, a married woman, had an illegitimate son, Hercules. Jupiter desperately wanted Hercules to be wholly a deity, to sit among the Gods. One day when the wife of

Jupiter, Juno, was sleeping, Jupiter had the babe taken to Juno to be suckled by the Goddess's breast milk, thereby making Hercules more god-like. Hercules was greedy in taking that milk, clawing at Juno's breasts. Juno sprang awake, fiercely angry that her milk was being stolen. She pushed Hercules away, spilling Her milk across the sky, creating the glorious Milky Way.

"Could such a majestic creation of the stars truly have no meaning for mortals?"

The two women shared a smile. "I had forgotten that story," said Maria Luisa. "It is true. There is majesty, and magic, in the skies."

Maria Luisa spoke softly as she took Juana's hand and led her to the sofa. "It feels as though we have met before, Juana. Do you think we have?"

The question seemed natural to Juana, for she felt the same, the same sense of déjà vu, the same comfort of a friend, the same anticipation.

"I should say that No, we have never met before, but I can't say that." She chose her words carefully, for they both felt they knew one another the moment they met. "I do not believe in reincarnation, but I do feel that I know you as I have never known another. I do not know where I saw it, but I do know this room. I do know you."

The two women, both in their early thirties, both immensely powerful in their own realms, both gifted in intellect and talent, stood on the brink of a relationship that neither could have anticipated.

A quick taptaptap on the door and an older Spanish woman in the dark blue skirt and white blouse of a servant peeked her head in. "He is here, Señora."

"Thank you, Consuela. Sor Juana, this is Consuela Lopez, my most trusted servant."

"Sor Juana Inés de la Cruz, if you ever need or want anything, please do not hesitate to ask. It is an honor to serve you." Consuela spoke humbly, sincerely, and stood proudly.

The snappy clapclap on the tile floor was unmistakable; it was the strong walk of a man in charge, his steady gait would stop for no one. Juana recognized him immediately as the new Viceroy, the Count of Parades.

"Buenos días, mi marido. You are home early." Maria Luisa rose to greet him.

"Buenos días, Excelencia," said Juana as she stood and bowed to acknowledge him.

"Husband, may I introduce Sor …" began Maria Luisa.

"Sor Juana Inés de la Cruz, of course!" interrupted the Viceroy. "Everyone praises your poetry, your drama, your brilliance. I am honored that you have come to call, and sorry that I was not here to greet you formally." He struck an elegant bow worthy of the Spanish court. "Since you had not come to call, I thought perhaps that you were displeased with our appointment in Nueva España."

"Oh, on the contrary, Excelencia," said Juana. "Your presence here does us more honor than our poor country deserves."

"I understand that you write poetry and plays, Sor Juana," stated the Viceroy.

"I try, Excelencia."

"Perhaps one day you can share some of your works with us. But not today." The Viceroy spun abruptly to face his wife. "Señora, it is time for us to dress for the Governor's reception. I want the government appointees here to understand that I do not idle. Sor Juana, I regret that I must cut our meeting short today. Perhaps we can talk another day."

"Of course, Excelencia," replied Juana, bowing as he marched out of the room.

Maria Luisa lingered a moment after the Viceroy left. "I am so sorry, Juana. That was simply rude. I think he is jealous because I met you before he had a chance to talk with you." Maria Luisa spoke gently, but there was a strong message beneath her words.

"Do not worry, Maria Luisa. I will make certain that our next meeting meets with his approval." She was already hatching a plan to entice the Viceroy to her side.

OVER THE NEXT few weeks Juana emptied her ink well day and night, tackling one by one the commissions overflowing her desk, and writing too about the most brilliant statesman ever to grace the office of Viceroy of Nueva España, comparing him to all the great Greek and Aztec Gods that ever were. She worked with energy drawn from

Maria Luisa's eyes, from a confidence knowing that they would meet again soon. She made sure that all the proper people saw these poems of the Viceroy. Archbishop Payo smiled wryly when he told Juana about the slender hand-bound volume of her poetry that he had created for the Viceroy, and how pleased the Viceroy was to receive it.

Juana's invitation to the fiesta celebrating la Virgen de Guadalupe arrived but a few days before the day, but it did arrive. Juana's plan had worked its magic; she would be welcomed at el Palacio. Hundreds would see her there, and the new Viceroy would see her as an ally.

SHE CARRIED two parchments to the fiesta at el Palacio, one for the Viceroy, and one for la Vicereine. The Viceroy stood with his beautiful wife on a platform, greeting guests. The crowd made way for Juana as she walked most regally to the couple, then dropped to a low curtsy in front of the dais. The Viceroy bowed to lift her hands and invite her to join them on the platform, which she gracefully did.

She then opened the parchment tied in a gold ribbon, and read a brilliant poem to the whole crowd, a poem extolling the unending virtues of such a Viceroy, and the many blessings his presence brought to Nueva España.

As the crowd joyously gave its approval, Juana handed the parchment to the Viceroy as a gift, and then opened the second parchment, the one tied with a purple ribbon. Juana stood as close to la Vicereine Maria Luisa as she dared, just a foot or two away, and presented a poem filled with beauty and cadence, soft melodies, and reverence.

The crowd fell silent. La Vicereine was in awe. The Viceroy was in awe. As the poem concluded, the crowd stood in total silence for a full eight seconds, then burst into applause.

Juana felt Maria Luisa's kiss on her cheek like a westerly breeze from the sea, a kiss of mystery and promise. Juana handed the parchment to Maria Luisa and with great ceremony she descended the steps and joined the revelers.

The musicians scattered throughout el Palacio courtyards burst with raucous, fierce dancing beats, with some musicians strumming ballads for courtship and conversation. Juana clapped in pure enjoyment while the flying fingers of a guitar player challenged a group of caballeros to jump higher, spin faster, plunge deeper, each caballero flaunting his masculinity. The audience roared its approval as the men finished their last spins. The music then softened a bit, as the men each sought a beautiful señorita as a partner. Skirts swirled, tossing rainbows of colors like dozens of prisms caught in a sunbeam, while silken shoulders teased the caballeros to come just a little closer.

Someone touched Juana's hand. She did not need to look to see who it was. "Come," spoke a whispering voice. "Let's dance."

Juana was a splendid dancer who enjoyed seeking out children on fiesta days. No man would ever dare to ask a nun to dance, certainly not in public. No ordinary woman would ever so dare either. But this was no ordinary woman at her side. And so they commanded the center of the patio. Juana lifted the skirt of her habit high enough so she would not trip on it, high enough so all could appreciate that she was indeed a gifted dancer.

They began side by side, their right shoulders nearly touching. As they circled each other, the crowd fell back, leaving these two alone in the waning sun light, everyone mesmerized by this couple. The measured beats of the guitar began the fandango with a quick paseo.

The women bent their knees slightly, holding their heads tall. Their crackling heels echoed a conversation of their own while the staccato notes of a flute led them into the quick step of the zapateado.

Maria Luisa dipped her shoulders in a seductive twirl; Juana matched her.

Maria Luisa spun, her skirt flying nearly waist high, her petticoats cascading, a field of sizzling wildflowers,

… while Juana matched her turn for turn, her starlight white skirts a counterpoint to Maria Luisa's brilliance.

Juana clicked her heels on the adobe tiles, and with undulating hips circled Maria Luisa;

Maria Luisa returned the favor.

As they spun to a climax in a crescendo of guitar and flute notes, the considerable audience that had gathered to watch them stomped on the floor, begging for more. Here was a Vicereine, and a nun, to reckon with.

As they slipped back into the crowd, Maria Luisa whispered, "My husband is leaving Tuesday morning to visit the western provinces. Will you come to see me Tuesday afternoon?"

"I will."

THE MINUTES FELL into slumber as Juana waited for Tuesday, then stretched to an eternity on Tuesday morning. Then Juana stood looking at Maria Luisa as if transported there by a wizard.

Consuela set the small table with coffee and sweets, then closed the door silently as she left.

"Tell me, Juana, where did you learn to dance with such abandon?"

"At the fiestas at nearby rancheros as I was growing up, and later as a lady-in-waiting here, at el Palacio.'

"You were a lady-in-waiting, but you chose to not wed."

"True. Marriage was not my destiny. My Abuelo taught me to read, taught me to learn everything that I could possibly learn … history, art, philosophy, biology, even astronomy. That was my destiny -- to study, to learn."

"And to write?"

"That came later. It was Archbishop Payo who challenged me to write, years ago when he was the Bishop of Guatemala." Juana told Maria Luisa the tale of how she dressed as a boy so she could visit la Biblioteca de la Universidad, and how the Archbishop had gifted her with parchment and ink. This is a story that she had shared with no one else.

"And, you, Maria Luisa, with the treasures in this room it appears that you also have a desire to learn, and perhaps even a talent for writing."

"Not nearly so much as you, Juana." Maria Luisa spoke of her severe tutor, and how he considered it a waste of his good time to teach a señorita to read, even a regal one. But he was paid well, and so he stayed with the family until she left to be married.

"Why did you marry?" asked Juana.

"Perhaps as with you, it was the best option available to me. I do not possess your gifts of learning and writing, Juana. I do love to learn, and to paint a bit, but my gifts are those of a privileged aristocrat, not those of a blessed nun. I was nearly thirty years old when we married, and truthfully, my options were limited. My parents had been playing a game of chess with my betrothal, and time had run out. When my madre passed, her title of Countess of Parades came to me, and that put me back on the bridal list again. Marriage with an aristocratic man, a wealthy aristocratic man from a highly respected family, was not such a bad option in my case, and my husband was glad to assume the title of 'Count of Parades' in honor of that marriage."

Juana and Maria Luisa stood at the glass doorway, silently watching the clouds slip into night, with an unseasonal rain just beginning. Maria Luisa leaned against the door frame, wrapping her arms around Juana, gently gathering her closer. Huge raindrops splattered in a syncopated chatter on the balcony as Maria Luisa lifted Juana's face, their lips aching to touch. One second? Or more? Their breasts touched with the softness of nightingale feathers. Their lips touched …

… *No… NO!* Magnificent agony rushed through Juana's whole body, igniting every niche so strongly that she feared for her very life, feared that her soul was bursting right there, right in front of her. *It is the Devil's flames! the witch's flames!* Wispy images of umbral banshees flew across the window.

Juana pulled away, afraid to even look at Maria Luisa, covering her face with her arm and rushing out of that room …

out the long long hallway …

down the interminable staircase …

running … running …

Juana did not even know what she was running from, but she could not stop. Flailing arms reached out from the shadows …

Roderigo sneered at her, reaching down from a low hanging branch, howling, *Come, little señorita* …

Sor Beatrix jumped at her as she sped around a corner, sneering …

There were so many ensnaring shadows that she could not distinguish one from another. She ran all the way home, not stopping until she reached the safety of her own cell. She fell, a dripping bundle, in front of la Virgen de Guadalupe.

"Dearest, most blessed of all Virgins," she begged as she had never begged before. "Please, I implore you … tell me … Why am I weeping? Why am I running? Has a witch twisted my heart and cast a spell on my body to make it feel as it has never felt before? Why do I ache? Why … why do I weep?"

She prayed, her head bowed. She prayed for mercy, for understanding, for guidance. But no answers came.

She stood and paced from side to side.

She poured herself a glass of wine, then paced some more.

She reached for one book, then for another, not opening any of them, just setting them back on a shelf.

Once again, she pitifully knelt before la Virgen, deeply praying for guidance. She slowly raised her eyes to behold the eternal face of la Virgen. La Virgen was not scowling, as she feared She would. No, She was smiling, a gentle, compassionate smile. All around, the room had filled with a soft aura, an aura wrapped around her that infused her with a strength and understanding she had never known.

JUANA RETURNED to el Palacio with a soft smile of her own and a lightness to her step that she had not felt in a very long time. Soon she stood, dripping, in Maria Luisa's chamber. Maria Luisa held her close while Consuela readied a warm bath with plumeria blossoms floating on it. She stepped into the whispery bath removing even the undergarment that she always wore, savoring the luxurious sponge that caressed her. Maria Luisa wrapped her in a soft wool dressing gown and they settled on goose down pillows in front of the fire.

"What brought you back, Juana?"

"I spoke with la Virgen de Guadalupe. I asked Her about the tremendous feeling that poured into me."

"What did She tell you?"

"She told me that these were the feelings of an ancient love, a deep love, a love more profound than even the love I felt from my dear Abuelo, the one person in the world who loved me unconditionally."

"Sor Juana, my beloved, we are blessed beyond measure. I know … I know… here are feelings that even I was not prepared for." They held each other's hands and softly, slowly kissed each other's fingertips.

Maria Luisa gently caressed her cheek as Juana turned her head to capture Maria Luisa's fingertips on her lips.

They kissed   …

   long kisses   …

      exploring kisses   …

kisses to please the other as she had never been pleasured before   …

kisses that reached from her brow to between her toes, kisses on her wrist, on the softness of her bended elbow, on the soles of her feet

…

   lingering kisses   …

   forever kisses.

Maria Luisa desperately wanted Juana to believe in her own beauty, in her own womanly power, and so caressed every curve

   every crevice …

   enticing her beauty to break loose.

Juana knew that she could never tell Maria Luisa how extraordinarily beautiful she was, but she needed to try. A gracious fire, the scent of wild willows, enveloped them in a night of wave upon crashing wave of pure passion. Juana had kissed women before, especially the ladies–in–waiting. She had even felt the gentle massage of curious fingers. But never … never … like this.

Never … Never had she ever known the fantastical joy of being a woman. She heard a scream of utter ecstasy.

The voice was her own.

Una mujer en su major momento (A Woman In Her Prime)

"JUANA, I AM surprised to see you entering the gates. The guard didn't tell me that you had left this morning." Sor Josepha's window looked directly onto the huge gates at San Jerónimo's, and she took this as a personal sign that she was to be the guardian of everyone's comings and goings. With dawn barely breaking, she was startled to see anyone, even me, the often-undisciplined Sor Juana Inés, coming through the gates

"I slipped out very early this morning, on a mission for Archbishop Payo," I explained. *Well,* I thought, *he did command me to go call upon la Vicereine Maria Luisa yesterday afternoon.* "Perhaps the guard had stepped away as I left." Being on a mission for the Archbishop also explained why I wore my ceremonial habit, now fresh and clean.

I returned to my cell to find Sara slumped over the dining table, her head resting on her folded arms. Sara jolted to attention, even as I tiptoed softly into the room.

"Señora, I was so worried about you," said Sara, her brow wrinkled from the night's speculation.

"I am truly fine, Sara. Please do not worry if I am not here. Sometimes I have business on behalf of San Jerónimo's or duties assigned by Archbishop Payo that carry me further from the convent than usual."

"Of course," said Sara. My gentle smile no doubt told Sara it was something more than business, but it was not her place to inquire. "Would you like some breakfast?"

"Yes, Sara, I would. And let us keep this a secret between you and me. I do not want to explain my duties to every gossiping woman at San Jerónimo's." I smiled, as did Sara who was delighted to be held in such trust by her Señora. Sara knew well the vitreous gossip so common in the convent, and sorely wanted to protect me from it.

My facility with finance is probably as recognized as my writings, having grown San Jeronimo's treasury substantially, as well as my own accounts, through wise investments, mostly by investing in properties that are rented out, for which I have Dona Angélica to thank. And the Archbishop does indeed call upon me to advise him on extensive investments by the Church, so it is reasonable that I have gone to advise him.

It is a blessing too that I have sometimes donated monies from my own treasury for repairs and expansion at San Jerónimo's, and with my architectural knowledge I have even supervised much of the work, for I now have a job that needs very confidential treatment. I know exactly who to call upon.

"HERE?" Don Manuel was surprised. He had built many things for me, but this request was unique.

"Yes," I told him. "Right here. I want a door just this wide." I held my hands about two feet apart. We stood on the outside of the convent wall, the wall that formed part of the perimeter fence around the Convent. Behind that wall was my cell.

"There is a library inside," I explained. "I want to be able to move a bookcase aside and step directly outside, onto the street."

"Ahhhh," he said. "And would it be helpful to have a few shrubs around to hide any curious eyes?"

"Exactly! Can you do it, my friend?"

"For you, Sor Juana Inés de la Cruz, I could build a stairway to the heavens. This door? Yes. I would be honored." Don Manuel bowed graciously.

"You understand this is quite confidential…"

"Of course! I have one worker, my nephew, who I would trust with my life. I will trust him – and only him – to help me with this."

My dear friend, Doña Bonita, the seamstress, clapped her hands in pure joy at being part of this conspiracy. "Aha! Don Diego needs a new set of clothes! What witchery is Don Diego up to now?"

"A most wonderous witchery," I said. "A most wondrous one."

I walk the path, and sing the air, of an Aphrodite. Yes, I am beautiful. Very beautiful. At times I hardly recognized myself. How can I love Maria Luisa any stronger? And yet I do.

Everyone and everything carries a magic, even sometimes grisly old Fray Miranda.

There is so much poetry to write. I must thank my dear Virgen de Guadalupe for fresh forevers that I can share with none but my lover.

A caterpillar is a curious creature, legs that latch onto journeys through fields and forest, a fuzzy, inconspicuous bug causing havoc to the unwary. Yet … when that caterpillar unfolds its butterfly wings, it covers the world with heaven-toned blues, with rose petal reds, proud sunflower golds, and violet eyes.

Let us sing to the gods, my Beloved,
and let us revel in our Beauty, you and I.

A pen takes flight, and yet it is not I who guides it.

I had a dream last night, a first dream, the dream of early rest when my love and I awake after the midnight hour, share a glass of wine, and each other.

The dream painted Goddesses caressing the Earth, singing Life to all they touched, following the call of the morning dove to every precious spot. The heavens were filled with beautiful Goddesses -- Aphrodite, Hathor, and Lakshmi, a Hindu Goddess. Hedone came too, and Xochiquetzal, the Aztec Goddess of Love. The lace of their gowns spun spirals of gossamer rainbows.

My love and I were there too, spinning in a circle of Love, opening the world to new blessedness.

Maria Luisa loved this dream, as she loves all my "first dreams." I have promised her a poem, just for her, with all these beautiful Goddesses singing, just for us.

Music is the most beautiful of all the arts, for it is the most orderly, stepping its notes up and down the scale, creating a harmony.

The most beautiful of all the Egyptian Goddesses? Isis. For it is she who is the very essence of intellect, it is she who invented writing.

And Cleopatra's legendary beauty? She who entwined the hearts of Emperors in her fingers. What was the source of her beauty? Yes, her library. She held in her grasp the most glorious library in all the known world, with untold knowledge at her fingertips… so breath taking.

Dearest one
  My heart flies on the hummingbird feathers
  Of the diadem – your gift –
And dreams of resting on your breast
Beloved one
  She who lifts on gossamer dreams,
  Come, take my hand
And let us discover our pleasures, together.

Find here sweets to tingle your tongue,
The sweetness of Eros, gifted to one
Whose sweet meats I'll savor
Soon … with great exultation.

Blessedly, there are no biographies of women, for if men were to write them, we would be a pitiful lot indeed. Woe to those men, for it is women's wisdom that unlocks the mysteries of the world.

Where do women belong in the eyes of men?
Where do women belong in the eyes of God?
Where do women belong in the eyes of women?

When God wrote of women, he wrote of judges, of warriors, of politicians and bravery. Debbora, the Queen of Sheba, Naomi, Sarah, Mary Magdalene, Hannah, Miriam, and dozens upon dozens more. He knew that women were strong, intellectually, spiritually, and physically. So why have men forgotten that?

Why have we forgotten it too?

Maria de San José, my dear niece, is writing her autobiography at the request of the Bishop of Puebla. She is a blessed visionary, called to the life of a perfect nun, hearing the voices of la Virgen and saints, devoting hour upon hour to their soft songs. I sometimes yearn to be like her, but that is not my place on this earth.

I do not listen for soft songs; I write to stir the soul and the senses. God gave Maria de San José the gift of whispers; He gave me the gift of letters, the gift of curiosity.

They say I am wealthy.

I am. I have a vast golden treasury of a love that is mine alone. There is no greater wealth.

If God had not wanted me to use analytical skills, He would not have stuffed my brain with so much intellect. But the intellect is there. I cannot un-stuff it, so there it is.

Our blessed Virgen Maria,
the Queen of Heaven,
the Queen of Earth.
By God eternal She conceived His son,
washed clean of all sin.
She walks in glories,
She walks in graces.
In but a moment, God freed Her of all blemish,
and made Her His Madre.

Mirrors bring your image back to you. Echoes bring your voice. What is it that brings your soul when it wanders? Love. Simply love.

A magnifying glass makes your vision increase. A speaking device makes your voice fly. What makes your soul take wing? Love. Only love.

And when there is a gallery of mirrors,
a plethora of echo boxes,
the world sings in freedom, learning, teaching, writing,
power.

Don Sebastian shied from shaking my hand. Does he think women diseased? Perhaps writing with black inks until one's hands are calloused is a disease. Indeed, my fingers are even blacker than Sara's. No matter. They were a gift from Archbishop Payo long ago.

These are not the hands that once enchanted the rogues at el Palacio.

These are the hands of one who swims in ink, joyously. No gloves for me, thank you. If you want Juana's touch, respect the ink.

And the callouses.

Sometimes it feels the pen flying by itself, an ocean of ink spilled from the heavens.

Lots of kisses on your slippers
I give you with my love
For kisses freely gifted
Will kisses also know

I awoke from my first slumber last night with visions of a wild ocean and I, a huge octopus that wrapped my beloved in my many arms.

Maria Luisa laughed when I told her.

Then we cried, for no matter how close I held her, I could never hold her close enough, not even were I a creature of a thousand arms.

I watched Sara as she took a pinch of this, a dab of that, a stirring of aromas to create her culinary masterpieces. Of course! If I met the Blessed Virgen Maria, I would tempt the Holy Señora with flavors She had never tasted.

I snuggled this nugget of insight into the theme of a hymn that I am writing for the Feast of the Assumption, with tempting flavors enticing la Virgen to stay, just a little while longer.

I stood behind the Velázquez family as they paid their final respects to Don Pedro Velázquez de la Cadena, my godfather in so many ways. Mass was said at la Gran Catedral de la Ciudad de México with all due decorum. After my elegy in poetry was read, after the eloquent speeches, after the hymns and communion, after all the farewells, I turned to leave.

"Sor Juana, do you have a moment?" Young Ignacio Velázquez, now the head of the Velázquez estate, touched my arm gently. His voice already held the authority of a general's command, although he was but a dozen years old. He was the only child of Don Pedro Velázquez de la Cadena, born after the Velázquez family had stopped hoping for children.

"Of course, Don Ignacio. I can stay as long as wish."

He thanked me for my most eloquent poem, then said, "There is something you do not yet know about my father. When he was ill and ready to join our Christ, he told me that I should forever take care of you ..."

"Me?"

He smiled. "Yes, you. It was his dying wish that I should help you with whatever you might need, always, although in truth I cannot imagine anything that the blessed Sor Juana Inés de la Cruz might ever need."

I was so very touched by his kindness, and now whenever he comes to la Ciudad de México he brings sweet oranges and treats, and we sit in the locutory and talk.

I read a treatise by a gentleman I had not met, but one whose analysis of Pliny's history intrigues me. I wrote him a note.

> *"Most Honorable Don Hernando"* it began, *"should the hand of God find you in our beautiful country, please do come to visit us at San Jerónimo's. Visitors from around the world are most welcome at my locutory, and do bring your tales from far-away places."*

Don Hernando wrote back.

> *"I had not planned on a visit to your glorious city, but now I must! Your brilliance and wit shine even here. Shall I come next spring?*

> *"I have told many friends about you, dear Sor Juana Inez de la Cruz, and all have wished to bask in your glorious commentaries. Would it be acceptable should a few of them visit your locutory as well?"*

I shall write again to him soon.

"Of course, my honored Don Hernando. All are welcome."

God and mi madre Isobel have indeed blessed me with a kind and loving servant. I saw her last night, long after she usually retires.

"Sara, where are you going with that bucket? It is the middle of the night."

"I didn't know you were still awake, Señora. A few of us are going to clean the dining room tonight."

"At this hour?"

"Sí, Señora." She left without another word.

This morning I discovered that Fray Miranda had ordered that Sor Lucia should clean the dining hall floor with her tongue for two weeks, as penance for speaking ill of a learned priest.

And for two weeks Sara and her friends will ensure the dining room floor is spotless before dawn.

What does love sound like?

Surely something so strong, something that commands every inch of your being, surely it has a sound.

Perhaps the song of a swan,
 or an imp's whisper,
or the sound of a cannon shot by an angel.

"Josepha, my dear sister, you have come to la Ciudad de México for the fiesta!" She looked only a bit shabby in her purple and rose fiesta gown, but her down-turned eyes led me to know that something was amiss.

Josepha is now alone with three children. Her most recent lover has returned to España. Maria, our older sister, the one who went to Las Amigas, the girls' school, lives at Panoayan now with her lover and four children. Panoayan is too small to house two families, so Josepha needs to find other accommodations.

"I feel like an old woman with no home since my godparents died."

My dear sister Josepha is no beggar, but simply a sister who needs help. I am so honored that I can care for so many of the members of my extended family.

And this one is easy. I will just sell some of my own jewels and purchase a lovely hacienda for Josepha near Chalco, one that will grow maize and cows and chickens enough for her growing family.

"Sor Juana, thank you for rushing over!" the Viceroy smiled broadly, honoring me as a celebrated guest. "Do you recall the Count de Andalusia?" A portly gentlemen regaled in France's finest silks presented an elegant court bow.

I looked as I returned the acknowledgment. Well, yes, he did look familiar, but I could not quite place him. He must have seen my puzzlement.

"Several years ago, I visited the Marquis de Mancera, then Viceroy of Nueva España. You and I were both guests at his fabulous gathering, but you were still a lady-in-waiting back then."

"Yes!" I clapped my hands in merriment. "I do remember!"

It was one of the most splendid evenings that la Vicereine Leonor had ever created, with free-flowing wine and liqueurs from around the world, gold plates at dinner, and massive bouquets of plumeria, roses and ferns. The women were all regaled in silk gowns with the laces and flounces and gems that were the trademark of la Vicereine Leonor's parties, and the men were just as regal.

After dinner, the Viceroy invited me to join him in the large parlor where he had assembled over twenty men, politicians, and scholars, each certain that one as young as this Doña Juana Ramírez could not possibly know very much – I was only in my late teenage years then.

They were to question me on any topic, while the Viceroy stood proudly aside. What merriment! They asked me questions about Plutarch, Kino, Machiavelli, Euripides, esoteric corners of science and philosophy, and so much more, mostly simple questions, I thought.

Every time I answered a question correctly, they all toasted my health, and got a bit drunker, passing pesos around for who won what bet about my abilities. By the end of the evening, they were all loose laundry, shouting love songs.

One man had asked, "What is the relationship between poetry and painting, according to Plutarch," and I replied, "Painting is silent poetry, and poetry is painting that speaks."

Another asked how Euripides thought friends showed love, and I replied that friends show their love in times of trouble, not just in times of happiness.

The final question was How many rooms are there in this Palacio? and I replied that there are as many rooms as there should be. Everyone roared, and drank more wine

My favorite question was my estimation of the finest extant scientist, and I replied without hesitation that it was Kircher, the scientist who studied Egyptology, language, medicine, music, and had even invented an Aeolian harp.

"You were the one who asked what St. Augustine said about Pride," I said to the Count de Andalusia.

"And you answered correctly, that St. Augustine said it is Pride that changed angels into devils, and it is humility that makes men as angels."

"Yes, I do remember! Forgive me for not remembering your name, but that was over a decade ago. I am so delighted to meet you again, Excelencia."

"You know, Sor Juana – for it is Sor Juana now, not Doña Juana – you know, your reputation had already begun spreading through España and Portugal when you were still a child, and now you are a luminary in our skies. When the King asked that I come to la Ciudad de México, there was one thing I knew I had to do. Come, Sor Juana, I have a surprise for you."

He led us to the center of the room where something sat on a marble table, something almost flat, about three feet long, with a silk cloth draped over it. He ceremoniously waited for the Viceroy and Maria Luisa to join us, then lifted the silk cover to reveal a strange contraption made of wood that sort of looked like a lyre, with a dozen gut strings of varying widths held in place with wooden pegs.

"An Aeolian harp! It is one of Kircher's Aeolian harps!"

I could hardly believe my eyes. "I have heard of these instruments. It is said that King David had one hung over his bed to capture the evening breezes. Only Kircher has been able to create such a harp. I never dreamed that I would ever actually see one."

"That is precisely what it is," said the Count. "I have borrowed it from a friend in Lisbon who said he was honored that Sor Juana Inés de la Cruz might play it a bit. Sadly, I cannot leave it in Nueva España, for I must return it to Lisbon."

"How is it played?" asked Maria Luisa.

I could not stop myself. I stepped forward, picked it up and blew on the strings … just a gentle breath … and the harp rewarded us all with truly angelic sounds that it held onto for a long time as it filled the room.

I returned many times to el Palacio to play the Aeolian harp, both indoors and outside with natural breezes. Maria Luisa sat the harp on a pedestal at night where it could capture evening breezes and lull us to slumber.

All too soon the Count had to return to España, but he left with one of my lyrical poems in his hand, and another splendid poem for the owner of the harp in Libson, thanking him for this magical visit.

O that my Achilles arm
Could toss off the crowd
Around you
And ravish you, inch by inch,
Right now

Prohibido (Forbidden)

WITH A FIERCE arm Maria Luisa waved the servants out of the room, and with the same arm she picked up a silver vase and hurled it at Juana. Juana knew she deserved it and did not even try to dodge it. The vase struck her left shoulder and with a thud ricocheted to the floor.

"My whole body ached." Maria Luisa glared at her with an intensity that Juana had never seen before. "I begged for you to come, but you did not come. My time came. I needed you. I desperately needed you, but you … were … not … here." Maria Luisa paced around the room, a leopard stalking its prey.

She screamed her accusations through clenched teeth, seething anger. "You did not even come to the baptism, Juana! I sent Consuela to personally deliver an invitation to you, and you did not come. Do you know how it cut into my gut that you … that YOU could not pry yourself away from your damned desk to come to our son's christening?" Maria Luisa grabbed a heavy wooden chair and slammed it into the wall, shaking the whole set of bookcases. "Why did you stay away for weeks and weeks despite my begging you to come? Did you think I was repulsive because I was with child?"

"No, no, my beautiful Maria Luisa. You are eternally breathtaking, even more so now." She fell to her knees, her tears flowing over Maria Luisa's slippers. How could she explain to Maria Luisa the isolation, the desertion, the abandonment, even the jealousy that she had felt these past weeks? How could she even explain it to herself? Massive swarms of angst overtook her as she touched her own stomach, knowing full well that she would never bear a child.

She knew she was being unreasonable, for with but a nod to any number of priests or wealthy landowners she could become pregnant herself. She knew she was desirable, but even the thought of having intercourse with a man nauseated her, her memory still ramming into the dark shadows of Don Roderigo's brutality.

Nor was this something she could take to her confessor, Fray Miranda. Men do not understand the depth of motherhood, and priests certainly do not. To someone like Fray Miranda, someone who could not even look at a woman, such feelings would be incomprehensible, if not repugnant. Fray Miranda had in fact summoned her to his confessional, again … berating her for wasting so much time on secular poems and songs, again … and declaring increasingly severe penance, most recently demanding self-infliction of lashes, and denying her the right to compose anything for a full month.

Perhaps, too, she was drenched in some of the agony that had permeated every niche of la Ciudad de México since the arrival of the new Archbishop.

THE BISHOP OF PUEBLA was right – he was not selected as the next Archbishop of Nueva España, nor was the ambitious Fray Miranda awarded the position, no matter how much he thought he deserved it.

The Bishop of Puebla did indeed believe, albeit briefly, that he had been appointed as the new Archbishop, for a colleague in España told him so.

He was in la Ciudad de México when the letter had arrived with congratulations and celebration.

> *"…You may have heard by now, my dearest friend and colleague, but if you have not, may I be the first to congratulate*

you on your appointment as the Archbishop of Nueva España! Truly, my friend, the appointment is yours. I am so proud to know you, so overwhelmingly joyful for your success..."

Not only was this a personal tribute to the abilities of the Bishop of Puebla, but all the work that Archbishop Payo had begun – the chapels, the hospitals, the homes for unmarried women, the schools, the programs for the poor, the celebration of the arts – it could all now be continued. He was elated.

He hastened to share his joy with Archbishop Payo, for it was this honorable Archbishop who had so vigorously presented his accomplishments to the King. He discovered Archbishop Payo in a shaded courtyard, his head bowed, his shoulders drooping.

"Excellencia!" called out the Bishop. "Have you heard the news?"

The Archbishop looked up, his face ashen, motioning the Bishop to sit beside him. "Come, my friend," said Archbishop Payo. "The question is rather: Have you heard the devastating news?"

The Bishop took the letter that Archbishop Payo held out to him, his face falling in utter disbelief. The letter said that Yes, the Bishop of Puebla was appointed the new Archbishop of Nueva Espana, but there was more.

No sooner had the Bishop of Puebla's appointment been announced than legions of conspirators working on behalf of Fray Francisco de Aguiar y Seijas y Ulloa descended on the Spanish Palace, bombarding their venom on the King and those around the King, using every diabolical machination, every gutless form of bribery, every slimy phrase of flattery, to have that appointment overturned, and Fray Francisco de Aguiar named as the new Archbishop in his place.

Within days their mission was accomplished.

"Can this be true?" The Bishop of Puebla was stunned beyond belief. He knew that he might not be granted the appointment himself, but to lose it to this gutless worm? No! And under such filthy, vile circumstances? No! It could not be true.

"A missive from the King sits on my desk," said Archbishop Payo sadly. "No doubt this worm has received his formal notification as well."

Fray Francisco de Aguiar was not totally inexperienced, although his experience was limited. Only three years earlier the King had appointed him Bishop of Valladolid de Michoacán, a province along the western coast of Nueva Espana. Even from that vantage point, Bishop Francisco de Aguiar worked tirelessly to position himself as the new Archbishop of Nueva Espana, and now he had succeeded.

"I will be leaving la Ciudad de México tomorrow," said Archbishop Payo, "and if I were you, my son, I would keep my distance from this Francisco de Aguiar."

The Bishop of Puebla did just that. In all the years that Francisco de Aguiar sat in the Archbishop's chair, never once did the Bishop of Puebla speak to him. Not once.

A FEW DAYS later this new Archbishop slithered into la Gran Catedral de la Ciudad de México under cover of darkness. Darkness had reigned ever since. Archbishop Francisco de Aguiar's excesses and aberrations were destined to pour waves of catastrophe throughout Nueva España, to systematically destroy everything that Archbishop Payo had created. The flourishing arts, the strong religious institutions, the proud clergy – all began to slowly crumble under the new Archbishop's reign.

But what could one expect from an Archbishop who wouldn't even show his face in God's sunlight? thought Juana.

Archbishop Francisco de Aguiar's carriage was totally encased in black leather to prevent even a ray of starlight from entering. Even the windows were covered in black. It was, of course, the fault of women that forced him to this extreme. He could not bear the sight of a woman, not even a gloved hand. He covered the windows of his carriage so he would not accidentally look out and perchance see a woman, and he arrived in the middle of a moonless night to forego any chance whatsoever that he might see a woman's shadow as he disembarked from his carriage. The path from his carriage to his private quarters was covered in new tiles, tiles that had never been touched by a woman's hand or shoe.

No woman, no nun, even one designated as Madre Superiora, was allowed anywhere near the Archbishop's private quarters. The windows in his office were blacked out up to eye level so he could never glance out the window and see a woman, even one far away on the street below. The windows in his private quarters were blacked out entirely. The story was told how he once had a whole foyer floor ripped out and replaced because a woman had stepped on a few tiles. Archbishop Francisco de Aguiar embraced the eccentricities of Fray Miranda, and multiplied them a hundred-fold.

Had Archbishop Francisco de Aguiar known a father who might have guided his path, that path might have been different. But he did not.

Had he enjoyed the pleasures of youth, chasing butterflies, bugs and señoritas, he might have come to respect life. But he did none of those things.

Had his madre not sent him to a monastery housing a severe swarm of men who found pleasure in tormenting boys in their care, shouting obscenities at every turn, his view of life would have been quite different. But she did dump him at a monastery where even his confessor took pride in humiliating him, especially when he wet his cot at night. "Stupid ingrate cur!" his confessor screamed as he rubbed the stinking sheets in the boy's face.

He developed an unpredictable, irascible temperament, and an uncontrolled paranoia that fed his many eccentricities, a paranoia fueled by his hatred of women.

"Watch your step, Juana," advised her friend, the Bishop of Puebla. "This is not Archbishop Payo." Indeed, he was not, but no one in Nueva España realized the extent of the new Archbishop's deranged rule before his arrival.

Although this Archbishop possessed the requisite education and influence, it was his family's heritage that foretold his future, for in his family tree was a knight of Julius Caesar, or so he claimed, and there was a tale that it was one of his ancestors who reputedly met the apostle St. James on the coast of España -- two resplendent stories that Archbishop Francisco de Aguiar repeated so often that they were accepted as validation for his appointment to high positions.

His mottled countenance, a frozen grey mask, reflected the shadows of his existence, and a taut square goatee announced his single-mindedness. He favored old torn garments and scourged himself thrice weekly. The more he scourged his body, the stronger the lust that haunted him.

One of his most vile gifts was his penchant to wring charity out of those who could least afford it, leaving the truly wealthy to wallow in their treasury.

Juana could handle most of Archbishop Francisco de Aguiar's eccentricities, for she had dealt with Fray Miranda's similar ways for many years, but unlike Fray Miranda, who left others to their own wrongful ways so that his imagination might simmer in their sins, this new Archbishop demanded that many of his beliefs be inflicted on all of Nueva España, with focused severity on nuns and writers. Juana, as both a nun and a writer, felt the sting of his edicts.

One of the Archbishop's first edicts was to ban all locutory gatherings at San Jerónimo's -- all of them. She knew that some of the gatherings were little more than drunken singing and dancing, and she understood why those might be banned. But her locutory gathering, the one pulling together the literati and politicos of Nueva España, the one that lured travelers hundreds of miles out of their way, even that one was banned.

"Please," she begged Madre Superiora, "please. We will meet in the afternoon, in daylight, on the roof where no one will see us. These guests have brought so many treasures to San Jerónimo's that we cannot shut the door on them. Our locutory gatherings must continue."

"I am sorry, Juana, truly. But we cannot risk having the wrath of Archbishop Francisco de Aguiar crash down upon us, now, when he has just arrived, and indeed it could. He could destroy us entirely. No, let us see where this game leads us before we defy him."

Juana continued to welcome small groups of one and two and three guests, scholars and clergy and politicians alike, but these modest gatherings lacked the vibrant repartee of the larger groups. Her locutory education came to an abrupt halt.

Gone too were all the public and private performances of secular plays, even plays presented at el Palacio, for Archbishop Francisco de Aguiar had banned them too. Juana had written some uproariously funny comedies that were performed at el Palacio de Viceroy with invited guests. Doña Caterina Rosa relished the naughty debauchery and playful flirting in Sor Juana's plays, sometimes even sitting on the laps of men, and women, in the audience, or rubbing their faces between her breasts. It was great fun, earning Caterina and Sor Juana very nice bonuses. One of them, "The Trials of a Royal House," had actors hiding under the skirts of the actresses, and even had actors talking with audience members and sitting amongst them, something entirely new in the plays of Nueva España.

Ironically, "The Trials of a Royal House" was being performed at el Palacio de Viceroy the night that the new Archbishop was due to arrive, with a steamy Doña Caterina Rosa in the lead role.

"Sor Juana," ventured the Viceroy. "Wouldn't it be a splendid welcome to the new Archbishop if you added a song about him at the end of your new play?"

Indeed, thought Juana, *it would be a wonderful welcome*. So, she did. She composed a cheerful tune, welcoming with wonderment the bright light that was the new Archbishop. It is unlikely that Archbishop Francisco de Aguiar even knew of this play, or of Sor Juana's song for him, and had he known, he would no doubt have condemned it as evil frivolity inspired by witchcraft.

Juana felt the heavy foot of the Archbishop when he banned her locutory, but she managed to convert the time to studying and writing. She even had time to teach Sara how to copy her writings into final form, something Sara had been begging to do for many months. Sara did not understand what she was copying, but her hand writing was quite exquisite.

She could find no good in Archbishop Francisco de Aguiar banning secular plays. The Bishop of Puebla surmised that this edict against secular dramas secured the Archbishop's domination of Nueva España's society, even that of the Viceroy himself, and she had to agree. Archbishop Francisco de Aguiar could not allow his ego to step aside for any man, certainly not for a secular figure, no matter how important that secular figure was. Sadly, the Viceroy, Maria Luisa's husband, had neither the intelligence nor the backbone to challenge the cyclone that was Archbishop Francisco de Aguiar.

When the Archbishop commanded that all nuns should be totally sequestered, a collective gasp gripped La Ciudad de México. If nuns could not leave the convents, how could they go out and assist the poor? How could they travel to forests and fields, plucking just the perfect flowers and leaves to create essences needed in the hospitals? How could they walk to the schools for girls that they had established? How could they join in the religious celebrations, the joyous celebrations on the Plaza Mayor, or even visit la Capilla de la Virgen de Guadalupe? Strict orders like the Carmelites were already totally sequestered, and they snubbed their noses at their undisciplined Sisters. Liberal orders felt smothered by this edict.

Ultimately, the religious orders of la Ciudad de México, priests and nuns alike, reached an unspoken compromise. Nuns would not flaunt their independence, but they could leave the convent for their religious duties, but only for their religious duties. Since nearly everything that a nun did was in religious service, from teaching to nursing to harvesting their orchards, or even writing, they managed nicely with this edict. With his windows blacked out, the Archbishop's myopic eyes never saw a nun on the street below him, and no one dared to tell him that they were there.

WITH RUMBLINGS of book banning, and even book burning, Juana became increasingly concerned about her own biblioteca, which, except for la Biblioteca de la Universidad, was the most extensive and most diverse biblioteca in all Nueva España. There was no doubt that her biblioteca held some titles that someone like the Archbishop would consider lewd.

At first, she hoped to hide some of her most valuable tomes at the homes and shops of dear friends, like Doña Bonita, the seamstress, but she knew if they were ever discovered, the wrath of the Archbishop could crush her friends forever. She needed other options. She called in Don Manuel, the contractor who had built her private entry, and together they contrived hiding places for several dozen of her most valued titles – in the walls, under the bookcases, in hidden shelves behind the bookcases, even in small dugouts under the floor. Having those irreplaceable titles protected set her mind at ease so she could continue writing.

With her private door and Don Diego persona, she continued much as before.

Until Maria Luisa got pregnant.

SHE TRULY could not grasp the magnitude of the feelings that swelled up inside her.

Early in the pregnancy she visited Maria Luisa often, writing charming and saucy poems about this person inside her, about her blossoming breasts and the milk that flowed from them, comparing her to the great Goddess Gaia who birthed the earth.

Even if she had recognized her strange feelings sooner, she could not have spoken to Maria Luisa about them, for nurses and attendants fussed over la Vicereine every minute. They had not a moment alone. As the time drew nearer, she stopped visiting, saying that she had to devote more time to her writing. It was not true. With no locutory gatherings and few visitors of her own, and Sara copying her writings into final form, she had more time than she had had in a long time. But she just could not make herself go to el Palacio de Virrey.

Now, standing accused, she fell to her knees and held Maria Luisa as close as is possible, burying her face in Maria Luisa's still soft tummy.

And she wept. Salty fierce tears, poured down her face. "I do not know … I do not know why I did not come. I can only tell you how sorry I am. Please … please find a corner in the goodness of your heart to forgive me, just a little."

Maria Luisa took Juana's hands to help her up, then crushed her as close to her breast as she could. "Juana, Sor Juana, my beloved, I do forgive you … more than just a little. Oh, Juana, how did it happen that such tears flow from your eyes?"

"Perhaps it is only because I dared to love you more than life itself."

Maria Luisa understood. Attending to all the joys of impending motherhood, she had felt that something was missing. The loss of this treasured woman, her Juana, her beloved, was missing. They held that embrace for a long time, soaking up the glow that formed around them.

A gentle tap on the door and Consuela's voice. "Excuse me, Señora, but little Don Juan Maria has woken from his nap. Do you want to see him now, or shall I take him to the wet nurse?"

Maria Luisa doted on her child, cherishing the moments she had with him. His suckling sent massive waves of ecstasy through her whole body, equal only to the joy that Juana's intense love-making gave her. But Maria Luisa also treasured her own rest, so sometimes the little Don went to a wet nurse who lived at el Palacio, a lovely Criolla, a devout Catholic, who always wore blue "to soothe the babe."

"Bring him to me, please, Consuela. I would like our dear Sor Juana to meet him." In but a moment her babe was in her arms. "Juan Maria, please meet Sor Juana Inés de la Cruz, our beloved, our madre."

"Oh, no," scolded Juana gently as Juan Maria clutched her finger. "I cannot be Juan's madre. That is your honor alone."

"Not true, Juana," said Maria Luisa as she settled Juan to her breast, aching to burst with the milk it held. "Who but you cast my womanly body into such a crescendo that even I could not ignore it?"

"It was Nueva España itself that did that." In a sense, Juana knew she was right, for it was a given that many couples, even those who had been barren previously, burst into fierce romantism, and fertility, upon hitting the shores of Nueva España, creating legions of Criolle babes. The dynamic passion of Nueva España was no legend, it was there in every Spaniard's household to see.

Maria Luisa smiled. "Perhaps. But Nueva España alone did not accomplish this. It was you … you in Nueva España that opened my womanhood. Did I ever tell you that even my monthly bleeding had stopped while I was in España?"

"No, you never mentioned that."

"Well, it did. And it began again, with a flourish, when you came into my life. My husband was needed for his seed, but you were the catalyst of my passion. That is why I named you as a parent of my son."

"A what?" Juana was incredulous. A nun could not even be named as a godmother of a child, for nuns were forbidden such responsibilities lest they be forced to leave the order to care for a child. But being named a parent? Never!

"Yes," said Maria Luisa. "There is a document in the top left drawer of my writing desk. It is a copy of the entry in the record book at la Gran Catedral de la Ciudad de México." Juana retrieved the document. "Read it, Juana." Juana slowly opened the document. In a flourishing script the very formal looking document read:

In the Records of
la Gran Catedral de la Ciudad de México,
Nueva España

Name of child: Juan Maria
Date of Birth: June 15, 1683
Madre: Maria Luisa Manrique de Lara y Gonzaga, Countess de Parades
Padre: A child of God
Godparents: (Maria Luisa's brother and sister)

Juana was simply stunned. Long ago she had told Maria Luisa the story of her own birth, as best she knew it. Now here it was reflected in the birth certificate of Maria Luisa's child, in a reference that only she and her beloved understood.

"And the baptismal certificate?" asked Juana.

"The baptismal certificate shows my husband as the padre, and that is the record that most people will see. But I wanted the Church to know – I wanted you to know – that a child was born because of you."

Little Juan Maria finished his snack and Maria Luisa held him out to the nun. "Would you like to hold your son?"

Juana held out her arms to cradle him, gently rocking this small person who had grabbed onto her heart. All eternity stopped as Juana softly rocked this tiny enchantment.

"Oh, dear," said Maria Luisa, "my milk is over-flowing." She caught a few drops of the nectar on her fingertip, holding that finger out to Juana's lips. "Here, would you like a taste?"

She would. Juana licked Maria Luisa's finger and suckled it as she had suckled Maria Luisa's breasts a hundred times before.

"Be careful, my love," said Juana. "That is so sweet that I might come back for more."

"Please do."

Primer sueño (First Dream)

SHE SAT AMONGST her treasures, the writings that she had kept copies of for decades, the writings that still touched her heart, wondering what to write next. A pile of commissions waited on her desk, but she was drawn to something else, to something new, but she did not know what it was.

Yes, perhaps a *villancico*, a fabulous poetic play with a full chorus and actors, celebrating religious holidays. As the matins services shrouded themselves in pale dawn, parishioners from many miles around converged on local cathedrals to see spectacles of entities, real and unreal, indigenous gods and mythological creatures conversing with Catholic saints, with props and costumes surpassing even those of the nativity plays. Huge choruses shot songs soaring to heaven's portals, with guitars, flutes and maracas leading the way, and if it was presented at la Gran Catedral de la Ciudad de México, the massive organ shouted out its melodies. The greatest joy of all was when the *villancico* was one composed by the nun at San Jerónimo's. Juana had indeed composed dozens of these musical dramas, with her work performed all over Nueva España. Her most favored of all were those that celebrated la Virgen Maria in all her various glories.

When she picked up a piece of parchment from the middle of her box of writings that sat next to her desk, she was pleased to see that it was from the *villancico* depicting la Virgen Maria as a scholar of theology who had studied all disciplines, becoming the Mistress of the Supreme Choir, the one who directs all the others.

Another parchment in the box was a poem written in Nahuatl, the local Indian language, with Indian ceremonial choreography woven in.

She relished drawing from the lives of extraordinary women, knowing that – on some level -- she had known them personally. There were two women who shared the spotlight of Juana's religious poems: Santa Caterina and Cleopatra.

Santa Caterina was the brilliant nun blessed with immense intelligence, the nun who had been tortured inhumanely for that gift. She defied the Church padres, for when they moved to strap her to the wheel of excruciating death, that wheel fell asunder at her simple touch. They then beheaded her, a much more merciful death. This was the saint that Juana most closely identified with. Juana knew Santa Caterina's voice would always be stifled by the Church hierarchy in Nueva España, at least as long as Archbishop Francisco de Aguiar maintained in control, just as her own voice was.

Cleopatra, her other idol, held the knowledge of the known world at her fingertips in her celebrated library, and took her own life as her treasured scrolls were devoured in flames.

With captivating themes and stylistic innovations, Juana's renown grew, unequaled anywhere in Nueva España, by any other poet or dramatist. Her notoriety gave her freedom to choose commissions, whether they paid especially well or were of a kind that she enjoyed writing.

The wealth that she acquired from her writings gave her the choice to help others as she wished, such as when Sor Alicia was reprimanded one Friday afternoon for not contributing to the Convent's treasury. Juana, the Convent's treasurer at the time, liked this gentle nun, and so said boldly, "Oh, but she has contributed. I simply neglected to enter it into the books." That Juana would neglect to enter such a contribution stretched imagination beyond belief, but the very next day such a donation did appear in the books of the Convent. Her Sisters simply smiled.

"Here, Señora, here is a bit of hot cocoa for you." Sara set down a tray with a warmed pot of frothy hot cocoa and warm biscuits, barriers to keep at bay the chill in the air that afternoon. "And here is some incense that my friend Pedro, the seller of spices, sent to you. He said a poet like Sor Juana Inés de la Cruz would truly enjoy it."

Juana sniffed at the soft grey smoke floating from the hot coals in the incense burner. "It is heavenly sweet," she said, "sort of like the myrrh burned in la Gran Catedral. Do thank Pedro for me."

Sara nodded, content that she had done well, and left, leaving Juana with the cool breeze, the hot cocoa, and the sweet incense. Juana stood at the window, looking toward Popocatepetl, toward home, remembering the times her Abuelo took her to the sea. With the warm winds tossing shards of sand on her bare legs, and huge waves tumbling into tangled foam, she had laughed like a land-locked mermaid. She picked up the conch shell that Abuelo had given her those many years ago, hearing the echo of Neptune and mystical Gods and Goddesses calling to her. She saw her soul soaring, reaching for visions she had never seen before.

Maria Luisa had joined her husband on a journey to distant provinces. Juana was alone, melancholy.

She picked up her quill, dipped it in ink, and a story began to appear. It was a dream story, the story of a soul soaring toward its destiny, a soul yearning to learn.

FIRST THE WORLD goes to sleep, casting a huge dark pyramidal shadow, silencing all save the muffled cries of nocturnal birds, like Minerva's wise owl. Bodies fall quiet and lips are sealed. Even fish are rendered doubly mute, for they were mute before.

While Jupiter's bird, the eagle, does not give itself to slumber, all men sleep alike, whether they wear the crown of the Holy Roman Empire or huddle in a shack.

The vision that emerges is the fantastical flight of the Soul. The Soul sees all, hears all, feels all, as it soars ever higher … higher than Olympus … higher than an eagle in flight. The Soul reaches higher … further … sometimes faltering, but never retreating. The Soul, with the sharp eyes of Intellect, surveys all of Creation.

The dream calls upon a multitude of deities, mythological entities made real in an un-real world, deities like:

The three faces of the Goddess Diana reflected in the moon's light;

Nyctimeme, the nymph transformed into an owl because of her incestuous relationship with her padre, she who defied male authority;

The three daughters of King Minyas, punished for defying male authority in not honoring Dionysus;

Ascalaphus, who betrayed Persephone's immense authority and was changed into an owl;

Harpokrates, the God of Silence;

Alcyone, the sorceress who changed her suitors into fish;

Actacon, he who discovered Diana swimming nude, thus being changed into a deer, pursued by his own dogs;

The eagle, the Queen of Birds, who keeps herself alert by clutching a stone she dare not drop;

Phaethon, the youth who reaches for the heavens in flight, even knowing he could not reach it, ultimately drowning in the sea of his own tears.

Neither God, nor Christ, nor the Holy Spirit appear in this vision. The eagle of Patmos and the statue of Nebuchadnezzar are the only Biblical references. This is the journey of an independent Soul reaching, roaring, yearning to know.

The dream ends with Phaethon on the brink of his ill-fated flight, with an Amazon defending her dark path against the dawn, shards of light slicing her retreat. The sun returns.

So overwhelmed is the Soul with all that it sees, that it can do no more than form a tiny germ of a notion, then its ship is anchored, its mast destroyed, her rudder worthless. The Soul has not found what it sought. There is no great revelation at the end of the journey. There is only the question, *Should we dare to fly?*

The dream asks if it is better to know just a little, and know it well, or if it is better to reach for the heavens, knowing the heavens cannot be reached. The answer, unequivocally, is FLY! Fly, for that is the destiny of the Soul. While the subject of the poem has no name, no age, no gender, in the last line the word "I" appears, ultimately identifying Sor Juana as the dreamer, the Soul in its quest for knowledge.

In many respects this journey of a soul told of Juana's personal journey, her constant striving to know, her searching, her unabashed yearnings, her missteps and determination. In the end she had no Answer; she had only The Question, *Should I dare to fly?*

It is nearly a thousand lines of poetic mysticism. It is her masterpiece. Scholars would study it for days on end, trying to glimpse its meanings; mystics would simply understand.

SHE WOKE, the sun dipping to the horizon, sheets of parchment neatly piled on her desk. She glanced through the poem written there. Some of it she remembered writing; some of it she did not. Yet there was not a single word she wanted to change.

"Señora, you are awake." Sara spoke softly, as if Sor Juana might still be sleeping.

"Sara, how long have I slept?"

"You went to sleep early this morning."

"How long have I been writing this poem?"

"More than three weeks now. You slept a bit from time to time, and ate a bit, and once you walked to la Capilla de la Virgen de Guadalupe. But otherwise, you wrote."

"Three weeks? Didn't I go to any of the daily prayers?"

"No," said Sara. "I told the Sisters that you weren't feeling well. Since you never left your cell, they believed it." Juana's health was indeed challenged, a weakness that constantly haunted her, so Sara's lie was quite believable.

"My goodness," laughed Juana. "That certainly explains why my habit is so wrinkled, and so dirty."

Juana noted a pile of pages, freshly lined for music, on the corner of her desk.

Sara smiled. "You hummed a melody sometimes when you worked, and I thought you might be writing a new *villancico*, so I lined some parchment for you."

"Thank you, Sara, but no. No *villancico*. This is a poem, a writing just for me."

WHEN JUANA and Maria Luisa met again a week later, it felt as though eternity had slipped by in but a moment. The kisses, the embraces ... they were all there. But there was something more, something deeper, much deeper.

"I missed you so," whispered Maria Luisa, "and yet it felt as though you were sitting beside me the whole journey."

"I know," said Juana. "I was."

"Oh, but look!" Maria Luisa reached to pick up something wrapped in a tilma. "I've brought you a gift."

Juana unwrapped it, finding a guitar. But this was not just any guitar. It was not even the most exquisite guitar Juana had seen. It was a unique guitar, one that Juana thought she recognized. It was decorated with mother-of-pearl and abalone shells, a richly embroidered strap glistening with silk threads, images of peacocks and roses intertwined. She could not be certain, but it looked so very much like the guitar that the Roma, the wanderer from Spain, had played at his campfire so many years ago.

Maria Luisa and Juana had exchanged many gifts ... turquoise bracelets, Aztec antiquities, pearl rings, tapestries, curiosities, chocolates ... everything special, everything beautiful ... and from Juana, no matter how small the gift, a poem. But this gift, this guitar, was different from all the dozens and dozens of other treasures they had exchanged.

"Where? How?" Juana's forehead crinkled. She could not quite believe what she was seeing.

"It was a middle-aged man, a strong man with rich grey hair and long agile fingers," explained Maria Luisa. "We had stopped to water the horses along a trail on the outskirts of a village. Consuela and I took a walk into the forest bordering the trail, and this man appeared from behind a tree. He held out this guitar, offering it to me. I tried to pay him for it, but he said No, it was a gift. Then he disappeared. At first, I thought it was a gift for me, but even as I accepted it that day, I knew it was a gift for you."

Juana held the guitar humbly. The world had come full circle, returning her to sounds she needed to hear again. She heard the echo of the old woman, saying, *You will live longer than your years.*

Juana found herself softly strumming the guitar as though it had belonged to her forever, the vibrant notes swirling around her, passion engulfing her. Her fingers paused, and silenced the strings. She set the guitar aside, in awe of its presence.

"And you have brought a gift too." Maria Luisa spoke as a child at Christmas, looking longingly at the parcel Juana had set on her desk.

"Yes. It is a poem."

"Will you read it to me?" Maria Luisa so loved Juana's poetry, listening in raptured joy at each piece, hearing the words left unspoken, the syllables in between.

"After dinner I will read it to you."

After dinner they settled themselves on the goose down pillows in front of the fireplace, Maria Luisa setting her glass of wine on a stool nearby. Juana sat next to her, their shoulders touching. Juana began. The world fell still, just as it had in her dream poem.

As Juana finished reading, she felt Maria Luisa's tears on her hand and heard her fervently whisper, "Oh, FLY, Juana, fly!"

They held each other in a long embrace that night, their bodies pressed together, flowing and merging in torrents of passion, inviting the shadows of starlight to join them.

When they awoke after midnight that night, Maria Luisa begged Juana to read it again. And she did. It was their first dream.

Cisma (Schism)

"HE SAID what?" Juana was stunned.

"He said -- he screamed -- you are incorrigible." Sor Gabriela was nearly in tears from her encounter with Fray Miranda. She and Juana had been good friends since Juana first entered San Jerónimo's, when she was the Madre Superiora. "Yes, Juana. Fray Miranda stood in that room and shouted that you are obstinate and incorrigible. Not only that, but a dozen friars and bishops were standing beside me when he spoke."

Juana stood, perplexed, shaking her head. "But he is my personal confessor. How could he allow himself to make such an accusation?" Fray Miranda's criticisms of her had grown increasingly common, and more severe, but this, in public, in front of Church leaders, was a massive slap in the face.

"I understand that you are upset, Juana. I am upset too. No confessor, not even the sometimes-erratic Fray Miranda, should speak publicly in such a way about his charge."

"Gabriela, what did you say that prompted such an outburst?"

"Nothing! I swear, Juana, it was nothing I said. I went to Fray Miranda to ask his advice on donating some rather distant properties to the Jesuit Order, something that you had recommended that we do. I made a comment about how much I enjoyed a loa you had written for la Catedral de Puebla, and he burst into a rage about your conduct." Gabriela herself was so upset by the incident that she returned to the Convent, so upset that the even Sor Josepha, she who guarded the gates, knew that something was amiss.

The surprise was not that Juana was considered difficult; she was difficult, often ignoring advice given by others, often defying regulations. The surprise was that her personal confessor – Fray Miranda – would dare to make such an accusation to anyone at all, let alone shout about it to one of the nuns at San Jerónimo's, and in the company of others.

Nor was this the first time he had erupted into spasms of criticism of Juana. These outbursts began many months earlier, but kept increasing in frequency and intensity.

She felt the ground beginning to quake below her, her footing with the Church becoming unpredictable. The Inquisition had recently banned another playwright, Fray Juan de Montalban, with Fray Miranda as the Chief Inquisitor. Sor Juana had long looked to Fray Miranda to guard her from the storms of the Church hierarchy, and from the Inquisition, especially since the arrival of Archbishop Francisco.de Aguiar. Until recently it seemed he had done so. Now … now she felt the winds changing.

Now it was common knowledge that her personal confessor could no longer tolerate her. She felt like she was walking, naked, through a sand storm. She was on the brink of becoming an outcast, and but for the protection afforded by the Viceroy and la Vicereine Maria Luisa, she well might have been. The Church did not want a confrontation with the government of Nueva España, especially over something so ridiculous as one nun, so for the most part they left her alone.

Juana, however, was enraged. Such a public insult could not be tolerated. She really wanted to march to la Gran Catedral, tear down the stupid wall that Fray Miranda sat behind, and punch him in the gut. Fortunately, she did none of that. What she did do was what she often did – she walked out to la Capilla de la Virgen de Guadalupe, where she knelt and sincerely prayed all night through, asking for guidance.

At Aurora's first light she knew what she had to do. As always, her dear Virgen of Guadalupe guided her thoughts to the only resolution possible. She had to give Fray Miranda the option to cease being her confessor.

She approached this task with all the diplomatic skills at her command, which were considerable. She had no example to follow, for this was simply not done.

A personal confessor is not treated like a stray dog, and no nun had ever dismissed Fray Miranda. The nuns who elected Fray Miranda as their confessor took pride in the fact that they carried out his often-severe penance, the scourging and fasts that he demanded, even the crawling on the floor, cleaning their cells with their tongues.

Fray Miranda dealt a different severity to Sor Juana, denying her times for writing for several days, or several weeks, and once even for two whole months. Those periods of penance were far more painful for her than it was for the nuns crawling on their hands and knees. She retained immense gratitude for Fray Miranda's arranging for her admission to San Jerónimo's Convent, for without his intervention she trembled to imagine what her life might have been.

Over the past decade she had felt an encroaching meanness in his demeanor. Perhaps it was envious anger that he had never been appointed Archbishop, or even a bishop of one of the provinces, a station he had certainly earned. Perhaps it was his age and creeping ailments brought on by his severe way of life that ate away any compassion that he once possessed. No matter the cause, this was not the confessor of a decade ago.

And now this. To publicly humiliate her was so hurtful, so inexcusable, that Juana could find no other way. She had to open the door to part ways.

The letter was a long one, brimming with praises for his work, bursting with gratitude for all he had done for her, even opening the door for Fray Miranda to deny that he had ever said such a thing, leaving the door open for a reconciliation.

… Reverencia, I must say that my heart is overflowing with complaints that I might have addressed over the years, and as I

pick up my quill to write them, rebutting one I venerate so highly, it is only because I can tolerate no more, as I am not as humbled as other daughters in whom your teachings would be better placed. I am simply too tired.

…

Thus, I beg of you, Reverencia, if you no longer choose to favor me (for that is voluntary) please think of me no more for as I would regret the loss, I shall speak no complaint. … God has made many keys to heaven, … for salvation lies in my own desire, and I will find that in myself, not in my confessor.

The comment that "God has made many keys to heaven" no doubt stunned and irritated him like a burr in his shoe, for he believed that his guidance was the only direct route to heaven for his charges, for all who ever listened to him. Nor could salvation lie in her own desire, for it was universally accepted that a priest's intervention is needed for true salvation, especially for women who were naturally lacking analytical ability.

He sizzled too when she called upon the works of Santa Caterina, St. Gertrude, and Santa Paula, reminding him of the blessings of learning that women can bring to the Church. It was a bold letter, but one she felt she had to write. And he read her ultimatum: "If you cannot find it in your heart to think of me kindly, then please cease to think of me at all."

She gave him every reason to dismiss her, yet she knew she would accept any hint of apology or denial from Fray Miranda.

But none came. He had ceased to think of her at all.

It now remained for Juana to find a new confessor, one strong enough to accept her despite Fray Miranda's assessment of her. She chose Fray Arellano, a highly respected Jesuit in La Ciudad de México whose charges already included many nuns. His piety and scholarship were unquestioned, as was his integrity.

She was pleased. She had broken with Fray Miranda, but not with the Church itself, and that was very important to her. She had felt no repercussions from the break, assuming that he was pleased to be rid of her. She was meant for the life of a nun, and trusting in Christ the Redeemer and the compassion of la Virgen was part of her whole existence. From time to time, she simply needed protection from the fickle temperament of the Church hierarchy, and for the next several years Fray Arellano, in conjunction with the political shield of the Viceroy, was able to provide that protection.

Las llamas de Filotea (Filotea's Flames)

"JUANA, DO YOU THINK that if we had met many years ago, when we were still quite young, that we might have wed?" There was a sparkle in the eyes of the Bishop of Puebla, but more than a thread of truth in what he spoke. The Bishop and Juana had been close friends for nearly twenty years.

Juana's eyes wrinkled in merriment. "Me with no dowry, and you with no fortune or family? My dear Bishop, we would have been miserable!"

Their laughter mingled with the slurping of the creek nearby. They had walked to an open meadow on the outskirts of La Ciudad de México, both edgy from the constant stomp of the Archbishop's boot.

It was the summer of 1690. While España was settling Texas, while LaSalle had claimed Louisiana for France, and John Penn founded Philadelphia for the Quakers, the world seemed to be expanding at an alarming rate. Juana's world often felt trapped in the past.

"You know, Juana, he takes my money without so much as a thank you, then dumps it into the pockets of his chosen priests to have churches and hospitals built in their names." He absent-mindedly picked up a stone and threw it as far as it would go. "I could have built twice the church that Fray Alejandro built, at half the cost, with monies remaining for a glorious tableau at the altar."

Juana did not have to ask who the Bishop was referring to. "Perhaps it is a good thing that God does not judge us by the number of churches we build. You have accomplished miracles, my friend, no matter the obstacles."

"You've never given up on me, have you, Juana?"

"Never. And I never shall."

They sat on a fallen tree, watching the sun creep away, its blazing glow the backdrop for the forest of oaks lining the creek.

"He seems unusually quiet about your brilliant writings, Juana."

The first edition of Juana's writings had reached Nueva España a month earlier, the glorious volume that her dear Maria Luisa had supervised, the one that introduced the play "*Divine Narcissus*" to the world. Maria Luisa had arranged to have the play produced in Madrid, but no one outside of Madrid knew of it until this volume, "*Castilian inundation*" was published.

"I have heard from dozens of colleagues who saw the production of 'Divine Narcissus' in Madrid, most noting how envious they were that I actually know this brilliant playwright, this 'Sor Juana Inés de la Cruz.' " The Bishop smiled his broad smile.

"Did you tell them that this brilliant playwright has been a pain in your neck for decades?"

He laughed his wonderful laugh. "Yes, and I also tell them that once many years ago I kissed your hand and have remained enamored of your soul ever since."

The Spanish court and intelligencia were indeed impressed with this new play. The introduction, the loa, spoke of how native Aztecs and Spanish spar over religious ideas, ultimately realizing that they have a great deal in common, a concept they had heard of but had never seen presented so brilliantly. Juana had previously compared the Catholic communion with Aztec blood sacrifice, just as the Jesuits had done, so this perspective came naturally to her.

"Juana, there appears to be a great deal of controversy on the meaning of the character of Narcissus. Some say he represents an egotistical devil, and some say he represents Jesus Christ. And Echo too. Some see Echo as the Devil, yet when she can only repeat the words of others, she becomes very wise. What did you intend?" He raised one eye brow, as if conspiring with her.

"Truly, my friend, I wrote with no clandestine intention, malicious or otherwise. The characters speak as they are meant to speak, and perhaps that is the ultimate meaning, that there are many interpretations of God and Devil, of Good and Evil, and that our path in life is to find our own best way of serving the Good. It asks us to examine what we believe in."

"Do you think our Archbishop would agree?"

Juana shook her head. "Probably not. He does not seem to agree with much that I do, and on this work, he has been woefully quiet. Too quiet. He may attack you by theft, but he silences my voice in a black pit of nothingness."

She had expected an outcry from the Archbishop, a condemnation of her childish scribblings from the pulpits across la Ciudad de México. But there was not so much as a whimper from him, as though she did not exist. Blessedly, the entire intelligencia of La Ciudad de México flew into action, their voices and pens flinging her praises to the skies. Still not a syllable from the Church.

THE DECISION to print these works was not an easy one. It was during the last year of Maria Luisa's stay in la Ciudad de México, the times when they sought out every moment to be together. After seven short years, the Viceroy's term was ending.

"These works must be published," Maria Luisa had insisted. "They must!" She sat on the floor, Juana's poetry and plays spread out around her.

"No, not unless we want the wrath of the Archbishop to crush the poor printer." Juana shook her head. "No, I don't think we want to do that to any printer."

"You are right, Juana. They cannot be published here. They must be published in España. The Archbishop cannot touch them there."

"No!" was Juana's instinctive response, but it took little to convince her that this was the right path. Juana had never felt quite so humbled, quite so happy at the prospect of having her work in print, and that printing managed by Maria Luisa. Printing was a validation of one's prominence in the literature of Nueva España and, while Juana had often hoped to see her work in print, she did not honestly think it would happen.

A very determined Maria Luisa set out three boxes: a small box for those pieces that would be published, a large box for those that would not be published, and a special box for those that she would keep in her personal possession.

The last set was just too dangerous to leave in la Ciudad de México, but too beautiful to destroy. Maria Luisa knew she would read, and re-read, and re-read again the poetry that Juana had written just for her, most of the words sizzling with passion. She had already captured them all to memory, but there was a sensual touch in holding them close to her heart as she whispered them over and over. Several years later, when she passed away, this special set of poems would find its way to a dark storage room in Madrid where her belongings were stored, only to be discovered decades later by a valet who assumed the "J" in the signature was a "Junipero" or even a "Juan." He destroyed these blazing writings to protect Maria Luisa's reputation.

"It feels sinful to keep these majestic pieces out of sight," Maria Luisa had said as she set another "private" poem into her box. "Love isn't a sin," she insisted. "You know that. Not among women. These poems are magnificent. I'm angry that I must hide them." She knew why she had to hide them, but was just irritated at the mores that made her do so.

Juana knew too, and smiled at her, most mischievously. "Were your husband not so possessive, so jealous, I would run through the streets shouting my passion to all the angels. No," whispered Juana as she took Maria Luisa's hand, "it is refreshing to have a love that belongs just to us."

The last few months that Maria Luisa was in La Ciudad de México found them sorting through all of Juana's work, all that Juana had copies of. Most of the scripts for the fiesta plays were lost, as were many of the poems written on commission. It was not until Sara began assisting Juana that true copies of most writings were kept.

"Yes, 'First Dream' We must include that," insisted Maria Luisa. "It is your masterpiece."

"No. That poem is the only piece that I ever wrote just for myself. All the others were written on behalf of someone else, or for someone else. That is the one piece that I wrote just for myself. In fact, that is the only copy I have ever had. I am not even certain that I wrote it, it just appeared in my heart one day, just sitting on my desk, waiting to be read." The matter was settled, it would not be included in this volume, on the condition that Maria Luisa be allowed to take a copy with her.

All too soon, much much too soon, it was time for Maria Luisa to leave.

They spoke of Juana settling in España, even joining a convent there

> *"Will you show me the windmills in La Mancha that Don Quixote chased?"*
>
> *"Sí! Sí! And we will speed over the fields of Andalusia on white horses!"*
>
> *"And the theaters in Madrid?"*
>
> *"Absolutely, all of them, and in Seville too. Please come. The thought of living without you …"*
>
> *"I know. I know."*

… but in the end, they decided that Juana belonged to la Ciudad de México, as Maria Luisa belonged to España. It was a belonging that rooted the soles of their feet touching the soil of home, beginning before they were born; there was no beginning, no end, it just was.

There was an empty chasm of emotions and thoughts that each wanted to say, but there simply were not enough words in any language for their feelings. In the end all they could do was embrace, fiercely.

> *"I cannot bear to tell you farewell when others are present."*
> *"Nor can I."*
> *"My beloved, we will meet again."*
> *"Yes, I know."*

At their last meeting Maria Luisa slipped a ring on Juana's finger, a ring with a miniature painting of Santa Caterina that she had made herself, with diamond dust and rubies intertwined, creating the wheel that this blessed saint was meant to be tortured on. Juana always wore this ring, but not on her finger, for it was not something she wanted to share with the world. She wore it on a gold chain around her neck, close to her heart, beneath her habit, always reminding herself that, with but a whisper, Maria Luisa was always there. It was a constant reminder, too, that any time she could be silenced by the Church as Santa Caterina had been.

Juana gave Maria Luisa a ring too. This was a miniature portrait of Maria Luisa herself, painstakingly painted by Juana as Maria Luisa had taught her. "It is for your first finger, so that you will always know that my love points to you."

The last glimpse that Juana caught of Maria Luisa was as her carriage pulled away from el Palacio.

MARIA LUISA and the Count lingered in Nueva España for a while until his next appointment was announced. In 1689 he was appointed Major Domo to Queen Maria Anna, the position he had been working toward his whole career. He was thrilled. His 200,000-gold crown investment in his new position had done its job, it had guaranteed him substantial status as a lifetime grandee. Juana was pleased too, for it gave her a strong arm alongside Queen Maria Anna, should she ever need it.

While still in Nueva España, Maria Luisa had sent Juana's completed manuscript ahead to a printer she knew well in Madrid. When she arrived back in España, the printer had set the print, the proofs were ready, and soon the first copies came off the press to be bound in a beautiful leather cover with silver embossing. *Castalian Inundation* contained some of Juana's greatest works, including the play *"Divine Narcissus"* and several dozen of her finest poetic pieces. It was dedicated, of course, to Maria Luisa and was shipped off to Nueva España in 1689, and to booksellers throughout España and Portugal. Its arrival in la Ciudad de México caused a glorious uproar.

"Such majesty! Such wit!"

"Such a magnificent command of the Spanish language"!

"Such cadence in the rhythms!"

"Inspired rhymes tease our ears and imaginations!"

The city fell at Sor Juana's feet, honoring this nun they were proud to call their own. Huge honorariums and equally splendid gifts covered her desk.

But the Church was silent.

Not a word from the Archbishop, or from any priest in any pulpit or conversation. It was as though she did not exist. It felt eerie. Juana had never shied away from a lively discourse, or even criticism, but there was no discourse, no criticism from the Church at all. The Church always proffered its assessment of poets, sometimes honoring them, and sometimes banning them. But silence? No, the Church was never silent.

THE BISHOP OF PUEBLA skipped a stone over the ripples in the creek. "Just once … just once … I would like to get the better of him." The Bishop could not rid himself of his disgust with the gutless personage who had ripped the position of Archbishop from behind his back, and who now sat in the Archbishop's chair, the chair that he himself had earned.

No other minister of the cloth would be insulted by being the Bishop of Puebla, for Puebla was a prestigious province, second only to La Ciudad de México itself. But it was second. The Bishop of Puebla would always answer to the whims of the new Archbishop, a situation that did not please Bishop Manuel Fernández de Santa Cruz.

The hatred was mutual. Even after all these years, the two of them had never spoken. Ever.

"Yes," said Juana, "and just once I would like for him to acknowledge that I actually have a reasoned idea, or any idea at all."

"I've got it!" The Bishop surprised even himself with a marvelous idea that hit as he bounced another stone off the creek.

"Got what?"

"How we can make His Reverence sit up and take notice of you." He could not help himself, he grinned with laughter.

"Oh?" Juana was intrigued.

"Do you recall a few years ago when the issue of the nature of Christ's love was debated at your locutory? Someone mentioned the epistle by Padre Antonio Viera, the epistle he wrote decades ago."

Juana nodded. It was a heated discussion, one with solid arguments from all sides. Padre Viera, a highly distinguished Portuguese Jesuit, was widely recognized for his brilliance and courage, organizing a chain of missions in Peru, being confessor to Queen Cristiana, and fighting tirelessly for abolishment of slavery. When brought before the Inquisition, he pled his own case, and won. This was indeed a priest who might challenge Jesuit philosophy, as he did in a sermon about the nature of Christ's love.

Padre Viera posited that the greatest demonstration of Christ's love was that He left the earth, left the people He loved so dearly, leaving nothing behind. This contradicted not only St. Augustine, St. Thomas, and St. John Chrysostom, but the entire Jesuit Order that believed Christ's greatest gift was to bestow the gift of the Holy Sacraments to His people, and to offer humility as a sacred action as demonstrated when He washed the feet of His disciples.

In the locutory debate Juana had defended the Jesuit position brilliantly. At the end of the gathering, everyone stood and applauded her pointed analysis, the crystal clarity of her arguments. While this debate may have seemed arcane to ordinary people, within the Church hierarchy it was immensely important, gaining Juana kudos from then-Archbishop Payo and others in service to the Church. This was the argument that the Bishop now suggested that she put into writing.

"But to what end?" she asked. "Everyone has already heard it."

"Not quite. Our current Archbishop has not heard it. In 'Divine Narcissus' you touch upon the nature of God's divine love. The Archbishop would seriously disagree with you, but rather than debate the issue, he keeps silent. Let us encourage him to speak to the issue. The presentation you gave at your locutory is the perfect entry for that."

The Bishop clapped his hands, welcoming this splendid notion. "The Archbishop wasn't required to comment because 'Divine Narcissus' was not presented here. It was only presented in Spain. Your new treatise will be published here, on the press in Pueblo, so he must comment on it.

"And let us make it even more interesting. Let us suppose that someone, a 'Sor Filotea' perhaps, sees one of the very limited copies and writes a rebuttal to it. What is our good Archbishop to do? Shall he back a heretic nun – yourself -- who defends the Jesuit dogma just as he must, or back an unknown nun who criticizes her? It will be the talk of the entire clergy, so he will have to take sides, putting him in a pretty predicament. What fun!"

They both knew that Archbishop Francisco de Aguiar and Padre Viera shared a long-time friendship, so to place the Archbishop in a position where he had to support Padre Viera and an unknown nun on one side, or the entire Jesuit order and Sor Juana on the other side, was truly brilliant.

"Either way he must support the view of a woman, either Sor Filotea or me. What a splendid predicament to set before our Archbishop!" Juana laughed out loud at the Bishop's outrageous suggestion. If worse came to worse, the Archbishop might just ignore it, and that would be fine too.

So it was done, a comical conspiracy.

SOR JUANA SET her pen to parchment and, as only she could do, set out the labyrinth of logic to defend the Jesuit's dogma on the issue of Christ's demonstration of love for mankind. Point after point hit the mark, like a lumberjack felling a forest, and when she had finished, she had cut through every argument, leaving those arguments bereft of any strength or even any branches. It was brilliant.

She did not think of it again until the Bishop of Puebla sent her a copy of the final printing, with "Sor Filotea's critique" included. Juana laughed out loud when she read this critique, so artfully and pitifully crafted by the Bishop. Juana's logic could not be critiqued, so this fictitious nun, this Sor Filotea, attacked her with all the tired arguments about the dangers of being an educated woman, paragraph after paragraph of regurgitation of the silly arguments that Juana had heard so many times before. She wrote that women should not be allowed an education, that Christ forbade women to learn, that women were simply not smart enough. Yet here was Sor Filotea, theoretically an educated woman herself, making all those arguments. Juana simply thought it was funny. It was a short, humorous little treatise.

Everyone knew that the insolent Bishop of Puebla had printed it, and had probably written the contribution from Sor Filotea, for the Bishop made no secret of the fact that it was printed on his printing press, and Sor Filotea signed herself "Sor Filotea de la Cruz," a conceit that only the Bishop of Puebla would dare use. Clearly Sor Juana had not written this piece, for it was for too short and too flimsy for a gifted writer like Sor Juana.

The Bishop of Puebla did write this treatise, presenting "Sor Filotea" as an addle-brained old woman who spewed out tired old arguments, and did not even do that very well. The inference that anyone who supported Fray Viera's argument was also an addle-brained old woman lit a fire of hell in the Archbishop.

No, Archbishop Francisco de Aguiar did not think it was "funny." The intelligencia of la Ciudad de México elite was indeed reading it and laughing about it, and what could the Archbishop say? That Sor Juana Inés de la Cruz wrote a brilliant sermon? That this unknown nun, this "Sor Filotea," was quite perceptive? He felt trapped. The Archbishop took it as a personal insult, even more so because he and Fray Viera had been close friends since childhood. Such debates were welcomed amongst the clergy, but from a nun? Good God, Never!

It irritated him, like a cactus thorn in his big toe, that the Bishop of Puebla had written the "Sor Filotea" critique. He knew that he had thrown the Bishop of Puebla off the chair that rightfully belonged to him, and that the Bishop had no doubt been plotting revenge for years.

Just what could the Archbishop do? Attacking the blasted thing was not the answer, nor was silence. Both the Bishop of Puebla and Sor Juana Inés de la Cruz provided an inordinate amount to his treasury, something he did not want to relinquish by punishing them, and they were both highly revered by la Ciudad de México's elite.

"Track who is saying what, and order a special sermon in every church in la Ciudad de México," the Archbishop instructed Fray Miranda. "I will be visiting some of our provinces."

"Is that all?" asked Fray Miranda.

"No, that is not all. But it is all we will do for now. She shall be condemned from every pulpit in La Ciudad de México. The time will come when we can do a great deal more. Some day we will punish her as she deserves to be punished. In the meantime, give that Bishop and that nun some rope and they will hang themselves."

ARCHBISHOP FRANCISCO de Aguiar left La Ciudad de México, being unreachable for nearly two months, giving the two blasphemers enough time to hang themselves.

When the Sisters of San Jerónimo's entered their church for services the following Sunday, there appeared a priest that they did not know, as was the case in nearly every church in the entire city. Every single pulpit shouted condemnation like cracked bells in every belfry, each pointing a finger at Sor Juana's girlish ideas, rating her discourse as nothing more than pitiful. Amazingly, the pews in most churches were nearly empty that Sunday. Word had gotten out that Sor Juana was to be condemned from every pulpit, and the people simply did not want to listen to such blasphemy.

Madre Superiora of San Jerónimo's had asked a Valencian priest, Francisco Xavier Palavincino Villarrasa, to present a sermon, and he did just that, disagreeing with both Viera and Sor Juana, saying that Christ's greatest gift was to conceal himself during the sacrament of the Eucharist. He also praised Sor Juana as "The choicest intellect of this blessed century, the Minerva of America," yet he lamented that she was handicapped by being a woman.

Rather than quench the fire that Filotea wrought, these sermons became fuel for the fires both for and against Sor Juana and the Bishop.

"RIGHT HERE will do fine," Juana told the smiling rancher who had given her a ride out to the countryside in his pony cart.

"Here?" he asked. "In the middle of nowhere?"

"Yes," she smiled. "I am meeting a friend. God bless you for your kindness, señor." She waved, heading across the field of wild roses to the creek and the crumbling old stump where they sometimes met. She so enjoyed these conversations with the Bishop of Puebla. On this chilly winter's afternoon, he had sent an urgent message to Juana to meet him at the creek where they last spoke. He sat slumped, his head in his hands, but snapped to attention when Juana approached. She knew without asking that something was very wrong.

They embraced warmly. "You seem distressed, my friend," she said. "What is it?"

"You must reply to Sor Filotea's accusations," insisted the Bishop. Everyone was talking about it – clergy, booksellers, learned men of all ilk.

"No," said Juana. "We have had our fun. Let us just let it pass." But she knew that people were still talking about it, even now, nearly three months after it was published. Others begged her for a reply as well; booksellers loved the sales they were making, and some members of the clergy who had no love for the Archbishop stoked the fires.

Juana had survived numerous outbursts from envious poets who mocked her wit, from haughty businessmen who envied her influence with the Viceroy, from priests who saw her independence as an affront to religious hierarchy. For them all, Juana simply ignored their accusation; they were not worthy of her time. Critical debates settled down, yet these criticisms of the Sor Filotea papers continued.

"Juana, you have got to reply to Sor Filotea."

"What? Reply to a fictitious, arrogant nun who wrote an amusing critique?"

"The Archbishop does not find it amusing." She knew this to be true but refused to recognize how serious it could be. She also knew that the Bishop had not told her everything.

"What is it, my friend?" she asked. "There is more…"

He shook his head slowly, sadly. "Juana, I am so, so sorry that I got you into this. My arrogance overpowered my better judgement and I am on the brink of destroying one I love dearly. My punishment is to never feel the pleasure of your friendship again, to never even see you again."

"What? You cannot be serious. It was an amusing joke, that is all."

He spoke deliberately. "It is not only the Archbishop. Many others in the Church hierarchy do not consider it an amusing joke. They see it as an attack on the Church itself." He now chose his words very carefully. "Juana, you and I are being labeled as conspirators against the Church. Heretics."

A conspirator? No! A heretic? No! She was stunned. In all the accusations piled on her head, never once had she been accused of conspiracy against the Church, something that could indeed be a matter for the Inquisition. Her writing had been called "frivolous," "childish," "foolish," and Fray Miranda had constantly reminded her that she should focus on religious themes. But she had never been accused of being a heretic, a charge that could fling her into obscurity and degradation. A "conspirator against the Church" was an even more serious charge, the consequences of which she did not want to ponder, consequences that could most certainly include excommunication. As someone ripped from her entire heritage, she would no longer have friends, colleagues, or even acquaintances. She would truly be an outcast.

She knew well that for everyone counted as an ally, there was another opposing her every breath, another jealous of her success, another who wanted her destroyed. The lines had now been drawn.

The Bishop's voice filtered through a haze. "Juana, use your pen to cleave a rift between us. Separately we can survive. I pour mountains of treasure into the Archbishop's war chest, and can do more. I rarely come to la Ciudad de México, but hide away in my own province. I can be ignored."

The Bishop knew well that, not only was Puebla a very wealthy province economically, but that under his guidance its landowners contributed more than double what the businessmen of La Ciudad de México gave to the Church. This was an important source of revenue for the Archbishop, one he would not relinquish easily.

She nodded.

"With your wit and popularity, the Archbishop dare not do anything too dramatic to silence you. You can survive in La Ciudad de México, relatively safely, by yourself."

Again, she nodded.

"But together we are seen as a powerful conspiracy, which in truth, should we choose to use our power, we would be. I do not want such a confrontation with the Church."

"Nor do I."

Juana paced, tracing her steps around several of the massive oaks as if looking for someone, or something, to spring out with an alternative, pacing through the trees as if in an insoluble labyrinth.

A half hour passed. An hour. No alternative emerged. The Bishop sat, deep in contemplation. She could see no other option.

"Are you certain?" she asked at last.

"Yes … yes. Juana, I am very certain"

Juana would never presume to have that much power herself, although she knew her influence was substantial. But her power, combined with that of the Bishop, yes, that would be a formidable opponent to anyone. Any astute administrator would shatter that power before it took him down.

"Juana, I am so sorry …" His arms fell, battle worn and weary.

"I know, my dear friend."

They sat in silence for a long while, each searching for ideas, for words. There simply were none.

"I know, my dear friend," she finally said sadly. "Know too that you will be in my every prayer, and perhaps one day we can meet again."

"Yes. Perhaps."

There by the brook they stood in silence, each silently hoping that the damned Archbishop would get out of Nueva España, out of their lives, that their beloved city would shine once more. He pressed her hands to his heart, their hearts broken as only two dear friends can feel when they part … forever. They had crossed the line in the Archbishop's world, and now, to protect each other, they had to pay the price. He watched her for a long time, slowly trudging back to San Jerónimo's, the approaching storm clouds obliterating every trace of her shadow. He had protected her in the only way he knew. He prayed it would be enough. It was now up to Juana to create the public rift between them.

SEVERAL DAYS PASSED before Juana could even take out a piece of parchment, and when she did, she sat and looked at it for a very long time. Words came easily to Juana. Poetry flowed easily, plays nearly wrote themselves, and writing complex *villancicos* brought her immense joy.

But this writing was so different. It was not poetry, or a play, or a celebration.

Yes, she thought, *Sor Filotea's epistle is an irreverent bit of humor. So shall this be.*

Yes, Sor Filotea spoke to Church doctrine. So shall I.

Yes, as the Bishop said, I must sever our ties, for his sake and mine.

But NO, I will not, I cannot be silent. If indeed the Inquisition gags me, then this writing must set forth my strong conviction on the right of women to learn, to study, and to teach. I must defend myself as an intelligent woman.

Ultimately this brilliant epistle reeked of solicitous irony, and serious attack.

"My most illustrious Señora," she began, launching into a lengthy apology for not replying sooner, respecting the humorous persona of this "Sor Filotea de la Cruz," and qualifying the qualities of "silence," no doubt a veiled aside on the Archbishop's silence toward her. She flowed into several amusing, but less than accurate, anecdotes about her childhood, like how she learned to read when she was only two years old, alerting her reader that if he so chose, he could read the *Reply* as a light dissertation.

She commiserated about her lack of instruction in logic, rhetoric, physics, music, arithmetic, geometry, architecture, history, law, and astrology, then proceeded to prove her expertise in every single discipline.

She lamented the fact that men had a great many more choices in their lives than women. She acknowledged her own lack of religious knowledge, then proceeded to draw on the collective wisdom of dozens of illustrious, educated women. She looked to religion and found Debbora, the Queen of Sheba, Abigail, Esther, Rahab, and Anna. She looked to the classics and noted the Sybils, Minerva, Polla Argentaria, Tiersias' daughter, Zenobia, daughter of Aristippus, and many more. She called on other educated women in contemporary society – Queen Isabel, Queen Alexandra of Sweden, and others.

But, of course, she was but a woman, a simple nun.

She built a strong case for older, educated women to teach younger women and girls.

And, yes, she condemned an unnamed person for betraying her trust. It was a small mention, just the kind astute readers love to discover.

Bam! Bam! Bam! In her finest style she led the reader to stand beside her, to light up the absurdity of the arguments against her.

The whole of its pages – of which there were many – spilled knowledge that few, if any, in the world of Nueva España letters could begin to challenge. The treatise was not her chosen form of communication, but she used it here with precise aim at her critics.

She made only three copies, placing them in the hands of prelates "to review," knowing full well it would be copied again and again, spreading its venom throughout Nueva España. While the *Reply* did not overcome the vindictive hatred of the Archbishop and others in the Church hierarchy, it did quell public mumblings against her, and in severing her relationship with the Bishop of Puebla, it served to protect him.

She too was protected, for the time being.

SHE STOOD in the small locutory where her dear friend Sor Sophia had played the songs of birds on her little flute, aching to hear those songs again.

The golden canopy of autumn had settled in. A gentle rain blessed the trees, dripping down her face and drenching her habit. She deeply wanted someone to talk with, but there was no one … no one. Doña Leonor had passed away years previously, as had Sor Sophia. Writing to Maria Luisa was not the answer, for she was certain that their letters were intercepted.

And now even the Bishop of Puebla was out of reach. She turned to the only person she knew she could completely trust, and knelt before la Virgen de Guadalupe.

"*Por favor*," she whispered. "*Por favor*."

$$\mathcal{R}eclama\ los\ cuerpos,\ uno\ por$$
$$uno\ (\mathcal{C}laim\ the\ \mathcal{B}odies,\ \mathcal{O}ne\ by$$
$$\mathcal{O}ne)$$

May 1691

"POR FAVOR, SEÑOR, por favor," begged Juana's friend Xipil. "Just a little grain for my children."

Xipil stood with his friends at the entrance to one of the grain silos near La Ciudad de México, armed guards aiming their rifles at his chest.

Now in its third year, this famine, this incessant rainfall that drowned crops, spewed havoc on all of Nueva España. Three years of torrential rains, three years of decayed crops, three years of no sustenance for any but the ruling classes. What began as simply high prices morphed into rationing, then into oblivion. The poor could not even resort to theft, for there was none to steal. All the meager crops were stored in silos under armed guard ruled by the Viceroy. The only hope was to bribe the guards, guards who more than once had killed pilgrims at the silos.

"Please señor, I can pay for the grain." Xipil held out the hundred pesos that Juana had given him. She came often to his hut with bread and wheat and sometimes even vegetables, things that would keep them alive.

"Give it here!" The Major in charge held out his hand.

Xipil rushed up to the Major, putting the hundred pesos in his outstretched hand, elated that his family would eat that night. The Major stuffed the hundred pesos in his pocket, then raised his gun over his head, and with direct aim smashed the butt of his rifle into Xipli's shoulder.

"Get out, you stinking turd! Come back when you have real money." The guards sneered, like they were watching a cockroach being smashed.

Xipil, stunned, with his shoulder in pain, started to rise. "Por favor, señor, the hundred pesos," he begged. "I need it to feed my children."

The closest guard let fly with his heavy boot, kicking Xipil under his chin, sending him careening backwards, leaving him sprawled, face down in the mud. Two of Xipil's friends rushed to carry him to safety.

Xipil returned home, empty handed, with no food, no money, his whole body aching, torn up from the beating. Juana was waiting for him at his hut, and with the nursing skills she had learned serving at the Convent's hospital, set to work to put him back together. She came often to their hut, sneaking out of the convent in the shadows. With men's clothing and a brown cape, she slipped easily through back alleys, bringing them food that kept them alive, and money to buy more. Tonight, she looked sad, but determined.

"Xipil, I cannot continue to bring you as much food as I have been. Even our rations have been cut and the nuns who were helping me cannot give as much."

Xipil's anger spilled out. "Are we all to starve? All but the rich government officials and soldiers?" He slammed his fist on the wall, collapsing, his head on his arm.

"No, Xipil," said Juana. "I have a plan. As you know, most of the bishops all over Nueva España hoard the grain and sell it at exorbitant profits or have relinquished their grain to be stored here, under the authority of the Viceroy. All except the Bishop of Puebla. He has been stock piling the grain in his region too, but he is different. He sells the grain at a low price so everyone can afford it. Puebla is a rich agricultural area, and the Bishop has been helping many hundreds of families."

"What is that to us, Sor Juana?" asked Xipil. "He is not our bishop."

"Xipil, that Bishop is my dear friend. He will help you. Here," she said, placing her ring in his hand. "Show him this ring. Tell the Bishop that this is the ring that Archbishop Payo placed on my finger at my initiation ceremony at la Gran Catedral de la Ciudad de México, and that I am begging him to help you. He will understand. Do not speak with anyone else, just the Bishop. And here," she said as she handed Xipil a few coins. "Please visit la Capilla de Nuesta Señora del Rosario and light a candle"

"In whose honor shall I light this candle?" he asked.

"In honor of the love that Christ has brought to our lives."

The Bishop of Puebla did help Xipil, very generously, and told him and his two traveling companions to return any time and he would personally ensure that they all had food.

SOR JUANA WAS at Xipil's hut when he returned a week later, as she had been every day, ministering to Tochtli. This once saucy little dancer laid in bed, her cheeks caved in from hunger, her spindly arms at her side. She had been giving her meager portions to her grandchildren, starvation now taking its toll on her tender frame.

The family floated, ghostly shadows preparing a tea for her from bits of wood and leaves scrounged from the countryside. Juana's small packet of food, scraps that Sara had gathered from other nuns, had already gone into the soup pot. Juana knew she was not bringing much, even with her own meager rations included, but it was all she could find, and she trusted the family to make a soup that would help them live for another day.

"Tonight we shall eat!" declared Xipil, setting down his bundle of food.

"And tomorrow?" Xipilli, the *Jeweled Warrior*, Tochtli's son, sat, holding his madre's small body in his arms.

"We will eat for a few days," said Xipil, the patriarch of the family. "We will share what we can. In a few days everything may change." His voice carried an ominous foreshadow.

"What is it?" Sor Juana asked.

"I am not certain, Señora, but I know here …" Xipil hit his gut with his fist. "I know here that something will change. Soon." He paused to gather in the whole family, his brothers, their wives, the children and grandchildren, everyone crowded around. "All along the journey, both going and coming back, we heard tales of misery. Children are dying of starvation. There is no food. There is no money. Whole fields of crops lay drowned in torrential rains, fit only for the weevils to eat. And yet the Governors eat. The soldiers eat. The wealthy eat. Everywhere but Puebla. In Puebla everyone eats."

He stooped to kiss Sor Juana's shoe. "Blessed Sor Juana, you will be in our prayers every moment of every day, for your kindness alone is saving our family."

A young man stepped forward. "Uncle, what are we to do?"

Xipil spoke with the authority of a military captain. "First, we will gather information. We will spread out through all the sections of La Ciudad de México. We will gauge the temper of the people and discover what is being planned. And we will gather weapons – anything we can find … knives … clubs … bows and arrows. Whatever happens, we must be prepared to defend ourselves."

Then, three days later, it happened.

THE OMENS had all lined up. In August 1691 a solar eclipse foretold of ill times, followed by the devil's rains that destroyed adobe homes and flooded La Ciudad de México, followed by a plague of weevils that ate all the maize and wheat left standing, culminating in the country-wide starvation. Coal, firewood, fruit, vegetables, meat, and fowl all disappeared from the Mexican landscape.

The Archbishop launched the clergy into a melee of religious action with prayers and public flagellations in every monastery, in every convent. Even the *Virgen de los Remedios* was taken from her usual throne to become the centerpiece at la Gran Catedral de la Ciudad de México in the heart of La Ciudad de México with constant prayers begging her intercession for mercy.

The Viceroy, Count Galve, was young, only thirty-five years old, and woefully inexperienced. His Excellency, Gaspar de la Cerda Silva Sandoval, 8th Count of Galve, Lord of Salcedon and Tortola, this Viceroy with more names than brains, this Viceroy in his esteemed wisdom, did what he always did -- he held meetings. Lots of meetings. But he did nothing more than guard the silos for his own use. He was condemned from every pulpit, condemned by Criolles and village clergymen alike. A sermon by Fray Antonio de Escary on Easter Sunday in la Gran Catedral de la Ciudad de México was so vicious that it was a virtual call to violence. Viceroy Galve blocked out this inflamed sermon, even from his pew in the front row.

In April, Viceroy Galve had commandeered all the grain throughout central Nueva España and had it brought to tightly guarded silos in la Ciudad de México.

All except for the province of Puebla.

When soldiers approached the silos at Puebla, they found the Bishop at the gates, blocking their way. "The grain will be soaked in my blood before I allow you to take food out of mouths of my people!"

There was no doubt that he meant it. The Bishop of Puebla had purchased all the grain in his region, at very high prices, and had re-sold it to the people of Puebla, at very low prices. He was not about to allow fat politicians get it.

All the rest of the grain was centralized in la Ciudad de México, and now rumors had spread that supplies had run out. People from every corner of la Ciudad de México rushed the granary doors, desperate to grab onto whatever handfuls of grain they could. The guards pushed everyone back, but people kept coming … dozens of them … hundreds of them … all starving people, torches and improvised cannons demanding access to their only source of food.

*"Food for my children…"   "My beloved madre is starving…"
"Mercy, I beg of you, mercy…"   "My son has eaten nothing
in four days … nothing…"   "My baby is so hungry he can't
even cry any more …"   "Your heart cannot be this hard…"*

"Only a little, por favor, just a little …"

Pleas piled on top of pleas, each more desperate than the next. All classes of Nueva España – the Criolles, the Indians, the Chinese, the Mezita, every mixed blood – merged in this desperate attempt to grab onto a few grains of the last remaining food in La Ciudad de México.

The smoldering pot that was La Ciudad de México spewed fumes for two more months, but now, on June 7th it blew apart.

The guards stood firm, shoulder to shoulder.

"My baby, my baby. He needs just a little, por favor, por favor." A pregnant Indian woman rushed forward in front of the crowd, stepping up the incline toward the silo, raising her arms to beg for just a bit of grain. A young soldier stomped forward to stop her. His eyes grew large, his beardless chin quivered as he raised his heavy gun and smashed it into her belly. His eyes bulged, disbelieving what he had done, as he fled the hill, vomiting.

OOOOOOOH. A collective gasp ignited the crowd.

Then silence.

The Indian woman held onto her belly convulsed with pain. She reached under her belly, trying desperately to stop the birthing pains shooting through her. A coterie of women from all classes knelt around her, protecting her, helping her. But their ministrations did not work. In but a few minutes there was a small fetus, stillborn, and a few minutes later the Indian woman took her last breath, her face skewed in pain, her blood staining the mud for yards around.

The crowd passed a wooden plank and set it beside the woman. Xipil and his brothers stepped forward, offering to carry the dead Indian woman and her baby. A Criolla woman respectfully turned them away.

"This is for us to do," she said.

The crowd fell to its knees, praying for Christ's mercy.

Eight women, Criollas and Aztecs alike, gently set the two bodies on the plank, and slowly carried the plank to the Plaza Mayor. Across the Plaza, step by step, the whole entourage quietly embraced their journey. They went to the huge door leading to the offices of Archbishop Francisco de Aguiar. This Archbishop who could not set eyes on any woman refused to see them.

The women led the hundreds of protestors slowly across the Plaza Mayor to el Palacio del Virrey, asking to speak with Viceroy Galve. They desperately wanted to show him what his cruel policies had birthed, but were again refused entry. It would not have mattered if they were allowed in, for Viceroy Galve and his wife had already left el Palacio for the relative security of a walled monastery. There the Viceroy made a decision. Now that the outlying silos were empty, he ordered that all militia within a two day's journey to come to the capital immediately, readying for any battle that might erupt.

It was Friday night. Members of the insurrection kept vigil over the two corpses all night, and on Saturday hundreds gathered to bury them in the church graveyard, led by several priests sympathetic to their cause. Sor Juana stood by Xipil and his family at that service. Hundreds of people recognized this small nun in her black and white habit, bowing their heads as they passed her.

Many had been injured in the rush at the silo, so Juana set to work with the meager supplies she could gather from the hospital.

"My little parakeet, is that you?"

It was the irrepressible Doña Caterina Rosa, not in one of her resplendent gowns, but dressed in a simple pale blue frock, carrying a large basket. She was about twenty yards away, her contagious smile brightening a grey day as Juana rose to greet her dear friend. Caterina began to run toward Juana just as thudding hooves shook the ground around them. A contingent of thirty mounted militia flew around the corner behind Juana. Juana spun, frantically waving her arms to stop the horses as they careened closer.

"STOP!" she screamed, her voice silenced by the thundering hoof beats.

Xipil grabbed Juana around her waist, dragging her out of the path of the horsemen.

"AIIIIEEE!" It was a woman's scream, a scream that echoed long after Doña Caterina had been ripped apart by the raging steeds. Caterina could not get out of the way in time. In but a few seconds her beautiful face was split in half, her pale blue gown ripped in shreds and soaked in her own blood, her body torn apart, one severed hand still holding the basket that spewed fresh vegetables, bread, and medicines for yards around, all now smashed into the mud.

Juana rushed to Caterina's side. "You bastards!" she screamed to the skies. "Look what you have done. Just look. She brought you nothing but joy, and now look. Just look." There was no one to kick, no one to punch. All she could do was pound her fierce fists into the open air.

Weeping uncontrollably, she picked up pieces of Caterina's body, as if trying to glue them back together again. She picked up a severed foot, searching the mud for the leg it once belonged to. Xipil lifted Sor Juana by her shoulders, gently leading her back to Tochtli's hut.

"Why? Why?" Juana was in stunned disbelief. "What was she even doing here?"

"She once lived here," said Xipil. "She took her family to live with her in a beautiful hacienda in the center of la Ciudad de México, but she has been coming here for years, with food, medicines, clothes, just like you have, Sor Juana."

Juana could pinpoint the moment when La Ciudad de México began to change, for her memories returned to Fray Payo's time as Archbishop and Viceroy, to the quiet times, to the bountiful artistic times, then to the arrival of Archbishop Francisco de Aguiar and the stinking pall he threw over the land. Although she chastised herself for doing so, she could not stop herself from wishing – yes, praying -- that Archbishop Francisco de Aguiar were dead.

SATURDAY PASSED with an undercurrent of discontent in la Ciudad de México as Viceroy Galve's armies converged on the city to quell any uprising. Both sides, however, were poised for whatever came.

At Sunday mass the Viceroy was pummeled with threats from other worshippers and from poor Indians lining the streets outside the church. And the crowd grew. What was once a few dozen protestors grew to several hundred, then to thousands, crowding every street throughout the entire city. – men, women, and children from every caste. "Justice!" they demanded. "Food!" they demanded.

They got neither justice nor food. All they got were armed militia forcing them back, then further back, and when they could go no further, the soldiers opened fire on them. Thousands of shots rang through the streets of La Ciudad de México, indiscriminately killing hundreds of men, women, and children. The entire Plaza Mayor was awash with the blood of protesters, bodies piled on top of bodies.

Those protesters still standing tore apart the wooden vendors' carts in the Plaza, setting the makeshift flares aflame, and tossing those flares into the windows and courtyards of el Palacio de Virrey, and setting fire to the buildings housing the homes and offices of government officials throughout the entire central region of la Ciudad de México.

Families came to claim these bodies – their children, their mothers, their fathers, their brothers and sisters, their neighbors -- and buried them in the graveyards of the churches throughout the City.

As the attacks continued into the night, Xipil escorted Sor Juana back to San Jerónimo's. He could not bear the thought that she too might be killed in the melee.

"Look!" said Juana as they passed a government office building. "There is another sign, just like the others." The sign read in scrawled letters "For rent: This chicken coop for local cocks and Spanish hens," a gross insult to the local government. The protesters made it clear that it was the local government that had caused the problem, not the government of España.

The protests continued for days. There was no leader of the protesters; rather, it was a spontaneous uprising. With no leaders, Viceroy Galve claimed he had no one to negotiate with, and no apology ensued. He simply let word get out that the people of la Ciudad de México had "misunderstood his actions," and he wrapped a net around several hundred more protesters at random and had them all killed, men, women and even children. The killing was again in the Plaza Mayor, with the bodies laid out in the sun for everyone to see, children still gripping the skirts of their madres.

And the families came – again – and claimed the bodies – again. And again, they were buried in church graveyards, officiated by local priests.

Xipil came to claim the body of Xippili, *the Jeweled Warrior*, his nephew. With such limited food, Tochtli had died too.

Miraculously, the Church was not held responsible for the tragedies that crashed on La Ciudad de México. After all, it was not the Church that withheld food, and it was not the Church that sent militia to kill the protesters. And local priests stood beside them as the dead were buried.

The people desperately needed to believe in something, and that "something" was the Church.

The people's hatred soaked the local government, especially Viceroy Galve. Oddly, the Spanish government did not see it fit to recall Viceroy Galve, and the discontent simmered for many years, even when signs of famine finally eased throughout the country.

It was but a few weeks later, with starvation still ripping la Ciudad de México apart, that Fray Arellano, Sor Juana's confessor for the past decade, summoned her to his office.

Los cuernos del diablo (The Horns of the Devil)

"I CAN NO LONGER protect you as I had wished. I can no longer be your confessor." Fray Arellano spoke gently.

"Are you dismissing me?" Juana was startled, and sad.

"No, Sor Juana, no. I will be here as long as you want me to be here. But there are vicious winds blowing in la Ciudad de México, and you may need more protection than I can give you. You would do well to seek that protection now, before it becomes more serious."

She too had felt an icy wind, a wind with no beginning and no end, a cyclone that engulfed the entire city.

Fray Arellano was not timid. His long-respected presence in la Ciudad de México had taught him well how to wend his way through a labyrinth of confrontations, but he could no longer avoid a severe clash with the Church hierarchy.

Juana knew it too. That ill wind was challenging her ties with the intelligencia of Nueva España, as fewer commissions arrived at her desk. Now she was standing on a precipice. She stood on one side of her survival, with Fray Miranda and Archbishop Francisco de Aguiar on the other. If she had ever hoped to flourish again, to write again, to publish again, she had to find a way to mend that chasm.

Juana did have strong support in the Spanish court. Maria Luisa's brother-in-law was now the Chief Majordomo in España, with the ear of Queen Maria Anna, a formidable post. Both former Viceroys, the Count de Parades, and the Marquis de Mancera, had always been staunch supporters of Sor Juana. The Marquis de Mancera's two brothers also held high posts in the Spanish court. Without the former Viceroys uttering a word, Archbishop Francisco de Aguiar knew that the Crown would smash him should he challenge Sor Juana too openly. But they were in España where even important communications consumed months of letters. Those months of waiting gave the Archbishop Francisco de Aguiar more options than he had ever had. The door of his revenge was cracking open.

This was especially true since the current Viceroy, one Count Galve, placed his loyalties at the seat of Archbishop Francisco de Aguiar before his loyalties to lower ranking prelates, and certainly above his loyalty to nuns. Viceroy Galve did not dislike Sor Juana, he simply placed her lower on his scale of importance. La Vicereine Galve followed her husband's example. Clearly Sor Juana could not look to them for protection.

She needed protection in Nueva España.

With few options remaining, she had to lure Fray Miranda to be her protector once more. The odds against her accomplishing this on her own were incalculable, and anyone else would have given up before trying. But Sor Juana Inés de la Cruz was not anyone else. As one of the most brilliant negotiators of her generation, she knew she could find the way. She was no stranger to the politics of the Church. She had to believe she could find the way again, for the alternative – isolation and ridicule – was too horrific to imagine.

She knelt in front of la Virgen de Guadalupe, the one that her nurse Rosita gave her long ago, and she prayed. She prayed for guidance. She prayed for mercy. She prayed with a full heart and a bleeding soul. For days and days, she prayed, barely stopping for a sip of tea. Her devoted slave Sara cared for her, with a shawl to stay the evening chill, with tea and broth to build her strength.

Finally, when the last tear was dry, when she had thanked the beloved Virgen de Guadalupe a hundred times, finally with the aid of Sara she stood slowly, stepped to her writing desk, picked up a piece of parchment and selected a sharpened quill. She waited until her hand stopped its incessant shaking, then began.

Your Reverence, Most Righteous and Honorable Fray Antonio Munez de Miranda,

I write on bended knee in awe of the relentless work you have done in aiding the poor, the humbled, the distraught people of our country. Truly, your praises are sung in every chapel, in every cathedral, in every home in the land, as well they should, for the unceasing work you have done for God's people. Truly, I do not believe the world has ever known another of your stature, or your kindness. I think upon the thousands of souls you have brought to God's sanctuary, the thousands of poor who have benefitted from your blessed generosity, the tireless work you pursue day and night to bring God's word to the far reaches of Nueva España, and I am humbled beyond measure.

… I do not know what angel led me to your ecclesiastical nobility, only that I was very blessed to have received the wisdom of Your Grace's counsel when I needed it the most. My deepest regret is that I did not listen to your guidance as I should have, I did not mold my ways to meet the demands of the Church as I should have, I did not focus on the beauty of the Church that surrounded me every moment as I should have, and in neglecting all of this I did seriously err.

… I write to you now as your most humble servant, as one who has felt so deeply the loss of your wise counsel, as one too miserably unworthy to see even your shadow. Yet I must crawl to you, prostrated in grief that I was so foolish that I tossed aside the wisdom of your counsel. It was your sage counsel that brought me to San Jerónimo, and for that I shall be forever indebted to you. It was your wise counsel that summoned me to use my God-gifted talent as a celebration of Him -- I could rip my heart out in grief that I did not follow your counsel. It was your wise counsel that guided me for years through the crooked corridors of life, a counsel that I very foolishly set aside.

… My soul yearns for the wisdom of your guidance once more. I ask of you – yea, I beg of you – to permit a conversation between us. I yearn to prove to you that I am worthy of your wisdom and kindnesses yet once again. You have gifted me as many kindnesses as there are stars in the heavens, and I do hesitate to beg for more, and yet I must. You are truly, most Gracious and Generous Counselor, the only one who can lead my soul to salvation.…

I remain the most wretched of all women, and the most humble of all your servants, S. Juana Inés de la Cruz

The words flowed easily onto the parchment, guided by the hand of the Virgin herself. Juana re-read the letter, now several pages long, and, satisfied with its message, sent it to Fray Miranda via messenger.

Then she left the convent grounds, walking slowly toward la Capilla de la Virgen de Guadalupe on the outskirts of La Ciudad de México. Too many pilgrims pushed up to the image, lighting candles and touching the cloth, so she waited.

Long after the first stars of the night had appeared, she stood alone in the chapel, close to her beloved Virgin. Touching the cloth softly, she knelt once again and begged for Her intercession. The mystery of la Virgen de Guadalupe continued to awe Juana, as it did all in Nueva España. The cloth that she just touched was over 200 years old, and it should have crumbled in her hand, or at the very least should have felt like soot from the dozens of candles lit nearby, all day, every day, for years on end. But the cloth did not fall apart, and it did not feel odd. It felt like freshly woven cotton, the traditional cloth of the peasants of Nueva España. She remained all night, standing to leave only as new pilgrims arrived at first dawn. Fray Gilberto stood at the door, ready to greet Sor Juana, as he so often did.

"What troubles you, my child?" he asked. "You appear to be wrapped in a burden."

"I am, Reverencia," she replied. "I came to la Virgen, hoping for a solution."

"I have seen you here many times, Sor Juana, always beseeching the Blessed Virgin for intercession. Perhaps if you used your gifts to write a poem for the Virgin Herself, well, that might influence Her some."

"I've written many dozens of poems and songs in honor of la Virgen de Guadalupe," she said, a bit confused.

"Yes, but they were all commissions. You were paid for writing those poems and songs. Now write something just for Her."

Juana smiled. She recalled when sadness overwhelmed her at the death of Leonor, and how writing soothed her; and the death of Sor Sophia, and how a simple plea to the Virgin quieted her restlessness. She understood, and rushed home to San Jerónimo to write the most splendid poem she had ever written. For the next several days she wrote relentlessly, not caring that her fingers ached or her back groaned from bending over her desk. The words flowed miraculously, and when she finished, she knew she had written a poem unlike anything she had ever written before.

"May I copy that for you?" Sara offered her assistance.

"No. This is the only copy I need."

She returned to la Capilla de la Virgen de Guadalupe that night, and again waited until she was alone. She knelt before la Virgen and read her poem softly, not spoken to an audience, but spoken to Her Lady's heart. She sat for a while and let the gentleness of the moment settle around her. Then she took a white candle from the altar and lit the parchment, letting it turn to ash in a silver dish. She left early the next dawn, content that The Lady had received her gift with joy.

THEN SOR JUANA WAITED for a response from Fray Miranda.

She waited all that day. And the next. And the next. She waited for over two weeks, sitting patiently in her cell, trying to focus her feelings, each day becoming a bit edgier. Yes, there were hundreds of reasons why Fray Miranda might not have responded to her letter, but what if he simply ignored her? What if he refused? What would her life become with absolutely no one to speak on her behalf? Would she never greet another guest in the locutory? Would she never have another commission for a loa, or a song? Would no one ever call her name again? The people who turned their backs when she passed, that cut the deepest, an old rusted knife churning her gut.

Finally, she could stand it no longer. She took up another piece of parchment and wrote a much shorter letter. She wrote that she prayed for his well-being with every breath, and she asked him directly,

> *"Please, most exalted Reverencia, what can I do to bring you to forgive my unforgiveable arrogance? I will do as you request."*

THE LETTER was delivered to Fray Miranda when he was talking with Archbishop Francisco de Aguiar. Fray Miranda started to toss it in the open fire.

"Miranda, what angers you so much that you would burn it?" asked the Archbishop.

"Another empty plea from the heretic nun. She wants me to return as her confessor." Fray Miranda knew better than to utter a woman's name in the presence of the Archbishop.

The Archbishop pounded his huge desk. "That ingrate who dared to criticize the respected clergy of Nueva España? The enchantress who lured the eyes of España to her blasphemous ramblings? The conniving nun who dared entwine three Viceroys to her will of demonic practice?"

"Yes," confirmed Miranda. "She arrogantly dismissed me as her confessor a few years ago, in favor of the spineless Arellano, and now she has decided that I am the only one who can save her soul. Pure poppycock!" Her face emerged through the cracks in the wall. Miranda smashed his fist into that image, leaving but veins of rage racing across the wall.

The Archbishop held up his hand. "Perhaps she is right, Miranda." The Archbishop spoke deliberately, slyly, for now he saw that his own prayers were answered. "Your gift for salvation of souls is recognized throughout the land. This girl needs strong guidance from someone who can silence her screeching voice, from someone who can strangle her spells and lead her back to a religious life."

Fray Miranda swung around to face the Archbishop. "Are you commanding me to accept this assignment?"

The Archbishop knew Fray Miranda well from decades of being allies. "No, Miranda, I am not commanding you. I only ask that you consider it. You may be the only one in all Nueva España who can silence her. Pray upon it." He paused, then added, "Shut … her … up." He picked up the inkwell that sat on his desk, and with an immense fury he threw it into the fire, visions of the heretic witch winding through the smoky flames, launching him into a diatribe of profanities.

"Do you know what that heretic witch has done? She had turned the entire Spanish clergy against me. Just look at this." He handed a sheaf of parchments to Fray Miranda, and there it was, page after page after page of praise for this disgusting woman:

> "Brilliant! …" was but the first word of an effusive, multi-paragraph praise from a highly respected Spanish cleric.

"For decades she hid behind a Viceroy. Well, she cannot do that anymore, so she crawls like a slimy worm, begging for protection behind the sacred vestments of the Spanish clergy." Little did the Archbishop know that it was the Countess Maria Luisa who approached each priest individually, asking for such endorsements, and with her long list of extremely generous donations, they were eager to please.

"Sor Juana Inés de la Cruz takes her place among the greatest theologians of Europe…" began another entry that stretched over three pages.

"This screeching heretic stirs coals in her evil well, the hand of the Devil himself on her shoulder. They have never deigned to praise the theologians of Nueva España with such drippy words." The Archbishop was beyond being furious.

"Stunning ideas wrapped in gossamer poetry…" The priest who wrote this gave example after example of her exquisite writing.

"The Unique Queen of Poetry" wrote another, claiming that "the verses of Sor Juana are as pure as she is."

"Clearly, gender does not comprise intelligence…"

"… matchless theologian …"

"… celebrated woman and of all illustrious women the exemplar…"

"… We have found our Tenth Muse!"

"This woman is a man in every respect."

Over forty sheets of parchment, all in praise of her poetry, written by over twenty respected priests in España. Four of those priests were even Jesuits. Not even one admonished her for her devotion to petty secular letters.

While that would have been enough to enflame any sensible priest, the Chief Inquisitor in Madrid, Fray Miranda's counterpart, had the audacity to write that the writings were in keeping with the teachings of the Church, and praised her for her religious work.

"That arrogant Chief Inquisitor has no authority to judge her; that judgment is for Nueva España's Inquisition alone. It belongs to me!" Fray Miranda's eyes bulged at the gross insult from the Spanish Chief Inquisitor.

The Archbishop paced -- hard, measured steps -- slashing his hands in the air as if to gore her. "She has lured the clergy of España into her den of hell. She has snatched authority away from me – and you! – making us look like trained monkeys, subservient to their whip. She has placed herself above all other writers and theologians in New Span – all of them – when she is nothing but a savage, spineless girl better suited to the sewers than a convent."

"She hides behind the fact that other nuns are allowed to write."

"Pure poppycock! Other nuns write sweet devotionals calling on visions of the Virgin. No other nun writes the blasphemy that this one does. The Devil himself cast flaming coals into her quill, each word that she writes is entangled in lewd black magic, not in righteousness. She has cast devious spells on our Spanish brethren, and uses them for her erotic purposes."

The Archbishop paused, then slowing, added, "She is but a cur who hides behind Spanish robes. Are we no more than peons in the fields? No! We are the rulers of Nueva España. It is our duty – OUR duty -- to return her to Christ."

"Where are the poems that these priests refer to?" asked Fray Miranda.

"I have not got copies of them yet. My colleague in España felt these pages were so savage that he had them copied and shipped to me immediately. I expect to get the witch's writings in the next shipment." He could not deign to call them "poems," they were simply "witch's writings." He turned to face Fray Miranda and said again, "SHUT … HER … UP."

FRAY MIRANDA KNEW his assignment, and it was not optional. Before he responded to Sor Juana's plea, there was one thing he had to set to rest. Rumors still flew about her questionable heritage, and he knew she was from the province where he once took a babe late one night. And once, in a dream trance, he had seen her face on the babe that he took to Fray Miguel. He did not know what it meant, and until now it did not matter. But now it mattered.

He summoned Fray Miguel de Asbaje, the country friar who once took a babe from his charge.

Fray Miguel felt the urgency in the summons, and arrived in la Ciudad de México the very next day. He was escorted to Fray Miranda's sparce cell, where he waited for over two hours. Fray Miguel dared not to even sit, for he knew well Fray Miranda's notorious temper. The cold damp walls of this cell pushed the chill into Fray Miguel's bones as he wrapped himself ever tighter in his cotton robe.

Fray Miranda flew into the room, bringing the fire of Hell with him. The interview was abrupt.

"Fray Miguel, do you recall the baby that I brought to you nearly forty years ago?"

"Yes, Your Reverence, I do recall that event."

"What happened to that child?"

"I entrusted her to a local family."

Fray Miranda spun, facing this insignificant friar, nose to nose. "Her? Was it not a boy child?"

"No, Reverencia, it was a girl child."

A girl? Fray Miranda had always assumed it was a boy child, although he had no reason to make that assumption except that a female baby would be an unforgiveable affront to its father. "The name? What was its name?" Fray Miranda was now highly agitated.

Fray Miranda had previously admonished him to not name the family, so even now, decades later, Fray Miguel spoke only of a "local family." "I entrusted her to the Ramírez family, to Doña Isobel Ramírez."

Fray Miranda shook the walls with his shouting. "Its name? What was its name?"

Fray Miguel quivered in all ill-defined trepidation. "Juana Inés Ramírez."

Madre sagrada de Jesús! No! Fray Miranda refused to accept it, spitting the words through his teeth. His voice plummeted to a raspy whisper. "What happened to the child?"

Fray Miguel took a step backward. He did not know why, but he did not want to be the one to bring the news. "She became Sor Juana Inés de la Cruz, at San Jerónimo convent. Surely you know her, Reverencia."

Fray Miranda hit his fist on the table, ripping it in half.

"That will be all, Fray Miguel." Furious, Fray Miranda turned away.

"But there is something else I must tell you, Reverencia." Fray Miguel did not want to speak, but it had to be said. He froze, unable to move an inch.

"Well, speak man, speak!" demanded Fray Miranda.

"Once, many years ago, there was a cousin of the child, a young man, a Don Diego Esteban Ramírez, who inquired about this child. I denied any knowledge of her, of course. But he left angry."

"What does he know?"

"He saw only the church ledger, listing her name and identifying her as a 'child of God.' Nothing more."

Fray Miranda waved the old padre away, then sank onto his chair. He sat silent, his head in his hands. Confusion swirled around his scrawny form, crushing his shoulders. Then he bolted upright. *Yes!* he thought. THIS was what he needed to end this curse, to bend her to his will. He could silence her blasphemous pen forever, as the Archbishop wished, and he could make her regret that she had ever challenged his authority. And, yes, her soul would be saved in the process. This was truly the God-given path to follow.

SHE TRUDGED over the cobbled streets to the interrogation room, as she had every day for the past week, a murder of crows hunched down on the dank wall bordering the path to the nearly hidden doorway. A small, sparse space in the catacombs of the Archbishop's palacio, it exuded more steamy putrid odors than sweet salvation. She took her place on one of the two chairs, the one facing away from the tiny window so that she would not be tempted to look out, explained Fray Miranda. The only decoration in the room was a simple wood carving of the Crucifixion and a plain wooden panel that Fray Miranda stood behind.

She lit the one candle on the small table, and waited.

She was to wait until Fray Miranda arrived, no matter when that occurred. The waiting was not accidental, for Fray Miranda had been the Censor of the Inquisition of Nueva España for many years and had honed his skills of interrogation well.

"Wait, you witch," he told her silently. "Just sit and wait. And pray."

"How much do you want to re-enter the good graces of the Church?" His question was cold, and direct.

"Very much, Reverencia." Her response was even tempered. "With every breath that I take."

"Enough to relinquish all your books?"

Her books. Her beloved books, even some that had belonged to her Abuelo. It was a bigger demand than she expected, yet it took her only a moment to decide that the books could be replaced once her position in La Ciudad de México society was re-established. "Yes, Reverencia, even that much."

"You are doing this willingly, of your own free mind?"

"Yes, Reverencia."

And so they began.

DURING THAT FIRST WEEK of interrogation Sor Juana had agreed to all of Fray Miranda's terms. She was to provide a complete confession of all her sins in preparation for the celebration of her twenty-fifth anniversary as a nun, and submit to whatever penance Fray Miranda demanded.

She could then submit her petition to the Inquisition itself for forgiveness of all her sins, and begin fresh in her twenty-fifth year of service to the Church. The Inquisition had relinquished the rack as punishment, as well as the other diabolical instruments it once used. Its punishments now focused on saving the soul of the petitioner.

How she yearned to take her place once more among the intelligencia of la Ciudad de México. No matter what Fray Miranda obligated her to do, she knew the reward at the end, so she knew she could do it.

This day she simply waited.

Fray Miranda had spent the night in his dank cell, a single candle lighting the pages of the Second Edition of her Works. The Archbishop's copy, the only copy in Nueva España, had just arrived. He saw the forty pages of absurd praise at the front of the volume. He saw the poetry from the First Edition, and the critique of Vierya's sermon. Then he saw something radically new, a poem titled "First Dream," a fireworks of blasphemy.

The words of this poem pulled at him like a ferocious magnet, his soul devouring the unholy visions of its tale.

How dare she believe that everyone … everyone, Popes and paupers alike … were equal?

How could she reach for pagan goddesses to help her, without so much as a mention of Christ?

Then he saw the last line, the line that identified the "soul" in the poem as feminine. It hit like a battering ram, slamming him into his seat, where he sat, stunned for the rest of the night.

It was time for him to strike.

THE BELLS FOR MATINS rang, and she slipped onto the concrete floor, sincerely praying for guidance, and thanking the Lord for granting her this opportunity to change her life. The sharp edges of the rugged stones on the floor cut through the callouses on her knees, forcing streams of blood to soak her habit.

Rising, she heard quick, slogging footsteps arriving, the sound of Fray Miranda slipping through the dark corridor.

She was ready for the interrogation on her treacherous times, knowing that to win her freedom, she could not win this debate. Fray Miranda had to feel superior, had to feel that he had conquered her, had to feel that he had forced out of her some juicy secrets he had not known before. Her years of writing dramas had prepared her well for this confrontation, this drama in the airless basement room.

Fray Miranda wasted not a minute in casual talk. He was on a mission.

"Yesterday you mentioned being admitted to la Vicereine Leonor's inner circle as a lady-in-waiting, your arrogance with the silk gowns and popularity amongst the Viceroy's guests." Sor Juana remained silent. Although she had not taken vows as a nun when she was at el Palacio, she was a Catholic, and she was responsible for her errant conduct even then. She had confessed those sins yesterday. Why was Fray Miranda bringing them up again?

"How often did you give alms to the poor?"

"Not nearly often enough. Indeed, rarely did I do so. I do confess that I deeply sinned."

"How often did you sell one of the fancy jewels these men gave you and donate the money to the Church?"

She could not tell the truth, that she was rarely gifted such jewels since she offered no sexual favors. He would not believe the reality, so she said, "Only once, Reverencia. I am guilty of greed and pride in the highest degree, and arrogance in not caring for those less fortunate than I. I do regret that I so deeply sinned."

"How often did you leave your frivolous life and pray devotions to Christ and to the Virgin?"

"Rarely, Reverencia. I am truly guilty of ignoring my salvation as a Christian, and I do confess to that."

"You went on various excursions with the lords and ladies of the Court, didn't you, Sor Juana?"

"Yes, Reverencia, there were many such excursions." What was he getting at?

"Did you or did you not protect your sacred virginity during these excursions?"

"Yes, Reverencia, I did indeed protect my sacred virginity." She was not alarmed at this line of questioning. She had known from the beginning that Fray Miranda fed on the sexual aberrations of his charges, that in fact he did not even like being bothered with "small" sins.

He stopped pacing and stood with his back to Sor Juana. "Who is your father, Sor Juana?" He did not have to look at her to feel her jerk to attention. He knew the effect that this question would have on her.

She spoke in a harsh whisper. "My mother Isobel tells me that my father is Don Pedro Manuel de Asbaje."

"Do you believe that?"

"Why should I not believe my mother?" Her voice was higher, and louder, than she would have wished.

"Do you know that Isobel Ramírez is truly your mother?"

Her mind spun, desperately searching for a reason for the question. "Why should I not believe that she is my mother?"

He paused dramatically. Then … "Because it is a lie."

He paused again, waiting for her to absorb the fact that he knew. "Don Pedro Manuel de Asbaje is not your father. Isobel Ramírez is not your mother."

"Then who is?" She heard herself blurt out the question, and instantly regretted it.

He saw the door of opportunity fling open. This was the moment of truth. He spun to face Sor Juana, smashing the wooden divider as he flung it to the wall, and for the first time in over four decades he looked into a woman's eyes, boring hatred into her deepest soul.

"You do not want to know, Juana. I do know who your father is. I do know who your mother is, and I promise you this: If you lie to me again, even once, I will tell the world what your heritage truly is, and you will not like it. Trust me, you … will not … like … it."

The searing hatred in his voice soaked into every crevice of the room now cloaked in drunken strokes of candlelight, into every inch of Life. He turned his back to her. She could not see the smirk on his face, the total satisfaction he felt for all those years of her taunting him, of belittling his authority, of snubbing her nose at the Church hierarchy.

Now she would be punished.

Instantly his smirk twisted into painful agony as he realized that the witch had plied her dark magic again, that she had lured him to look at her, a woman, something he had not done for decades, and see Lucifer himself, something he cowered to see.

The image of this nun burned into his soul, the image of a black hulk with white horns, laughing at him, her skewed smirk mocking him. His myopic eyes could see no more than this shapeless form engulfing his every thought. It was Satan himself! She was indeed the Devil! His agonizing screech caught in his throat as he bolted from the room.

Confusion tumbled on her. What did he know? And how did he know it? Did someone else confess the sin of fathering her, or birthing her? Did someone simply go to him for help? Who? Why? A million questions flew through her mind, but not a single answer. Not even one single answer.

She was trapped.

She fell to her knees in front of the Crucifixion on the wall, hiding her face in her hands. No! she refused to cry. She turned to confront the mirage of Fray Miranda, to challenge whatever allegations he might have. But he was gone. Gone. Only the jerking shadows of the solitary candle remained.

AS SHE ENTERED the convent grounds that evening, several of her Sisters were there, anxiously waiting for her. Sara was there too, terrified.

"Señora! Señora!" cried out Sara. "Soldiers are in your cell, taking everything!"

Juana was livid. That was not the agreement. The agreement was that books, and only books, would be relinquished. She expected, too, that the Church would have the courtesy to let her pack up her books. Blessedly, she had hidden the most treasured tomes years ago, and they remained safe. But to take everything? No! she would not tolerate that. She raced down the hallway to confront the soldiers.

"NO!" she shouted as she entered her cell. "STOP! Stop at once!"

The soldiers were indeed smashing everything into boxes and baskets, from cookware to clothing, enjoying their mayhem immensely. In her adjoining cell they were totally emptying her shelves, even tossing her treasured conch shell into a box, shattering it.

She pushed the soldiers away from the shelves with the force of ten nuns.

A burly sergeant grabbed her arms from behind. "We are only doing as ordered."

"No!" she shouted. "You were ordered to take the books. ONLY the books. That is all that I agreed to."

She pulled away from the sergeant and began emptying the baskets and boxes, putting microscopes and kaleidoscopes, paintings, and masks, back on the shelves. Her arms flew about in desperate haste, her habit askew from the tussle with the sergeant. The soldiers began laughing at her, this small nun fighting half a dozen armed soldiers, only to retrieve a few trinkets. It was the disgusting, demeaning laugh of drunken sailors that filled the entire wing of San Jerónimo's.

In the melee one of the soldiers flung his arm around and knocked down Juana's beloved stature of la Virgen de Guadalupe, the one that Rosita has given her when she first joined the convent. Holding his stomach and laughing, the soldier stepped back, crushing the statue with his heavy heel, splintering it into a thousand pieces. He thought it was great fun and laughed even more.

Juana fell to her knees, trying desperately to collect the shards of the statue, holding them close to her breast.

No, they will not make me cry. "You bastards! Get out of here!" she screamed.

"Here," guffawed the sergeant as he tossed some coins on the floor. "Go buy another."

With all her might she threw the coins at his face, which only made him roar more.

Sor Gabriela appeared at the door. "Get out!" she demanded, her voice carrying immense authority from her years as Madre Superiora. "Gather what you are authorized to take, and get out. This is a convent, not a cock fighting arena. Your presence desecrates the sanctity of our worship. You have three minutes to remove your stinking carcasses from the convent or we shall pummel you with the wrath of God Himself."

"Okay," said the sergeant, sneering along with his men. "Let's just get the books today. We will come back for the rest later."

For all their bravado, the soldiers still felt the wrath of God in Sor Gabriela's voice, and so did as she commanded.

When they had left, Gabriela held Juana as she wept.

EARLY THE NEXT morning Sara set out to find the studio of Don Alberto, a master wood carver. She turned down streets and alleys, stopping every turn or two to make sure she was headed in the right direction.

In a narrow side street, she stepped a large studio, a half dozen apprentices already at work. This cavern was lit with cathedral windows to mimic the light found there. Several large statues were in various phases of development, and one very large retable of the journey of the Magi was set against the wall, destined for one of the larger chapels at la Gran Catedral de la Ciudad de México. A large rough-hewn carving of the Archangel Michael dwarfed her as she took a step inside.

"Por favor," she inquired of the closest apprentice. "Is Don Alberto here?"

With the mention of his name, a strong wiry elder with a long grey moustache appeared from behind a large statue. "What brings you to my sanctuary, little señora?" his deep voice asked.

Sara curtsied, saying, "I come looking for a small statue of la Virgen de Guadalupe, a glorious statue with gold dust encircling her blue robe."

"Small?" called out the apprentice she had first spoken to. He waved his arm around the workshop. "There is nothing small here. Go back home and play with your dolls." His guffaw joined the laughter of the other apprentices.

Sara, embarrassed that she dared to ask, turned to leave. Then she stopped, and spun around, defiant. "It is for Sor Juana Inés de la Cruz, my Señora. The miserable soldiers shattered her cherished statue that she so dearly loved. Madre Superiora at San Jerónimo's told me that you are the finest wood artist in all Nueva España, and so I have come to you for help."

"Wait! Wait right here," said Don Alberto as he disappeared into a small room alongside the studio. He returned a few moments later, placing a beautiful small statue of la Virgen de Guadalupe in Sara's hands. It even had gold dust along the edge of her robe, just like Rosita's statue. "I didn't know at the time why I made this statue," he said, "and I have no others. But I knew this would be for a special person."

Sara reached in her pocket to hand him a pouch of coins that she had saved from the food money, but he closed her hand around the pouch, gently declining them. "Our Lord has already paid for this statue," he said.

That evening Sara gave the statue to Juana.

"I know it is not the same one," said Sara softly, "but when I went to the gallery of Don Alberto, and told him what had happened, he went to a back room and brought out this statue. He said he did not know why he had made it, for he did not carve such statues, but he knew it would be for someone special." Sara handed the statue to Juana.

"It is beautiful, Sara. Thank you. Take some gold coins to pay Don Alberto for his work."

"I tried to pay him, Señora, but he would not accept payment. He said this statue was made by the hand of God and that it was already paid for."

Together they placed the new Virgen de Guadalupe on the wall. Then Juana sat down and wrote a lovely poem, one just for the artisan who created her. The goodness that erupted in the world never ceased to amaze Juana, especially amid such misery.

AFTER A FITFUL NIGHT of calling upon all the angels of heaven to protect her, she trudged the road to the interrogation room the next morning at dawn. She barely had time for a cup of coffee and a slab of bread before she left San Jerónimo.

She waited all day, in prayer to the Virgin. But Fray Miranda did not come. The same thing happened the following day, and the day after that. She knelt in prayers each day, every day, going over and over in her mind all the questions that he might ask, searching for answers to those questions. Sometimes she sat in the chair, idly counting the angles in the cracks in the wall, tracing lines in the floor to follow footsteps from centuries of interrogations. She could not stop herself from analyzing these things, no matter how useless the information seemed.

She did not know that Fray Miranda was doing penance; that he was scourging his soul for the sins of breaking his vow and looking directly at a woman. Lash after lash beat upon his body, now bare even of the hairshirt that he always wore. The lashes cut into his flesh, calloused from decades of thrice weekly scourges. But this was worse – much worse – than his typical lashings. Now his scourging reached epic proportions, again and again beating himself until he fell to the floor in a puddle of blood. He willed himself to rise and do it again. Then again, day after day, begging Christ to tell him how He could have thrown the devil incarnate at him.

For days on end, he begged for mercy. "Dear Christ, son of God, how could I have sinned against Thee? How could I let the temptations of flesh rend the soul that you gave to me? How could I have shattered my vow to you not once, but twice? How can I presume to live when I am but a turd in a sow's pen? I plead … dear Christ, accept the blood of this impure soul. Lead me to find a way so that I might prostrate at your feet in the hereafter. Mercy, O God, I beg. Mercy." From his early childhood priests had pounded into his head that he was worthless. Try as he might, he could not shake that knowledge, and sins of the flesh once again twisted his convoluted soul.

He finally totally collapsed, unable to move or speak. As he awoke from his frozen stupor, the answer came. God allowed the Prince of Darkness to throw these evil spirits at him so that he could endure all the temptations that were to come. He rose from his blood-soaked cell having conquered his devils, just as God demanded. He could proceed with the interrogation of Sor Juana Inés de la Cruz.

AFTER TEN DAYS of absence, Fray Miranda walked to the interrogation room, finding Sor Juana deep in prayer, just as she should have been. He began with no greeting, no ceremony, from the beginning again.

"Who was your father?"

"I don't know, Reverencia." She spoke softly, defeated.

"Who was your mother?"

"I don't know, Reverencia."

"Are you, in fact, Criolle?"

"I don't know, Reverencia." The admissions seared her heart.

"What are the sins of your childhood?"

She began again, confessing the sins of her childhood, the indecencies and desires of a young girl. She confessed to feeling pleasure as her curious young fingers discovered her breasts and watched as her nipples stood firm when she rubbed them, and discovered the pleasure hidden between her thighs. She confessed to the amazement she felt as she watched through a crack in her madre Isobel's bedroom door as her madre screamed and groaned with a lover, two sweaty pigs in heat. She told him about the encounter with the boys at the pond, and about her enchantment with the Roma, and how she longed to go with them. She told the basic story of the Roma that she had told the ladies of the court, but without the dramatics, and without the old woman's prediction for her success. The prediction of her success sounded arrogant, even to her.

With each confession, he nudged her on, listening for new details.

The day ended with Fray Miranda smug. These were confessions she had not made before. He would indeed get it all out of her. That night he went back to his room and again scourged himself for all the sinful images that had infected his mind all that day, all the while thanking God for this opportunity to save a soul.

The next day she confessed sins committed while living at el Palacio de Virrey. She confessed how she loved wearing fancy gowns because the silk fabrics felt alluring on her skin. She confessed about the luxuries of the bath, how it felt to have servants wash her. She confessed how smug she felt when men courted her, admiring her wit and her beauty.

"The outings," he insisted. "What happened at the outings?" He knew well what happened, but he relished hearing it from her, a master storyteller.

She knew what he wanted. "We sometimes went on outings, especially to a waterfall where we swam nude and ate lunch."

"Is that all you did? Swim and eat lunch?"

"No, Reverencia. There was more. The ladies of the Court were tasked with teaching the men of the Court how to please a lady. So, we showed them what pleased us. We kissed each other, and as we dried off each other, we touched others all over their bodies and between their legs, and others touched us."

"Did you know men were watching?"

"Yes, we knew that men were watching."

"Did you enjoy your sinful lust?"

"We did not know it was sinful. We believed it was our duty to teach men how to make love to a woman."

"Did you enjoy your sinful lust?" This time he shouted through clenched teeth.

"Not at first. I felt very awkward. But yes, I did learn to enjoy it. Very much. I looked forward to these outings."

"After your time at the Carmelite Convent you returned to el Palacio de Virrey, to the indecencies of your former life." It was a statement, not a question.

"Yes, Reverencia." He knows this, so why is he questioning me again?

"You continued your Satanic rituals with the ladies of the court, did you not?"

"We sometimes met, yes, but truly we believed we were simply demonstrating how to please a woman to the male members of the court."

"The women touched you … your breasts … your thighs … your womanhood." He sucked the words through his clenched teeth.

"Yes, Reverencia … "

"And you pleasured them in return."

"Yes, Reverencia …"

"You had a physical and emotional experience with a number of different women, didn't you?"

"Yes, Reverencia, but there was no sin. A woman cannot spill her seed, and so no sin is committed." She was certain of this.

This is the opening he was waiting for. He spit out his accusation. "I am not speaking of spilling seed. This is something far more serious, Sor Juana. This is transforming yourself into a *whore*! An *equivocator*! You have perjured your very soul!"

She spun to face the wooden barrier, confused. "Not true, Reverencia."

"Oh? When was that ring placed on your finger?"

"When I took my vows at San Jerónimo's Convent."

"No. The first time. When was the ring placed on your finger the first time?"

"When I was admitted to the Carmelite Convent."

"When you … took … those … vows … the vows of the Carmelite Order, did you not vow, in most sacred terms, to devote your life, your body and soul, to Christ alone? To the service of His work here on earth?"

"Yes, Reverencia." She saw where this was headed, and she had no defense.

"How then can you use your body to please the lusts of men? Or women?"

"But I had left the Carmelite Convent. I gave them back the ring."

"You may have left a place, but there is no 'leaving' in a sacred vow. You cannot kick aside a sacred vow like you kick aside a bitch in the street. A sacred vow is there, part of you, body and soul, forever. Forever! Anyone who believes that she can ignore a sacred vow, a vow made to Christ himself, she is cursed to hell, to damnation forever!" His voice had raised to a screeching roar.

She heard him gasp as he fell to the floor, clutching his heart. She was angry, confused, desperate for an escape. There was none. She did not hear him leave, but when she looked behind the screen, he was gone.

So this is his strategy, she thought as she walked through the night. He will use knowledge of my parentage, and the taking of the Carmelite vow, to label me a heretic.

On reflection, she felt relieved. Fray Miranda focused on her life before she ever met Maria Luisa. She could be honest about her earlier life, but she vowed to herself that should an issue arise about her relationship with Maria Luisa, she would lie, she would do whatever it took to protect the one person in the world who loved her so completely.

She would rot in hell if need be.

ON HER WALK HOME that evening, a stranger stepped out of the dark shadow of an oak tree, and bowed to her most graciously. This sharply-dressed man was clearly a dignitary of some sort. "Pardon me for interrupting your meditation," he said.

"I don't believe we have met. Who are you?"

He spoke softly. "I am Don Jose Federico. More importantly, I am a trusted friend of the Countess de la Laguna, Doña Maria Luisa. She asked that I deliver this to you personally." He handed her a package sealed with sealing wax with Maria Luisa's signature ring design. The seal was intact.

"I travel under the protection of Queen Maria Anna on this journey. No one searches my trunks. Doña Maria Luisa suggested that you might have a letter that I could take back to her as well."

Juana was elated. She felt her heart lilt in joy, for she had true letters from her beloved, and now could write to her in open love as well, and even send her the passionate poetry that flowed from her pen so uncontrollably.

She raced home to write, to write joyously, with unabated love, with passion over flowing. She had not written like this, she had not felt like this, since Maria Luisa had left Nueva España. Her whole being ached with more love than she could ever put into words.

She read and re-read, and re-read again the love that poured out of Maria Luisa's letter. It gave her amazing strength to confront Fray Miranda, more energy to slice through his pretentious questioning.

THE FOLLOWING DAY Fray Miranda began questioning her on her various writings, asking who it was she was referring to as "the softest form" or as "she with the star-kissed lips." She felt comfortable saying truly that it was a poem or a song for someone's wife, or someone's lover. Hour after hour he droned on about the lewd lyrics, especially those that had been published.

Finally, it seemed that he was ready to leave, but he had one last question. "When did you learn of your dubious heritage?"

"You told me yourself yesterday, Reverencia."

"That is a lie. What about your cousin Diego Esteban Ramírez? When did your cousin Don Diego Esteban Ramírez tell you what he saw at the church?"

"Don Diego Esteban Ramírez, Reverencia? I have no cousin named Don Diego Esteban Ramírez. There are many named 'Diego' in my family. My half-brother is Diego Lozano, and a cousin is named José Diego de Torres; my step father is named Diego Ruiz Lozano. There must be some mistake. I have no cousin named Diego Esteban Ramírez."

Then it struck her what he meant. "Don Diego Esteban Ramírez" was the name she used when she herself went to the church to look at her birth records.

"What relative did you send to the church, and what was his real name? Who else did he inform of your dubious background?"

"I sent no one to the church."

"That is a lie!"

"Reverencia, I beg of you. That is the truth. I sent no one to the church, and I do not know who else might know my background."

Juana was telling the truth. She sent no one, she went herself. A grammatical quibble perhaps, but an important distinction in her mind. And truly she did not know who else might have guessed her background.

Decidedly upset, Fray Miranda left.

She pondered her situation. He got his information from the old padre at the church, a Fray Michel? No, Fray Miguel de Asbaje. Back to the question she asked many years prior: What does Fray Miguel know? And how did it happen that Fray Miranda spoke with him about this matter?

Questions. There were always so many questions.

She felt relieved, as if Fray Miranda did not, in fact, have a window into her soul. He did not have the answers to all the questions either. All he had was a bit of information that she lacked. He may know the circumstances of her birth, but she knew the rest of her life. She could handle this interrogation, this confession. If he could withhold facts, so could she. It was easy … she had been doing it all her life.

Just get through this, she told herself, just get through this and then, with the blessing of the Church, you can return to writing and to learning all the rest of your days.

Her footstep lightened as she neared San Jerónimo that night, confident that the Virgin had answered her prayer for a path forward.

THE INTERROGATION droned on for weeks. Fray Miranda was intent on pushing Juana until she melted in a putrid puddle in front of him, and so the war of these two thunderous bulls escalated, he calling on his God, and she calling upon her Virgen de Guadalupe. A parry, a feint, a blazing red cape tossed out, then tossed aside. She knew she had to appear to lose or she would never get her life back, so she faltered from time to time like the master opponent that she was.

The priest dug up stories of lurid sex amongst the ladies of the court, stories of lost virginity at Palacio soirees. None of this was new to him, he just took pleasure in hearing it from this virginal nun, this disciple of the Devil. Many nights he went to his cell after intense interrogations to flagellate himself for hours or days on end.

He was certain that Juana and Doña Leonor Caretta had been lovers. Everyone knew it to be true, and the written evidence was there in her own writing, in her own books. All he had to do was force it out of her. A woman as sumptuous as Doña Leonor would certainly prey upon a pretty little señorita in her charge. He had already heard Sor Juana's confession on the relationship of the men of the royal court, but that was old hat. Like a lynx on the prowl, he entwined Sor Juana in his rhetoric.

"No!" She was emphatic. "There was no romantic relationship between Doña Leonor and myself."

"None? How about a kiss on her hand?"

"Yes, often."

"A kiss on her cheek?"

"Sometimes."

"A kiss on her mouth?"

"No. Never!"

"Never? Really?"

"Sometimes, but only in friendship."

"A kiss on her breasts?"

"No!"

"Liar!"

"Yes, sometimes, but not as you imagine."

He went through every poem, every song, every play, demanding to know the erotic meaning of hundreds of lines. To all of these, she answered truthfully, for indeed she had not had an affair with Doña Leonor.

He never once asked about her relationship with Maria Luisa.

Rather, his dagger shifted to the religious content in her writings, especially to the blasphemies of "The First Dream." He knew he would triumph in this battle when he saw the one copy of her new collection of poems.

Oddly, the cartons of books being shipped to Nueva España disappeared from the dock in España, and the only copy that made the journey across the Atlantic was hand-delivered to Archbishop Francisco de Aguiar. Fray Miranda sat with that one copy for days, astounded at the blasphemy in its pages, building his case line by line against the heretic nun.

"DON IGNACIO VELÁZQUEZ, we don't often see you at the Congregation of the Knights of the Order of Santiago." Fray Miranda was indeed surprised to see Don Ignacio, but he, and his family's fortunes, were always welcome at this committee of elite businessmen.

"My heart saddens, for I don't often come into la Ciudad de México, Reverencia," said Don Ignacio. "Certainly not as often as I would like. I have come today to see Sor Juana Inés de la Cruz." Fray Miranda shot to attention. "I understand that she has been at la Gran Catedral a great deal, under your direction, Reverencia." Don Ignacio willingly accepted his father's wish that he protect Sor Juana, and his voice echoed now with the authority of generations of power.

Had Don Ignacio been alone, Fray Miranda's ego would have demanded a retort to smash this boy like a bug. But he was not alone. All twenty leading businessmen in the room stood in unison behind Don Ignacio.

Fray Miranda smiled his diplomatic smile. "She is well," he assured Don Ignacio. "We are studying so that she may renew her vows as a nun, as do many nuns."

Don Ignacio bowed briefly and sat, as did the other businessmen, ready for their homily of the day, another one addressing charity and kindness.

When Don Ignacio left that day, he boldly put a pouch into Fray Miranda's hands, leaving no doubt as to where the real power of Nueva España rested.

"SHUT HER UP!" screamed Archbishop Francisco de Aguiar again. He too had read the Second Edition of Sor Juana's book. He was incensed. "She screeches like a bat gone mad. If you cannot do it, I shall! I shall shut her up permanently."

Despite his disgust with her writings, Fray Miranda feared for his own soul were she to be silenced permanently. "I can do it," he said, with more confidence than he truly felt. His arm flew out in protest before he knew what he was doing, the cold stares of the elite businessmen still filling his brain. "I can do it."

So the interrogation continued.

HE HIT HER again, and again. For all the logic she put into her defense, she knew it was not enough. It would never be enough, for he was determined to prove her wrong.

After days of battling over "The First Dream," she knew she had to give in. Winning the fight over one poem, even one as treasured as "First Dream," was not the goal; gaining his backing in front of the Inquisition was the goal, and to accomplish that, she had to let him believe he had won. After all, the poem was already published, so the world would see it, no matter what.

"Reverencia, I have sinned fearfully in the composition of this piece. My soul is rent to think how I must have displeased you. Were it possible, I would rip this piece from the pages of every single book that is being published, but alas! it is not possible. I can only beg your forgiveness, as I do now."

Her tactic worked. His questioning shifted to other matters, minor issues. After weeks of inane questions, it seemed that he should be winding up, but he kept on and on, like a wild game hunter who had not yet bagged a cougar. He did not yet feel that he had "won."

She had one card left to play, an invented revelation that could draw the interrogation to a close.

On a hot sweltering day she said, "Reverencia, there is one part of my life that we have not talked about, and in the interests of full confession, I feel I must confess it to you."

"Oh?" He was clearly interested.

"Yes. My time at the Carmelite Convent."

"Of course. I already know that you were unhappy there." He knew the rumors of the Carmelite Convent and the diabolical nuns who ran it.

"But I have not told you, Reverencia, why I was unhappy. I was unhappy because I could not be good enough … I could not be sensual enough … to please Sor Beatrice."

"What?" This was a confession Fray Miranda had not even dreamed of.

"If I had pleased Sor Beatrice, I would have been given special privileges, perhaps even writing privileges, and those I sorely desired. But she was never satisfied, no matter how hard I tried." She paused, listening for a reaction from him.

"Go on, child."

She then detailed the physical contact between them, the rubbings, the kisses on her breasts, the pleasures between her legs, stretching each description out until she heard the erratic breathing of Fray Miranda, then she told him more, making him sweat profusely. She told how she begged Sor Beatrice to tell her what would please her the most, and how a bit of parchment would mean more to her than an extra potato at dinner.

Then she shifted her approach entirely. "When you came to visit me, I saw the glory of Christ's love surrounding you, heard angels in your voice leading me home. With the strength of your presence, I knew I had to find the courage to change my life's path; I knew I had to find that courage, even if I became nothing more than a gutter girl. Blessedly you and la Vicereine Leonor reached out your hands, generously pulling me from a ruinous fate."

She could not hide the sincerity in her voice, nor did she wish to.

"As my fame grew, I came to devour the approval of the masses, when I should have held on tight only to the Grace of God. That is what has brought me to this juncture today, this is the sadness in my soul. I am truly the worst of women, and I deserve nothing, nothing at all, from you, Reverencia. Were you being entirely just, you would leave me to rot in hell, alone."

"Enough!" he said. "Enough. That is all for today." He rushed out of the building, only to subject himself to days and days of severe flagellation for all the incredible images that she had carved into his mind that day.

SHE LEFT the basement that evening, her back straighter, her head held higher than it had been for many months. The confession, she knew, was not entirely true, nor untrue. It was simply what he needed to hear to set the matter to rest.

He sent word that they would meet again in four weeks to compile the full confession that she would read to the Inquisition Tribunal. In that written confession to the Inquisition there was no more mention of the Carmelites, nor was it ever mentioned again, for he did not want a fight with the entire Dominican order.

She had won.

Canta el silencio (Sing the Silence)

IT WAS over.

They had come, the Archbishop's militia, tearing through her cell, snatching all its contents – books, writing materials, drafts of poetry, scientific instruments, and curiosities – hundreds of them from all over the world.

She ignored the self-congratulatory sneers of the soldiers, no doubt some of whom had come before. It was now a cell bare of the reminders of so many friendships. They left her with a spare habit, a Bible, and some cooking pots. It was the price she paid to prove her sincerity to the Inquisition, to prove that she was worthy of taking anew her vows as a nun.

She watched barbaric soldiers toss all her belongings, even her most loved volumes, onto a pyre built outside her window, standing in stunned shock as these treasures turned to ashes. Archbishop Francisco de Aguiar did not want anything that she had touched to remain.

She did, however, see jeweled rings and small treasures slip into pockets.

It was over.

On February 17, 1694, she had signed the formulaic "Learned Explication of the Mystery and Vow Made by Sor Juana Inés de la Cruz to Defend the Immaculate Conception of Our Lady," in which she named St. Joseph, St. Peter, her guardian angel, St. Augustine, and others, but not Santa Caterina or any other woman.

On March 5, 1694, she had signed in blood her "Profession," asking forgiveness for her sins, and presented this to the Inquisition. She promised to never publish again. But she would not, she could not, promise to never study again. She would not, she could not, promise to never write again.

She had already forgiven Maria Luisa for publishing "First Dream" against her wishes, for had Maria Luisa not done so, the glorious poem would have been destroyed with everything else. She did relinquish all her worldly possessions – all of them.

She did all of this willingly, for there was no other path for her to reestablish her role among the scholastics of la Ciudad de México. It was a compromise she could live with. And so could the Church. The Church could not put her on the rack like her dear Santa Caterina, or send her to a leper colony, both of which would have suited Archbishop Francisco de Aguiar grandly.

Nor could the Archbishop silence her completely, as la Ciudad de México made so abundantly clear to him. When he tried to rid La Ciudad de México of her vile second book, the one containing "First Dream," he could not. Book sellers hid it from his clutches. Noblemen and priests gathered in salons to read and discuss her works, sometimes out in broad daylight.

> *"Your Most Excellent Reverencia,"* the missive from the Spanish Court read, *"would you be so kind as to forward to us any writings that you may have from your brilliant poet, Sor Juana Inés de la Cruz? Our courtiers are begging for more. You must be immensely proud that Nueva España has contributed such glorious talent to our realm."*

Her damned writings gnawed at the Archbishop's gut like an infected rat, and he could do little more than hope that she chose to live in obscurity.

So now it was over.

SHE RESTED a lot. The ordeal with Fray Miranda had wrung a lot of energy from her, challenging her weak health, as Sara cared for her day and night.

"Sara, what are these books on the shelf?" Juana picked up a treasured volume, a book from her Abuelo's biblioteca. "Didn't the soldiers take everything?"

"Oh, no, Señora, not those. Sor Josephina had borrowed those books, so they weren't here when the soldiers came. She just returned them yesterday."

Juana did not remember a "Sor Josephina," but there was a little note from her: "*Gracias* for lending me the books. I did enjoy them. Josephina." Perhaps Josephina was a new nun, one she had not met in all the confusion of the past year.

A couple of days later Juana returned from a walk and discovered some more books on the shelf, with the same little note, but in a different handwriting. Then it happened again. And again. Finally, there were nearly a hundred very beautiful volumes sitting on her shelves, always with the little note from "Josephina." Most of the books that showed up were ones that she especially treasured, valuable and rare editions, and some from her Abuelo's collection.

She went to the Friday afternoon meeting that week, the first time she had gone since the ordeal with Fray Miranda began. She stood and with her quiet smile said, "I've come to meet Sor Josephina, and to thank her for returning my books." She added slyly, "She must be a voracious reader."

Sor Gabriela stood, smiling. "Oh, no, dear. Josephina isn't here any longer. She did not profess, and so she has left the convent. We don't know where she went."

Juana looked around as all her Sisters shook their heads and shrugged their shoulders.

"I am glad you got some of your books back," said Sor Gabriela. "We all know how important they are to you."

The Sisters of San Jerónimo's could have been excommunicated themselves for defying the orders of the

Archbishop. The whole Convent could have been shuttered. They had risked so much, so much.

Juana wiped her face with her sleeve. "I seem to have gotten caught in the rain," she said as she caught the tears on her cheeks. "Should you see Josephina, do tell her *Gracias*! A million times, *Gracias*. I shall be grateful to her every moment of my life."

Yes, this is where Juana belonged. The angels that brought her here no doubt worked hard, but being at San Jerónimo's was the most blessed miracle of her life.

"*BUENOS DIAS*, Sor Juana!" Don Felipe the indefatigable bookseller threw open his arms and embraced her. "It is so good to see you again! Are you well? Are you writing? Will we see another book?" His questions came so furiously fast that they both laughed.

"I am well, *gracias*, Don Felipe. And you? And your family?"

"Yes, all well. Since your books arrived, I have done more business than ever before. Everyone wants copies of your books. I am afraid that I sold out long ago, and I do not even have a copy to give to you. More will be coming soon. When will you publish again?"

"No more publishing, I am afraid. But I do study, and I do write. I am here today to find a book or two on the scientific nature of sound. I have been intrigued with sound since I was a little girl and my Abuelo placed a conch shell to my ear."

She had heard the mystery of the conch shell. She had listened to the crashing waves. She had played with air, teasing notes from the Aeolian harp, and had coaxed the little flute that Sor Sophia gave her … and churning air of the massive organ at la Gran Catedral de la Ciudad de México … and the little hammers in music boxes. The songs of nightingales had fascinated her for years. Sounds! So many wonderful sounds! Now she had time to study these sounds.

"Do you have something, Don Felipe?"

"For you, Sor Juana, you may have the entire store. Truly. Four different gentlemen – FOUR of them!" And he held up four fingers. "They have all said that anything that Sor Juana wants, Sor

Juana shall have. Anything! The entire store is yours if you like." He swept his arms full circle, grinning ear to ear.

They found two books, one a lesser-known work of Kircher, and another that had been destroyed by Archbishop Francisco de Aguiar's soldiers in the fire. Juana insisted that those two books would keep her busy for quite some time, that she did not need the whole store.

HER WORLD began to open even more, day by day as her many friends discovered that she sat in the sunshine in her locutory most afternoons, quietly reading and writing.

Friends came with books and trinkets and inventions and oddities and even money for her treasury, each more pleased than the next to spend a bit of time with her again, and her shelves once again held treasured volumes from Lyon, Antwerp, Brussels, and Madrid.

"TELL ME, SOR JUANA, what is the one thing that you most want?" Her young friend Don Ignacio Velázquez had come to visit, and immediately asked, "What can I do?" He had become a strong young man since his father's death, respected in leadership and in scholarship. Because of him, the Velázquez family was still highly respected throughout the country.

"There is one thing I would appreciate, my friend. Would you bring your carriage and drive me out to la Capilla de la Virgen de Guadalupe? I am not certain that I can walk that far just now, and I would love to visit la Virgen to thank Her for all Her blessings."

The ride to la Capilla on a bright summer morning warmed her soul as people of all castes smiled and bowed to this honored nun.

As Fray Gilberto had once suggested, she now wrote an elegant poem, a poem just for Her, and whispered it to Her at Her altar, beginning

Beloved Queen of Heaven,
Your shadow
Casts the symmetrical harmony
That graces all below
The slow pick of guitar strings
The staccato of a banjo.

It was over two hundred lines of pure devotion, with la Virgen as the Prime Conductor of all that is beautiful. She also wrote a poem for Fray Gilberto to thank him for his many kindnesses whenever she was in distress.

"*Millon de gracias*," Fray Gilberto said. "I will keep this blessed poem here, beside the other magnificent pieces in this book." She saw him take her book, the controversial second edition, from the top drawer of his desk and carefully place her new poem inside its cover.

As Don Ignacio Velázquez helped her out of his carriage at the entrance to San Jerónimo's, she placed a small scroll in his hands.

"I deeply thank you, Sor Juana. Is this a poem mi madre may have requested?"

"Our Lord commissioned this one, a humble *gracias* for your family's faith in me for so many decades."

"Our Lord blessed us when my father met your Abuelo, and talked with him and with you on your veranda. My life has been blessed by simply knowing you, Sor Juana Inés de la Cruz." He kissed her hand most reverently. That poem remained on the wall of the elegant entry hall of the Velázquez estate, exquisitely framed, from that day to forever.

SOMETIMES SHE walked around the convent grounds, sometimes visiting the gravesites of friends who had passed to the Other Realm, offering prayers and poems, and sometimes talking with Sor Sophia.

"*Did you find a love, Sor Sophia, Madre? Who was it? Or was it a love inflicted on you?*" Juana herself had served as midwife for several such "inflictions," and knew the pain they wrought when a babe is ripped from its mother's arms.

"Did you find your God, Madre? What is it like in God's world? Do the birds talk with you? Sing with you?"

Often Juana sprinkled a few crumbs on the grave enticing wrens and robins to come sing at this grave, which they gladly did.

For hours on end she was now able to follow a dream quest, to explore all those intriguing questions about sound that had nibbled at her brain for many years, questions like *"Why does the lark sound different from the eagle?" "Why do echoes sometimes sound like your voice, and sometimes not?" "What is the song the breeze whispers in the willows?"*

She began to organize her discoveries in a new book that she titled "The Conch Shell" ("*El carocol*"). She saw the spheres of music as a spiral, not a circle, but a spiral ascending and descending from heaven to earth and back again, drawing inspiration from her extensive studies and experiences with her "speaking trumpets," echo chests and Aeolian harp.

She saw the conch shell itself as Love, for it was in the shape of her Beloved's heart.

Always, always, she dreamed of being with her beloved, her Maria Luisa again, pouring her heart out to her daily.

> Oft I sought mad Chiron's raft
> A path to slash the firmament
> And hold you just once more.
>
> Yet Penelope's weft
> Of gossamer hue
> Flies to you,
> and back
> To here, the most blessed of all,
> A tapestry of our love.

April 17, 1695

SARA SAT with her all night, the hospital wards still blazing with activity as more women were brought in. A vicious illness was consuming San Jerónimo's.

Fray Miranda had died February 17, 1695, from complications of cataract surgery. About six weeks later an epidemic hit San Jerónimo's. This was not like the plague that had engulfed La Ciudad de México several months earlier; this was an epidemic focused on San Jerónimo's – only San Jerónimo's. No one knew what – or who – caused it. They only knew it was deadly.

The women of San Jerónimo's fell ill, one by one, some taken to bed at the convent, the sickest taken to the hospital, white shrouds passing to the graveyard every day. Sor Juana had dropped everything to help her Sisters, the Sisters who had so generously helped her so many times, the Sisters who had risked everything to save her books, the Sisters who sang with her, who prayed with her, for decades.

At first, she joined the daily penance of the nuns as directed by Archbishop Francisco de Aguiar, walking the halls of the convent, lashing themselves by candlelight, inflicting themselves with blows to draw blood. They even wore away their tongues as they licked the convent walkways repeatedly.

Sara's Señora had begun feeling ill, but when she learned that her Sisters needed help at the hospital, she flew over with more energy than she thought she had, knowing full well that for all ten women who entered the hospital, only one emerged alive. For three days she tended the ill, changing their bedsheets, helping them drink a little water, assisting the doctors with blood-letting, and the priests with final rites. There was nothing else that anyone knew to do, for no one knew what plague had ensnared the women of San Jerónimo.

On her fourth day helping at the hospital, Juana collapsed too.

That was yesterday. Sara stayed with her all night, and at 4:15 in the morning she called to the priest. Her Señora had passed to the other world.

Still Sara stayed with the body now wrapped in a white linen shroud, waiting for the ward to quiet down as the nuns said Matins at six o'clock. Sara had a treasure in her pocket, and there was one thing more her Señora asked of her. As Juana rushed from her cell to help at the hospital a few days earlier, she handed Sara her most valuable possession, the ring that Maria Luisa had gifted her, saying, "Sara, please guard this ring until I can wear it again." Sara tied it safely in her apron pocket, and then in the quiet of the morning when her lady was wrapped in white, she took the ring from her apron, opened the shroud, and placed the ring by her lady's heart.

Soon the grave diggers came, as they did each morning, to take those who had died during the night. Open graves laid waiting. Sara accompanied the shrouded body, catching a glimpse of a lone hawk flying above in circles, as if it were tethered to this spot.

As the grave diggers set the shrouded soul in the grave and began covering it, Sara said quietly, "This is Sor Juana Inés de la Cruz, my mistress, my Señora."

The men fell immediately to their knees on this now sacred spot, repeatedly crossing themselves. One man walked away as the others, slowly and respectfully, resumed their task. Soon a church bell began to toll, resonating with dignity and grace. Then another. And another.

The bells of la Gran Catedral de la Ciudad de México were silent.

"What is all that racket?" shouted Archbishop Francisco de Aguiar.

"The bells are ringing for Sor Juana Inés de la Cruz," replied his aide. "She has died this morning."

Archbishop Francisco de Aguiar turned his back and hid his smirk. "Good," he said. "Let la Gran Catedral bells ring loud and long. This is a day we celebrate."

As the bells of la Gran Catedral de la Ciudad de México rang out, a glorious symphony of sorrow embraced the whole city.

Sara looked up to soak in this wonderment of the bells and saw two hawks flying, circling each other, their shoulders nearly touching as they danced in circles in the sky, disappearing into the clouds.

Before the bells had stopped ringing, Archbishop Francisco de Aguiar's soldiers once again stormed the heretic witch's cell, taking all her writings, her notes, her books, her jewels, everything … even a single letter on her desk, an unopened letter from Madrid telling her that her beloved Maria Luisa had died.

Appendix:

After Word
Real? Or Not?
For Further Reading
My Brow Lowered, I Thank You
If you enjoyed this story …
For thoughtful discussion

After Word

Archbishop Francisco de Aguiar y Seijas y Ulloa was to live nearly three years more, until August 14, 1698. Upon his death a petition for sainthood began, citing his good works and generous soul. The petition was denied. Sor Juana has been honored in hundreds of ways – in stamps, in currency, in operas and films, in murals and eulogies over the world, even in tributes from writers, famous or not, including me, her most humble servant. Were it not for Sor Juana, the legacy of Archbishop Francisco de Aguiar would be locked in hellish obscurity.

Fray Manuel Fernandez de Santa Cruz, the Bishop of Puebla lived a few months longer, until February 1, 1699. He was never named Archbishop, although Viceroy Galve once offered him the interim position of Viceroy. The Bishop declined, citing his own poor health.

There is no record of Sara's life, or death.

Sor Juana, My Beloved

Real? Or Not?

There is a lot that we simply do not know about Juana Inés de la Cruz.

Truthfully, we don't even know where or when she was born.

We do not know her genetic heritage, i.e., her parentage.

We do not know anything about her childhood, and very little about her adult life, even after she entered the convent.

We have poems and plays that were attributed to her, but I know that many are missing.

There are a few things we are relatively certain of, such as:

* There was an Abuelo who had a big library. Some scholars see him as a fierce father figure; I see him in a kinder light.

* There was a Tia Maria and Tio Juan who took her in when she was in La Ciudad de México, and who took her to the Vicereine as a lady-in-waiting.

* We know she spent three months at the Carmelite Convent, but we do not know why she went there, nor why she left. Most writers say her doctors "told" her to leave; I do not believe that – if Sor Juana had wanted to stay, she would have stayed.

* We know that she became a nun at San Jeronimo's, and that she served as Treasurer for a while, and as Historian for a while.

* We know she had one of the most extensive libraries in all the New World, perhaps The most extensive.

* We know that Fray Miranda was every bit as eccentric as I described, and probably more so. We also know that he was once her personal Confessor, and that the relationship broke apart, then came together again. We do not know the Why or When of these events.

* We also know that Fray Miranda was the Chief Inquisitor, and that he was the one who interrogated her. We have no record of the actual interrogation.

* We know she was a friend of Archbishop Payo and the Bishop of Puebla. Many historians will tell you that the Bishop of Puebla turned against her during the Sor Filotea era, but I do not believe that at all. He was her friend, forever.

* We know that Archbishop Francisco de Aguiar was her arch enemy, and many of his eccentricities are widely reported.

* We know that Maria Luisa had some of Juana's works published in Spain, and that nothing was published in Mexico.

* We know the date and circumstances of her death.

* And we know there was a plague that focused solely on San Jeronimo's Convent. There was a city-wide plague a couple of years earlier, but the one that took Juana's life was a very defined event.

There are HUGE gaps in her life that we know nothing about. Women were not worthy of being written about, so they were pretty much ignored in official writings. Even duchesses and vicereines had no biographies, and certainly a nun would have nothing written about her life.

Theoretically she did write a brief autobiography, but it was more a defense of her belief in the right of women to study than a true biography. The "facts" she presented were questionable, at best, such as the statement that she could read before she was three years old.

Historical fiction fills in the gaps, the parts we do not know. For example, I know that Sor Juana had a love relationship with Maria Luisa, for I have read her poems of that era. I cannot call her a "lesbian" because that term was not coined until centuries later. But they were in love, deeply in love. Contemporary biographers gloss over this part of her life, many denying it entirely, calling it a "friendship". My heart tells me it was a lot more than a friendship.

It was common for privileged women to enjoy physical pleasures from one another, and Dona Maria Luisa and Sor Juana were certainly "privileged women." Men were not theoretically allowed such pleasures, for they would be spilling their seed. I say "theoretically," for there is a report from a traveler who tells us otherwise.

If you study the formal history of that era, you will likely see references to the rebellion lasting only a day or two, with no causalities mentioned. Again, a journal from an obscure traveler said something quite different.

When reading the works of scholars, remember that woefully little was written about women of that era, and what was written was overwhelmingly from a male perspective.

The story that I have written is Juana's life as it could have been. There is no way to determine if I am completely correct; in fact, I probably am not. There are many possibilities.

I wrote what my heart told me. Others will write what their hearts tell them, and all together we may discover who she really was.

Sor Juana, My Beloved

For Further Reading

Sor Juana Inés de la Cruz is an intriguing person who lived in a fascinating era of Mexican history. Should you wish to learn more about her, her writings, and her times, here are some starting points.

Should you be thinking of writing about her yourself, please do. She is worthy of all the attention her works and her life have generated.

You will see conflicting information in books about Sor Juana. Even primary sources are not consistent, even in relating historical events, so it is only your heart that will determine what is most accurate, and what is not.

.

SOR JUANA, by Octavio Paz. Pub. By the President and Fellows of Harvard College. © 1988. Translated by Margaret Sayers Peden.

This is, by far, the most significant study in English of the life and times of Sor Juana. If you are looking for a deep dive into that era, and her writings, there is no second choice. Dr. Paz and I do not completely agree on what the ultimate "facts" of Sor Juana's life are, but I bow to his depth of knowledge.

.

WOMAN OF GENIUS: THE INTELLECTUAL AUTOBIOGRAPHY OF SOR JUAN INÉS DE LA CRUZ. Translation and Introduction by Margaret Sayers Peden. Published by Lime Rock Press. © 1987

This is not an "autobiography" as we know it, but a treatise on her philosophy regarding women and the Church. It includes some anecdotes that are repeated often, which may or may not be true – she was always a splendid story-teller. One of her anecdotes tells how she was not yet three years old when she learned how to read. This is a writing that says, "This is how I would like to be remembered." If you were writing such a treatise about your own life, what would you include/exclude?

GUADALUPE.MYSTERIES: DECIPHERING THE CODE, by Grzeborz Gorny and Janusz Rosikon. Pub. By Ignacius Press

A lavishly illustrated, meticulously researched study on The Virgin of Guadalupe. It steps into the history of the Aztecs and Spain's influence on the area as well. Truly captivating information.

THE TENTH MUSE: SOR JUANA INÉS DE LA CRUZ, by Fanchon Royer. Pub. By St. Anthony Guild Press, © 1952.

This is a relatively obscure book about Sor Juana, and for the most part is a paean to her life and works. It does, however contain rich information about her sources, and even photos of the church where La Vicereine Leonor was buried. Royer's translations are quite eloquent, but the poems included are only in Spanish. Considering the difficulty of translating poetry, this is not surprising.

SOR JUANA: BEAUTY AND JUSTICE IN THE AMERICAS, by Michelle A. Gonzalez. Pub. By Orbis Books, © 2003.

An astute examination of Sor Juana's life and works, I found myself returning to it several times for glimpses into Sor Juana's core beliefs. Here was where I discovered that Sor Juana's later years were the years that liberated her, years that gave her time to explore ideas and write only as she chose.

POEMS, PROTEST, AND A DREAM: SELECTED WRITINGS, SOR JUANA INÉS DE LA CRUZ, translated with notes by Margaret Sayers Peden. Introduction by Ilan Stavans. Published by Penguin Books.

Poetry is a monster to translate, with meter, rhyme, word play and innuendo intertwining in a mythical web. This excellent volume presents the Spanish and English side by side. Includes translations of "First Dream" and Sor Juana's Response to Sor Filotea, as well as a number of her poems, and selections from her plays.

.

SOR JUANA INÉS **DE LA CRUZ: SELECTED WORKS**, translated by Edith Grossman, with an Introduction by Julia Alvarez. Pub. By W.W. Norton & Company, ©2014.

A splendid selection of poetry, including "First Dream," as well as the letter from Sor Filotea to Sor Juana, and Sor Juana's Response. Completely in English. A wonderful index of the people and places contained in these writings.

.

SOR JUANA'S LOVE POEMS, translated by Joan Larkin and Jaime Manrique. Published by University of Wisconsin Press, ©1997.

A slender volume, but an important one. This is the book that reminded me that Sor Juana was no prissy, sequestered nun. No, she was a very real, very sensual woman in every respect. Spanish and English, side by side.

UNMADE HEARTS: MY SOR JUANA, by July Westhale. Published by Harbor Editions: Small Harbor Publishing, ©2024.

Not a "translation," but a poetic conversation with Sor Juana. All I could say was Yes!

Sor Juana, My Beloved

I Bow My Head ...

How can I begin to thank all the amazing people who helped this story become a reality? I cannot. There were simply too many. For those I have omitted, please forgive my feeble-mindedness and know you are in my heart.

First, a huge Thank You to **Bill Rauch**. When he was the Artistic Director of the Oregon Shakespear Company in Ashland, Oregon, he commissioned a play about Sor Juana. It was a good play, but it felt like something was missing. This play inspired a three-year search for the Sor Juana beneath the play. Without seeing that play, I am not certain I would have ever felt so driven.

Thank you to all the readers and writers and friends who kept me on my toes, especially to several Key Readers:

* **Heather Cumming**, who took her Peace Corps experience in Africa and turned it into a lifetime mission of bringing water to villages throughout west Africa (*see* www.ssaap.org);

* **Julia Raneri**, a gifted healer who has settled on a wooded wonderland with a river running by, and her dog as a special buddy;

* **Kathryn Henderson**, a professor emeritus, with a lifetime focused on women's spirituality and the goddess world;

* **Libby**, the vivacious young woman destined to see the world, the one who prompted me to see that this book was for younger women too.

* **Maria Geigel**, an intrepid traveler and international business consultant;

* **Patty Duggan**, who traced the footsteps of the deer (and sometimes bears!) in the wooded watershed every morning, and reads voraciously;

* **Char Hersh** and her wonderful gathering of women remind me often of the compassion all around us. **Annie O'Boyle, Janet Ligon**, and dozens more.

To all the readers groups and writers groups who devoted time and energy to help me become a better storyteller. Each of you contributed so much.

Thank you all so, so much.

And thank you to all of those in Ashland who have created such an astonishing artistic, inspiring environment. There are far too many actors, writers and artists of all ilk to mention here, probably a couple of thousand, but let me give a quick bow to the Artistic Directors of a few of our theaters: **Tim Bond** of Oregon Shakespeare Festival, **Jessica Sage** of Rogue Theater Company, **Gwen Overland** of Camelot Theater, and a dozen or more.

To you, my reader, my sincerest heartfelt Thank You. You make it all worth while.

If you enjoyed this story …

All authors (me too) treasure any bit of help/comments from readers. If you are so inclined, there are several, relatively painless things you might do.

Do **tell your friends** about it, whether in **person**, or via **emails**, or on your favorite **social site**.

Jot a note, short or long, at your favorite spot, perhaps on **Amazon** or **GoodReads** (just search for "Sor Juana, My Beloved") or other review page. You cannot imagine how important these notes are to writers, even if they are short.

Tell your **local bookstore** about the book.

Tell your **local library** how much you enjoyed the book.

Letting others know about a book is a tough assignment. Any word of assistance that you can provide is a blessing!

Book Club Visits

Do visit my website: https://www.maryannshank.com. You can reach me via the Contact information there. I would be thrilled to visit your book club via Zoom or other online hookup. Chatting with readers is one of my most favorite things to do.

I do hope you enjoyed reading Sor Juan's story as much as I enjoyed writing it.

Thank you. Thank you so much!

For thoughtful discussion …

Imagine. If you were blessed with the incredible talents of Juana Ines, what would you do with your life? How would your life change? How would the world change in your eyes, and how would the world see you differently?

..

Is there any poet or playwright that you know of who might compare with Sor Juana? (My thoughts turn to Emily Dickinson, for they were both immensely creative and both truly dreamed in poetry, but there are probably others.)

..

Take a simple poem, something like "Humpty Dumpty," and translate it into any language that you know. How did you do? Now try it the other way. Take a simple poem in a foreign language, like "Sur le pont d'Avignon," and translate it into English. Any better?

..

If you were Sor Juana's advocate at the Inquisition with Fray Miranda, what would you advise her to do? Hold firm in her beliefs? Acquiesce to his demands? Or something else?

You might also enjoy these books:

Rooted in Sunrise
By Beth Dotson Brown

A tornado destroys Ava's comfortable life. Rather than crumbling under the loss, she feels a load lifted. Maybe something beyond the familiar is calling to her, especially via the strange suitcase that landed on her lawn during the storm.

Song of the Wooden Sparrow
By Isabel Tutaine

1894. A widow practicing medicine in a town hostile to female doctors befriends a carpenter who's shunned for having murdered a man while robbing a bank. Their struggles to belong challenge the fragilities in their strengths and reveal facts don't always convey truth.

The Mystical Land of Myrrh
by MaryAnn Shank

A young woman in a forbidden land, savage warriors, kindness beyond any expectation, and a Goddess who protects them all – this, and so much more in this land called Somalia.

"A captivating read..."
Barb Dickinson, We'Moonager of We'Moon Date Book: Gaia Rhythms for Women

(http://www.maryannshank.com)

The Scent of Distant Family
By sid sibo

"What begins as a lost-dog story quickly develops into an unfolding tapestry of life. Families and strangers, along with animals, wild and domestic—from a herd of horses to a hibernating boa— are woven into an intricate mosaic of relationships of which, ultimately, you yourself will become a part —Michael Mountain, cofounder of the Whale Sanctuary Project and founding editor of *Best Friends Magazine*

Sor Juana, My Beloved

Sor Juana, My Beloved

Sor Juana, My Beloved